Escardy Gap

Peter Crowther & James Lovegrove

TOR®

A TOM DOHERTY ASSOCIATES BOOK
NEW YORK

This is a work of fiction. All the characters and events portrayed in this book are either products of the authors' imagination or are used fictitiously.

ESCARDY GAP

Copyright © 1996 by Peter Crowther and James Lovegrove

All rights reserved, including the right to reproduce this book, or portions thereof, in any form.

Cover art by Mark Elliot

A Tor Book
Published by Tom Doherty Associates, Inc.
175 Fifth Avenue
New York, NY 10010

Tor Books on the World Wide Web:
http://www.tor.com

Tor® is a registered trademark of Tom Doherty Associates, Inc.

ISBN: 0-812-55539-2
Library of Congress Card Catalog Number: 96-8306

First edition: October 1996
First mass market edition: January 1998

Printed in the United States of America

0 9 8 7 6 5 4 3 2 1

For Nicky and the boys . . .
and, of course, for my mother:
here's a strange tale, and no denying . . .—PC

For my parents,
without whom this book (and I)
would not have been possible.—JL

Acknowledgments

To Susan Gleason, who cast the line . . . and to Natalia Aponte and Tom Doherty, who took the bait: may the waters you travel continue to be calm and fruitful.

—PC and JL

I am riding on a limited express, one of the crack trains of
  the nation.
Hurtling across the prairie into blue haze and dark air go
  fifteen all-steel
    coaches holding a thousand people.
(All the coaches shall be scrap and rust and all the men
  and women laughing
    in the diners and sleepers shall pass to ashes.)
I ask a man in the smoker where he is going and he
  answers: "Omaha."

—Carl Sandburg,
"Limited"

Beginning

Dregs and dregs.

I was dividing my attention between my drink and the big mirror behind the main bar at Bunyan's, between the remains of a fourth martini and the aimless shift of humanity traveling along Bleecker Street, heading for the West Fourth Street station or up to Washington Square.

Dregs and dregs.

There they went: businessmen and bums, young couples and swaggering homeboys, crazy kids and crazier old farts like me, all wandering through the now-remembered warmth of an early-spring evening.

Dregs and dregs.

Sometimes, if you repeat a word often enough, it loses all its meaning. Unfortunately, this wasn't one of those occasions. I knew the meaning of the word "dregs" far too well.

I tossed the olive into my mouth and snapped the cocktail stick into a nearby ashtray. "I wish I was dead," I said into the glass. A breath-ghost appeared inside the rim, faded, and vanished.

Shouldn't that be "I wish I were *dead"?* the editor in me wanted to know.

Was, were—it didn't matter. Damn it, they were only words.

I drained the martini. The liquor hit the back of my throat, stayed there for a second, then dropped, the brief sting reminding me that I was still alive. I hissed my enthusiasm for this state of affairs through clenched teeth.

Out of the corner of my eye I caught the waitress looking at me. She snatched her eyes down, pretending she had an important appointment with a speck of dust on her sleeve. I cleared my throat, smiled feebly, and waved my empty glass. She glanced up, smiled back, and nodded. Both of us were making as if nothing had happened, as if she hadn't witnessed me hold a conversation with my drink, as if we were just any old customer and waitress in any old bar in all the world.

She came over and loaded the empty onto a tray that featured a picture of Paul Bunyan scratching his back with a giant redwood.

"Another?" she said, holding up a finger.

"Another," I said, holding up a finger. "But just the one."

She didn't say anything else. She didn't need to. Her expression said it all. Every day she saw dozens like me, hundreds, all of us sinking further and further into our personal mires. It wasn't her job to rescue us, throw us a line, offer a word of sympathy or anything like that. All she was there for was to make our suffering less; like a vet, painlessly put us lame horses out of our misery.

Not that I was just any old boozehound. Oh, no. I was worse than that. Far worse. I was, in fact, a writer without an idea, and in the Lowest Form of Human Life sweepstakes, the writer without an idea beats the old boozehound by several lengths. In fact, a writer without an idea is just about the dumbest, most desperate creature in the world. From dawn till dusk he is haunted, hounded, hunted by invisible demons. Nothing contents him, nothing comforts him. There are no satisfactions, no consolations for him. None. Not a one. Not even a well-mixed martini in a warm, softly lit bar on a pleasant street conveniently off the main drag in the depths of Greenwich Village on the island of Manhattan in the great city of New York, tarnished but still-shining jewel in the crown of that last and mightiest of empires, the United States of America.

The waitress placed the fresh martini in front of me. I drank, and it was good. I set the glass down on the Budweiser coaster.

Even in the mirror behind the bar, in the reflection of the street window, filtered through a pall of pollution, the sunset was impressive, with fat cerise clouds slowly dissolving into a lilac and saffron sky and the low light glowing in the faces of the passersby, lending even the most taut and drawn and worried of them a kind of gilded serenity. Caught by the sinking sun's sidelong rays, the ferroconcrete-and-glass sides of the skyscrapers smiled. Everyone in the city, everyone in the whole wide world, seemed to have discovered the key to inner contentment. Everyone except me. I probably threw away the mail-order catalogue they'd printed *that* offer in.

I thought about my neighbor, Prima, who had spent the last year telling me all about yoga classes, how I ought to try some of that stretching and bending, find myself, discover my

true inner being, the whole nine yards. But what she didn't
know was that the reward would hardly be worth the effort.
The revelations wouldn't justify the trip. It was a ticket to
nowhere. And the only stretching and bending I was ever prepared to do was stretching back on the stool and bending my
elbow to drain my martini.

So I did just that, letting the hot tang of the gin afterburn
flow back over my molars. Then I called the waitress over
and asked for the check. I left her a fat tip in the saucer. I
could barely afford it and she wouldn't thank me for it, but
she had a pleasant face, nice teeth, nice tits, no conversation.
You couldn't ask for more. Then I got up and strolled outside.
I took a minute to get my bearings, scanning around for a va-
cant cab at the same time, pulling in jumbo-sized lungfuls of
carcinogens.

The cabby fate eventually allotted me was an immigrant il-
literate. Sign language just about served for directions, but the
almighty dollar spoke louder and clearer.

We set off through bomb-blast puffs of steam and smoke,
riding through the Village onto Sixth Avenue, which we followed doggedly, swerving around potholes and mounting the
sidewalk whenever necessary, jolting around in our seats like
a couple of pioneers in a chuck wagon. We took a left on
Twenty-third and a right onto Eighth Avenue. Stopping at
some lights, the cabby plucked a prize booger out of his nostril and munched on it while I stared out the window at a
bunch of kids throwing bored bodies routinely around to the
pumping roar of a ghetto blaster. One spotted me and flipped
me the bird.

The lights changed and the cab pulled away. We passed an
old lady with a mustache who was rooting around for food in
the spillover from the trash cans outside a burger joint. She
straightened up, spat in her hand, and rubbed her fingers
around in the spittle, divining. Then she bent down again.
We passed a shop doorway in which a dirty-faced girl who
had probably never been beautiful sat splayed out with a scrap
of cardboard in her lap. The card read, *I Fuck for Food*. A slat-
ribbed dog beside her licked the eczema flakes from her fingers. I debated, not entirely as a joke, whether to stop the cab
and take the girl up on her offer.

We drove on (left on Thirty-fourth, right onto Tenth Avenue), shuttling through the city loom.

Two blocks from the river, west of Times Square, I saw a young black kid toting a carrier bag along the street, a spring in his air-cushioned step. The bag came from a major chain of bookstores, and it didn't look like it had books in it—clothing, drugs, something bulky and shapeless like that—but nonetheless at the sight of it I got to thinking about books, other people's books, *successful* authors' books, and I pictured them, row upon row of fat hardcover extravaganzas, stacked in piles so high they mirrored the towers and excesses of New York itself. *Big* books. Bricks, doorstops, cinder blocks. Books written and sold by weight. A welter of slabs propped up like headstones in the graveyard of literature.

Maybe that was what I should do. Maybe that was the way out. Write a blockbuster. I could just imagine it. *Yeah, I'm gonna sit right down and write me a blockbuster. Gonna bust me some blocks, boy! I'm gonna write me a boner fidey ball breaker. Yeah! My publishers are gonna love it, the critics are gonna hate it, and Steve King's gonna say on the dust jacket . . .*

Dust jacket.

Dust jacket.

Dust.

I shook my head and blinked three times at the luminous balloon of my face reflected in the cab's side window. Somewhere in the barren wasteland at the back of my mind, somewhere made tiny by distance, something glimmered. Was it? . . . Could it be? . . . Dare I hope that there was the tiniest possibility that it might even conceivably be . . . ?

An idea?

I closed my eyes and concentrated, but the glimmer had gone, swallowed back into the emptiness that spawned it. It must have been a flashback, a phantom memory of a time when I *did* have ideas, and good ones, and often.

The cab started to slow and I opened my eyes. Up ahead, ambulance lights flashed, spinning arcs of red onto the sides of buildings. We dropped from ten miles an hour to around four or five. A man was lying across the gutter by a secondhand record store and a soft-porn parlor, looking like he was asleep and having good dreams. He wasn't.

My driver cursed in his native tongue, whatever that was (Tagalog? Croatian?). A cop waved the cab by. I closed my eyes again and checked for the idea, hoping against hope that it might still be there. But whatever I had glimpsed in the middle of that arid desolation couldn't have been anything more than the shimmer of a mirage. Could it?

I settled back into the seat, suddenly needing to piss badly, and we followed the nose-to-tailpipe crawl of traffic toward home.

Home: a shoe-box apartment in the upper nineties. Sometimes at night you can hear what sounds like firecrackers popping up in Harlem. This isn't some mistimed Fourth of July celebration. The firecrackers are small arms and Uzis, and for every one that goes off someone oohs and aahs and dies.

The elevator was out of order again so I schlepped up the stairs. Outside my door, I fumbled with my key. Somewhere down the corridor a television was playing. I strained, but couldn't make out what show was on. A siren Dopplered along Riverside Drive and I thought I heard a distant scream but it may just have been car tires. Then there was a dog bark, and another, then a man's voice yelling something in Spanish peppered with good old Anglo-Saxon obscenities.

I let myself in. The weak light from the hallway seeped in around my legs, showing up throw rug, comfortable armchair, coffee table, and less comfortable director's chair in faint relief, and trapping my spindly shadow silhouette within it like an insect in amber. Its head—my head—was canted against the foot of the desk. On top of the desk, in front of the window, squat and dark against the ghostly starshine of New York City, sat the hooded shape of my Smith Corona. Gateway to dreams. Ticket to despair. Waiting.

Well, good of you to drop by, the typewriter said, voice muffled by its dustcover. *And what fucking time d'you call this?*

"Fuck *you*," I replied, tossing my keys onto the coffee

table, kicking the door closed behind me. The light from the hallway narrowed and slid shut.

When I had completed my transaction with the toilet bowl, I sauntered into the kitchen, to be met by Hudson demanding food, now. I fed her the reeking remnants of an old can of cat food, then rummaged through the refrigerator for something marginally more fit for human consumption. I came across a bottle of San Miguel lurking behind a carton of milk that was well past its sell-by date. Alcohol being a luxury I could afford only in small quantity but hungered for in large amounts, finding the beer was like striking gold.

The clean, earnest face of a boy just scraping into his teens peered from the side of the milk carton. The text below declared he had been missing since last September. He looked like a nice kid: clean, thoughtful, grown-up but not in a precocious way . . . and now almost certainly decomposing at the bottom of a lake somewhere, naked, hog-tied, throat slashed, colon full of semen, asshole mashed to hamburger.

I took the beer to the study and sat down in the more comfortable of the two chairs, my right shoulder mere inches away from my old buddy, the Smith Corona. It would be so easy, wouldn't it, just to shift over to the desk chair and roll a sheet of paper into that baby and start to type. I reached out and raised the cover, which I had put on so that I wouldn't be able to see the typewriter . . . and so that the typewriter wouldn't be able to see me. Bared, the keys looked dull and unused. Betrayed.

I let the cover fall, then leaned back and selected a volume of poetry from the bookshelf on my left. I settled down into the chair's stuffing. I popped the cap on the San Miguel and beckoned to Hudson to come and join me for a small celebration. She declined, hopping up onto the windowsill instead, hunkering down, tucking her forepaws beneath her breast and turning her head away to gaze out with her amber eyes on her distant namesake as it crawled its way to the sea.

I flipped open the book of verse and took a sip of the beer. I chose this pastime, rather than flipping through the TV channels, because there was a chance that one or other or both of my only two friends in the world might drop in, and it wouldn't do for them to catch the only writer they personally knew in the act of watching *television.* As far as I was aware, neither Chip, who lived on one of the floors below, nor Prima, who lived on one of the floors above, had anything better to do this evening but come and bug me. While I sat and waited and hoped, I read some of the poems, cradling the beer bottle to my chest. Then I threw the book away in disgust. It wasn't that the poet was bad. Far from it. He was good. No, he wasn't even good. He was *great.* He threaded those old well-worn, familiar words together into new and eloquent configurations. Each line was a guitar string waiting to be plucked and sing its sweet note of emotion. That was why I couldn't read him.

Television was better. Television beats reading by a mile, because television is the Glass Teat—someone else came up with that; I could never have thought of *that*—on which the world suckles and gluts itself and is pacified. Never mind Prima and Chip. Who gave a damn what they thought? I switched the set on and flicked through the channels until I found some sport. Pretty soon I was cheering away as a football team I had never thought much about romped to victory over another football team I couldn't have given two shits about.

When the game ended, I shambled into the bathroom to urinate again. I glanced at my watch, and decided to brush my teeth and shower. No one was coming to visit this bored asshole tonight.

Soon I was tucked up all snug as a bug in bed, without a good book, my glasses minding their own business on the bedside table. I hadn't drawn the curtains. Fuzzed by myopia, the city beyond the window was an undersea fantasy of drowned lights, great coral pillars of soft phosphorescence swimming in wine-dark depths. An ache of despair throbbed in the pit of my belly. I wished I was dead.

Were dead.

Goddamn subjunctives.

The following morning promised to be a morning just like any other, the next link in a chain of days stretching back more months than I cared to remember to the time when I had last written something good, something worthwhile, something that didn't die on the page gasping for air.

The coffee had perked, and Hudson had been fed and was licking her paws in a what-next kind of a way, and the bed had been made, and there was nothing really honestly worth reading in the newspaper, and I had rolled a fresh sheet of letter-sized paper into the Smith Corona and the machine was sitting there, sticking out its white-paper tongue like some Shinto demon god, laying down the old challenge: *What's it to be, big boy? Me, or a trip down to Cosmo's coffee shop for breakfast; or me, or a handful of pointless phone calls to your agent and your publisher and the tax office; or me, or a morning on your fat ass in front of the tube laughing at cartoons and game shows and talk shows and daytime soaps, or me?*

"Bully," I whispered.

The typewriter stared back with blank black ribbon-reel eyes and grinned a glitter of key teeth.

I poured myself a coffee, milking and sugaring it for energy, then walked back to the desk, swerving at the last possible moment to take in the view from the window, which I had seen only, oh, about eight million times before. The traffic was thin down on the street. The early-morning rush had given way to the midmorning dawdle. Still, even the diminished rumble of cars was reassuring. So long as the cars rumbled, the world turned. Recently I had begun to dread a moment when the noise would stop and an awful sibilant hush would fill the air, a high hiss-whine heralding The End.

The End. Of me. Of everything.

An end to the drought of stories. An end to the dearth of ideas.

I sipped my coffee.

Maybe an End wasn't such a bad thing after all.

A high hiss-whine.

I turned away from the window and ambled, pretending not to hurry, over to the typewriter. A yard, a mere three feet from my chair, I veered off again into the bathroom. (It was the coffee. It had got to the stage where even the smell of the stuff sent my bowels into spasm.) I reemerged shortly to the gurgle of flushing water, brisking my palms together. My stride was purposeful now, oh, yes, now there were going to

be no more interruptions, there were going to be no more
bullshit diversions, now I was really going to do it, I was really . . .

A couple of the books on the shelves had somehow gotten
out of alphabetical order. (I'd have blamed Maria, the cleaning lady, if I hadn't had to let her go a couple of years back.)
I went over to correct the error.

This author! When had I last read any of *this* author? Oh,
God, and I used to love him so. Used to worship him! When
I was much younger, much much much younger, I'd read
everything the guy had ever written, every novel at least once,
every short story at least twice—all in the space of a year.
Annus (as they say) mirabilis. The year that turned my head
around and set me going on the right path, with this author
slapping me on the butt and yelling *Giddap, there!*

So what was his secret? How did he put the words together
so immaculately, so fearlessly, so goddamn effortlessly? A
quick flick-through might reveal the trick.

I flicked.

I looked.

I cursed.

Bastard! How dare he! How dare he be so talented! How
dare he be so much better! How dare he be so . . .

So dead.

I hated him for that, for being dead. Because there was
nothing to look forward to from him. Because there were no
new books expected of him. Because he had left behind a
complete and perfect legacy of joy and wonder for all time (or
for as long as people remember how to read).

I wished . . . I wished for him to be *alive.*

So come back to me, wheedled the typewriter, *come back
to me and let's do our stuff together, you and me, me and you,
bucko. Partners. Hero and sidekick. Man and wife. Best buddies. Fred and Barney. Fred and Ginger. Batman and Robin.
Let's free associate all the way from the beginning to the end
of the tale. Run your fingertips across my keyboard, caress my
carriage return, fondle my platen, twiddle my bail bar. . . .*

"It's not so easy!" I cried, clutching the air above my bald
scalp where there had once been hair before I wore it all out.
"It's. Not. So. Easy. Any. More." My eyes must have looked

smaller than ever behind my glasses, like tiny fish eggs in big glass bowls. "I haven't got a clue how. I don't know where to start. I don't know where to end. I can't come up with anything that half a dozen, a dozen others haven't come up with already!"

Hudson had been watching me all this while with her big steady amber eyes, watching this extraordinary demigod half-wit dancing back and forth across the narrow dusty apartment. Now, bored, she padded off into the bedroom.

Of course it's easy, said the typewriter. *Starting's the easiest part. "A journey of a thousand miles must begin with a single step." All you have to do is hit a key.*

"Hit a key? *Which* fucking key?"

Any key.

So I sat down and I typed: 　

```
Once upon a time in a shoe box on the
eighth floor of a crummy apartment
building there lived a lunatic who
talked to his typewriter.
```

Then I tore the sheet of paper out, crumpled it up, slam-dunked it into the wastebasket and rolled in a fresh one.

The Smith Corona accepted this mutely, cynically.

And I typed:

```
Whether I shall turn out to be the hero
of my own life, or whether I'll be just
another meat-beating son of a bitch,
these pages will show . . . in spades!
```

I tore that sheet out, too, and crumpled it up and slam-dunked it and rolled in another fresh one.

The Smith Corona remained resolutely silent.

And I typed:

```
The crazy writer who couldn't write
thought: officious little prick. And
then smashed his typewriter into a
zillion tiny pieces. The End.
```

That sheet went the way of the others.

Still not a peep from the beleaguered machine.

And I rolled in a fourth sheet and stared at the blankness of the paper.

And then the Smith Corona said, *"A high hiss-whine . . ."*

"Eh?"

That's how it starts. With a high hiss-whine.

"No, it doesn't."

How do you know? How come all of a sudden you know so goddamn much about writing, asswipe?

"I don't. I just know that there's nothing in there anymore," I replied weakly, shaking my head and hearing my brain rattle.

Well, at least you've got a dried pea in there. That means you can whistle. You know how to whistle, don't you? You just—

"I know! I know! Why the fuck won't you leave me alone?"

Never. We had a bargain, you and I. Till death us do part. I haven't given up my side of it. I still work, don't I? Sure, I need a service now and then, but basically my innards are sound. What's your excuse?

"I look inside myself," I said, "and all I see is . . . nothing. A big brown expanse of nothing. A long time ago I detonated a series of explosions in there, chain reactions of ideas, and for a while they shone. They shone so fiercely. They shone brighter than a thousand suns! And for a while their light illuminated the farthest reaches of me, the darkest corners. But now . . . now there's only desert and desolation. I'm dry. I'm a dry old fool."

Is there really nothing in that desolation? No sagebrush? No snakes? No scorpions? No cacti to cut for their moisture? No rattlers to roast over a campfire for their flesh? No grinning geckos or lurking lizards coiled in the cool underground waiting for just the right conditions to crawl up to the surface?

"Nothing!" I wailed.

Nothing? Nothing at all? Look closer.

"There's . . ." I hesitated. "There is something glimmering."

Glimmering. Good.

"I can't quite . . . A line. Two lines."
Good. Good.
"Iron."
Very good.
"Tracks!"
And what lies in between them?
"Sleepers."
Words, moron! Words!
"Sleeping words."
Wake them!
"I can't."
What's coming?
"I can't see."
No, but you can hear it, can't you? You can heeeaaarrr it.
". . . yes . . ."
Quick! Sit down! Sit down now!
". . . yes . . ."

And I scrambled into my chair, not caring that I spilled coffee over the desktop and down my pants leg, and I shot my cuffs, freeing my wrists, and I articulated my fingers, each hand performing a small Mexican wave, and I hunched my shoulders as though anticipating a tremendous blow, and I leaned forward . . .

. . . and the idea was hurtling toward me. I *could* hear it. I could *feel* it. Coming so fast I didn't know if I could stop it in time. Maybe I couldn't. Maybe it would race past, lost forever.

But I *would* stop it.

Or die trying.

One

1

The heat had a sound like a note plucked from a taut wire. Within the shimmering harmonics of the note could be heard the chirrup of insects sawing on their bowlegs and the keening of black-backed birds yelling warnings and the yelp of prairie dogs staking their claim on the land. And woven through this tapestry of sound like a single silver thread was a hum from the railway tracks that sliced across the land from way over here to way over there, a high hiss-whine vibrating in the hazy air and reverberating deep in the ties laid down long, long ago by convicts and Chinese laborers.

And in the far distance, on the quivering horizon, a thin solitary plume of dry black smoke rose and dissipated in a swirl of gray cotton-candy streamers.

A train.

This was the message carried by the twin iron telegraphs over miles and miles of dead earth, beneath miles and miles of empty sky.

A train. A train is coming.

The prairie dogs scurried for their burrows. The black-backed birds took to the wing. The insects scattered like a handful of rice. A train was coming.

And such a train! A train like none of these creatures had ever fled from before. A monster of a train with a glittering beast of a locomotive, all jet black and silver from cow-catcher to running boards, with shining steel pipes running the length of its cylindrical boiler, and a black tender detailed in silver to match and loaded with glistening coal. A train that was all smoke and steam and blur, eating up the track, roaring along the track, groaning, whickering, *bellowing* down the track . . .

. . . suddenly past, the hiss-whine tailing away and pure silence rolling after it like tumbleweed, and, suspended in the train's wake, a tang of burning, and a faint buzzing, and a faint echo of laughter.

2

A few miles down the line a town waited, and its name was Escardy Gap.

Escardy Gap: a tidy gridwork of streets and avenues, tree lined, verdant, residential, quiet. Oh so quiet.

Escardy Gap: home to fewer than eight hundred souls, and all of them good and all of them decent.

Escardy Gap: pinned firmly on the axis of Christianity, democracy, and good neighborliness.

Escardy Gap: an oasis of humanity amid blasted wastes of badlands, a tiny pocket of perfection in a region God seemed to have left half-finished.

Escardy Gap: a home for midmorning front-porch murmurings, and afternoons spent fishing for trout until the sprawling summer dried out the creek bed, a haven for seemingly endless and everlasting early evenings.

Escardy Gap: a place where nickel chocolate bars and Tootsie Rolls were on sale in the one and only general store alongside spinning racks of comic books filled to the brim with four-color wonder, and all for a dime, just one thin dime, folks, just one tenth of a dollar!

Escardy Gap: where kindly, wintry old men in plaid shirts liked to crowd in snug-warm back rooms, smoking pipes and playing checkers for matchsticks while a Chesterfield-toting

Ernie Bilko smiled down benevolently from an old tin plaque tacked on to the back wall.

Escardy Gap: where a father's idea of living dangerously was to roll up his shirtsleeves and say "golly!" or "land sakes!"

Escardy Gap: where a mother would clasp a wooden spoon in guilty delight to her apron breast whenever an especially juicy morsel of gossip came her way, and still be sure to have dinner on the table by six, secure in the knowledge that her children would make it home in time, safe and sound.

Escardy Gap: where the only noise to disturb the sleepy stillness of a weekend afternoon was the crack of a BB pellet fired from a Daisy rifle or an echoing whack as a well-wielded baseball bat connected with an incoming pitch in Poacher's Park or the dull rattling thud of the latest copy of *Grit* or the *Saturday Evening Post* hitting the wood or the mesh of a screen door.

Escardy Gap: where on three hundred and seventeen radio sets, the Shadow knew, and the old tomb door to the Inner Sanctum creaked on in deliciously deadly earnest; where on forty-nine phonograms the Four Freshmen crooned and the heart-stopping promise of rock and roll hung paused with a baby-faced kiss-curled Bill Haley just about to open his mouth to sing "One, two, three o'clock . . ."

Escardy Gap: where in the town square, every afternoon just before three, the shadow of the town-hall clock would strike the window of the Merrie Malted Soda Shoppe, telling its proprietor Old Joe Dolan that it was time once again to mix up the Double Chocolate Shrapnels and the Rocket's Red Glares ready for the moment when the end-of-day bell pealed out at the schoolhouse and in they would storm, a flurry of breathlessness and squeaking sneakers, their schoolbooks (buckled up with old leather belts in neat and sometimes not-so-neat bundles) thrown forgotten for the day onto Old Joe's thick-padded diner stools or propped on his counter against jars of hard candies and chrome napkin dispensers, the wide-eyed, cowlicked boys and ponytailed girls, resplendent in their gaudy baseball jackets and worn jeans and simple skirts, spared once more from the toils of Knowledge to sit and suck at and gulp down and just generally never, not ever, get enough of those two-scoop, three-scoop, sometimes even four-scoop multicolored wonders of ice cream and syrup and rainbow sprinkles and homemade wafer biscuits, and knowing in that instant, in that special impossible eternal fraction of time which was about as near to a thousandth part of a millionth of a nanosecond as you could get, that school was well and truly out for the day.

Escardy Gap: where, every evening and all Saturday morning and for the best part of Sunday afternoon, in the Essolodo Motion Picture Palace on the corner of Main and Delacy, the same wide-eyed kids, their stomachs groaning with popcorn, their bladders bulging fit to burst with 7UP, gazed up in awe at monochrome marvels of mirth, mystery, and masked avengers.

A few miles down the line Escardy Gap waited, dozing in the summer heat like an old dog too dumb, just too darned lazy, to think of moving into the shade.

3

The train raced along the tracks, a gleaming metal millipede, eating up the old wooden ties and spitting them out behind.

Three women rode the locomotive, clinging to the pipes that crisscrossed the black boiler, pipes so scaldingly hot no one human could have held on to them without earning a palmful of blisters. Leaning into the wind and laughing, their long manes of hair snaking out behind them, their scanty silken robes sculpting their bodies, the women's faces were masks of manic glee. They looked young, these female creatures, teenager fresh, peachy of skin and ripe of flesh, but they were older than that, much older. They were as old as flint.

And in the writhing white clouds of smoke that billowed from the locomotive's mushroom-shaped funnel, it was possible to make out faces—faces screaming, faces crying, faces pleading, faces like theatrical masks of tragedy, faces twisted into all the shapes of suffering.

And from behind the drawn blinds of the two trailing carriages not one of the dozens of passengers within peered out. The women riding the locomotive trembled and shuddered in anticipation, chattering their teeth in time to the tune of wheels on rails—*chitter-clack, chitter-clack, chitter-clack*— but for those hidden within the carriages there was no excitement, no yearning, no elation or trepidation. For them there was only a stifling, wearying sense of necessity. They looked forward to the performance that lay ahead of them the way the average human being might look forward to the next breath of air, the next sip of water, the next decent meal. The urgency of the train, its steam and sweat and blur, was a sham.

A sign came up beside the track. It said:

ESCARDY GAP—2 MILES
WHISTLE

The train shot by, faster than a speeding bullet, and the sign whirled like a windmill in its slipstream. And the train did not whistle.

4

Of all the wide-eyed, cowlicked boys in Escardy Gap, it was generally agreed among the grown-ups that the brightest and the best was young Joshua Knight.

Sure, in many ways Josh was no different from the other boys. The knees of his blue jeans were more hole than denim, his shirttails and his waistband shared a permanent mutual aversion, and the laces of his sneakers often forgot what it was like to be tied. But what set Josh apart from the rest was his quiet, gentle, reflective nature. He was intelligent, polite, levelheaded, less prone to fits and starts than his peers. Folks reckoned this had a lot to do with Josh's parents leaving him, and this world, when he was at a tender age. He had had to grow up fast, faster than was natural, and learn all about responsibility at an age when most kids were learning how to be utterly irresponsible, and this was looked upon with sympathy and regret by adults who had watched their own childhoods whisk by too quick to savor and mourned them from the troubled vantage point of experience.

So while the other kids loved to charge out of the Essoldo Motion Picture Palace after the Saturday-morning screening was over and hurtle down Main Street with their tongues down around their ankles, sprinting to the Merrie Malted as if ice cream might, just might, be declared illegal tomorrow, Josh preferred to walk away from the movie theater slowly and with the air of someone who had just woken up, someone still tethered in the traces of a dream. Josh could never quite understand how the other kids managed to shake off the celluloid spell so easily, or even how they could sit there hooting and hollering and howling during the showing of the movie as if there were still a part of them down there in their seats, as if not every single ounce of their consciousness was up there on the silver screen. Kids—other kids—were a mystery to Josh. But then, by the same token, Josh was a mystery to most other kids.

By the time Josh reached the Merrie Malted this Saturday morning, his peers were already halfway down into their sundae dishes, and they called out to him with smudged clown mouths, "Hey, Josh!" and "Come on in and join us, Josh!" and "This has to be the best Vanilla Lime Miracle I ever tasted, Josh!"

But Josh kept on going. He strolled right by Old Joe Dolan's emporium as if it weren't even there. And inside the Merrie Malted the kids watched silent for a few seconds, ice-cream floats sinking into caramel and chocolate goo like dying mastodons into tar pits. Then, all at once, they resumed eating.

Josh kept on going, oblivious, on and on until he came to his house. There he halted, looked up, blinked around, glanced back, and wondered why his feet had taken him this far when he was sure he had told them to stop for an ice cream. He stared down at his sneakers and flexed his toes, then squinted up into the sun. If a guy couldn't trust his feet then what *could* he trust?

He debated whether to head back to the Merrie Malted. He turned around and stared back along Muldavey Street, watching the heat rise from the roadway and juggling his

twenty-three cents—a dime, a nickel and eight pennies—
around and around in the pocket of his jeans.

He lifted his face and sniffed the afternoon breeze. Nothing but the usual smells of dust and heat. He squinted up at
the sun to see if it was still describing its daily orbit. It was.
He glanced around at the smooth lawns, the painted mailboxes, the white picket fences, the red roofs, and the shadowed porches of his neighbors' houses. Nothing different
there. Escardy Gap was the same as it always was. So what
was it he was feeling? What was this sense he had that something was about to happen, something very bad?

Then he heaved his shoulders up in a huge shrug and said
to himself, *Well, whatever it is, wherever it's coming from,
there's nothing I can do it about it right now.*

Besides, a triceratops had arrived in the post this morning
and demanded to be assembled.

Josh turned again and skipped up the porch steps to where
his grandfather and his lunch (and the triceratops) were waiting for him.

5

The train was very near its destination now and the
women—sisters of a sort, though they were related in
ways unfamiliar to you or me, sisters only in the weird
sense—chattered their delight louder than ever *(chitter-
CLACK, chitter-CLACK)*, for the air hereabouts hummed
with happiness, glowed with goodness, stank of selflessness
and sacrifice, and reeked of respect. The women inhaled,
heads back and eyes closed and teeth bared, and they relished
the smell, sucked it in deep, swilled it around in their mouths
like connoisseurs, and their eyes rolled behind their lids like
the bellies of storm clouds that boil and swell just before the
rain comes.

It was a smell they knew. It had a taste. The taste of barely
healed belly buttons, of toothless smiles and scuffed knees, of
still-unplucked cherries and still-slumbering scrotums, of fatherhood and motherhood, of matinee tears and twilight
promises. . . .

And suddenly the rain brimmed and broke from the women's stormy eyes and coursed down their shivering cheeks to mingle with the thick emissions bubbling from their mouths. Bliss! *CHITTER-CLACK!!!*

Now, above the shimmering whir of the wheels, it was just possible to hear noises from the two carriages as the passengers also got wind of the scent: rustlings, stirrings, dry-leaf whisperings, stealthy foot paddings, finger-to-mouth hushings, and a swishing of curtains, like the myriad silent activities of a formicary, sensed but not seen.

The train whisked by another sign. . . .

ESCARDY GAP—1 MILE
PLEASE WHISTLE

. . . and snapped the post in two with the force of its passing. And again, the train did not obey.

6

Nobody had called the mayor of Escardy Gap anything but Mayor since his first and last uncontested election twelve years ago, although in his time he had been known by many names, so many he would have needed an entire address book to catalogue them all.

Indeed, Mayor had had so many names he couldn't always remember the one he had started out with in the first place, not without looking at one of his old posters. And there it would be:

AND DOUGLAS B. RAYMOND AS
UNCLE MATTHEW

Or perhaps:

FATHER MENDACIOUS . . . DOUGLAS RAYMOND

Or even:

PLUS DOUGLAS RAYMOND

And sometimes:

WITH D. RAYMOND

But most often:

FEATURING A CAST OF THOUSANDS!

Nor would he ever let anyone forget his illustrious former career. "Did I ever tell you about the time Ethel Merman trod on my toe?" Mayor might begin a conversation, way before a hello or a how-do-you-do. Or, beaming with pride, he might inform even the most passing of acquaintances in the most casual of conversations, "The critics said my Hamlet had 'all the expressiveness and subtlety usually associated with the Great Dane.' " ("Great Dane the morning," was the response on one such occasion when Mayor was passing a few moments of the day with Big Ben Burden on the stoop of Wilbur Cohen's general store. "It was pearls before swine, I kid you not," Big Ben told his wife Janey later. He knew *she* would appreciate the pun.)

Some people listened to Mayor's theatrical anecdotes and Hollywood reminiscences because he was the mayor and it would have been impolite not to do so. Others *pretended* to listen to him, but their eyes would gradually glaze over as their thoughts strayed to what they were going to have for dinner that evening or what was going to happen in tonight's Fireside Theater. Still others simply nodded and changed the subject. Quickly.

The truth was, mayor was Mayor's most fulfilling role by far, the one he felt he was born to play. That he executed it with style, verve, flair, and perhaps even panache, few would argue, although, equally, few could agree on who Mayor "had been" the last time they had seen him. Depending on the day, or even the time of day, or even what he had had to eat for breakfast that morning, he could be any one of several noted character actors. Raymond Massey, Cary Grant, Gregory Peck, and Claude Rains were regular masks donned by Escardy Gap's thespian town official, but there were also occasional appearances in the town square or along Main Street by such screen luminaries as Peter Lorre and Pat O'Brien (and W. C. Fields or Slim Pickens if he'd been at the whisky).

So it was far simpler just to call him Mayor, because that was all he was now. All? It was more than enough! Dressed up in his finery for July Fourth or Labor Day, Mayor would take a look in his old faithful, truthful makeup mirror, and grin and wink at himself—mayor!—as he went over his speech once again, all atingle at the prospect of stepping up to the podium and delivering his well-chosen words to the assembled folk of Escardy Gap while Old Glory waved high overhead against the blue and several hundred miniature versions fluttered in the crowd's hands and the band sat just itching to strike up "The Star-Spangled Banner" (which, if he was feeling particularly mischievous, Mayor might well sing as Groucho Marx or Sidney Greenstreet). Here was an audience who loved him uncritically, their mayor-of-a-thousand-faces, who hung on his every pause and nuance and applauded like crazy when he finished his speech—perhaps as James Cagney—on a choked, heartfelt "God bless Escardy Gap, and God bless the United States of America!"

Mayor should have known things were about to go wrong that Saturday the moment he woke up as Bogart. He hated Bogart. He climbed out of bed and shrugged his way to the bathroom, his posture stooped and sagging as if the weight of several worlds rested on his shoulders. He urinated slowly and cynically.

Over breakfast at Billy's Bar & Grill down by the railway depot, Alice Tremaine, who worked the early shift, was surprised when Mayor walked in, sat down, adjusted his belt, pulled up his top lip to reveal his teeth, and asked for some flapjacks with a sibilant, sardonic lisp. (" 'Fapdjash' is what it sounded like," Alice told her husband, Bob, when he came by later to pick up a few beers on his way to help Ike Swivven mend his fence out on Boundary Hill. "Fapdjash! I ask you!") And when it turned out that the coffee had stewed in the pot, Mayor informed a profusely apologetic Alice that maybe it didn't amount to a hill of beans in this crazy world, but if she didn't bring him some fresh coffee right now, this could be the end of a beautiful friendship.

"Is something the matter?" she asked him.

"Pour it out, Sam," Mayor replied, and shook his head as if he could rid himself of a sense of foreboding the way he could shake a stone from his shoe.

As he went about his mayoral duties—which on a Saturday morning generally meant dropping by as many people's houses as he could and having a chat, some coffee, maybe a cookie or two—a noticeable change came over Mayor. Simply put, he stopped being Bogie and became himself: Douglas B. Raymond. And as Douglas B. Raymond he started slipping innocent-seeming remarks into the conversation, to gauge whether anyone else shared his indefinable doubts. For example, he might say, oh so casually, "Mighty strange weather we're having, don't you think?" in the hope that somebody would pick up on it and agree, and then he could lead the conversation by the nose the way he wanted. All he got in reply, however, were puzzled smiles and "No stranger than normal, Mayor," and even "Say, I don't think I recognize that one, Mayor, who is it?"

It occurred to Mayor that he might be the only one who felt like this. If so, what did that signify? That the threat was directed at him alone? That the danger he sensed applied to him and no one else? No, it was larger than that. It was hovering over the whole town, *his* town, like a huge thunderhead. And pretty soon, he reckoned, it was going to break open and send down rain.

7

The train was nearing the low swell of a hill, and the black mouth of a tunnel loomed, fringed with an array of perfect stone teeth. The three women crouched down against the boiler, still cackling, still chitter-clacking.

With a swooping whoosh, the locomotive dived headfirst into the tunnel, lugging the carriages along with it. Roaring darkness enveloped the women, and the smokestack belched copiously into their faces. They loved it!

Obediently the train followed the sinuous twists and turns that had earned this tunnel its name, the Snake. Through the intestinal darkness, with no light visible ahead or behind, it raced. Orange sparks flickered around the women's heads, and they joyfully snapped at these, extending their tongues and gulping them down like a trio of greedy frogs catching fireflies.

8

Ike Swivven could see the clock tower on the town hall from where he was working, wrapping wire around the posts of the fence that marked the edge of his homestead, and that also marked the steep drop where the railroad sliced into the northern edge of Boundary Hill. The clock tower was all Ike could see of Escardy Gap. The rest of the town was hidden beneath trees, the occasional break in the canopy indicating where a four-way road junction or the center of a municipal square lay. Over to the far west of town Ike could just about make out the glittering ribbon of water that was Fleischer's Creek.

It was a quarter after eleven, or as near as never mind. Bob was due to arrive shortly with a bag of beers. He was probably down at Billy's Bar & Grill right now, kibitzing with his ladywife, Alice. Ike smiled a touch ruefully.

He finished stapling a length of the wire to the post he had just resunk, then stood up with a long groan, a hand bracing his aching spine. He wiped his forehead with his glove and swallowed hard. A whorl of wire lay at his feet along with a claw hammer, a pair of wire cutters, and a bundle of fence posts he had bought from Wilbur Cohen at a reasonable discount; Ike, at least, thought it was reasonable, though Wilbur had had his own ideas about that. Ike had been hard at work since seven that morning, and he was looking forward to seeing Bob, not for the help so much as the company.

Things had been quiet for Ike Swivven these past two years since Emily had died. Too quiet, perhaps. He was glad Emily hadn't suffered any, but her departure had left a hole in his life and an absence in the home that just couldn't be filled. It was as though there was a color missing from everything and, no matter what he did, Ike simply couldn't put that color back. So he busied himself instead, hoping that if his mind was occupied enough it wouldn't notice anything was gone.

At seventy-three years of age, Ike still rose with the rooster and got out into the fresh air as fast as he could each morning. He always had to be doing something, even if only for doing something's sake. The fence, for instance, didn't really need mending. The cleats holding the wire in place were strong and true, and the wire itself had barely rusted, and only rarely did some burrowing critter dislodge a post. But it was good for the body and the soul to get down on your haunches and wrestle with a problem every once in a while. It was better than sitting around downing the beers at the Bar & Grill, which only got you drunk as a skunk and fat as a neutered tomcat; and much better than sitting at home on your own, thinking too much, thinking so much that your thoughts tied themselves up in knots.

So Ike was glad of the occasional visitor, and Bob was the closest thing he had to a best friend, even though there was a gap of several decades between them and Bob had some pretty funny ideas about some things, particularly about the Russkies, who, according to Bob, were responsible for everything bad in the world today. They were even responsible for bad weather, if Bob was to be believed. On account of their nuclear testing, see. That was why the past few summers had been so long and hot, the past few winters so ferociously cold.

Ike had neither the heart nor the patience to try to explain to Bob that the Russians were human beings just like the rest of us, and that those he had fought alongside during the Big One had been brave, generous souls, icy when you first met them but soon thawing out as you got to know them; and that over in the Nevada desert and down in the South Pacific the U.S. government was up to some nuclear monkey business of their own, tinkering with the atom any which way and curious to see what came of it; and that the past few summers had been no longer or hotter and the past few winters no more ferociously cold than the summers and winters before them.

Speaking of which . . .

Ike sniffed the air. Was that rain he could smell? The sky

looked clear enough but there was a promise of *something* hovering in the breeze, mixing up with the flies and the wasps and the soft watery taste that blew up the river past the train tracks. Then, thinking that he had heard a noise, he glanced back at the house.

"Rufus?" he said, and then remembered with a sudden dull throb of regret that Rufus, like Emily, was no longer there, would never be there. He pictured the big dumb old brown mutt in his dotage, flopped out in the shade of the maple over by the garage, dreaming about the days he used to run every-where chasing any rabbit or raccoon too stupid not to have heard those huge paws come crashing over the earth.

"We all dream about those days," Ike told the wind. "Yes, sir."

His head snapped up. There it was again, that sound he had thought could be Rufus whining in his sleep but wasn't. Maybe it was time to go visit Doc Wheeler and get his ears checked out. Maybe he was getting a touch of tinny-tits, or whatever it was called.

The wind had risen a little. The branches of the maple were twisting and rustling, ducking and bobbing every which way, throwing filigree shadow patterns over the empty and dusty dry patch of ground where Rufus used to love to lie and loll.

Slowly the sound grew clearer, gained focus: the churn of pistons, the puffing of steam, the hiss of wheels.

Ike both smiled and frowned simultaneously. It was just a train. But there wasn't a train due, not till Tuesday. After sev-enty years of living on Boundary Hill, Ike thought he knew the railroad timetables pretty well. Minor fluctuations he could understand, but a train arriving in town a full three *days* ahead of schedule? That demanded investigation.

As the locomotive emerged around the foot of the hill, looking for all the world like a black-faced, silver-whiskered cat sneaking out from a bush, Ike Swivven felt the first speed-ings of his heart in his chest. Were those *people* hanging on to the engine? Scampering all over it? *Women?*

And as Ike watched, with a great show of effort the train began to slow, hauling on the brakes, squealing to a halt plumb below where Ike stood at the top of the escarpment.

They stood there for a while, Ike and the train. There was

silence apart from the seethe of steam bucketing out from under the locomotive's stilled wheels and the boiler hissing in a rage of impatience.

Then the three women stepped down from the running boards that ran the length of the locomotive's chassis on both sides. One glanced up and smiled at Ike. It wasn't a warm friendly smile. It didn't say *Well, hi, there, and how're you today?* or *Hot enough for ya?* or *Mind telling us how far to the nearest town?* It said other things, in a tongue that Ike didn't cotton to at all.

Rooted to the spot like one of his own fence posts, Ike watched the three women move past the tender to the first carriage and open one of the doors and take the hands and arms of a big man and guide him down the high last step. He was the biggest man Ike ever saw, and looked like some type of a vagrant, with all kinds of tiny bottles, all sorts of colors, dangling from his ragged coat on pieces of string or twine or something, twisting and turning and sparkling and shining in the wind. Ike marveled at the big man's big head, which was even bigger than it should have been for that big, big body.

The women left the man beside the locomotive, which was ticking over as though the metal were straining to get on, move on down the track, get where it was supposed to be going. Without their assistance the man seemed to be finding it hard to stay upright, his head so heavy it threw his sense of balance off-kilter, and he teetered from side to side at the whim of the wind. Chitter-clacking to themselves, the women moved back to the carriage to help someone else out: a woman.

Ike recognized her instantly. He knew her from the way she held herself, straight but not proud, steady but not stiff, and he knew her from the glossy waterfall of chestnut hair down her back, and he knew her from the exquisite blue eyes that turned up to look at him, brimming with love and tears.

"Emily," Ike whispered, long, low, and lovingly. Then, louder, *"Emily!"* And then, shouting, *"EMILY!"*

And without another thought, Ike Swivven started down the incline toward the track, his feet skidding, his eyes ablaze, his old heart thumping like new against the inside of his rib cage.

9

A short while later the train hit the outskirts of Escardy Gap, rumbling across the canal bridge, rolling past the lumberyard, heading for the heart of town as unerringly as an arrow aimed straight at the bull's-eye. The three women danced over the locomotive with chilling surefootedness and grace, oblivious to the track speeding by mere yards beneath them. They cackled and chitter-clacked while behind them, like a big hungry stomach teased by a single candy and now hankering after a handful, the inhabitants of the black-windowed carriages murmured in anticipation. Slumbering appetites had been whetted.

Weaving from side to side on its chassis like a drunkard pickled on the finest moonshine, the train rocketed past a sign that said, almost apologetically:

ESCARDY GAP
POP. 792
LET US KNOW YOU'RE HERE

And—at last!—a shrill, momentous whistle burst from the engine, rising high into the blue air on a plume of scalding steam.

And the sign exploded into a thousand thousand tiny splinters that rained down on either side of the track like confetti.

10

A nd everyone in Escardy Gap stopped whatever it was they were doing and cocked their heads this way and that, angling their ears to the sky. Fathers whitewashing picket fences broke off midbrushstroke. Mothers latticing apple pies let the pastry strips droop from floury fingers. Grandfathers bottling elderberry and dandelion wines cussed silently as they almost dropped their precious burdens onto musty cellar floors. Grandmothers crocheting shawls and comforters paused between purl and knit. Infants stopped squalling and sat gape-mouthed, dumbstruck. Elder brothers waxing the hoods of the family Chevy Bel Airs, Hudson Wasps, and Nash Ramblers in their driveways glanced up, cloth in hand. Big sisters pulling the last curler from their hair puckered their freshly plucked and penciled eyebrows into a frown. Dogs in cool shade snapped their ears to attention, red rheumy eyes clicking open. Fresh-faced kids spun around on the stools in the Merrie Malted Soda Shoppe, heads jerking outward and upward, ice cream dripping from their spoons onto old Joe's linoleum in soft plops.

And in his bedroom a young-old boy called Joshua Knight looked up, a triceratops's horn in one hand, a hornless triceratops in the other.

And at the town hall a mayor sometimes known as Douglas B. Raymond stumbled to his window, the morning paper crumpling between his fingers.

And over at Ike Swivven's place Bob Tremaine arrived to find Ike there . . . and not there.

TWO

1

Walt Donaldson finished adjusting the station clock to match the time according to his fob watch. He closed the glass cover of the larger of the two timepieces and gave its brass trim a brief but loving polish with his handkerchief. Then he climbed carefully down the stepladder on which he had been perching, folded it up, and leaned it against the wall.

A portly man, Walt didn't so much walk back to his office as waddle, and when he sat down in his desk chair, it was not without a certain amount of squeezing, levering, and grunting. Before he picked up his copy of the latest issue of *Weird Tales,* he mopped his damp palms with the same handkerchief he had used to polish the clock. Then, having run a tongue across his sweat-shiny upper lip, he continued with the story he was reading.

The story was called "The Plane Tree's Plaint," and Walt was relishing every sentence, every word, every syllable, every single letter of it. Going out to set the clock during a break between the short chapters only served to enhance his enjoyment of the story still further, like a brief, appetite-whetting pause between courses of a banquet.

Apart from the fact that it was well written and gripping

and thrilling and enthralling and enchanting and all the things a good short story should be, "The Plane Tree's Plaint" laid one further claim to the attention of Escardy Gap's redoubtable stationmaster. Its author was a regular contributor to *Weird Tales* and other anthologies, a lady by the name of Sara Sienkiewicz, who happened to live in none other a town than Escardy Gap and who was just about the most beautiful creature Walt had ever set eyes on.

Walt, indeed, loved her. He loved her the best way a man can love a woman: from afar. Which meant he loved her without complication or qualification. His adoration was constant and unwavering; it was, above all, pure.

He was quite certain that he loved Sara and that his love was pure because whenever he came within speaking distance of her, he became a gibbering, tongue-tied wreck. As a result, he had never exchanged more than a few basic pleasantries with her. This didn't trouble him. He *knew* Sara. He knew her kindness and compassion and her sheer humanity. He knew everything there was to know about her from her stories, which he clipped solicitously out of the magazines where they appeared and kept indexed and in chronological order in a special binder.

Did *she* love *him?* Walt didn't think so. Walt didn't think she was aware of his existence as any more than an overweight civic functionary in a uniform. Sometimes he allowed himself to draw hope from the way she dropped her eyes shyly whenever she passed him in the street and returned his spluttered, stammering good-morning with a secretive, coquettish, winning smile. But this was his only encouragement. In his heart of hearts, he doubted she saw beyond the uniform. But that was all right. It was undeniably a handsome uniform. It had a dozen brass buttons bright as tiger's eyes set into its rich navy blue worsted cloth, and it was cunningly tailored to show off Walt's figure to the best advantage, making all the things that bulged and sagged look hard and perhaps even muscular. As status symbols went, it was just about the best. And every Sunday, when no trains came or went, Walt's landlady Miss Ingrid Ohllson—also Escardy Gap's schoolmistress—would clean and iron the uniform for him, smooth out the rumples and resurrect the crisp creases and reinvigorate the cloth and scent it with a whiff of lavender, so that Walt could go to work the next day looking and smelling like a million dollars. First thing every Monday, Walt prayed that this week, please, Lord, this week Sara might suddenly realize that within that wonderful, freshly pressed, sweet-smelling uniform, beneath that massive girth, lurked the soul of an eligible and humble and oh-so-loving man.

Personal neatness and keeping the station clean and tidy were things Walt concentrated on largely because they were his duty, but also in order to impress Sara Sienkiewicz. Should Sara ever choose another man, take as husband any-one other than Walter Roderick Donaldson, it was almost too horrible to contemplate what would happen to the state of Es-cardy Gap station and its stationmaster. The gleaming varnish on the teak benches in the waiting room would grow dull. Dust would settle on the timetables and baize bulletin board, never to be feathered away. The great brass station clock would wind down and fall to rust. Walt himself would begin an irreversible decline, forget to brush his hair or comb his mustache, lose weight, grow pallid, pine, dwindle, and even-tually, inevitably . . .

Walt was nearing the end of "The Plane Tree's Plaint," and already anticipating a second reading before he went for lunch, when the whistle blew. The sound of that steam scream sent a chill racing deep into the marrow of his bones. He sat there transfixed, unable to move, unable to breathe, unable to think, while the echoes bounced and batted over the rooftops. When they finally died down, his mind started to turn over as sluggishly as a car's engine on a frosty morning.

The express from Harrisburg via Wayneville wasn't due to arrive until Tuesday, and if there was a special today, the rail-road company would have informed him at least a week in advance. Had it even been a train whistle? It had sounded more like Fay Wray trying to outdo King Kong himself, deci-bel for decibel.

There was only one thing for it.

Before bustling out onto the platform, Walt had sufficient presence of mind to fetch his red and green flags and silver whistle down from a shelf and grab his stationmaster's cap and jam it on his head.

He pulled up short of the platform's edge and leaned out, peering up the track to where the rails narrowed to a knife point.

Nothing.

Then: there! A speck that became a dot that became a spot that, in no time at all, became the face of a black-and-silver locomotive, plumed with smoke like a circus pony's feathered headdress.

Soon the train was pulling level with Walt, immersing him in clouds of smoke and steam. Temporarily blinded and suffocated, it took a great effort to remember where he was and who he was and what he was and what his duties were, and then he started to jump up and down and wave his flags madly, yelling at the top of his voice, *"ESCARDY GAP! ESCARDY GAP! TRAIN NOW ARRIVING AT ESCARDY GAP!"*

2

Over at Billy's Bar & Grill, lunchtime had just begun, and the Evett brothers and Big Ben Burden were running a sweepstakes on whether or not Moose Rollins could fit a whole three-quarter-pound burger into his mouth in one go—bun, catsup, dill pickle and all. Earl Evett maintained that he could and here was a dime to prove it. "Ain't nobody," replied Earl's brother Carroll, *"nobody* can fit in one of Billy's three-quarter-pounders all in one go. Nobody!" And he put down a dime on top of Earl's, and Earl saw that dime and raised it a nickel, which Carroll met with another nickel. Being brothers, and not just brothers but *twins,* Earl and Carroll rarely saw eye to eye about anything, and bickered constantly, and sometimes even came to blows, but loved each other madly and would have defended the other to the death if need be.

"Fellas, fellas," said Big Ben Burden from behind his thick sagebrush beard, "fellas, are we men or are we mice?"

Earl and Carroll frowned for a moment and then replied in unison, "Men." Then they looked at each other and said, "Mice." And then they both swore roundly, and Earl said, "Hell, what's it matter, anyway, Big Ben?"

"Because," said Big Ben Burden, "if we were *men,* we'd be betting with *real* money, not nickels and dimes. Not even kids bet with nickels and dimes." So saying, Big Ben flourished a fresh, crisp smacker and laid it down on the checked tablecloth next to the tomato-shaped catsup dispenser. "I say Moose can do it," he announced, glancing over at Moose, who was exercising his massive jawbone, working it around and around in readiness for some serious mastication.

Earl and Carroll reached for their back pockets simultaneously, each bringing out a billfold and unfolding a bill. They moved in perfect synchronization, like swimmers in a Busby Berkeley spectacular, even to the extent of licking their thumbs to peel off the bills at the exact same moment, in the exact same way, with the exact same amount of lick.

"Okay," said Big Ben. "Here's the plan. If Moose manages it, Earl and I get a buck fifty each. If he doesn't, Carroll gets the lot."

"That ain't fair!" cried Earl.

"Sure it is," said Carroll.

"Who says?"

"It's the rules."

"Yeah? Well, who made up the rules?"

"Jeez, I don't know," said Carroll, "the man who invented gambling, I suppose. Course, I'll buy all you guys a drink when I win," he added magnanimously.

"Hey!" said Moose, butting in. "Hey! And what about me? What do I get out of this?"

"For you, Moose, our resident burgermeister," replied Big Ben, chuckling over the pun (even though he realized none of the others would get it), "a free burger."

Moose considered this and decided it was fair and reasonable. Food was just about the only currency Moose dealt in, and a free burger was a free burger and a free three-quarter-pounder was a godsend. So he nodded and went back to pumping his jaw.

Big Ben Burden's boy, Jim, and some of the other kids were in the habit of playing a similar game down at the Merrie Malted Soda Shoppe with Moose Rollins's son, Moose Rollins, Jr. On these occasions, everyone present chipped in to buy a pint of a chosen flavor of ice cream and then each kid would bet something of value—a baseball card, say, or a prized comic book, or a particularly fine ball of string— that Moose, Jr. couldn't get all the ice cream into his mouth and swallow the lot without spilling a drop. They all of them knew that Moose, Jr. would manage it, so that rendered the bets a little pointless and pretty much killed the suspense, but they were kids and hadn't quite grasped the win-or-die ethic of gambling. They just loved to watch Moose, Jr. shovel in spoonful after spoonful of ice cream; they loved the way it made his eyes roll and his cheeks bulge out like huge flesh balloons. And when it came to that final almighty gulp, when it looked as if Moose, Jr.'s head might burst with the pressure, they loved to cheer and roar their admiration. Only once had he let them down, when, just as he was spooning in the last dribbles of a pint of raspberry sherbet, some mischief maker (mentioning no names, but his first initial was J and his father was known as Big Ben) slipped an ice cube down the back of his shorts. The explosion spattered every surface and person within a ten-foot radius. The air turned pink, and then, when this wonderful ice-cream mist had cleared, Old Joe Dolan's epithets turned it a darker shade of blue. The culprits—Jim, Moose, Jr., Tom Finkelbaum, Andy Gallagher, and in fact almost every kid there except Josh Knight, who had looked on with mild amusement but had not been directly involved— were handed damp cloths and told to get everything sparkling again, which they did willingly, between helpless sniggers and gut-aching guffaws. And even Old Joe, struggling to keep his expression stern and his eyebrows fiercely knitted and his arms resolutely folded, couldn't suppress a smile.

So when Jim Burden told his father about the game one afternoon as they were out fishing in Fleischer's Creek, it seemed such a fine and dandy idea to Big Ben that he decided then and there he would try it out with Moose, Sr. just as soon as he possibly could.

Three dollars now lay on the table (the earlier coin wagers having been returned to Earl's and Carroll's pockets), and three pairs of eyes were fixed on them, all bright with hope, and now Billy Connors was bringing over the three-quarter-

pounder itself, that which the menu deemed the Monster, a
great succulent mouthwatering mound of meat and bun that
dwarfed the plate it squatted on and streamed juice and fatty
ooze everywhere. He set it before Moose Rollins, and Moose
felt the saliva sluice over his tongue, and everyone in the
diner, and some people who weren't, heard the far-off earthquake that was Moose's stomach rumbling. Moose grabbed
for the burger but Big Ben shook his head and said, "Unh-
unh," and stayed Moose's hand.

"On the count of three," said Big Ben. "One."

Earl Evett crossed his fingers and prayed that Moose's
mandibles were in top-notch form today.

"Two."

Carroll crossed *his* fingers and prayed that Moose was
coming down with a toothache.

"Three!"

And Moose Rollins snatched up that three-quarter-pounder
Monster (bun, catsup, dill pickle and all) in his two ten-pound
hands, his fat fingers sinking into the soft bun until it was almost impossible to tell what was bun and what was finger,
and Moose brought the burger up to his face, and the juice
cascaded down his chin, and he opened his mouth wide, and
wider, and wider still, so wide you could see the little pink
wiggly thing hanging at the back of his palate, and yet *wider*
until every tooth stood revealed, like blunt stalactites and sta-
lagmites in the roof and floor of a vast cavern, and just when
everyone thought that that mouth couldn't go any wider, not
without Moose's head splitting apart or a rift appearing in
the space/time continuum, wider it went! And where Moose's
face had been there was nothing but an unplumbable depth of
yawning wet redness. And into this went the Monster.

"No," said Carroll, meaning *No, it ain't possible.*

"No," said Earl, meaning *Yeah, Carroll, it sure is.*

"No," said Big Ben, meaning *Can it, you guys.*

Because it wasn't over yet. Moose had to close his mouth on
the burger all the way so as his lips were sealed, and then he
had to chew and swallow without losing a grain or a drop or a
crumb. Those were the rules Big Ben had hastily drawn up.

Moose's head seemed to have swollen to twice its natural
size and his cheeks were the color of cranberries and his eyes

were damn near popping out of their sockets and from somewhere deep inside him there was coming an *mmf, mmf, mmf*
sound, like a man suffocating beneath a pillow. That got Big
Ben worried. It wouldn't do to have Moose die of asphyxia-
tion, not for the sake of a dumb bet, although Moose probably wouldn't have minded "hamburger" listed under cause of
death on the coroner's certificate, nor would he have objected
much to the epitaph on his tombstone being, "Here lies
Moose Rollins. He went for the big one." But just as Big Ben
was about to tell Moose to spit it out, all bets were off,
Moose's huge maxilla started to move, slowly at first like the
piston of some giant engine grinding into life, working itself
up and around and down and around again, slowly, slowly,
but gathering pace and confidence, and Earl's and Carroll's
and even Big Ben's own jaws were dropping open and their
eyes staring in frank amazement, as were those of Billy Connors and Alice Tremaine and all the clientele of the Bar &
Grill, some of whom were holding full forks suspended in
midair halfway to their lips, some gripping forgotten glasses
of ice-cold beer, some absentmindedly stirring their coffee
sloppily, all looking over to the table where the three-quarter-
pounder burger sweepstakes was now nearing its climax.

Then the whistle blew.

Moose's mind, like that of his son when an ice cube was
slipped down his shorts in the middle of a titanic feat of eating, was so devoted to the task at hand that a sudden sharp
and wholly unheralded shock brought about an instant and
complete reversal of the process of ingestion. It was as though
someone had detonated a stick of dynamite in Moose's
mouth, and indeed some of the eyewitnesses thought that this
was precisely what had happened and shrieked as half-
chewed ground beef and some indefinable brown matter flew
toward them, believing for one startled second (and for several disgusted seconds afterward) that they had been show-
ered with parts of Moose himself, and reaching for napkins
and handkerchiefs and corners of tablecloth and anything to
swab themselves clean. When they realized it was only
burger, nervous not-quite-laughter permeated the diner.

At the epicenter of the blast three men sat frozen, their
faces dripping globs of meat and bun, none of them willing

to catch the other's eye, all gazing at the three dollar bills lying in a mess of brown lumps and juice spatters in the middle of the table. Moose himself still had his lips pursed and his back arched, reminiscent of those figures found at the ruins of Pompeii, men turned into statues at the split second of eruption.

And then somebody said, "What, for the love of Pete, was *that?*"

And somebody else said, "I do believe it was a screech owl."

And somebody else: "No, sir, it was a car braking."

And another: "A big cat yowling."

And still one more: "A baby."

But they were just saying this, because everyone knew deep down in their bellies that it wasn't an owl or a car or a big cat or a baby.

Big Ben Burden smeared cooling, congealing debris from his forehead and plucked a couple of morsels out of his sagebrush beard, and then he said, "It was a train. God knows what kind of a train has that kind of a whistle, but that's what it was. And it sounded like the goddamned Fifty-Foot Woman catching sight of a goddamned fifty-foot mouse."

"Darn tootin'," said Earl Evett.

"Mmmf," said Moose Rollins.

3

Summoned by the sound and fury of that extraordinary whistle, a slow exodus of perplexed individuals traipsed out of the Bar & Grill, crossing the street to the station as though they were walking barefoot over broken glass. They could see billows of steam purling up above the station roof and dissolving into the blueness of the sky. Now they were crowding through the entrance, now passing through the ticket office with nothing but murmurs and shuffling footfalls for accompaniment, and now out onto the platform. Here, all eyes turned to Walt Donaldson, who was standing right by the locomotive with his flags in his hands and his silver whistle around his neck, looking up at three exquisitely beautiful young women on the running boards. The women kept glancing at one another and chattering, a sound that had nothing to do with words and everything to do with the clicking of teeth on teeth (though Walt could have sworn it wasn't coming from their mouths). *Chitter-clack,* they went, clambering over that hot boiler as though it were no more than a child's jungle gym.

Earl and Carroll Evett disagreed on many things, but on this one matter they were as close to unanimity as they would ever get: those three girls were just about the loveliest creatures they had ever clapped eyes on. Of course, when Earl said later that he had never seen lovelier, excepting Sara Sienkiewicz, Carroll had to cap it by saying that he would never again see lovelier in his lifetime, Sara Sienkiewicz excepted; but the principle was the same. On the Earl-and-Carroll Ladder of Loveliness, these girls perched together on the next-to-top rung, just below the incomparable Sara. If there was a quality they possessed that Sara lacked, it was a wanton wildness, a fluttery-frocked freedom from shame that the immaculately reserved, tightly buttoned Sara could and would never possess, nor indeed want to possess. Sara, for instance, would not have been seen dead in a dress as diaphanous and as revealing as the gossamer robes that barely covered the women's statuesque figures.

One was blond, one was brunette, one was redhead, but even a man's natural preference for a particular hair color was irrelevant here, because the blondness of the blond was cornfields and summer wine, and the brunetteness of the brunette was milk chocolate and buffed leather, and the red-headedness of the redhead was twilight and copper beeches, and a man would have willingly abandoned a predilection just for a chance of running his fingers through any one of those gorgeous flowing manes. And as for what he would have given for a kindly glance from any one of those pairs of eyes . . . Well, it didn't bear thinking about.

A silent subconscious whisper had passed through the crowd and elected Walt spokesman, because he was wearing the uniform and he was the stationmaster and this was his duty. Now everybody waited for him to speak.

Walt gazed up at those girls. He pushed his cap back up his

head. He exhaled. Finally he said, "Ladies, welcome to Escardy Gap."

4

What else would the sound of the train whistle do to Mayor except turn him into John Wayne?

All right, so the connection may not immediately be obvious, but think: how many trains has John Wayne defended from Indians and bandits in his time? Right. Union Pacific must have him on permanent retainer. Wayne, J., Official Marauding-Indian and Bandit Repellent. At a few dollars and a bottle of red-eye a week, cheaper than the cavalry, and you never have to wait for him to arrive.

So it was as John Wayne that Mayor walked out of the town hall, six weeks' worth of imaginary saddle soreness keeping his knees apart and his legs stiffly bowed, and the jingle of spurs and the picking of a lonesome Spanish guitar were all but audible as he made his way down Main Street in his tidy suit and a clean pair of wing-tips, twirling an unseen toothpick from one corner of his mouth to the other with a grim, slightly constipated look on his face.

Around him people were beginning to emerge from shops and houses, all looking in the direction of the station. When they caught sight of Sheriff Mayor striding barrel chested and wide thighed along the dusty street, it was hard for them not to let out a loud hurrah. Quickly they fell in step behind him. Among them were Jed the barber with a straight-edge razor in his hand, and Quincy Hogan, projectionist at the Essoldo, with a towel round his neck and shaving foam lathered over one half of his chin; Wilbur Cohen and his pretty daughter, Josie, who liked to help out at her papa's store on Saturdays; Miss Ohllson, schoolmistress, all pinched cheeks and black shirtwaist and drab skirt; Old Joe Dolan and a gaggle of sundae-stuffed kids; Hannah Marrs, the dowdy, respectable lady who ran the library; and two dozen, three dozen others, all following their mayor to investigate the source of that whistle because in all their days they had surely never heard a whistle like that, like a terrific scream hurtling out of the throat of some monstrous she-beast, and they wanted to know, quite rightly, what it was that had announced its arrival in their town so demonstratively.

Mayor led the swelling ranks of his posse to the station. They followed him through the waiting room to the platform. There they waited, watching Mayor take stock of the situation: the train, the small crowd already gathered, the three young women in their flowing robes. From his expression it was hard to tell if he was thinking anything at all, unless it was whether he should start shooting now or ask a few questions first. He looked for and found Walt Donaldson, and made his way over and patted the stationmaster on the shoulder.

"Mayor!" said Walt. "Am I glad to see you."

"What's the situation here, Walt?" Mayor drawled.

"They won't say anything, Mayor. They just laugh a lot. I figure maybe they can't speak, maybe they're a little slow in the head."

"All right," said Mayor, nodding slowly. "You better leave this to me."

Walt moved aside, eagerly abdicating responsibility.

"Ladies," said Mayor, stepping forward and extending the hand of friendship, "may I be the first to welcome you to Escardy Gap."

"I already done that," whispered Walt from behind.

"Oh," said Mayor. "Then, ladies, may I be the second."

The girls giggled and chitter-clacked.

"Reckon you're right, Walt," Mayor muttered out of the side of his mouth, whirling an index finger around his temple. "Okay," he said, hiking up his waistband and resettling his balls in the crotch of his pants. "Now, the truth is, ladies, we don't get many strangers visiting Escardy Gap, so forgive me if I'm just a mite rusty on the protocol. Assuming that you're staying and not just passing through, I think it's safe to say that our town is your town and that you should make yourselves as comfortable here as if this was your own home, wherever that may be. If you're looking for a roof to put over your heads, Jack Chisholm's place out on Furnival Street is as good as any. Take it from me, the beds are the softest duck down money can buy, and you won't eat a finer buckwheat pancake than Cora-May Chisholm's, no way."

"That's right!" said Jack, who was in the crowd. "The best service and the most competitive rates in all the state."

The women giggled and chitter-clacked again, tossing their glossy heads of hair this way and that so that they shimmered like the gleaming, curried coat of a horse in the sunshine.

"D'you think you're getting through to them, Mayor?" Walt asked.

"I reckon I'd need a crowbar for that," Mayor replied over his shoulder. "Is there anyone in the cab? An engineer?"

"I ain't seen anyone," said Walt. He had looked, but the cab of the locomotive was entirely enclosed with iron plates and the small circular windows were glazed with smoked glass, making it impossible to know if there was anyone driving the train at all.

"May I make a suggestion, Mayor?" It was Big Ben Burden.

"Sure," said Mayor, squinting at Big Ben's face. "Say, what's all that stuff? It ain't blood, is it?"

"I'll explain later," said Big Ben. "Meantime, my suggestion is this. Why doesn't someone go along and try them carriage doors? I can't believe that this whole train's come all this way carrying only these three ladies here, but the way the blinds are all drawn in the windows, you just can't tell."

"That's a good idea, Big Ben," said Mayor. "Who do we get to do it?"

"Well, I was thinking you, Mayor, you being mayor an' all."

Mayor chewed this over for a while, frowning, then said, "I ain't read anywhere that the mayoral duties include opening train doors. That sounds to me more like a *station-master's* job."

At the word "stationmaster" Walt Donaldson visibly whitened. You could see him trying to shrink down inside his uniform and not be there.

Big Ben nodded. "Yeah, that makes sense. A stationmaster should have to deal with everyone and everything that comes into his station, ain't that right, Walt?"

"Right," said Walt faintly.

"I mean, this is a *station* and you're a *station*master, Walt, am I correct?"

"Stationmaster, yep," said Walt. He didn't seem any too

happy right then about the job he normally loved. He didn't seem too happy about those carriages sitting there all black in the beating sun, containing who knows what from God knows where, or about going up and trying any of the doors, not knowing what might leap out or lurch out or stalk out or even simply peer out from the blackness within. Of course there might be more beautiful women inside, more beautiful speechless, chitter-clacking blonds and brunettes and red-heads, but somehow that just didn't seem likely. What seemed most likely were things conjured up by Walt's imagination, which had been heightened by one too many weird tale, one too many astounding story—things he didn't much care for and didn't much want to meet.

But Walt *was* the stationmaster. And this *was* Walt's sta-tion. And so, with an "Excuse me a moment, ladies" to the three young women, who smiled coldly at him in reply, Walt went over to the first of the carriages and raised a trembling hand to the handle of the nearest door, glancing back at Mayor and Big Ben, who just nodded their heads and raised their eyebrows in an encouraging kind of way.

There were as many as fifty people on that platform, shaded from the midday sun by the great wooden awning overhead, all curious, some nervous, huddling together, clutching their own and one another's hands, and swaying forward from their ankles, half willing Walt to get on with it, half praying he would lose his nerve and back off, all long-ing for and at the same time dreading their first glimpse of whatever might be waiting within the carriages of that strange, screaming train.

5

It is a little-known fact that mankind and the dinosaurs *did* actually live side by side, during that period of history known as the Neverseen Era.

This may be in contravention of all the accepted theories of archaeologists and paleontologists, who will swear till they're blue in the face that sixty million years and an Ice Age divide little us from the big lizards. But then how many of those guys have ever *seen* a dinosaur in the flesh, large as life and twice as ugly? They've nothing but fossils and bones to go on, and when they have sucked those dry of all their secrets they resort to supposition and fancy, and just because they have polysyllabic job descriptions, everyone believes them.

Take it from Joshua Knight. During the Neverseen Era, not only did man and dinosaur roam the earth together, they actually got along pretty famously. Oh, sure, there was the occasional hiccup, but then even the best of marriages and the closest of friendships have their moments of friction. And if a tyrannosaur happened to feel like snacking on a little human flesh or the hill tribes decided to club together and bring down an oviraptor for a nice big barbecue, so what? It wasn't as if one paltry human or one gangling timid reptile was going to make any difference in the long run, not when you looked down like Josh from the vantage-point of Time and saw History stretched out over the millennia like a victim on the rack.

Through the forests primeval (and plastic) of the Neverseen Era that Josh had built in his bedroom iguanodons stalked, and in the (polystyrene) swamps brontosaurs munched their way through (rubber) ferns, and in the skies above pteranodons and pterodactyls wheeled on wings (and fishing twine), while down on the sandy (sawdust) plains dimetrodons and edaphosaurs raised the skin sails along their spines to catch the rays of the (forty-watt-bulb) sun and warm their blood, and just below the surface of the (sink bucket) lake an ichthyosaur lurked, grinning. Around the mouth of a (papier-mâché) cave several early humans stood or sat or poised on one leg as though running. One was stoking up a (red tinfoil) fire, another demonstrating how to throw a stone-headed spear, while a handful of children scratched around in the (genuine) dust mere inches away from the ponderous tail of a grazing diplodocus. Such a scene as History and experts would deny ever existed, whereas Josh Knight and a hundred movies, good and bad, would be happy to suggest otherwise.

It was as Josh was putting the finishing touches to the triceratops that his grandfather had bought for him by mail order, for no other reason than Grampa Knight liked giving his grandson presents, that the infamous whistle went, sending a sloosh of ice-water down Josh's spine. In that sudden all-splitting shriek, and in the seconds of hush that followed, Josh knew that it was all over: Escardy Gap, the world, everything. Everything he loved and dreamed and hoped, doomed. Don't ask him how he knew. He just did. And the knowing made him scared and sad. He put down the triceratops, stood up and stepped over the Neverseen Era, a boy-giant dwarfing the largest of the thunder lizards a hundred to one, his footsteps bigger than God's, and he went out of his room.

"Josh?" called out Grampa Knight from beside the stove where lunch was bubbling. "Josh? Did you hear something?"

"Yeah, Grampa," Josh replied as he trotted down the stairs. "I was just going to have a look. I think it came from over by the station."

Grampa came out into the hallway, his hands clown huge in a pair of oven gloves. "So is it any business of ours?"

"I think it may be. That's why I've got to go look."

"Well, okay," said Grampa, after pretending to consider for a moment. "You go and investigate, Sherlock. Just make sure you're back in time for lunch."

"No worry, Murray."

"No prob*lem,* Clem."

Grampa watched Josh scurry out through the front door and felt the customary stab of pride that he was, at one generation removed, responsible for the creation of this fine human being. Lord, the lad was nearly as tall as himself, and not yet thirteen! He was going to be a big 'un, no doubt about it, and handsome (*just* like his grandfather). And he was going to be a success, too. Although in theory it was too early to tell, Miss Ohllson was already predicting great things for Josh, on the strength of his grades and application in class and general aptitude for learning. Perhaps, she had said only the other day, a scholarship to one of the more prestigious colleges. Berkeley, Yale, even—whisper it—Harvard. In fact, it was clear that Escardy Gap was going to be too small to contain Josh Knight. Only the whole world was going to be large enough for that boy.

6

What Josh felt wasn't quite curiosity and it wasn't quite compulsion but a little of both and something else besides: a horrible dark sense of destiny. It dogged him all the way to the station. It shadowed him in the cool darkness of the waiting room.

Through the doorway to the platform he glimpsed people craning their necks. What they were trying to see was lost in the too-bright shafts of sunlight beyond the awning. The people were next best thing to silhouettes, flesh-and-blood three-dimensional townsfolk made flat and insubstantial.

A murmur arose. Josh moved around the side of the crowd to the edge of the platform and looked along, sorting away the train in a recess of his mental filing cabinet for future consideration because what was happening on the platform was of more pressing importance. There was Mayor, looking somehow larger than his slender self. There were Jim Burden's pa and the Evett brothers, all mooning over three very pretty women Josh had never seen before. The women, too, would have to be filed away for later, because the action was really centered around Mr. Donaldson and the first carriage of the train. Mr. Donaldson was about to open one of the doors, his expression saying he would rather be facing a pride of hungry mountain lions or tightrope-walking blindfolded across Hank's Gulch or even asking Sara Sienkiewicz out on a date. . . . Anything but this.

Now Walt was reaching up and drawing down the silver door handle.

Later, people would pretend they hadn't been surprised, and you could bet that the ones who claimed so the loudest were the ones who had jumped the highest. It was a phenomenon Josh liked to call the boo count, a theory he had formed from his own observations made down at the Essoldo. Those who came out of a horror flick claiming they hadn't been scared when the hand crept out of the corner of the screen to tap the hero/heroine on the shoulder were almost without exception the ones who had left a damp patch of

Coke or Dr. Pepper on their seats and spilled popcorn down the neck of the person sitting in front. Those who protested they hadn't felt even a slight tingle of apprehension as the Creature and the Victim got closer to one another in the dark woods were either too busy with their dates in the back row or too dumb to deserve to be allowed to go to the movies at all. But the rationale was simple: say you weren't frightened, and say it loud enough and long enough, and pretty soon you might start believing yourself. Given a few years and a college education (a *Harvard* education, perhaps), why, Josh might even have written a thesis on the subject!

Someone, at any rate, must have been surprised when all the doors of the carriage flung themselves open at once, because the cry that went up came from at least fifty throats, male and female alike. Earl and Carroll Evett grabbed each other. Mayor went for his guns only to find empty pockets and deep embarrassment. As for Walt Donaldson, he took one gigantic step backward and several little dancing ones, and then started fluttering his flags madly as if this were what he had been meaning to do all along. Even Josh felt his heart miss out a couple of bars before returning to the tune. In fact, the only individuals on that platform *not* surprised were the three women. It was obvious that they had known this was going to happen all along.

With unearthly abruptness and precision those doors flipped open together, and thin coils of some kind of dust or smoke drifted out from the interior of the carriage, reminding Josh of the way an old book from the library gave off a puff of age when you lifted the cover—an exhalation from King Tut's tomb, a taste of mist from Avalon, a breath of volcanic ash from the Jurassic Period, a swirl of the fog blanketing Old London Town.

Then the passengers began to emerge.

In ones and twos and threes they came, perhaps forty in all, maybe as many as fifty, some walking, some limping, some erect, some slouched, some clothed, some near naked, some hairy, some bald, some pale, some dark, some bloated, some lean, some stunted, some tall, some wrinkled, some smooth, some sighted, some blind, some laughing, some solemn, some shivering, some still. They filed out and they gathered on the platform until there were two crowds facing each other, one filled with amazement and awe, the other's emotions difficult to divine.

There was silence.

Then Mayor exclaimed, touching the brim of his nonexistent Stetson, "Good gravy! I do believe the circus has come to town!"

7

Bob Tremaine leaned against the mailbox marked Swivven and wiped the sweat from his eyes before lifting the flap of the mailbox and checking to see if anyone had written Ike this past week. There was nothing inside, of course, but it didn't hurt to look. Ike had become pretty lazy about things like that, the things Emily always used to do, like fetch the mail and pay the bills and take fresh eggs down to Wilbur Cohen's store and keep the icebox stocked. Sure, Ike was good with his hands and could always remember when he had to mend a fence or secure a wobbly chair back, and would do it and do it well, but when it came to dealing with the little day-to-day practicalities that had been Emily's province Ike was about as much use as a racehorse with a wooden leg. That was the reason they had made such a fine partnership, Ike and Emily. Ike without Emily was only half as effective, half as whole.

Together they had always been welcome dinner guests at the Tremaines', Ike charming with Alice in just the right way and Emily forever fussing over little Sandy, telling her she was just about the prettiest creature on God's green earth, which was true, and at the end of the meal Ike and Bob would sit out with a beer and would talk about anything and everything or simply share one of those long silences that true friends can safely enjoy, and maintaining this weekly tradition was all the more important now because Ike wasn't very good at feeding himself and generally looking after himself, but it hadn't been the same and it wouldn't ever be the same since Emily passed away. Then, it had been reassuring to know that while Ike and Bob sat out on the porch their womenfolk were inside discussing womenfolk's things, that the two halves of each whole were operating the way they were meant to, like proper, honest-to-God married Americans, and that all was right with the world (even if the Russians were doing their best to make it otherwise). The age difference between him and Ike meant nothing. Ike never spoke down to Bob or felt that gray hair automatically conferred wisdom on the head that wore it. He listened with an understanding ear to Bob's schemes and dreams and whims and crazinesses, and then came back with his own. Even an old man was entitled to crazinesses every once in a while. Heck, that was about the one thing for which a head of gray hair was a *license*. Ike could float mad thoughts up to the sky as freely as Bob, perhaps more freely. After all, he had had longer to think them up.

But now, with no Emily, there was no longer that sense of completeness. It was nobody's fault, least of all Ike's, but somehow Bob couldn't help blaming him for it. Because he *was* older, and it wasn't fair, it was downright *wrong* that he should have diminished himself with the loss of Emily. Ike should have remained a constant: reliable Ike, faithful Ike, ornery old Ike.

Some good had come of Emily's death, though. Whenever Bob felt he wasn't showing Alice the sort of appreciation she deserved, he only had to think about Ike and he would rush out and buy flowers or a big box of candy, or else simply snuggle up closer to her in their big brass bed and whisper "I love you," whether she was awake to hear or asleep. Because who could tell, tomorrow he might not be there.

Brrr. Grim thoughts on a gorgeous afternoon.

But as the years added themselves to Bob's round thirty, the more often they came to him, these thoughts, unasked for and unwelcome but unstoppable, all through the long nights and the dog days. Thoughts and fears. Inklings. Odd little anxieties. Was he a good enough husband? Was he a good enough father? Did the wife who clearly doted on him and the daughter who plainly adored him *really* dote on and adore him? Did they not see him slowly but surely heading the way of Ike, into hoary oblivion? He wasn't forty yet, for God's sake! But he felt that a peak had been passed, and that the downhill run wasn't an exhilarating toboggan ride—you just ground down deeper and deeper into the snow. And should it finally happen, should the Russkies come storm-trooping over the hill, all slant eyed and slab faced and brainwashed and emotionless, would Bob be up to defending his home and his family? Would he be able to protect his womenfolk from suffering unmentionably at the hands of the Communists? Bob was afraid that when the moment came, he would be too old. He would be found wanting.

He set off up the path to Ike's house. The air was still. The wind had settled down. Not a breath of a breeze stirred the bleached grass. The leaves on the tips of the topmost branches of the maple, just visible over the roof, looked as if they had been etched into the sky. Bob found it both alarming and comfortably humbling that he could recall the day Ike had planted that tree. Bob and the tree had grown together, until around eighteen he had reached the peak of height while the maple had just kept on going upward and outward. Hey! That sounded like something the Reverend King could have used in one of his sermons. Bob made a mental note to suggest it to him. Not that God's cassocked carny barker was ever short of ideas.

Then, faint but clear, came a sound from the town, a brief shrill *eeeeeee* that cut through the stillness sharp as a razor.

"Now, what in heck was that?" muttered Bob to himself. "Sounded like . . ."

A scream.

"Ike!" he called out. "Ike, you hear that?"

No reply.

"I said, Ike, you hear that?"

Again, no reply.

Suddenly a numbing pattern of dread was working its way through Bob's body, starting at the belly and spreading out to the chest and the crotch, tightening everything it touched, shriveling his balls to walnuts.

Ike was getting on and his constitution, though healthier than a man his age had any right to expect, wasn't what it had once been.

Please, prayed Bob, please let it not be *that*.

He rounded the house, and there was the maple scattering its shade, and over there was Ike, sitting on his butt, fence-mending paraphernalia scattered around his feet. His back was turned, so Bob couldn't tell if he was just resting . . . but he *was* still. Terribly still.

Bob broke into a trot.

"Ike!" he yelled. "Ike, speak to me! Ike! Move! Twitch! Stir!"

Ike didn't move, didn't twitch, didn't stir.

"Ike! You okay, old-timer? Want me to fetch Doc Wheeler?"

As Bob Tremaine drew up next to his friend and surrogate father, Ike Swivven slowly moved his head, slowly brought his eyes up, slowly stared at his friend and honorary son.

The Reverend King had a glass eye. He had lost the real one in a childhood accident with a firecracker. The replacement was nothing short of ingenious, and in certain lights and from certain angles you would have been hard-pressed to tell which was the real eye and which not. The reverend used the fake to great effect in his sermons, fixing it on the congregation and letting it glitter frostily as he intoned one of the Good Book's bleaker passages, or else widening his eyelids to catch the light that filtered through the chapel's stained-glass windows so that the glass orb flashed sun yellow or saintly blue or blood-of-Christ red. He had even used his eyes as an analogy for the way the Lord regarded mankind, with compassion on the one hand and utter unremitting coldness on the other. Like any good showman, the reverend understood that if you've got it, you should flaunt it.

Looking at Ike Swivven, Bob was reminded of this because Ike seemed to have installed a *pair* of glass eyes in his head, as blank, as shiny, as bitterly lifeless as the reverend's one, as incapable of warmth or interpretation, as impenetrable and mercy free. Eyes that neither twinkled with laughter nor glistened with tears, eyes that held nothing in love or fond regard, eyes that simply did not *see*.

The next thing Bob noticed was the smell emanating from Ike, the smell of an outhouse during a dry spell, the all-too-familiar rich loamy fustiness of crapped pants.

"Aw, shoot." Bob sighed. "What's happened to you, Ike, old pal?"

A smile spread across Ike's face, extending from ear to ear, but not as if Bob had said something funny—the needless smile of a baby in its cradle, happy just to be living.

A thin clear line of drool eked from Ike's lower lip and inched its way down his chin.

Three

1

A question: what is beauty?

Is it a sound, like a lone bird calling out to who knows what, who knows where, when the last faint red glows of sunlight make ready to fade from the day? If so, what is it about the bird's song that makes the heart ache with a special kind of crying/laughing happy/sadness? Perhaps it evokes an echo of other times, quieter times, when the world seemed simpler, more at ease even with its own self. Or maybe this is nature's casual reminder that time is passing and nothing waits for those who cannot accept. Are these things, then, these thoughts, the essence of beauty?

Or is beauty simply the *appearance* of something: a pretty dress, a milk-pure, breeze-fresh young face turned up to the sky flushed with wonder and naive acceptance? Or the contours of the body of someone you love, freed of garmentry, in the evening-cool confines of a bedroom so redolent with the promise of intimacy that the pungency of the very atmosphere shames the scent of the ripest of fruits? Or the way a forest river swirls and chuckles as it passes on its way from far away to far away, reflecting in its snaky back the sun-dappled boughs and leafy branches of trees that have stood and watched and puzzled for untold years? Or the cloud that tip-toes across a summer sky, all feather-downed and curlicued, trying in vain to dodge the soft shadow sliding across the plains beneath it? Or the way a book's page turns and, turn-ing, promises, hints, and hides, bears messages and masks se-crets with the thinnest of word veils? Is *this* a thing of beauty?

A smell. Perhaps beauty is a smell. The deep and dank-cool aroma of a dog's coat, wet from the creek, gently drying be-fore an open fire. The thick drift of browning pastry, of chicken pot pie, of sweet potatoes, of apples or blueberries powdered with cinnamon, and canned during the eternal af-ternoon sweep of summer. The faint and stinging pheromones tumbling from the dampness between the legs of lovers mo-mentarily lost in the heady business of arousal. The not-quite-discernible scent on the breeze, borne aloft from the warm south, come to ease the passage of a sunlit after-lunch doze.

Or maybe the mouth holds the answer. Maybe beauty is a taste. The lingering musk of a lover's kiss, perhaps, or the re-assuring feel of a bedtime nipple-thumb firmly planted be-tween the lips when the dark night beckons and the house goes quiet around patchwork quilts tucked tightly over day-weary bodies on which the playful shadows of early evening roam.

All of these? None of these?

The answer may well be Sara Sienkiewicz.

If ever there was/is/will be a paragon of Beauty, in all the books left to write, in all the days still to tumble dazedly into the maw of History, in all the songs still to be sung, in all the softly blurred cinematographic images that unfold across big screens in movie theaters the world over, in all the lonely star-crossed comets that burn briefly across the night sky and are gone, then Sara Sienkiewicz was/is/will be that definition.

Certainly in Escardy Gap it was commonly (and correctly) held that Sara Sienkiewicz was not just a beauty: Sara Sienkiewicz *was* beauty.

It wasn't just her physical appearance, though she was truly a delight to behold. Nor was it simply the soft bell-like trilling of her voice that caressed and soothed the air through which it traveled. Nor was it merely the fragrant woman/little-girl aroma of sweet jasmine and a million moonlit night-scented stocks that wafted after her as she moved along the streets and alleys past the stores and houses of Escardy Gap. Nor could it have been the taste of her, for none could say what that taste might be, though many—Walt Donaldson, notably— had spent long hours in twilight secrecy just wondering. Her beauty must lie somewhere else.

The petal, if released from the ungainly stem, is a frail and useless thing, a parody of itself. It may be courted by an amorous butterfly, but that dandy-winged romantic soon flouts petulantly away when his advances are rebuffed. A bee may bustle around it, but quickly learns the error of his ways and finds a better business prospect elsewhere. Starved of necessary ugliness, the tiny perfect petal slowly browns and shrivels. When the clumsy foot finally comes along to crush it, this is a merciful release.

For every light there is a dark. For the purest of lightnesses, there must be the deepest of darks. Beauty cannot survive alone, pure, ungrounded. Perfection is balance.

In the case of Sara Sienkiewicz, noted authoress, town spinster, tale spinner, beautiful lady and all-round good person, all her darkness went into her stories, and thus was the balance preserved and her continued perfection ensured.

Strange and bizarre were the word tapestries Sara wove, of cemetery dwellers and folk that liked the dark more than the light, of far distant planets and long-lost civilizations, of failed loves and dark motivations, of childhood and death and the death of childhood. She loved without qualification arcane agreements and pagan pacts. Her predilection was for the recently interred and the morgue at midnight. So great was her affection it even encompassed sinewy-thewed barbarians and hapless space travelers.

Her tales regularly appeared in the pulp anthologies, rubbing up alongside the weird scientologies of Clark Aston Smith and A. Merritt or squatting nose-to-tentacle with fantasies from the pens of H. P. Lovecraft and August Derleth, and some folk disapproved of the things she wrote (Miss Ohllson, schoolmistress, for example) and some folk lapped them up (Miss Ohllson's lodger, Walt Donaldson, for example). Some folk were just proud that Sara's name was known outside of Escardy Gap (in itself a small miracle). The only other living resident who could share that particular honor was a certain Douglas B. Raymond.

2

While the infamous train was still drawing toward the innocent town, all sparks and steam and whir of motion, Sara was writing. Of course she was writing. She did little else *but* write.

Even by her standards, this story was an unusual one. She had begun it this morning shortly after breakfast, with the words:

> When the population of the city reached a billion, the problem was not overcrowding. Overcrowding was certainly a cause for concern, and shoulders brushed shoulders and elbows jostled elbows a little too often for comfort, and tempers frayed (though seldom snapped). In fact, citizens were too exhausted simply fighting for room in which to live and breathe to battle one another. No, the real problem, the tragic irony of living among the many million soul-weary bodies that thronged the sidewalks and crowded the subways and occupied every square inch of available space, was loneliness.
>
> On the electrically powered omnibuses, in the pneumatic tunnel-trains, riding the conveyor-belt walkways, flying high above the gleaming towers of the city in the municipal airships, strangers stared at strangers. Unknown faces greeted one another at every turn with mute, uncomprehending looks. Casual words of friendliness were not exchanged. The time of day was not idly passed. In the robot cafés, where robot chefs rustled up unappetizing meals for robot waiters to ferry to the tables to the accompaniment of robot music, the human diners hid behind their miniature television newspapers or watched movies on their personal 3-D wristscopes and ate and drank and never talked. In hundred-story office buildings, workers hunched over desks in small featureless cells, juggling figures for vast conglomerates whose names

they did not know and spared not a thought for their next-door neighbors, whose names they also did not know.

There lived a man in this overpopulated, lonely city who owned nothing but a thousand clocks. Clocks of every description, clocks of all shapes and sizes, clocks from all periods of history, from sundials to the very latest thing in chronometry, a device with a sensor that calculated time by the position of the sun. This man owned stately horologes of pendulous solemnity and double-quick-ticking alarm clocks whose hands raced to their appointed destinations. He had hourglasses that sifted the seconds into microscopic subdivisions and he had silent electrical clocks that kept their own counsel. He had solid gold fob watches with solid gold movements and he had water clocks that drip-drip-dripped the minutes away. He had, indeed, nothing but clocks.

He rarely went out. His days were spent winding, polishing, cleaning, winding, taking apart, mending, checking, and winding some more. He had no friends, this man of clocks. He lived alone in his apartment.

And on she had carried through the morning. The words had tumbled onto the pages of her notebook, each letter finely crafted in the unmistakable swirl of her penciled script, every apostrophe and dot, every cross and colon exquisitely honed, not a stroke wasted. Her pencil had scurried along the ruled lines while, on the wall behind her, her very own grandmother clock lazily measured out the commas and the consonants, the vowels and the parentheses.

Around eleven she had fixed herself a fresh cup of tea, sharpened a fresh pencil, and resumed writing:

No fewer than three times during the next week did he see the beautiful neighbor who had accidentally knocked on the door to his apartment. On the moving staircases (she going up, he descending). In the automated elevator (she entering, he leaving). In the lobby, under the electric eye of the robot concierge (she on her way out, he on his way in). Each time he thought he ought to say something. After all, they had already *spoken. The ice had been broken. But he was scared to, in case she might think him presumptuous. Was the exchange of a few murmured excuses and pleasantries significant? No, it was just another random collision between two of the billion molecules that fritted and spuled aimlessly around the city in human Brownian motion.*

At this, Sara had sat back in her chair with a pleasantly puzzled frown. "Fritted and spuled"? Were they in *Webster's*? Oh, well, she could always change them later. Onward, ever onward.

The pencil had flown again. The pages had been filled and turned, filled and turned:

"Sometimes," she said, her gaze turning to the city spread out below them, "I think that all of us exist in someone's imagination. Someone dreams us alive and keeps us living only by the act of constantly remembering us, and the moment whoever it is forgets, that's when we die."

"Do you mean God?" he asked.

Her laugh was slender and secretive, easily borne away by the light winds that prowled around the rooftop.

"Do you really believe God would dream all this?" she said, waving an arm to take in the smoke-wreathed towers, the burning chimneys, the stately whalelike airships attended by small swarms of jet planes, all the majesty and misery of the city.

"Maybe He did," he said.

"And maybe we dreamed God," she replied.

Abruptly, Sara glanced up from her notebook. It was now approaching twelve o'clock. The fateful scream-whistle was still some minutes away. She looked glassy-eyed around her. It took her a moment to recall that it was Saturday, nothing special, just another merely wonderful day to be alive. And yet something had disturbed her from her writing. The air seemed to be alive, vibrant with a momentous tingling, filled with the silence that precedes the first thunderclap of an approaching storm. She looked around her room at the free-standing radio, the sofa, even the vase of sweet williams on the table right in front of her pinning down a square of fretted lace tablecloth, finally at the Rockwell-illustrated cover to the edition of the *Post* in which a story of hers had appeared, framed on the wall. All seemed to be bracing themselves. She glanced back over the line she had just written, and chewed her bottom lip. Lifting a straggling piece of hair off her forehead, she crooked her elbow, returned pencil to notebook, and continued. The end of the story was nigh. She wrote faster than ever.

Sara had written many, many stories in her lifetime. They thronged around her on the shelves of her room like an admiring crowd. Magazines like *Dime Mystery, Weird Tales, Argosy*, the *Post*, and even the *New Yorker*, scattered in untidy piles beside anthologies such as Bleiler's and Ditky's *The Year's Best Science Fiction* (volumes eight, ten, and eleven), Robert Bloch's *Sour Kisses*, Ray Bradbury's *Timeless Stories for Today and Tomorrow: Volume Two* and H. Russell Wakefield's "groundbreaking" collection of tales of graveyard retribution, *Unsettled Soil*.

Her success had come enviably, almost embarrassingly, easily. At the age of nineteen she had sent off her first offering to *Argosy*, receiving a note of acceptance and a request for more by return of post. In the years since, that had become the unvarying pattern. Story written, sent, accepted. Simple as that. But her work, as well as bringing her financial security, also brought her comfort, made her feel safe and content. A bulwark against the world. In the privacy of her home and the anonymity of authorship, no men stared at her in awestruck admiration, no women in jealousy. In her home, at her desk, with her words, she was safe among friends.

3

But outside her home . . .
Ahead of the coming train flew the smallest of things, traveling zephyrs and updraughts and currents with consum-

mate ease, heading single-mindedly and with malignant purposefulness toward the little house on Carver Street that contained this creature of incandescent beauty called Sara Sienkiewicz.

A fly. And not a fly.

It was unlike any fly ever pictured in biology textbooks or etherized and pinned down in any museum. It was the size of a golfball, and its abdomen gleamed in the sunlight like jade, and its eyes were rubies set in iron, and its legs were fringed with tiny hairs of spun gold, and its crystal wings glittered. It was a piece of jewelry brought to life, and it carried within it the soul and intellect of a human, and a human it could sometimes be, if it so desired, if circumstances required. It preferred the life of a fly, however. It preferred insect quickness and the freedom of flight over the clumsy, gravity-bound lot of humanity, and it loved, oh, it simply *loved* to sup on the tears of a dying child, tasting sweet misery, to crawl over a freshly laid dog dropping, eating its fill, and to carry uncleanness into clean homes, spreading the taint of disease all over. For a human being, there were restrictions on such pleasures.

Hurtling through the air, the werefly *grinned* at the thought of what lay ahead. (It was, at least, as close to a grin as its tiny mouth would allow.)

Coming closer now.

Closer.

4

Sara was in the home stretch now. Her pencil was a feverish blur, the notebook nearly full:

> *"All dreams!" cried the beautiful neighbor, hailing her arms toward him in the futile hope that his solid fingers might be able to grasp her evanescent hands and draw her back from the abyss of oblivion. She slipped through his fingers like milk.*
>
> *"I still believe in you!" he cried desperately, clutching at air. He*

could see the pattern of the wallpaper showing clear through her face. "I still want you!" Her skirt wafted like a gossamer veil in front of the walnut-paneled grandfather clock. "I still love you!"

"Not enough!" Her voice, too, was wispy and growing faint. "Not enough!"

"But I can," he begged. "I will. Give me time. That's all I need. Time."

"No time, no time!"

Then he could hear no more. Her voice was no louder than the sift of ashes in the embers of a dead fire as she mouthed words at him. Vows? Promises? Reassurances? He could not tell.

Now she was no more than a white shadow, a shift in the light that had the shape of a woman, a ghost again, and he watched what was left of her melt away to nothingness, blurred through his tears.

He was alone in his apartment. His clocks ticked on around him, counting time, adding time, subtracting time. He was alone as he had always been alone, with the thousandfold counterpoint of ticks and tocks and drips and subtle siftings that were his constant loveless companions. Slowly, he moved his eye from one clock to the next, over their numbered faces. Then, taking a cloth and inserting his finger into one corner of it, he picked up a nearby ormolu and carefully began polishing its gilt intricacies. As he polished, he murmured to himself: "Time? No time? But that can't be. Impossible. Ridiculous! How could anyone say there's no time? I've got all the time I want. All the time in the world."

Sara threw herself back in her chair with a gasp. Finished!

5

Like a shimmering bullet the werefly traveled, homing in on the frequency of Sara's words, attracted by their decency like a moth to a porch light. Purity! Honesty! So bright they made the werefly wince.

Sara's house loomed ahead. The werefly circled it once and dropped into the flower bed along its west-facing side, the night side. (Purely a habit.)

There was a whoosh, as of escaping marsh gas.

Then there was a man.

In the flower bed.

Carrying a package.

A present.

"Special delivery," he said softly, so that only he could hear. And all around him, Sara's marigolds and stocks and roses wilted as though in shame.

Unobserved, the man walked around the house, trampling through the wilting flower bed, to the front door.

Where he rapped loudly.

6

The whistle screamed, and the scream echoed and vibrated across the town, filling streets and houses with its shrill arrogant *I am here!*

Before Sara had time to recover her startled wits from the shock of that sound, there was a rap at the door.

She glanced around her room at the books, the magazines, the radio, the Rockwell cover, the small mementos and knick-knacks, fragments of a life. She was breathing in short bursts, hyperventilating, her tongue darting in and out of her mouth, moistening her top lip.

The rap came again, harder, insistent.

Sara stood up, laid her notebook down and, pencil still in hand, walked to the door slowly, unwillingly, to open it.

"Miss Sara Sienkiewicz?" The visitor gave a small and polite bow, sweeping his hat from his head.

She acknowledged her name with a nod and said, "As a matter of fact, I happen to be working. Would you mind coming back la—?"

"Ignore this ignoble intrusion," the man interrupted with all the brash pomp of a Fuller Brush salesman or a sideshow barker. "Neville N. Nolan's the name, alliteration the aim and greetings the game." He smiled and returned his hat to his head. "Little lady," he went on, "I have traveled from far, fording field, fence, and furrow, forging fast—"

"You can't ford a field."

"Sorry? Say again?"

Sara squinted up at him, trying to angle her line of vision so that the man's head was between her and the sun. "I said, you can't ford a field. Or a fence or a furrow. You can only ford water. A stream, or a river. You could ford a fjord, I suppose."

He waved an arm apologetically.

"Please," she said, "I'm terribly busy. What do you want?"

The man began again. "Neville N. Nolan, emissary extraordinary, at your service." Another bow. "Yours is the craft of creation, the telling and teaching of tall tales, the weaving of wonder, the science of soliloquy, the purveyance of purple prose."

"Get to the point," said Sara.

He held up his hand in front of her. In it was an envelope addressed to her.

"A gift," he said simply.

"A gift? For me? Whatever for? Whoever from?"

"Ah," said Neville N. Nolan with a smile Sara did not exactly like. "Your fame travels far, farther than far. This is . . . shall we say, from ardent admirers. Fanciers. *Fans.*" And he held out the envelope for her to accept.

Sara looked at it, then at him. "What is it?"

He grinned widely and shrugged. "The perfect present for *you,* Miss S."

"But what *is* it?"

"Have you no sense of suspense, no sympathy with surprise?"

Sara Sienkiewicz slid her pencil into a pocket in the front of her skirt, took the envelope in both hands and inspected the handwriting on the front. It bore a marked resemblance to her own. In fact, it was so like hers as to be almost indistinguishable. An impressive piece of forgery.

"Open it, operate it, why don't you?" urged Neville Nolan. So she did.

Inside the envelope there was just a slip of paper. On the paper, in *her* handwriting, as if she herself had jotted it down just a moment ago, was a message. It said:

A
MISSPELLED
PAUSE,

Immediately the critic/editor/nitpicker in Sara's head clucked over that comma. Some people's standards of grammar were not as high as her own. A period if you must, but never a comma.

A misspelled pause. A poors? A paws?

As she peered at this conundrum, she saw the words start to dance. She was used to this. Sometimes she could stare at a page and see nothing except letters performing polkas of punctuation and grammatical gavottes, and she would know that it was time to stop reading or writing and go and do something else instead, gardening or shopping or the laundry, something prosaic rather than compose prose.

But the words were starting to dance faster and faster, wheeling and whirling, and suddenly they skipped off the paper, flying upward, growing huge, getting bolder. Suddenly Sara's vision was filled with the letters' blackness. She could see nothing but the darkness of print. It rolled over her in an oily tide. She was wallowing in it. She was being drowned in words.

She wanted to look at Neville N. Nolan again, tell him to stop his silly chuckling right this instant, tell him to take his gift back, she didn't want it, please, take it back! *Please!* But the blackness around her was too deep. She leaned forward and in a last frantic effort groped for the door and slammed it, shutting out that awful laughter of his. Then she staggered blindly back into the room and fell to the floor, where she lay silent and very, very still.

The piece of paper fluttered down to the floor, where it lay for a while, then with a *woof* burst into flames, curling up and charring in an instant until all that was left was a small black ashy tongue.

Around Sara's house bees hummed and birds called, and from a patch of trampled marigolds and stocks and roses in her garden, a bright, large, jewel-like fly lifted up and buzzed off into the blueness of summer.

7

At the very moment that Sara Sienkiewicz collapsed in a swoon of cotton, her sensibly plain-patterned pleated skirt billowing up around her and then sinking back down with a sigh, another more formal instance of contact between people from the train and the folk of Escardy Gap was taking place on the platform, as a black-suited, raven-haired character of considerable dignity of bearing stepped forward, hand extended, to greet Mayor.

"Jeremiah Rackstraw," he said.

There was warmth and cordiality in Jeremiah Rackstraw's grip, as was only to be expected, but there was also something a little too extravagant about it, a touch too ornate, as if . . .

As if he's acting, thought Mayor.

When it came to acting, of course, Mayor was a match for any man, and the handshake quickly became a mutual thespian flourish, a truly hearty hail-fellow-well-met, Rackstraw patting Mayor on the biceps, Mayor laying a hand on Rackstraw's shoulder, both men grinning as if they had stepped up to the podium to accept a shared Oscar, neither wishing to appear one iota less pleased than the other.

"Mayor of Escardy Gap," said Mayor. "But you can call me . . ." (Damn! And he could have sworn he had remembered his real name a minute ago.) "Well, just call me Mayor. Anything else gets a mite complicated."

"Of course, of course," said Rackstraw. "And you'll call me Jeremiah."

"What else?" said Mayor in a friendly, jokey sort of a way.

The man's accent sounded like a poor version of Laurence Olivier or that young Niven fella. Although Rackstraw didn't exactly look like a Brit, his voice had the requisite china-teacup ring, the sherry-at-six, dinner-at-seven joviality, and it wasn't hard to imagine him escorting Grace Kelly down a long sweeping flight of stairs or going down on one knee before Vivien Leigh and confessing undying passion . . . except that his eyes didn't have the twinkle, the gentlemanly raffish spark that begged you to overlook his faults and warm to the man within. Nothing Jeremiah Rackstraw said or did extended to his eyes. His eyes stared constantly, seldom blinked.

Mayor kept on smiling. His and Rackstraw's hands parted, and on one side the residents of Escardy Gap and on the other the train people waited and listened and wondered just what was going to happen next.

"We're so happy to be here, Mr. Mayor," said Jeremiah Rackstraw. "This is such a fine and beautiful town. I think I can honestly say I've never seen another town like it. It has an ageless quality, I would say. The distilled essence of time, Mr. Mayor, bottled here forever in Escardy Gap."

Mayor chuckled. What the heck was this guy going on about? He slipped from John Wayne to Jimmy Stewart. A certain bumblingness entered his body and his face slackened into a permanent aw-shucks droop. In this guise, he said, "It's just 'Mayor.' "

"I'm sorry?"

"Not 'Mr. Mayor.' Just 'Mayor.' "

"My apologies," said Rackstraw.

"We don't pay any mind to official titles 'round here," Mayor explained.

"I see," said Rackstraw, although it was clear that he didn't follow Mayor's logic and didn't appreciate the subtle distinction between the formal "Mr. Mayor" and simply "Mayor." Then he said, "Mayor, I believe I speak for my colleagues as well as myself when I say that we are honored to be here, honored to be met with such courtesy, such kindness, such downright *niceness*. If you travel around like we do, you get used to hostile receptions. You tend to expect them. People don't look with favor on strangers. They seldom take to us straight away. But not *here*. Oh, no. Here we are met by dozens, welcomed the moment we step off the train. Oh, you wouldn't believe how that delights us, Mayor."

There was a universal mutter of agreement from the train people, a shuffling sibilant *yessss*, interspersed with one or two high-pitched titters, underpinned with the chitter-clacking of the three women. The townsfolk of Escardy Gap looked again at the new arrivals and a few of them donned smiles and some of them now even waved and said "Hi!" but not with any great deal of enthusiasm, all the while marveling at the bewildering breadth of variety in dress and size and shape that the strangers exhibited. Rackstraw was quite right: there wasn't an ounce of hostility in the people of Escardy Gap. But there was a permissible wariness. Let's face it, these strangers *were* strange.

"I don't suppose you'd think me rude," said Mayor, "if I . . . if I asked what you're doing here, why you've come."

"Absolutely not, Mayor. It's a perfectly reasonable question, given that you had no advance warning of our arrival. We would have liked to announce our coming beforehand, naturally, but such is the peripatetic nature of our work and the unpredictability of our traveling existence that planning ahead is not and cannot be a feature. We come and go when and where the wind takes us."

"The train, you mean," said Big Ben Burden.

Rackstraw flicked his gaze over at Big Ben.

"I don't think we've been introduced," he said.

"Mr. Rackstraw," said Mayor, "this here is Escardy Gap's very own beer-'n'-burgers philosopher king, Big Ben Burden."

"Delighted to meet you, Big Ben," said Rackstraw.

"Same here," said Big Ben, and they shook hands.

"Would I be right in thinking that's . . . hamburger on your face and in your hair, Big Ben?"

"You would be. We had ourselves a little accident over at Billy's Bar & Grill just now."

Earl and Carroll Evett glanced sheepishly at one another, while Moose Rollins blushed seven shades of scarlet.

"A fractious child?" asked Rackstraw.

"Not exactly," said Big Ben.

"You were about to tell us why you're here," said Mayor, who felt that the conversation had been sidetracked just at the point when some sort of explanation was imminent.

"Yes!" said Rackstraw. "My apologies. I think, however, that you of all people, Mayor, know the answer to that. Why, you gave it only just now."

"I did?"

"What was the first thing you said when my colleagues and I disembarked?"

Mayor's part contained a vast number of lines (indeed, it was the largest role he had ever had to play) but he was fine just as long as things moved along according to the script. If he had to backtrack to an earlier piece of dialogue, a different scene even, it took him a moment or two to adjust. A mental flicking of pages, a small prayer that there hadn't been a rewrite—then he was there: "I said, "Good gravy! I do believe the circus has come to town!"

"Correct, Mayor. Or as near correct as makes no difference."

"A real circus? Clowns and aerialists and bareback riders and lion tamers? *That* kind of a circus?"

"A show would perhaps be more accurate, because we lack the horses and lions, as you can see," said Jeremiah Rackstraw. "We call ourselves the Company, and each of us possesses a special talent or ability which we will be only too pleased to demonstrate in the fullness of time."

"Golly!" said Mayor, and he turned to his electorate, his audience, his responsibility, his friends, and he shouted encouragingly to them all, "Everybody hear that? We're going to have a show. A show! Here in Escardy Gap! Don't that just beat all?"

There was a ripple of appreciation, the odd cheer.

"Now, Mayor," said Rackstraw, taking his arm, "about your offer of board and lodging at . . . Jack Chisholm's, was it? That sounds like the ideal place for us but for one, ahem, slight difficulty." He coughed. He cast down his eyes. There, on his cheeks, was that a hint of a tinge of a blush?

"Shoot, Mr Rackstraw," said Mayor.

"Frankly it's a bit embarrassing, but . . . well, we're poor people. We live pretty much hand-to-mouth. We ask for little and we earn little, although we always give our all. This means that when we come to stay somewhere, we rather have to throw ourselves on the mercies of the local inhabitants. You understand?"

"I understand, Mr. Rackstraw. But Jack Chisholm ain't expensive."

"Expensive?" said Jack Chisholm, coming forward. "I reckon I could see my way to putting you people up for free." Jack was convinced that the Company would pay for themselves in novelty value.

"That's *extremely* nice of you, Mr. Chisholm," said Rackstraw, and you sensed from the way he said it—he said it too much with his teeth—that the abundance of kindness, the heaping of generosity on courtesy, he was beginning to find not a little irksome. "But we have grown accustomed to the practice of rooming with the locals, and we've even grown quite fond of it. Not only does it give us a better *feel* for the place, a more intimate sense of the atmosphere, but we *do* so like to meet people. We performers are gregarious folk. We love nothing more than to see new faces, make new acquaintances, forge new friendships."

"Say no more, Mr. Rackstraw," said Mayor. "Most everyone in Escardy Gap has a spare bedroom or two, and more than enough space in their hearts to accommodate you and your . . . Company. Ain't that so?"

The portion of Escardy Gap turned out on the platform were ready with a unanimous, resounding "Yes!" Their misgivings about the people from the train had been slight enough to begin with. It had been simple fear of the unknown, and now that the unknown had made itself known, there seemed to be nothing to fear anymore. And seeing Mayor there, talking, smiling, touching, laughing with the leader of the Company, this swept the last cobwebs of doubt from the corners of their minds. Little did they know that Mayor carried inside him more than enough doubt for them all. Such was his professionalism, however, his dedication to his craft—*the show must always go on*—that he would almost never let a private difficulty leak across into his public life. The two were kept in separate watertight compartments.

"Oh, thank you," said Jeremiah Rackstraw, clasping his hands together in unctuous glee. "Thank you all so . . . *very* much."

Four

1

Bob Tremaine came along the road that rolled out into the badlands, a narrow blacktop grayed by sunshine and whitened with dust. He came out of the heat haze, all but his feet, which remained lost in the watery shimmer. He came with the veins popping out in his forehead and forearms, face a grimace. He came in a stumbling, tottering agony of effort, with a sheen of sweat glazing his reddening skin. He came with his longtime friend and father figure, Ike Swivven, in his arms to the outskirts of town, where on one side stood the Evett brothers' grain and feed store with its tall gleaming silo, on the other the green-and-white Gothic excesses of Doc Wheeler's house.

And even at the end of his tether, with his strength reaching the limits of its endurance, Bob Tremaine didn't simply dump Ike on the doorstep to Doc Wheeler's place; he laid him down with the utmost gentleness, setting Ike's hat back on his head, dabbing a fresh streak of drool from Ike's mouth with his neckerchief, and still trying to pay no mind to the awful smell that had accompanied them (and drawn the flies) all the way. He raised a trembling fist to the door and knocked.

Then, and only then, did Bob Tremaine sink to his knees and permit himself the luxury of a groan.

"Ike," he whispered to his old friend as footsteps came closer from within the house, "Ike, we made it."

2

About this time, perhaps a little before, certainly not much after, there was a show of hands on the platform. Those who were willing to take on a lodger there and then raised their arms and said so. Almost everyone did. Those who did not either preferred not to take such a major domestic decision unilaterally, without consulting their spouses, or else were harboring vague suspicions about the Company. The latter category numbered only two: Josh Knight and Mayor. Josh's reluctance could easily be overlooked. Who was he to offer space in his grampa's home without his grampa's permission? He would have asked first if he wanted a friend over to stay (not that he ever did have friends over to stay, not even Jim Burden, who was the closest he got to a best pal). So a complete stranger? And a *strange* stranger at that?

Mayor, on the other hand, felt duty-bound to justify *his* reluctance. He didn't have a spare bed in his house, you see. Bachelor. A man of habits. Wouldn't have been fair on anyone to have to room with *him*.

"Quite, quite," said Jeremiah Rackstraw, as if he understood.

The traveling troupe moved toward the residents of Escardy Gap like tendrils of mud swirling through an eddying pool. Each of the performers seemed to have their sights (and perhaps their hearts) set on a particular prospective landlord, as if they had spent the past few minutes sizing up the assembled townsfolk for compatibility. An elderly lady wearing smoked-glass spectacles, for instance, bustled over to Hannah Marrs, town librarian, and introduced herself. A tremendously tall, white-skinned boy made straight for Tom Finkelbaum. A small gentleman—a midget, not a dwarf, because his proportions were perfect in every part—went up and tapped Jack Chisholm on the leg. Someone approached Mr. Macready, someone who crackled as he walked. The big, big-headed man who had so recently absorbed the interest of Ike Swivven (and it wouldn't be giving the game away to suggest that this was not *all* he had absorbed) presented himself before Old Joe Dolan.

It wasn't instant mutual attraction. It wasn't that insane certainty that drags a man, despite his slamming heart and swimming stomach and throbbing throat, across a dance-hall floor to ask her, that woman, that special stranger, if she would do him the honor of joining him in the . . . she *would?* Nor was it that subtle application of appreciative laughter by means of which a sly woman lets a man know she's interested, she wouldn't say no if he said maybe. It wasn't. Let's not make that mistake. What it was, was the bullying sperm butting the egg; the stallion sinking its teeth into the back of the mare's neck; the black widow spider smacking her mandibles; the sudden taloned swoop of cock on hen.

But not so as you would notice. Everywhere, tentative greetings were being exchanged. Agreements were being reached. Handshakes were happening. The first exploratory gropings toward conversation were being made. Talk was commencing. Then small knots began to break off from the main body of men and women, as the townsfolk of Escardy Gap and members of the Company wandered off together in twos and threes, out through the waiting room, out of the station, out into the street, away.

"A touching sight," Rackstraw remarked of the meeting and greeting.

"Quite warms the heart," said Mayor.

"Tell me, Mayor," said Rackstraw with a casual air, "who is that young fellow there?"

"Which one?"

"The one standing on his own, not talking to anybody, frowning a lot, over there."

Mayor followed the line of Rackstraw's index finger and found Josh at the end of it.

"That," said Mayor, "is Joshua Knight. Finest specimen of youth Escardy Gap has to offer, and in this town that's saying something, believe me, Mr. Rackstraw."

"I think I should like to get to know that young man," said Rackstraw.

"Say no more. Josh! Joshua! Joshua Knight!"

Josh pointed at his chest and mouthed *Me?*

"Come on over here and meet Mr. Rackstraw, Josh."

Josh hesitated. Then he came on over, sidestepping through the thinning crowd, and presented himself before Mayor and Mr. Rackstraw.

"Josh," said Rackstraw.

"Joshua," said Josh, accepting the proffered hand.

"Joshua," said Rackstraw. "And I am Jeremiah. That makes us both prophets. An interesting coincidence, no?"

"S'pose. It's a coincidence, anyhow."

"Coincidence is the father of many a friendship, Joshua, and I think that I would like very much to be your friend. Say, I don't suppose there's a spare room at *your* house, is there?"

"It's quite a small house," Josh said quickly.

"Not just one tiny little spare room?"

"I live with my grampa, and I don't know what he'd say. I'd need to check with him first."

"I think what Josh is trying to say—" Mayor began, still Jimmy Stewart, still the good-hearted if ineffectual soul.

"Oh, come now, Josh," Rackstraw interrupted, "a decent man like your grandfather would never say no to a fellow in need. And I am"—he looked to the hapless town official for support—"a fellow in need."

Josh could have further twisted and exaggerated the truth and could have kept on coming up with lame excuses till Judgment Day, but one thing he could never do was lie outright, and confronted with both Mayor, all straightforward reason, and Rackstraw, all sycophantic wheedle, there wasn't much else he could do except lower his head and nod once and mutter, "Okay. Sure. Fine."

"I *am* glad!" said Rackstraw, and yoked an arm around Josh's shoulders and hugged him to his chest, while Mayor looked on with a serene, beatific expression. Josh responded to Rackstraw's affection with all the animation of a scarecrow. The only thing for which he showed any enthusiasm at all was for Rackstraw to release him, and as soon as possible, if you please.

By now there was no one left on the platform except Josh, Mayor, Jeremiah Rackstraw, Walt Donaldson, the three women, and Big Ben Burden. Big Ben approached his mayor with an apologetic half-grin and said, "Seems like no one wants to come with me." His eyes were on the women. Their eyes were only for each other, and that bony chitter-clacking troubled the air around them.

"Did you ask them?" said Mayor, nodding at the triumvirate.

"Well, I would if I knew their names and if I could be sure they spoke English."

"Alecto, Atropos, and Aegle," said Jeremiah Rackstraw, "don't speak any language you would know. They have their own . . . well, I wouldn't even dare to call it a *tongue.* Let us say, mode of expression." Here he smiled to himself. "And they will be staying with the train, Mr. Burden. Someone has to keep an eye on it. For your benefit as well as ours."

"A lecture, a trophy, and a *what?*" said Big Ben.

"A Fury, a Fate, and a daughter of Hesperus," said Josh.

"Well *done,* lad!" said Rackstraw, giving Josh a pat on the head. Josh's face turned to thunder, but he buttoned his lip; the storm didn't break.

"Names like that, no wonder they keep giggling," muttered Big Ben.

"If you prefer, you could use the generic name we of the Company apply to them," said Rackstraw. "Which is the Man-eaters."

"I can see how they got that name," murmured Big Ben, raising a knowing eyebrow.

"Seeing as you're so keen to take in a lodger, Mr. Burden," Rackstraw said, "I think I have just the person for you. He's held up at the moment, but he'll be here shortly. I'll send him 'round to your house. You'll like him, this loquacious latecomer. He's very likable."

Big Ben said he had best make sure with Janey first but he couldn't foresee any problems. Then he said good-bye to everyone and set off home, with a short detour to the station restrooms where he cleaned the remnants of the Big One off his face.

"Er . . . Mr. Rackstraw, sir." It was Walt Donaldson. Events had been whizzing by so fast, it was only now that his sense of duty was beginning to reassert itself.

"Mr. Stationmaster?" said Rackstraw. "My, that *is* a fine uniform you're wearing."

"That's mighty kind of you to say so," said Walt, visibly flattered.

"You're welcome. How may I help you?"

"Well, I don't want to seem too rude or nothing, but . . . well, you can't just leave your train there."

"I can't? . . ." Rackstraw looked 'round at the great black-and-silver locomotive. "No," he said, "of course I can't."

"I mean, I don't know just how long you're expecting to stay here, and there ain't another train due till the two-thirty from Harrisburg next Tuesday, but . . ."

"Well, Mr. Stationmaster, what do you propose I do?"

"Well, uh, there's a siding about a couple of hundred yards back down the line. You could shunt her into there."

"A siding? Say no more."

Rackstraw gestured to the three women who, laughing and chitter-clacking, leapt up on to the boiler and, at some unseen signal, whoever was lurking inside the sealed-in cab let off the brake and the train began to move. The pistons slowly lunged and withdrew, the great spoked wheels turned, and backward the locomotive hauled itself, shunting its carriages ahead of it.

Just before the train reached the fork that led to the siding, the redheaded Man-eater alighted by the points switch and yanked the lever. Walt knew that lever to be a stiff, grudging cuss, but the redhead pulled it over with little effort. The train huffed and trundled forward again onto the other portion of track, rolling along until its rear buffers met the buffers at the end of the siding. There was a gentle, satisfied sigh of steam, then silence.

"Well, now, Josh Knight," said Rackstraw, "are you going to take me to your house, or do I have to find my own way there?"

"This way," mumbled Josh.

"Lay on, Macbeth," said Rackstraw.

Mayor nearly jumped out of his skin. Feigning jocularity, and not feigning it very well, he cried, "Macduff! Macduff!"

and flapped his hands in the air as though warding off an attacking crow. "Call yourself a performer?" he cried.

"How silly of me," said Rackstraw. "I do beg your pardon. I really should have known better, shouldn't I? Lay on, Macduff. Lay on, Macjosh! Ha ha ha."

3

Josh and Rackstraw leaving left the platform lonely. The disturbed air juggled its motes and settled. Mayor looked around. Himself, Walt Donaldson . . . Nobody else. The three women had disappeared, too, slipped away somewhere as soon as the train had parked itself, no doubt into one of the carriages.

"What was all that about, Mayor?" asked Walt Donaldson in a quiet voice. He was talking about the arcane paranoia surrounding the use of the name of the Scottish Play, but Mayor took him to mean the whole event, from the arrival of the train to now.

"I don't know, Walt," he said, and he was Douglas B. Raymond again (twice in one day!), frail, fearful Douglas B. Raymond. "I'm damned if I know."

4

Joshua Knight and Jeremiah Rackstraw walked side by side in the hot sun, Rackstraw gazing this way and that at the town around him and grinning with seeming delight at the houses and the mailboxes and the white-painted picket fences. Josh, meanwhile, kept darting sly, sidelong glances at his companion, trying to make out what it was about Rackstraw's face that he didn't like. It wasn't that Rackstraw was ugly, exactly. Most people would have said he was good-looking, in a large-nosed, sniffy sort of way. But there was a cruel turn to his mouth that made the smile that was fixed there look more like a sickle than a sign of delight.

His dark suit and white shirt were smart but at the same time fusty and funereal, and the large ring that he sported on

the third finger of his left hand—where one might expect to
find a wedding band—looked expensive but also tawdry. The
gold setting was about the size of a silver dollar, and inlaid
into it was the face of a clown picked out in brightly colored
enamel, a clown grinning hilariously, eyes wide in their mas-
cara crosses. It was a peculiar ring for such a somber-suited
man to be wearing, as incongruous as a Mickey Mouse watch
would have been, but at the same time it seemed appropriate,
embodying, by its very presence, the contradiction, the du-
plicity, that Josh sensed resided in the man by his side.

"Not far now?" inquired Rackstraw.

"Just to the end of Muldavey Street, sir," said Josh.

"Tell me, Joshua, what's your grandfather called?"

"Mr. Knight."

"That much," said Rackstraw with a polite cough, "I might
have deduced for myself."

Silence for a while.

"So. Are you going to tell me your grandfather's first name
or am I going to have to live in ignorance?"

"Here we are," said Josh, drawing to a halt outside his
home. Instead of walking straight in, he knocked. When there
was no immediate reply, he knocked again.

"Coming, coming!" came Grampa's voice from indoors, irritably. "Who is it?"

"It's me, Grampa," said Josh, "I've brought a—" A what?
A *friend?* No. "Someone with me."

Grampa Knight appeared veiled behind the screen, blinking through his thick glasses out into the dazzling sunshine.

"Who is it, son?" he said. And then, catching sight of Jeremiah Rackstraw, all he could say was "Oh."

5

Mayor was on his way back to the town hall, to contemplate and to ruminate on the day's events, perhaps even
to cogitate, and almost certainly to fulminate, when heavy
crepe-soled footfalls pounded up behind him and a middle-
aged woman in nurse's uniform came skidding to a halt, sending up a cloud of dust that floated past both of them and on

down the street. Mayor had a moment's leisure to marvel at
the fact that, even though it was the best part of half a mile
from Doc Wheeler's house (which was almost certainly
where she had run from) and the heat was fierce, Nurse
Sprocket hadn't broken a sweat and her uniform had stayed
crisp, clean, and crumple free.

"Mayor," she said. "Come with me."

Mayor was no fool. Nobody said no to Nurse Sprocket.

6

Upon returning home Big Ben Burden was, to say the
least, surprised to discover a guest already installed at the
kitchen table and enjoying a glass of Janey's lemonade, with
Janey looking on, delighted to have found another appreciative belly for the disposal of the ice-cold, thirst-devastating
concoction. It seemed scarcely credible that Rackstraw could
have got a message to his "loquacious latecomer" instructing
him which house to go to, and that said latecomer could then
have hurried over to the Burden residence without encoun-
tering Big Ben on the way. It had taken Big Ben less than a
minute to wash off the hamburger in the station rest room
and he was almost certain he hadn't passed anyone or anyone
had passed him during the six minutes' walk from the station
to here. And yet here the guest was, with a near-empty glass
before him, which, even considering how good Janey's
lemonade tasted, suggested the man had been here at least
two to three minutes. So it wasn't even scarcely credible, it
was nothing short of impossible. Even if the guy had wings
and could fly . . .

"Big Ben Burden!" the guest exclaimed, leaping to his feet
and wiping his lips. "Allow me to introduce myself. Neville
N. Nolan's the name and gulping down this luscious cold
lemonade's the current game. Big Ben, may I say how much
I envy you your beautiful, bounteous beldame. Such culinary
capability! Such exemplary expertise!"

"Oh, Ben," said Janey, laughing, "this man is just the *fun-
niest* person I've ever met."

7

Mayor and Nurse Sprocket reached Doc Wheeler's residence at the edge of town. A haphazard arrangement of cupolas, jutting angles, and interleaved stories painted cool white and peppermint green, a veritable clapboard palace of architectural indulgences, it towered over the street. A portion of the house was given over to the doctor's office and a couple of rooms with sickbeds, the rest of the two apartments were occupied by the doc and Nurse Sprocket. It wasn't quite a hospital, but that was how the residents of Escardy Gap thought of it and called it.

No one in town was ignorant that the relationship between doctor and nurse was somewhat more than professional, but the separate apartments and the pretense of separate lives were kept up so as not to offend the sensibilities of some of the town's older and more conservative residents—most of whom were only mildly concerned to know why Doc Wheeler and Nurse Sprocket didn't just make honest people of each other and have done with it. The situation was a little too precarious for that, however, Nurse Sprocket being possessed of a fiery temperament and Doc Wheeler being possessed of, well . . . another, perhaps fierier temperament. In the knowledge that they had their own bedrooms to retreat to, their own bathrooms to spend however long they liked in, their own apartment doors to lock and their own kitchens to stink up with the smell of frying onions, they found they could live with each other a great deal more easily. Marriage? It would have been like knocking two flints together seven days a week, twenty-four hours a day, in a box full of kindling. And a married couple living in separate apartments? Well, that would have been downright odd.

Doc Wheeler welcomed Mayor into the waiting room. The doc was doing his best to appear calm and unflustered and serenely professional, but he was never an actor.

"It's good to see you, Mayor," he said. "Hope I didn't drag you away from anything."

Mayor shook his head. "Nothing important."

"Good. It's just there's something I think you should see, something I'd like your opinion on."

"You're asking me for a second opinion?"

"Heh. You could put it like that."

Mayor then realized Bob Tremaine was in the room with them, slumped in a chair with a half-full pitcher of water and a glass beside him. Bob was sitting there so quiet and still it was almost as if he didn't exist. He looked all tuckered out, and he acknowledged Mayor with barely a twitch of his head. When Mayor laid a hand on his shoulder, Bob didn't even seem to notice it was there. All he said was, to no one in particular, "They got him. They got him."

"This way," said Doc Wheeler, taking Mayor's arm, adding sotto voce, "He's not making a lot of sense right this moment. Sunstroke, we think."

"Doctor," said Nurse Sprocket, "you're surely not going to look in on him, are you?"

"That I am, nurse."

"But I just gave him a sedative. He should be sleeping right about now," she said, ever so pleasantly but with steel in her smile, the implication being, You wake him up and I'll have your guts for my suspenders.

"Then I'll be careful not to disturb him, Nurse."

"Who?" inquired an anxious Mayor. "Who are we going to see?"

Doc did not reply. He led Mayor along a clean-smelling corridor and pressed a finger to his lips as he eased open the door to one of the wards.

There were two iron-headed beds in the room, one empty and the other bearing Ike Swivven, who lay on his side, knees drawn up, fists curled beneath his chin, facing the window and a prospect of land dead flat but for the verdant swell of Boundary Hill. If you peered, it was just possible to make out the roof of the Swivven place. Ike wasn't peering. He wasn't asleep either. He was staring, but his stare encompassed everything and took in nothing, a gazeless gaze from eyes of painted porcelain. The bedclothes had fallen off him a little way, to reveal a hospital robe that did not completely cover what looked like a pair of large padded undershorts.

"Are those what I think they are?" whispered Mayor.

Something more than an unwillingness to disturb Ike kept his voice hushed.

"We call them dignity pants," replied Doc Wheeler, equally low, "but they're diapers by any other name and they still smell as sweet." He went over and did his best to cover Ike up, tucking the sheets around him, the act a touch too ceremonial for Mayor's liking.

"Is he in pain?"

Doc Wheeler shook his head and indicated they should leave. Silently, soberly, the two men filed out of the room. Mayor was distressed to find that his dark feeling from this morning had returned, redoubled. Seeing Ike had brought it back, as though this wasn't just one man lying there silent and helpless and smelling faintly rotten, but the future of all Escardy Gap.

A minute later he and Doc were settling down in plush padded chairs on either side of the desk in the consulting room. The desk was size and simplicity itself, a great oblong block of polished mahogany with a minimum of ornament, the surface spread of tan calfskin spartanly adorned with a blotter and a pen set and a glazed china head marked off into the phrenological faculties. In one corner of the room a laughing skeleton hung by its skull from a steel frame.

Doc removed a fifth of best bourbon from a locked desk drawer, uncorked it, and poured out small tumblers of it for Mayor and himself.

"Your very good health, Mayor," he said, and they both swooped the whisky down their gullets.

Doc Wheeler exhaled a waft of liquor back over his tongue. "Bob brought Ike in," he said. "Told me he found him out in his spread, just sitting there all of a daze. He'd been mending his fences. Bob carried him all the way here. Carried him! I mean, the man's no ninety-four-pound weakling, but . . . Well, now I know I'm never gonna try and take him on one-to-one."

"Strength in adversity," said Mayor, because it sounded right. "What's happened to the old fella, Doc?"

"Mayor, believe me when I say I wish I knew. I was kind of hoping you might be able to offer a suggestion. You know everyone in town much better than I do. I only really see people at their worst, when they're sick, and after a while one sick person begins to look pretty much like the next."

"I don't see what you're getting at."

"We all know Ike's not been the same since Emily died. I was just wondering if lately he'd seemed any more, well, down than usual."

Mayor cast his mind back to the last few occasions he had bumped into Ike, when Ike was making one of his infrequent forays into town for supplies or on a visit to the Tremaine family. "Not so's you'd notice," he said. "You think Ike might have done this to himself, then?"

"Not so much *done,* more brought it on himself without meaning to." Doc shrugged impotently.

"I think you're going to have to be a little more specific, Doc," said Mayor.

"I don't think I can, Mayor," said Doc. "Let me be honest here. I really don't have the first clue what's the matter with Ike. If he's had a heart attack or a stroke or something, he isn't showing any of the typical symptoms. His ticker's in great shape, his reflexes are normal, and physically, apart from the incontinence, he's a fit, normal, healthy septuagenarian. If you really want to know what I think it looks like, I think it looks like someone went into his head and scooped out every thought from his brain." He spread his hands as if to say, Take it or leave it, Mayor. "That's the closest I can get to a diagnosis."

Mayor glanced over at the anatomical skeleton and at the incision around its skull and he felt a chill slither through him. Doc Wheeler had the sovereign remedy for this. He poured out another glassful of it for them both, and Mayor drank, and lo and behold, his chilliness was cured.

He said, "You know, after Emily died Ike started using that phrase about every cloud having a silver lining. Using it all the time. He really believed good can come of everything."

"We've both lived through a Depression and two World Wars, Mayor," said Doc. "We've seen how bad it can get. Hell, this town just about dried up and died in the thirties, though you wouldn't remember about that because you were gallivanting around Hollywood and romancing starlets."

"I sure was," said Mayor with a wistful sigh. "Did I ever

tell you about Mae West and me staying up all night and—"

"This is neither the time nor the place, old friend," said Doc sternly. "What I'm driving at is this: if you survive the worst the world can throw at you, you make a conscious decision that from then on you'll always see the best in everything. And that was Ike's philosophy."

"I thought it was up to God whether things turn out well or badly."

"Mayor, I'm a doctor. You want answers to questions like that, you go see the Reverend King."

"You know my feelings on that particular subject."

Doc laughed. Mayor was one of life's great agnostics.

"Come to think of it, Doc," said Mayor, "I'd like *your* opinion on something."

"Not your old problem again, is it? I've told you to cut down on the coffee."

"No," said Mayor, "nothing to do with that. You hear anything strange about an hour ago?"

Doc frowned, then nodded.

Mayor put on his storytelling hat, Doc poured a third round of drinks, and the events at the station were rehearsed. Mayor's impersonation of Jeremiah Rackstraw deserves a special mention, fired as it was with unusual, and uncharacteristic, venom.

Twenty minutes later, the two men sidled back into the waiting room, to be withered by the baleful glare of Nurse Sprocket, whose nose hadn't been so dulled by frequent use of calamine lotion, antiseptic, and disinfectant that she couldn't smell bourbon on a man's breath.

In there drinking while one of their friends lay insensible upstairs and another sat fatigued and sunstroked and shell-shocked down here!

Men!

8

A gift!" exclaimed Grampa Knight. "Really, Mr. Rackstraw, there's no need."

"There's every need," replied the houseguest.

"Well, then, what do you say, Josh?"

"Thanks," muttered Josh.

"You're welcome," said Jeremiah Rackstraw, grinning a grin that went far beyond obsequious. "It *is* customary to present your host with a gift of some fashion, is it not? Certainly it is where I come from."

"What can it be?" Grampa Knight wondered pointedly.

Josh turned the cubic parcel over and over, held it up to his ear, shook it tentatively, sniffed the plain brown paper wrapping.

"Open it and see," urged Rackstraw.

Wary fingers undid the string, unpeeled the wrapping. Cautious hands wrested a cardboard box from the torn folds. The hands and fingers stayed over the box, reluctant to proceed any farther.

"Go on," said Rackstraw. "Trust me, it's something you've always wanted."

How in heck would you *know?* Josh wanted to ask, but he kept silent.

It was a clock. There was a face on the clockface, a looning clown mask fixed into a broad yawning grin, with a pair of eyes bulging beneath the wavy lines of a furrowed brow— the very same face that Josh had seen on the ring on Rackstraw's finger, only this one was about ten times as large. The clown had to be some sort of Company mascot, he reckoned.

The alarm clock's hands stood at ten to four which, according to the steady old electric chronometer on the kitchen wall, was the correct time. The clock, however, appeared to have no tick, which was odd.

"That's good," said Grampa. "Josh hasn't got a clock of his own. Got a watch, but not a clock."

"Never wanted one," said Josh under his breath.

"Sorry?" said Rackstraw.

"I've always wanted one," said Josh, louder.

"Didn't I say so?" beamed Rackstraw.

"This is mighty kind of you, Mr. Rackstraw," said Grampa, feeling that Josh was managing not to overdo the gratitude a little too well.

"It's the very least I could do, seeing how I've been put up in such a pleasant room, with such a pleasant view, such a pleasant *smell*. You know, something the weary traveler never tires of is the smell of freshly starched sheets."

"I'm glad you like it," said Grampa.

"Like it? My dear fellow, I love it."

"I'm just about to make some lunch, Mr. Rackstraw," said Grampa. "Would you like some?"

"Lunch would be delightful," said Rackstraw.

"Josh, where are you off to, boy?" demanded Grampa, and the furtive fugitive froze in the doorway.

"Upstairs," said Josh. He was dismayed to find the clock still in his hands, but it presented him with a good excuse. "I want to put this on my desk. It'll look good there," he lied, and hurried out of the room.

9

The clock only began to tick and tock when Josh entered his room. The mechanism must have been stuck, he reasoned, and had just been needing a jolt to restart it.

Tick, tock, went the clock as he placed it on top of a pile of assorted copies of *Journey into Mystery* and *Tales from the Crypt*.

Tick, tock, went the clock as Josh leaned behind it to open the window and let in some cooler air.

Tick, tock, went the clock, hugely loud, as Josh turned and traipsed out of the room, thinking, *Just what I always wanted. Hah!*

Then nothing.

Josh halted in the corridor, poised, listening intently.

He took one slow step back across the threshold into his room.

Tick, tock, tick, tock.

Josh went out again.

Silence.

Step back.

Tick, tock, tick, tock. The hands told the right time.

Forward.

Silence.

He waited a full minute.

Stepped back.

Tick, tock, tick, tock. The hands still told the right time.

Forward.

Silence.

This was too much. Josh went all the way back into his bedroom and the loud steady *tick, tock* resumed as though nothing had happened. The balloon face of the stupid, dumb, unwanted clock grinned away.

Josh sprinted out of the room, pounded down the stairs and made for the front door, barely hearing Grampa's cry from the kitchen. "Aren't you going to have some lunch, Josh? Josh? Aren't you going to have some lunch?"

"Lunch, Josh!" cried Jeremiah Rackstraw, as if it was any of his business. "Don't forget your lunch!"

As the screen door swung to behind him, Josh heard Rackstraw say, "Well, that's a pity. But all the more for the rest of us, eh?"

And he ran on harder than ever.

10

There was going to be a game of baseball, for the wide-eyed, cowlicked boys of Escardy Gap had gathered in Poacher's Park. Stripped to the waists, batters-in-waiting were scything their Babe Ruth Specials through the air or darting from base to base, from Andy Gallagher's jacket to Greg Gregson's cap to Jim Burden's lumberjack shirt, slithering to a grassy halt and picking themselves up, brushing green flecks from the seat of their pants and running on. Their voices canoned and fugued like glass wind chimes.

When it was generally agreed that whoever was coming had come, the kids grouped in a huddle, and Jim Burden and Tom Finkelbaum, team captains for this afternoon, began to select sides. The early choices were easy to make, and it was only as the motley crew in front of them grew smaller and the teams behind them grew larger that Jim and Tom had to apply some brainpower to the process, determining not which of the dwindling huddle was better than any of the others but which was least likely to ruin their team's chances. Inevitably

Moose Rollins, Jr. was one of the last to be chosen, and offered a choice between him and puny Davey Higgs, Tom Finkelbaum had to settle for Davey. Moose, although highly prized for his skills with ice cream and associated foodstuffs, was not considered an asset to any baseball side.

The tall, stooped, pallid-skinned boy who had accompanied Tom to the game sat on the sidelines with his gloved hands resting neatly on his knees, palms up, the slender fingers spread like black petals to the sky. Tom hadn't yet been able to discover his name, so he just referred to him as the Boy. He could scarcely get a word out of the Boy, and the few lumps of conversational ore he did manage to prize out were useless and broken. Amazingly, or perhaps not so amazingly, it turned out that the Boy didn't know the first thing about baseball. Had never even heard the word. Can you believe that? Tom managed to fill the Boy in on the rudiments of the game and asked him, albeit unenthusiastically, if he would like to join in. He was not unrelieved when the Boy had said no, he would instead watch.

It was a royal pain in the butt for Tom that he should be saddled with the Boy, who had, after all, imposed himself on the Finkelbaum household. But Tom bore the inconvenience with a patient, suffering shrug. As for the other kids, they looked at the Boy with undisguised and undisguisable fascination, and that could only be good for Tom. The Boy distinguished him. He was the only one there with a peculiar companion, one of the Company. That had to count for something.

The Boy's face was extraordinarily flat and inexpressive, reaching a peak with its birdlike mouth and a small sharp nose. His skin was waxy and white, his eyes dark and also inexpressive. He rarely showed a flicker of emotion. He never cracked a smile. Someone at the softball game had whispered the word "vampire," and Tom had scowled and hissed "Ssh" at the culprit, while secretly thinking the word was as apt as any and possibly more accurate than "Boy."

The game was about ready to begin when someone shouted, "Hey! It's Josh!"

Immediately both Jim Burden and Tom Finkelbaum cried, "He's on *my* side!"

"It was my turn to choose," said Tom to Jim.

"Yeah, but I had to have Moose."

"So? I had to have *Davey Higgs.*"

"Maybe we should ask Josh what *he* wants to do," said Jim to Tom.

Josh was following his own shadow across the park, his fists balling out the pockets of his pants, his chin on his chest, as worried and care draped as ever.

"Josh!" said Jim. "Hey, dinosaur-boy! Mr. Iguana! Listen, we're about to start and you're on my side, okay?"

"Don't listen to him!" said Tom. "He's just sore 'cause he got that big booger Moose. You're playing for me, right, Josh?"

Jim felt like turning to Tom and saying, "He's *my* friend, pal! You find a friend of your own," but not only would this have been unfair and unkind, it wasn't strictly true. Josh wasn't really anyone's friend, not bosom buddies, not best of pals with any of the other wide-eyed, cowlicked boys or even of any of the wide-eyed, ponytailed girls. He and Jim did stuff together—read comics, knocked a ball around, explored the woods at the edge of town, sometimes shared a jumbo-size carton of popcorn at the Essoldo—but Jim never felt as if his presence was anything more than incidental to these pastimes. Josh could probably have got along just as well without him. Once, while Josh was engaged on that mighty Herculean labor known as Building the Neverseen Era, Jim had volunteered his help . . . and the offer had been gently but firmly turned down. "This is something I have to do for myself," Josh had said, and Jim had taken this philosophically on the chin, realizing (with a perspicacity that belied his tenderness of years) that Josh wasn't simply constructing a model landscape. It was something to do with Josh's mom and pop dying when he was so young. Something to do with coming to terms with loss. A kind of cure. Rebuilding himself by building something else. Recreating, reconstructing. Yeah. Something like that, anyway.

Josh came to a halt beside Andy Gallagher, southpaw pitcher extraordinaire, who was limbering up, rolling his left arm around and around to loosen the joints. Josh glanced around. There were a couple of dozen expectant eyes pinned on him, and an awful lot of hopes. Josh might have been a solemn solitary son of a gun 99.9 percent of the time, so on his own it was hard to be sure if he was aware anyone else existed, but put him behind a bat and on the plate and he could work miracles. He had been known to turn an entire game around in the ninth inning, and almost always supplied that crucial home run when and where it was needed. He played with dispassionate, almost clinical, precision, exerting not one more erg of energy than the situation required. In fact, there was something a little creepy about the way Josh batted. He was, if such a thing were possible, almost *too* good.

"Guys," said Josh. "Look, I don't feel much like playing ball today. You mind if I sit this one out?"

Disappointment reigned.

"Hey, I'm sorry. I'm just not in the mood, is all."

"It's okay," said Jim Burden, predicting that Josh would change his mind once the game got going. "Just be sure you root for the right team."

"Yeah," said Josh. He went off a little way and sat down on the grass, a few yards from the Boy. They glanced at one another, glanced away.

Andy Gallagher began his pitch by winding himself up like a mainspring, and then he leaned back on his left leg, raised his right toe cap off the ground, squinted, bit his lower lip, aligned his left index finger along the seam of the ball, nodded to Kevin Lieber at shortstop, winked, looked left, looked right, paused . . . and then unleashed the deadly snaking curve that was his trademark.

For an eternal fraction of a split instant the ball seemed to enter another dimension, one where the traditional laws of physics no longer applied, one where a traveling sphere of stitched leather could defy time and motion, make a mockery of relativity, soar from point A to point B via infinity and return to this world covered in stardust and space essence to fetch up snug and secure in the catcher's mitt with a joyous cowhide smack.

"Strike one!!!" everybody yelled.

And the game was under way.

Usually for Josh the simple geometries of baseball—the diamond, the short sprints between four points of the compass, the triple numerology of bases and strikes—satisfied a craving for order that not even lording it over the Neverseen Era could necessarily meet. When bat and ball made contact, whether it was for a low trundling grounder or a high arcing home run, when wood and leather kissed and parted, it was as if a connection were being made elsewhere in the world, a switch clicking into place and a light bursting into life; and boys became not just boys but spinning atoms following the steps of some quintessential nucleic dance. *This* was what it was all about, although Andy Gallagher sneaking yet another one past Freddy Zane, Jim Burden yelling red-faced from third base, Tom Finkelbaum yelling redder-faced from somewhere out in midfield, Stan Kirby stepping boldly up to the plate, Kevin Lieber hunkering down slapping bare fist into mitt, all with their caps on backward, all with their knees and backsides grass stained, all with their torsos browning in the sun, would never have known it. That knowledge was only revealed to one who sat on the sidelines looking in.

It wasn't easy being Josh Knight, being twelve going on thirteen and having a grandfather who doted on you, getting grades that were the envy of the class, being the best batter around—all this and builder of drool-making detailed prehistoric worlds, too! There were times when it seemed almost too much to ask that he act normal, that he belch and holler and rush and sweat and stink and play baseball with more guts than skill, just like any other kid. And you felt he would have willingly given it all up—grandfather, grades, batting brilliance, models—for a chance to escape the next ten years, to form a chrysalis tonight and wake up tomorrow a full-fledged adult. Skipping adolescence would have been no great loss for Josh. Childhood? He could take it or leave it.

For this was childhood in front of him, rushing around in the shockingly bright white light of the Saturday sun, yelling, yelping, thinking themselves free but actually abiding by the rules that someone—some *adult*—had laid down long ago.

Not Josh. Not today. Today baseball seemed utterly, irredeemably dumb to him. All that running and shouting. He wondered why he had bothered coming out here at all. But then anything was better than staying in his own house now that Rackstraw had installed himself. Darn Grampa for letting the man in! And darn himself for bringing Rackstraw there in the first place! And while he was about it, darn Rackstraw for giving him that clock, making him feel as if he owed the man something!

No, nothing Josh had seen today had given him any cause for happiness, not the sort of happiness he was witnessing right now, the blithe, blind happiness of these kids. Everything he had seen so far had only given rise to misgivings, to a stomach-hollowing unease. Boy, sometimes Josh wanted to take the town by the throat and shake and shake until he had shaken some sense into it. . . .

"Surely happy better than not happy."

"Eh?"

The Boy cleared his throat and said again, "You look not happy. Surely happy better than not happy."

"There are worse things to be," he replied.

"Oh, yes," said the Boy. "Lot worse." Those eyes winked darkly in the sun. . . .

. . . and the ball careened off Hal Fisher's bat at an angle that had nothing to do with baseball or ballistics, and its improbable trajectory took it across the park at alarming speed to strike Moose Rollins, Jr. square in the forehead, *thok!*

Had it been anyone but Moose, we might have been looking at a fatality here. At the very least, a severe concussion. But it was Moose Rollins, Jr., unfavored player of baseball, acclaimed consumer of ice cream, and the *thok* resounded hollowly as if the ball had hit the bole of an aging tree. The ball bounced off, and Moose blinked, and that was it. There was a loud cheer and Moose's fat face broke into a watermelon-rind grin.

Then he keeled over onto his back.

There was a gasp.

Then he got back to his feet, grinning again, and there was another cheer, and Moose took a well-deserved bow.

Josh turned and glared at the Boy. The Boy stared flatly, inscrutably back.

"You did that," Josh said in a low voice. "I *know* you did that. I don't know how you did it. I just know you did."

The Boy's shoulders lifted an inch in a nigh-imperceptible shrug. Josh felt like hitting him. He had never ever before wanted to hit anyone so much. If he didn't hit the Boy, he would have to hit *something*. So he leapt up and he shouted over at Jim Burden, "Hey, Jim, you need another batter?"

Jim scurried for his bat and held it out to Josh, Jim's own bat, Jim's very own Louisville Slugger, dented and dulled by every ball Jim had ever hit, the binding grayed and faded from Jim's very own sweaty palms. Jim trusted Josh enough to let him borrow his very own bat!

Josh accepted the bat humbly and stepped out onto the field, and a shout went up that sailed high over the rooftops of Escardy Gap, spread out beyond the town limits, a shout that could be heard as far away as Boundary Hill and Hank's Gulch, a shout of pure and selfless joy from two dozen pure and selfless throats.

Maybe it wasn't so bad being a kid after all, thought Josh as he took a few practice swings on the plate. Not all the time.

Five

1

Tick, tock, tick, tock . . .

Saturday afternoon stretched its arms and yawned. The sun slipped over the rooftops, gilding the eaves and gables and cornices and chimney stacks and lightning rods. In the soft and tranquil air a plethora of insects played, feathery stars dancing. Over the grass and shrubs of Poacher's Park wafts of cottonwood down floated like snow. From the creeks and narrow strips of woodland that fringed the town, keeping the badlands at one remove, the cries of loons and whippoorwills floated up, up, up. Bats darted erratically through the dusk.

The first wisps of Saturday night twilight filtered into the small town, slipping down Main Street like a shameful inebriate hotfooting it home. One by one the windows of Escardy Gap came ablaze. Against the cold of the coming night, the town draped a mantle of lights over itself: streetlights, porch lights, bedside lights, night-lights. Fireflies gathered and moths were drawn to consider the artificial warmth and sudden brightness, flying in closer for a second look, then a third.

From pool of light to pool of light early evening strollers

strolled, raising their faces to the cooling breeze. There were arms around waists and there were hands in hands, and sometimes there was just the tingle of proximity, fingers occasionally daringly brushing fingers.

Outside the Essoldo Motion Picture Palace a short queue had formed. The doors were open, the feature was due to start in less than five minutes, but no one felt like going in just yet. There was an evening to be enjoyed. There was a purpling sky to gaze at. There was the first twinkling star to wish upon.

In the bandstand in Poacher's Park a young couple sat and said nothing, for there was nothing that needed to be said. The near silence pleased them, but not nearly so much as brushing locks of hair out of beloved eyes, sharing kisses, making promises, vows. Nothing grubby.

Dirty-pawed kids were rushing home, the last frantic mad dash of the day before dinner (yay!) and a bath (groan!) and then, snug in bathrobes or pajamas, a book or a radio play (yay! again).

Escardy Gap at twilight.

Never such innocence.

2

*T*ick, tock, tick tock . . .

Hannah Marrs turned the huge key in the library door. Hearing the lock hit home and heaving a happy sigh, she turned her face to the roadway and hugged her book close to her chest. *David Copperfield.* She had read it so many times she had lost count, but every time, even before she had finished it, she couldn't wait to start it again. Tonight, though, was going to be different. Tonight was going to be special. Tonight, Hannah was going to share the experience with her houseguest. She was going to read *David Copperfield* out loud to the old lady whose eyesight was so poor that she must constantly wear those smoked-glass spectacles, read the book from "I Am Born" all the way to "A Last Retrospect"—if that were possible in one sitting, which (Hannah decided with some regret) it almost certainly wasn't.

When Hannah had suggested the idea of reading Dickens,

the old woman had laughed. That laughter, while initially unnerving the bookish Miss Marrs with its rich and raucous
depth, had filled Escardy Gap's resident librarian with a rare
sense of purpose. Here, at last, was someone to talk to, someone who seemed to share her literary enthusiasms. (The only
other person in the entire town with whom Hannah might
have felt so at ease, Sara Sienkiewicz, was too much her own
woman and too often lost in her strange solitary worlds ever
to be good company. Hannah thought it a shame that such a
fine writer should squander her talent on Science Fiction and
shuddery horror-things when she was so clearly capable of
more. She admired her nonetheless.)

   As she walked along Main toward the town square, Hannah imagined the two of them—herself and the blind lady—
sitting quietly in her small front room overlooking
Carmichael Avenue, gently sipping a hot chocolate or a weak
coffee, and then herself lifting the cover, licking her finger,
flicking through the table of contents and beginning the story.
Secretly, Hannah hoped she wasn't just foreseeing tonight. It
would be nice, wouldn't it, if the old blind lady could stay . . .
for a little while? A long time? *Forever?*

   Hannah almost shuddered in delight.

   Turning her eyes up to the day's first sight of moonlight,
she was reminded of a fragment of Whitman:

Splendor of ended day floating and filling me,
Hour prophetic, hour resuming the past,
Inflating my throat, you divine average,
Your earth and life till the last ray gleams I sing.

She hurried her step, the quicker to reach her guest who,
though Hannah didn't know it yet, was already making herself *very much* at home.

3

Tick, tock, tick . . .
   In the Merrie Malted Soda Shoppe, Old Joe Dolan continued to polish his already gleaming sundae schooners and

boat trays, gazing out of the large front window onto the town square. He saw Hannah Marrs scuttle out of Main Street and head across the square and across the window and into his own reflection. He stopped polishing and considered the portly aproned figure that eyed him back from behind the reversed letters of Malted.

"I bet she used to look pretty good when she was younger," said his guest, who had occupied a booth over in one corner of the shop most of the afternoon and all of the evening. The Fudge Fandango in front of him had been allowed to melt and deflate and degenerate, oozing whipped cream and hot fudge sauce down its sides, its crowning glacé cherry dethroned.

"I beg your pardon, Mr. Felcher?" said Old Joe.

"I bet she looked fresh as a peach and just about ready to pluck," said the big, big-headed man. "Am I right, Old Joe?"

"How—?"

"How did I know that was how you used to think of her?" Felcher said with a leer. "As a pluckable peach? I would say it was a lucky guess. 'Cept it wasn't."

With a creaking of wood and a squeaking of leather, Felcher slid his bulk out from the booth. The dozens of tiny multicolored bottles attached to his coat chinked and chattered. He moved over to the door gracelessly, as though unaccustomed to the size of his body, and Old Joe watched him flip the sign around to read Sorry, We're Closed.

Old Joe glanced at his wristwatch. He had *never* closed up earlier than eight. Ever. And he had a good mind to tell this fella so. But he couldn't summon the energy. He was starting to feel a bit dizzy, sick, as if he were on top of a high roof staring down at the world spinning below.

"That's better," said Felcher, and he carefully unscrewed the tiny cap from the tiny bottle hanging by the left lapel of his coat. "Now, let's see what else you remember."

4

T*ick, tock* . . .
"Hey, you see that?" Jim Burden.
"What?" Tom Finkelbaum.

"Old Joe's turned off the lights."

Tom stopped on the corner of Delacy Street and squinted over at the gloom inside the Merrie Malted Soda Shoppe.

"So what time is it?" said Jim to nobody in particular, least of all the tall, stooped, and permanently gloved Boy who accompanied them. *He* hadn't said a word since the baseball game.

"Why don't you look at the *clock,* dummy?"

Jim shrugged. He consulted the town-hall clock. It was getting on for half past seven.

"Kinda looks like we ain't going to be having any ice cream after all," said Tom. "Least, not tonight." He held up the two quarters his father had given him. Never had two coins looked more like worthless circles of tin.

"Tree."

"Huh?"

"Don't look at me," said Jim, pointing. "It was him."

"Tree," the Boy reiterated. "We go to tree?"

Tom glanced at Jim Burden.

"Hey, I gotta be getting home now anyways, Tom. I'll catch up with you guys tomorrow." He leaned over to try and get the attention of the Boy. "I'll see you tomorrow, yeah?" he said, raising his voice in the hope of breaking through that stonewall face.

"We go to tree?" was all the Boy said in response.

Jim rolled his eyes and nodded to Tom. "Be seeing you," he said and, spinning on his heel, walked off toward Main Street.

"It *is* getting kinda late," said Tom Finkelbaum, although, in truth, both he and Jim were used to staying out much later than this, whether Old Joe Dolan closed up the Merrie Malted or not. Over toward Main Street Tom heard Jim say, "Hi, there," to somebody, and he made out the shape of a woman rushing through the gloom with something small but heavy clutched to her chest. Miss Marrs.

"I want to go to tree," the Boy said, pointing again at Century Cedar, and the words were more an instruction or a demand than a suggestion or a request.

"Okay, okay," Tom muttered, "keep your shirt on." He started off across the grass toward the towering explosion of leaves and branches that had stood at the heart of Escardy Gap for nearly twice as long as its name implied. "Come on, then," he shouted to the figure behind him, adding somewhat viciously, "We go to tree. We *go* to tree."

The Boy began to follow, stepping as neatly and gracefully as a praying mantis. If Tom had turned around then, hadn't kept his back to his houseguest, he would have seen him, for the first time that day, break into a smile . . . and he would have seen him slowly, slowly remove his gloves.

5

*T*ick . . .
     "Who was that, dear?" Cora-May Chisholm asked of her husband as she heaped dirty dishes onto the stand by the sink.

Jack Chisholm had just stepped out onto the front porch to tap his pipe out against the steps, something of a nightly ritual out on Furnival Street. (Folks could set their clocks and watches by the tap, tap, tap and the rapid taptaptap that followed.) Then Jack had called out something about it being a hot one and no mistake. He had been addressing the Dickens-bearing Hannah Marrs, scuttling to her date with Destiny, and he told his wife so when he came back in, leaving out the bit about Destiny, of course, because he had no idea that this was what the woman in the smoked-glass spectacles called herself. Agnes Destiny, to be precise.

The screen door swung to with a loud creak, and Cora-May tutted to herself the way she always did when she heard the noise. How many times had she asked Jack to oil the hinges? And how many more requests would it take before Jack actually did what she wanted? "I'm putting some more coffee on," she said. "Will you ask Mr. Olesqui if he'll be joining us?"

"I'm right here, Cora-May," said a soft voice from the door to the kitchen.

Both Cora-May and pipe-filling husband Jack glanced over their shoulders.

There was the small but perfectly formed Mr. Olesqui, looking like Richie Rich in his well-made woolen suit, cornflower blue shirt and wide floral-patterned tie, all tailored impeccably to fit that child-sized frame. The doorway dwarfed him.

"I gather you're a smoking man," he said to Jack.

"That's right," said Jack. "Been one since I was sixteen, and there's been nary a day I've regretted it."

Now it was Jack's turn to feel a definite thaw in his frosty opinion of the diminutive member of the Company, for Mr. Olesqui, with a wink of complicity, held out a pipe of his own and informed Jack, "As you can see, it's one of my personal vices, too."

"Well, all I can say is a little smoke after a meal never did anybody any harm," Cora-May said as she dried her hands on a dish towel.

Although initially wary of the guest her husband had brought home, Cora-May had warmed to Mr. Olesqui over dinner, watching him plow his way through three helpings of her renowned biscuits, a double helping of sweet potatoes, most of a dish of carrot purée heaped with sour cream, two thick-as-a-sidewalk-slab lamb chops, and, to follow, two dishes of her apple-and-rhubarb pie à la mode. (How Mr. Olesqui had fitted all that into his small frame was anybody's guess, but he hadn't even *looked* as if he were having any trouble getting it down.)

"Why, thank you, Cora-May." Mr. Olesqui gave a small bow. It had to be a small one. Any larger and he would have cracked his forehead on the floor.

"So, Jack," Mr. Olesqui went on, "just what kinds of tobacco do you like?"

"I'm none too picky," Jack replied. "Whatever's going at Wilbur Cohen's store usually does me."

"Perhaps, then, you'd care to try some of mine."

"I'd be pleased to," said Jack, and he tipped his pipe out into his pouch.

"Excellent," said Mr. Olesqui. "And I do believe I'll have some of that coffee, Cora-May."

"Coming right up," said Cora-May cheerily. Humming a tune she didn't know the name of, she busied herself with some cups and saucers (always saucers for the guests, just like the British, she kept telling Jack) while the men left the kitchen for the living room. She let the tune fade from her lips as her husband switched on the radio and strains of Bing Crosby crooned through the wall. She heard her husband say, "That's a fancy pouch you've got yourself there, Mr. Olesqui. I don't think I've ever seen a pouch quite like that one."

Night was snugly dark beyond the windows. Bing was singing. Life was good.

6

*T*ock . . .

"Evening, Mr. Macready," shouted Hannah Marrs to the two men strolling toward the intersection of Carmichael Avenue and Carnegie Drive.

"Miss Marrs," replied Mr. Macready. "Oh, I'd like you to meet my new friend, Buzz. Buzz Beaumont, Hannah Marrs."

"Ma'am," said Buzz, with a charming smile.

Like many of the members of the Company, Mr. Macready's houseguest looked perfectly normal until you got close up. Up close, it was possible to make out the material that provided the pinstripe for the flannel of Buzz's suit: fuse wire. Yard upon yard of fuse wire, woven into the cloth. And for jacket buttons, small copper switches. Buzz sparkled as he moved, and his every gesture was burnished copper red.

Hannah paused, hand on her gate, and nodded politely. "Mr. Beaumont," she said warmly, while wondering just how comfortable that suit could be to wear.

"I was just telling Buzz here about my lightning rod," said Mr. Macready, jerking a thumb in the direction of Carnegie Drive and his prized roof ornament just visible across the rooftops opposite, die-cut into the shape of old Father Time and stained turquoise by the passing of the seasons; old Father Time, hourglass in one hand, scythe in the other, striding through the air from here to there, from has-been to will-be.

"Oh, how nice," said Hannah Marrs, anxious to begin her evening proper. "And are you enjoying yourself here in Escardy Gap, Mr. Beaumont?"

"That I am," he replied. "It's all very interesting. I'm going inside soon and Mr. Macready is going to show me all his electrical appliances. I'm fascinated by electrical appliances."

Hannah knew Mr. Macready was fond of gadgets. So, it appeared, was Mr. Beaumont. And Hannah suspected that it was the instinctive recognition of a shared interest that had drawn Mr. Beaumont to Mr. Macready in the first place, and Agnes Destiny to her, and all the other houseguests to their hosts. How funny that the tradition should be that opposites attracted when quite clearly the reverse was true.

"We're going to exchange notes," Buzz Beaumont went on. "Mr. Macready's going to show me his and I'm going to show him mine. I like to keep up on *current* affairs, you see."

Mr. Macready seemed to find Buzz's weak pun inordinately funny. Hannah looked from her neighbor to his houseguest and back again, and said, "Well, you enjoy yourselves, you two."

"We will," said Buzz, the man in the solenoid suit.

A nod, a wave, and the librarian scurried indoors, allowing the two men to recommence their journey home, both pairs of eyes fixed on the lightning rod.

"Will you *lead* the way?" Buzz said, grinningly, to Mr. Macready as they turned the corner.

"Lead!" guffawed Mr. Macready, slapping his thigh. "Ho, ho! *Lead!*"

7

Tick, tock, tick, tock, tick, tock, tick . . .

Six

1

Grampa Knight caught Josh on the stairs before he could reach his bedroom.

"Where you been all afternoon, son?"

"Around."

"Around where?"

"Here and there."

Grampa decided not to press the matter. The boy was old enough to look after himself, and if he wanted to be alone, let him. It was highly unlikely that he was up to no good. Not Josh. "Mr. Rackstraw's taking a nap," Grampa said. "Best not thump around too much case you wake him up." He lowered his voice. "Don't ask me why, but I reckon the longer we let him sleep the better."

"I'm sorry about all this, Grampa," said Josh. "I know I should have asked . . ."

Grampa waved the apology away. "Can't be helped. My guess is he would have persuaded you even if you weren't the polite and obliging kid you are. He's got a way with words, that Mr. Rackstraw. He could charm the fangs out of a rattler. Have you noticed, when he talks, it's like he's reading it all out of a book, like he's got *Webster's* and a complete Shakespeare sitting on a stand in front of him? Have you noticed that?"

"Yeah," said Josh, slightly ruefully, and this time it was his turn to change the subject. "I'm going to have a bath."

"You do that. Dinner'll be on the table by the time you get down."

"No sweat, Rhett."

"No fuss, Gus."

Josh entered his bedroom. There was the Neverseen Era, his world, all paleolithic swamp and campfire security. There was his closet with comics spilling from the door and his chest of drawers vomiting socks and underpants and the patient lines of drinking glasses bearing the white memories of milk that seemed to accumulate in his room without hope of release, like prisoners on death row.

He listened.

Tick . . .

And there, definitely there, inexorably there . . .

Tock . . .

The clock.

Josh stepped back into the corridor and pulled the door shut after him. Then he knelt down, placed his head by the keyhole and listened again. He pressed his ear closer to the door and he strained to hear until it seemed the skin of his eardrum could go no tighter without snapping.

Nope, nothing. Not a sound. Not a tick, not a tock. Just the sound of his heart pounding away like a timpanist.

He jumped up and whisked the door open, keeping a hold of the handle so that it didn't crash back against the wardrobe but sweeping it open as far as it could go, as if to say, I'm here now so you'd better stop whatever it is you're doing! and he strode over to where the clock sat on a pile of comic books on his desk. The balloon face grinned inanely through him to some far distant point in space.

Tick, tock . . .

It wasn't as if he'd asked to be given the dumb thir
first place. It wasn't as if he wanted Jeremiah Rac'
give him *any*thing.

He picked it up. The ticks and tocks reverber
the flesh of his palms. The clock felt oddly w?

Tick, tock . . .

So what was *really* wrong with it? Was it that the clock weighed far more than a collection of brass cogs and steel springs had any right to? Was it the happy-but-not-happy smile affixed to the mad clown face that filled most of the clock's circular frame? The telltale hint of temper promised by the wavy furrowed-brown lines painted onto the smooth enamel? Or was it the eyes? Greedy eyes, hard and shiny eyes, eyes that seemed to say, I see you . . . I see your room, I know where you live . . . and I know what you're doing. . . .

Josh turned the thing over in his hands. It had a fine brass-plated back into which there was set a small square door without a handle or hinges, held in place by four brass screws. He wasn't sure what the door was for but he suspected it was to make the clock-repairman's job easier when the time came for the clock to be repaired, when the effort of holding back all those seconds got too much for the mainspring and the teeth of the cogs wore down through gnashing.

He turned it over again. That was better. He felt more comfortable when he could see the face on the clock's face. As though, when he couldn't see it, it was doing things. He stared closely, minutely.

The face wasn't doing things now. Just . . .

Tick . . .

. . . ticking and . . .

Tock . . .

. . . tocking. It was a clock, nothing more.

And yet, since the arrival of the train this afternoon, everything seemed more than it had been. The train and all that it contained had impregnated everything with significance, the way the Reverend King tried in his sermons to turn the everyday into the extra-special, inflate the ordinary to a parable of the divine. Then again, a clock that didn't tick all the time wasn't *more* than a clock; it was significantly less, markedly worse. Above all, it was an intrusion into Josh's life, an alien artifact without true place or real reason to be here, especially ~ear his cavemen and dinosaurs, who did not have time for ᵊ, for whom Time was an awkward visitor who asked too ᵈifficult questions.

ᵗ the clock down again on the desk and moved over

to the Neverseen Era, which occupied a larger proportion of floor space than any item of furniture, resting on a raised wooden platform he had constructed in one backbreaking afternoon of sweat and carpentry. He hunkered down among the sauropods and the Neolithic men, turning his back on the clock, and he felt that he could be content for a while, just casting his eye over the intricacies of his handiwork and seeing that it was good, very good.

2

Down at Billy's Bar & Grill the conversation was turning around the only topic worth discussing, namely whose turn it was to buy the beers.

"Carroll's!" claimed Earl Evett.

"Earl's!" counterclaimed Carroll.

"Toss of a coin," said Big Ben Burden, whose turn it never seemed to be. He made a thumb catapult of his right hand and loaded it with a shining quarter. "Call it."

"Heads!" cried both Earl and Carroll at once.

"Tails!" they cried again.

Big Ben groaned. "Heads, Earl, tails, Carroll, agreed?"

Agreed.

The coin spun upward, its milled edges glinting in the light of the Bar & Grill's electric lanterns, and, reaching apogee, came tumbling downward, slap into Big Ben's palm, then slap onto the back of Big Ben's other hand.

He peeked, said, "Carroll, it's your turn," and pocketed the coin.

Without a murmur, Carroll got to his feet and went to the bar. Though the quarter had been heads up, it *was* Carroll's turn, since Earl had bought the last round before closing time yesterday. Only Big Ben had the wit and the wherewithal to remember these things, and for this reason, to save a lot of futile argument—what Earl and Carroll called "getting things straight"—he had devised the coin trick. It wasn't cheating his friends (he thought, reasonably enough). It was just a harmless piece of subterfuge to make everybody's lives a little bit easier.

Once the beers were on the table, frothing in their frosted glasses, the conversation could turn to other, weightier matters. Such as Big Ben's houseguest.

"So help me, that man is crazy as a rabid rat," Big Ben averred, sucking froth from his bearded lips. "Can't use one word where ten beginning with the same letter will do. Janey's taken a shine to him, though. Now, don't get me wrong, I don't begrudge Mr. Nolan the room or the food or anything, but I wish once, just once, he would talk like a normal human being, not keep firing off all them fancy words like a Gatling gun."

"Nothing wrong with fancy words," said Walt Donaldson, who had just come into the Bar & Grill and had caught the tail end of Big Ben's remark. "Sara Sienkiewicz uses fancy words."   .

Earl, who had his back to Walt, rolled his eyes to the others: *Sara Sienkiewicz! Does Walt ever talk about anything else?* The others managed to keep straight faces.

"Yeah, Walt, but only on paper," Carroll pointed out. "She *talks* just like you and me."

"Now, let's not do the lady a disservice, gentlemen," said Big Ben.

"So, who do you think's prettier, Big Ben, Sara or them three girls?" Walt asked, pulling up a chair and seating himself without needing to be invited to do so.

"Yeah, Big Ben, who do you think's prettier?" said Earl, mimicking Walt, but not so accurately that Walt would notice and take offense.

"Well, of course, I only have eyes for my Janey, but if you held a gun to my head I'd have to say there was no contest."

"No contest," agreed Earl, hoping that this would bring the conversation to a swift close.

Walt scratched his head. "So who wins?"

Big Ben was only too happy to elaborate. "When I say no contest, Walt, I mean how can there be any contest? We're dealing with two completely different classes of woman here. On the one hand you have Sara, okay? She's like this fragile thing, this rare Chinese vase. Makes you just want to keep looking at it and looking at it and drinking in its beauty, but you're kinda scared to touch it with your big clumsy hands, case it breaks on you." (Walt nodded his head vigorously to this. He knew exactly what Big Ben meant.) "On the other hand you have them girls, who are like"—Big Ben cast about for some suitable comparison and found it at the next table, where Moose Rollins, Sr. and his not incomparably large wife, Thelma, were tucking in to a heaped plateful of Billy's amazingly succulent cheeseburgers and crisp fries—"are like earthenware dishes. They look fine, they're made well, but you can still eat off them. Yep." With this last Big Ben reassured himself that the metaphor worked and was good and held water. "Besides, everyone knows Sara's got brains. Them girls . . ."

"Only giggle," said Earl.

"And clack their teeth," said Carroll.

"Giggle and clack their teeth," agreed Big Ben Burden. He drained his glass and nodded at Walt. "Your round next, Walt, I believe."

It turned out to be a long evening's drinking. There was much for these philosophers to discuss. Posterity, however, will be bereft of their arguments and their conclusions. There were other things happening in Escardy Gap that night, equally if not more demanding of attention.

3

Jack Chisholm took up residence on Cora-May's pride and joy, her early-American-style Hide-A-Bed sofa, which stood next to Jack's pride and joy, his Arvin High-Fidelity Velvet Voice radio. Mr. Olesqui hauled himself up into an armchair opposite Jack and settled himself in with his feet dangling down, heels rubbing against the valance, looking for all the world like some darling boychild dressed up by an overattentive mother for an evening with the grown-ups. Jack watched him take out a pouch from his pocket, ferret around inside it and pull out a thick fistful of shiny tobacco. The tobacco glistened and glowed like rich honey. Every shade and hue of brown was there. Jack's mouth fair watered at the prospect of tamping a wad of it down inside his Medico Crest filter pipe.

Jack knew about pipes, and the Medico was his favorite. Now four years old, he still reckoned it delivered the best smoke, and he fully endorsed the company's claim that their sixty-six-baffle filter system and bite-proof nylon stem did indeed cool the smoke and Trap Dangerous Nicotine and Tars, Bitter Juices and Flakes. He held it in his hand and waited impatiently for his guest to pass across the wedge he was busy putting together, stroking strands off the main lump and delicately dropping them back into his pouch. That pouch! Jack had seen some fancy tobacco pouches in his time but this one beat them all.

"That's a fancy pouch you've got yourself there, Mr. Olesqui," he said, trying desperately to contain the pool of slaver that was building up in his mouth. "I don't think I've ever seen a pouch quite like that one."

Mr. Olesqui gave a small why-thank-you bow and said, "I guess you haven't, Jack," while he finished unraveling an obstinate strand of tobacco. Jack couldn't decide which to look at, the pouch or that juicy tangle of tobacco, so his eyes darted anxiously from one to the other. The tobacco seemed mighty keen to get out into the air, like as though it wanted to be smoked.

But that pouch! It was made of some kind of glossy, thick leather, a mixture of earthy colors: soil browns, stone grays, sandy yellows and the red of rocks, shot through with streaks of orange like veins of iron ore. He thought at first that Mr. Olesqui must be squeezing and fondling the pouch between his fingers, to make its mouth swell and bulge and suck so, but then it occurred to him that the pouch was moving independently of its owner's hand. He didn't pay much mind to this. His attention was soon drawn to the tobacco, which squirmed in Mr. Olesqui's other hand like worms being loaded into a fisherman's jar.

"Give me your weapon, Jack," said Mr. Olesqui, smiling, "and I'll load her up for you."

"Why, thank you." Jack drooled. He couldn't understand what had come over him. He had never been quite so eager for a tobacco fix since he had quit smoking cigarettes a few years back, when he had had that bad chest and Cora-May was convinced that the smoking had something to do with it, or at any rate was making it worse. She was probably right, but still, it was only with the greatest of reluctance that Jack had moved away from his beloved Camels, first on to menthols such as Kool and then Salem—all of which tasted to Jack like indigestion powder—and then Spring, which promised only a "wisp of menthol" but still tasted like indigestion powder. It was Wilbur Cohen who finally suggested to Jack, one day when Jack was standing half slumped over Wilbur's counter staring mournfully at the range of cigarette packs stacked on the shelves lining the back wall, that he should try a pipe.

So he did.

At first, it was like sucking on the smell put out from the socks and shorts that Cora-May scorched with the iron, or the old wet moldy leaves that Jack raked together and burned in the backyard every fall. Then, slowly and surely, and almost imperceptibly, it got so he quite looked forward to sitting down and sticking the stem between his teeth. Smoking a pipe was more contemplative than pulling on a cigarette. Jack could imagine things when he smoked his pipe, could think and sort out the little problems that life threw up and which stuck up there in his brain and wouldn't work themselves out to a satisfactory conclusion.

He bought several pipes. A clay cob (for fun); a classic dry-smoking Peterson, all curly stemmed and silver collared, its reservoir perfect for salivating Jack, a wet smoker of some renown; a metal spiral-stemmed Falcon with a screw-on bowl (which he never much cared for because he thought it was a bit low-class); two beautiful English briars—Duncan and Dunhill—fashioned from finest walnut-colored wood; a cherry (also for fun); and a cool-smoking meerschaum, which had been Jack's bosom buddy for nigh on two years. It was made from cream-colored clay that had darkened the more he had smoked it, the bowl gaining a slight but definitely deepening amber tinge from the tobacco. Then came the Medico Crest. That had been *the* pipe for four years now, ever since he had bought it from Wilbur, along with the first of his packets of ten-for-a-dime "throw away nicotine" Medico filters.

Tobacco proved to be a slightly less important consideration. As Jack had told Mr. Olesqui earlier, he was none too picky when it came to what he filled his pipes with. He had tried them all. But it did turn out that there were a couple of brands that, if pushed for a preference, Jack would have to say were his favorites: Borkum Riff, flavored with bourbon (a delight, even though Jack Chisholm was not what you could call a drinking man) and Kentucky Club, which Jack felt held true to its advertising claim of being "The Thoroughbred of Pipe Tobaccos"—and anyway, he liked the tins. He had stacks of them stored out behind the back door beneath an old lean-to, which he gave out regularly to anyone who needed something to store things in. If you had checked the bedrooms of Escardy Gap's early-teen population, chances were you would find one of Jack's Kentucky Club tins. Sara Sienkiewicz used one to keep her pens and pencils in. (Jack had been only too proud to make his small contribution to furthering the career of the town's loveliest lady and successful authoress.)

Now this connoisseur of all things fuming yearned to try Mr. Olesqui's tobacco, and he fumbled with his Medico as he handed it over to the midget.

"You're going to find this a revelation, Jack," Mr. Olesqui said as he packed the writhing tobacco strands deep into the Medico's bowl. "It's an . . ." He paused for a second to find the right word. "Interesting flavor. Perhaps an acquired taste, I don't know. That's for you to decide."

"Interesting?" Jack was barely concentrating on what Mr. Olesqui was telling him, was barely concentrating on what he himself was saying. All he could see, all he could think of, was that tobacco. "Acquired?"

"There!" The little man finished filling the pipe and held it up almost for Jack to see. Thin strands of the tobacco were unfurling themselves and snaking over the rim of the bowl, only prevented from making good their escape because they were too tangled up in their brethren. Mr. Olesqui prodded the would-be fugitives back down with his thumb and returned the pipe to Jack. "Light it quick now," he said. "I've pressed a good-sized lump down in there and it's like to unravel itself in the blink of an eye."

Jack nodded and reached in his sweater pocket for his book of matches, unaware he was dribbling down his chin. Mr.

Olesqui smiled at him paternally and folded the flap of his pouch shut, apparently oblivious to the way the sides inflated and deflated in his hand. Then, pouch returned to his pants pocket, where it still moved, though more slowly and laboriously, Mr. Olesqui shifted himself back into his seat, little dangling legs swinging from side to side, and retrieved his own pipe from the ashtray where it had been smoldering throughout the filling of Jack's Medico.

Jack gripped the pipe between his teeth and tore off a match from the book. With trembling hand he lifted the flaring match to the tobacco and sucked in air, observing with only the mildest of disbelief the strands trying to wriggle away from the flame.

"How's that?" said Mr. Olesqui.

"Mm," said Jack, still pulling. "Mmmm."

The taste of the tobacco was indeed interesting. When it first hit his mouth it burned slightly, but only for a moment. Then it mellowed out some.

"Mmmmmmm, good!"

Jack removed the pipe to consider it in his hand, smoke curling up from the bowl. He shook out the match and dropped it into the ashtray, returning his beloved Medico Crest to its rightful place between his lips.

The little man from the train stifled a chuckle as the first plumes of smoke drifted out of Jack's ears.

Jack pulled harder on the pipe and, before long, he was doing something he had always sworn he would never do: he was inhaling. He swallowed that beautiful smoke, swallowed it in clouds, felt it travel down his throat and swirl around in his hollow insides.

"Mmmmmmmmm."

He took his hand from the stem and scratched his cheek. *Must've been bitten,* he thought distantly, rubbing off what felt like the crushed remnants of a mosquito and flicking it into the ashtray. A fresh drift of smoke wound its way lazily out, freed from his mouth by the tiny new exit Jack had thoughtfully supplied in his cheek.

Now his hand was itching, and the top of his leg. He scratched at the hand with a fingernail, not surprised to see the skin come away like warm butter scooped out of the dish. He rolled the skin tissue across the tops of his fingers with his thumb, still puffing on his pipe for all he was worth, and placed the resulting small gray-pink ball on the arm of the sofa. Rubbing the top of his leg, he smiled over at Mr. Olesqui, raising his eyebrows to indicate that his guest should look at the way the smoke rose from the hole in his hand. Mr. Olesqui gave a small laugh.

"Shquite a chick," Jack said around the stem of his Medico Crest.

"It most certainly is," replied Mr. Olesqui.

Jack got to his feet and unbuckled his belt, letting his pants drop to the floor. Wisps of smoke were twining upward from a red patch on Jack's left thigh, just below his shorts. He kicked off the pants and jammed a fingertip into his leg, wiggling it around and chuckling as more smoke wafted out around his knuckles.

"Mmmmmmmmmmm!" he said, savoring the taste of the smoke, gulping it down.

Keeping his finger inserted into his leg he sat down again and pushed his hand toward his knee. The leg split open obligingly, peeling back in two halves to expose bone and muscle encased in smoke, which billowed up gratefully from the wound into the thickening atmosphere of the Chisholm's living room.

Mr. Olesqui kept smoking, smiling his approval at each new discovery Jack made: the thick handfuls of stomach wall; the small purse of genitalia (not especially well endowed, Jack Chisholm); the little bonfire piles he had collected of fingers and toes, crowned majestically with his nose and left ear; and finally the sudden realization of just how pliable this exceedingly fine-tasting tobacco made his bones. They just bent and then snapped off.

It bothered him some that he no longer had any hands or teeth, and that most of his face had fallen away, but then Mr. Olesqui volunteered to stand by his side and hold the pipe in place so that what remained of Jack's head could suck and swill and swallow, and everything was fine again.

"Shanksh," Jack said with what he hoped was a look of gratitude. He took another puff. "Mmmmmmmmmmm . . ." Then his head, lacking anything in the way of support, sank down onto the wet gray pile of skin, flesh, and bone that had been his body. There was a hissing sigh, and then a final puff of smoke, the last of Jack Chisholm, gouted up and mushroomed out across the ceiling.

It was at this moment, with the Chisholms' diminutive houseguest leaning against the arm of the sofa, which now contained a large amorphous mass of something resembling wet cement topped with a single eyeball like the proverbial cherry on the cake, that Cora-May Chisholm chose to join in the fun. Her domestic duties discharged, she switched the lights out in the kitchen and came down the hall. Upon entering the living room, her nose started to twitch in pleasant puzzlement. Through the clouds of smoke she could just make out Mr. Olesqui. He was inserting a pipe, Jack's Medico, stem-first into the strange mess on the sofa and patting the mess on the head as if it were a good dog.

"Why, Mr. Olesqui, whatever is that smell?" she exclaimed.

"Wonderful, isn't it?"

"I don't think I ever smelled anything like that before. Is that some kind of foreign tobacco?"

"Have you ever smoked a pipe, Cora-May?"

Cora-May put an index finger to her cheek and frowned at the ceiling. "Well, no, I haven't, Mr. Olesqui, but I'd sure like to give it a try."

Mr. Olesqui plucked the pipe from the gray pile on the sofa, which was slipping down over the cushions now and dripping onto the floor in globs and splats, and removed his pouch from his pants pocket again.

"Then now's the time to try, my dear," he said.

And she did.

While beside her, unperturbed by the smoke, Jack's Arvin High-Fidelity radio launched Perry Como into the continuing chaos for what was to be, at least for the radio, a very long night. It might have saddened the sleepy-voiced Mr. Como to learn that no one present gave a good goddamn what Della wore.

4

Down at the Bar & Grill closing time arrived—as usual, with a suddenness that surprised and disappointed—and Billy Connors had begun washing and polishing glasses deliberately noisily so that his two remaining customers, Walt Donaldson and his friend Clem Stimpson, could be in no doubt as to the lateness of the hour and the imminence of their being tossed out. (Big Ben Burden, being a family man, had headed home long ago, and Earl and Carroll Evett had shortly followed suit.) Walt and Clem were sunk deep into their cups and were discussing matters of great weight, and were for these two reasons impervious to Billy's subtle hints. Clem, anyway, had made it his life's work to ignore the comments of others, and, in his role as official town soak, had developed a thicker skin than most.

"Just *knowing* alla them words ain't enough," Clem was telling Walt. "You gotta know how they all stack together. 'S'like I always say. You can know the lyrics and you can know the tunes—don't mean you can sing the songs." Sharp as a new razor, that Clem!

"I don't want to know if she can sing any songs," replied Walt, with a whiny note of complaint in his voice. "I just want to know if she knows how to kiss."

"Only one way you're going to find that out, Walt, old pal."

"Nah, she'll never want to have anything to do with me. She's a famous writer and I'm a . . . a stationmaster."

"But you're an important man around town now, Walt."

"No, I'm not. I'm just a fat old nobody."

"A woman likes a little bulk on a man, Walt. Brings out the mother in her."

"Is that so?"

"Hey, trust me, Walt. I know about these things," said the permanently unattached and decidedly ineligible Clem Stimpson.

"And I'm an important man around town?"

"Hey, it weren't *Mayor's* station that train pulled in to. It weren't the *Reverend King's* station. It weren't *Old Joe*

Dolan's or the *Evetts'* or *Doc Wheeler's* or, jeez, even *Wilbur Cohen's*. It was . . . What was I talking about?"

"It was *my* station?"

"Damn straight!"

"That what people are saying?"

"Sure it is," said Clem. Only the whitest shade of an untruth, that.

"Well, I wish someone'd tell *her.*"

"Someone can, Walt. *You* can."

Walt found the concept nothing short of astounding. "I go over to Sara Sienkewicz's and tell her I'm an important man around town?"

"Not in so many words, Walt."

"I walk up the steps and knock on the door and say, 'Good day to you, Miss Sara. I'm an important man around town now. Will you kiss me?' "

"I think you're taking this a bit too littible . . . Liberal . . . *Literal*. I think you're taking this a bit too literal, Walt. If'n you don't mind my saying so. Okay. Lemme put it to you this way. What you gotta do is you gotta go over there . . ."

"Yeah?"

". . . and invite yourself in . . ."

"Yeah?"

". . . and make all that small-talk stuff for a while . . ."

"Yeah?"

". . . and then, all casual-like, you start talking 'bout the train, and you say what you did, you know, open the doors an' that, and then you tell her how everyone was watching you and just how big a moment this was in the history of Escardy Gap, and I figure if she ain't kissin' you by the end of that . . ."

"Yeah?"

". . . then she ain't a woman at all."

The plan seemed simple enough and the logic was sound. Walt could find no fault with it except one: "What if I chicken out?"

"Criminy, Walt! All these years I been hearing this big talk about you and Sara Zinkywink . . . Sara Blinkatink . . . About you and her. About how you're gonna make that woman your wife, she's gonna make you the happiest man in the world, la di dah di dah. Every time she looks at you, it's like you just seen the face of God. You go 'round with this great fat grin on, you stumble and dance for the next couple hours. *But you don't do nothing about it!* How're you gonna make her your wife if you don't hardly ever talk to her? How're you gonna get her to fall in love with you if the only word she ever hears you say is 'Hi'?"

"I *know* what to say," said Walt, sounding more ashamed than hurt. "It's just, whenever I see her, she's so beautiful, my mind goes blank. My tongue goes all dry. I get the sweats."

"Like I said just now, like I always say—you know the lyrics, you know the tune . . ."

". . . don't always mean you can sing the songs. I know."

Clem dangled his empty glass by the handle in front of Walt's nose. "Your round, I believe, old buddy."

"It's always my round."

"My cash for this week's nearly all used up," said Clem. He didn't tell Walt that he had nearly used it all up buying three bottles of Wild Turkey from Wilbur Cohen's, one of which he had on his person and the other two of which he had tucked away in a secret hiding place beneath a loose floorboard in the bandstand in Poacher's Park. "I'll pay you back," he added.

Not convinced about this, Walt nonetheless turned to Billy Connors and raised his eyebrows beggingly.

"One more," said Billy, "and that's it. Then you boys are going home."

"Thanks, Billy," said Walt. "You're a pal."

"Well, at least someone here is," said Billy, twitching his eyes over at Clem Stimpson.

"So what you gonna do?" Clem asked Walt after he had taken a good, deep draught from his fresh glass. "You gonna go through the rest of your life wanting her and scared of telling her in case she turns 'round and says she don't want you? But what if she turns 'round and says she does? What if *she's* liked *you* all along but been scared to say so?" Actually, knowing Sara, this didn't seem any too likely to Clem, but it was the only thing to say to a drunken man with absolutely no self-confidence: suggest there were others like him, others who felt the same way.

It seemed to work, at any rate, because Walt said, "Dammit, Clem, you're right! I'm an important man around town. Damn straight! I'm good enough for her. I'm gonna go right out and tell her how I feel, lay it all on the line, be a man. Damn!" And he banged his fist on the table.

Billy Connors glanced 'round, frowned, and bit his lip.

"That's the spirit," said Clem.

"Damn right!" Walt took a fortifying sip of beer. "And I'm going to do it . . . first thing tomorrow."

5

Walt remembered everything about the journey home. He remembered bidding Billy a fond farewell and leaving the Bar & Grill with his arm around Clem and Clem's arm around him, and he had a strong recollection of the two of them pretending to be contestants in a three-legged race, joined at hip and ankle, staggering and stumbling and swerving along the street and laughing like there was no tomorrow. He definitely remembered Clem pulling a half-pint of Mr. Jack Daniel's invaluable contribution to the well-being of the world from out of his pocket, unscrewing the cap, taking a deep swig and then offering it to him, and he remembered declining on no particular grounds except that his head was beginning to seesaw and he didn't think he could match bottle to lips with sufficient accuracy to make the effort worthwhile. He also remembered his solemn, tearful parting with Clem at the corner of Main Street and Belvedere Way, their unabashed professions of lasting friendship and love, their embrace. He remembered, too, his solitary moonlit totter down Belvedere. He remembered going up to the porch and preparing to insert his key before realizing that the door was painted the wrong color, and he remembered how this had confused him for a good five minutes until he had realized he was trying to get into the wrong house, and he remembered sneaking back down the path, praying he hadn't woken the occupants. He remembered all this with great clarity, even though it had all seemed to be happening to someone else.

He only came to his senses when Miss Ohllson appeared in

the hallway just as he was tiptoeing toward the stairs and demanded to know where he had been.

Suddenly sober, cold with shock, Walt said, in a voice like a squeaky hinge, "Out," and fumbled with his fingers.

Ingrid Ohllson, in addition to her trials as Escardy Gap's schoolmistress, carried the burden of being Walt's landlady, and her home life seemed to be equally divided between correcting homework and trying to correct Walt's bad habits. In this latter task she had so far proved an abject failure. Walt, in the subject of habits, was not an apt pupil. It seemed that the best she could do with him was cluck and fuss and disapprove, in the hope that doing this often enough and consistently enough would eventually wear Walt down into submission.

"It's quite clear that you have been out, Walter," she said. "The question is, where have you been out?"

"Out and, uh, about."

"About?"

"Um, with friends."

"With Stimpson, you mean." Miss Ohllson could not bring herself to dignify Clem's surname with a title.

"Clem was there, yeah," said Walt. He yawned. "Gee, I'm kinda tired, Miss Ohllson. I think I'll just go upstairs and—"

"You'll do nothing of the sort," said Miss Ohllson, but not angrily. She was trying to force a smile upon her severe features, although the expression was refusing to settle there, unfamiliar with the territory. "You will come through with me and have a nightcap first. I have just put the milk on to warm."

"That's mighty kind of you, Miss Ohllson, but honestly . . ." Walt's fingers were now anxiously intertwining with each other, pulling and snapping the knuckle joints frantically.

"The milk will settle your stomach and the chocolate will help you sleep, do you not agree, Walter?"

Walt felt too weak to protest. He consented, mutely and meekly, to Miss Ohllson taking him by the elbow and leading him through to the kitchen. He let her pull out a chair for him and sit him down, and through a dull dry haze he watched her preparing two mugs of steaming chocolate. The sweet smell from the mug she placed in front of him did much to revive him, and the lip burn he gave himself with his first sip also helped considerably.

"I didn't know if you would be in tonight so I grilled two pork chops," she said. "The other one is in the larder beneath the fly cover. It will be there if you want it. If you get hungry in the middle of the night."

"Thanks."

"So, where did you eat?"

"Billy's."

"Billy's," said Miss Ohllson. As if she had expected Walt to eat out anywhere else. "Anyone there whom I might know?"

"Unh-unh," said Walt.

"We do not say 'Unh-unh,' Walter, we say 'No.' "

"Uh-huh. I mean . . . okay."

Miss Ohllson was determined that she was not going to lose her temper. "Was it not exciting at the station this afternoon? I must say, they are a strange lot, do you think? The Company. The name sounds rather Biblical to me. Does it sound so to you, Walter?"

"Can't say it does."

"Biblical and . . . theatrical. Of course, I would have offered to put one of them up, but, well, I only have one spare room, and that is taken, is it not? Are you sure you might not like that chop now, Walter? I know it is cold, but with a dab of relish and some of the Ma Kettle's Best Baked bread it could be quite palatable."

"Thank you, really," said Walt, and he chugged down the last of his chocolate, scalding his tongue and the roof of his mouth quite badly, but the pain was a refreshing shock, dispelling the last of his drunkenness. He knew he had to get upstairs and into bed as soon as possible, otherwise . . . Well, let's just say that if Walt didn't get to bed in the next five minutes, Ingrid Ohllson would almost certainly have to think twice about renewing his tenancy.

So he made his excuses as politely as he could and strode carefully out of the kitchen. Miss Ohllson sat there and sighed. The truth was, she was very fond of Walt Donaldson.

Awfully fond. There wasn't an earthly reason why she should be, but she couldn't help herself. She felt the same for him as she might for a wayward pupil who cannot see, or deliberately turns a blind eye to, his own brilliance. Pity and affection vied within her, but there were other, stronger factors involved. Physically, she found Walt oddly appealing— size and all. Their proximity at night, with just two doors and a length of corridor between their bedrooms, sometimes left her feeling flustered and short of breath. She wanted to look after Walt, care for him more than she already did, she wanted to improve him, she wanted to better him, she wanted to turn him out to the world a new man and say, "Look what I have done! Look! The material was poor and the process was long and arduous, but look what I have made of him!"

Miss Ohllson was not ignorant of Walt's infatuation with Sara Sienkiewicz, but equally she was convinced it could not last. One day, sooner or later, the Sienkiewicz woman would reject Walt. She might simply choose another man, or Walt might pluck up the courage to admit his feelings to her and then Sara would, of course, have to turn him down flat. Either way, Ingrid Ohllson would be there waiting to pick up the pieces.

These daisy chains of unrequited love are not unusual in small towns in out-of-the-way places in sparsely populated states. They wreathe themselves from house to house, from bedroom window to bedroom window. They garland themselves across streets and gardens and roofs and plots, strands of passion never spoken, never revealed, but always tended and always nurtured with care. In the course of time some may snap abruptly, some may gradually wither and fall away . . . but a few, a very few, will last right up until death, which breaks all ties, and dashes all dreams, and ends all loves.

6

Josh Knight lay in bed. Josh Knight listened. Hard.

The ticking and the tocking were muffled. Three T-shirts, two sweaters, and an old pair of baseball pants that Josh used to wipe his brushes after a stint painting dinosaurs had done the trick. The mound of cloth sat snugly on the desk.

He dared the clock to tick.

Dared it to tock.

It didn't.

Or if it did, he didn't hear it.

But if he slept, would the clock? Would it continue to tick and tock silently to itself? Would he wake up tomorrow and find it still telling the right time after a night's muffled clandestine work?

What was the matter with it?

What *was* it?

And suddenly there came to Josh, quite unbidden, a memory. He didn't even know it *was* a memory because he had never remembered it before, but it couldn't be anything else. It was a vision of a woman whom he didn't recognize but whom every instinct told him was his mother. A truly beautiful woman. A paragon of love and kindness. Dressed simply but elegantly, she was bending over him, and her huge cool hands were caressing his forehead and her face was bent low to his face and she was crooning softly, a gorgeous soothing melody, lulling the words over and over and stroking her fingers across his brow in time to the music. And Josh found himself staring up at her in awe and wonder, at the serene vastness of her face, at the milky smoothness of her pale skin, at the bright moonlight of her eyes. Then there was another voice, this one low and rumbling but equally full of tenderness, and Josh knew that his father had entered the room, pushing a delicious earthy man-smell before him. And his mother glanced 'round and smiled at her husband. Then they both peered down at Josh from above, his mother on the left, his father on the right. And Josh looked from one to the other and back again, and he was speechless with happiness, awestruck with love.

Then the memory faded. Just like that, as abruptly as it had appeared. It left Josh feeling empty and deprived. One moment he had been cresting a wave of inexplicable joy, the next he had come crashing down onto a dry barren shore. He wondered why the memory should have chosen now, of all times, to make itself known. He had a feeling it was something to do with the clock and Mr. Rackstraw and all the weirdness that was going on in town and in their lives. The past had reached out to him and stroked a comforting hand across his troubled brow, telling him that yes, the present was fraught with uncertainties and difficulties, but the past was always there, and always safe, and always secure, and could never be changed, never improved upon.

Josh was heartened. All the same, it was a long time before his fear would allow him to sleep. A very long time indeed.

He lay there, yearning for the quiet hours to pass.

7

Quiet.
Hours.
Passing.

Night arching over Escardy Gap, encapsulating that small sweet town like a bell jar, like the glass dome that Superman built to protect the miniaturized city of Kandor. Snug beneath the stars, Escardy Gap sleeping.

If you could rise above the town, if (like a certain winged werefly, for instance) you could soar up a quarter of a mile, half a mile, a mile, and hover there gazing down, you would see Escardy Gap laid out beneath you, tidy and orderly and just about damn near perfect. The streets running in straight lines. The houses camped on either side, their tented roofs silver in the moonlight. To the south, the glittering ribbon of Fleischer's Creek. To the east, the gentle grassy swell of Boundary Hill. You could watch a hundred twinkling streetlights give the town a shape in the darkness like a constellation or a small galaxy. You might even hear the hum of happiness, the snores, the sleep murmurs, the nuzzlings of true lovers and husbands and wives and small children gripping their favorite stuffed toys; a gasp here, a sigh there, and then hush once more. It would be hard to keep from smiling. Like a parent over a baby asleep in its cradle, you would look down on the face of utter contentment. You might wonder what was going on in the sleepers' heads, what filled the emptiness behind their sealed eyelids. Or you might prefer simply to imagine good dreams of happy lands of plenty.

Certain houses did not sleep, however. Lights burned in certain wakeful windows the whole night through.

Continuing

Chip left earlier than usual for the annual Hemingway Look-alike Competition in Key West. He went in July, even though the competition didn't take place until September. He wanted to acclimatize himself to the suffocating heat and the afternoon rainstorms and to go big-game fishing if his budget stretched that far and, if it didn't, to drink himself into a stupor at Sloppy Joe's. He wanted to get the true feel of the place. Go native.

Chip felt he had a real chance of winning this year. Of course, he had said that twice before and had twice come home empty-handed, but this time was different. Not only had he adopted the habit of smoking a lot of fat cigars and speaking in short enigmatic sentences, he had grown himself a white beard that would have made Zeus jealous and had taken to wearing a pair of round-framed glasses on a chain around his neck. I told him they made him look more like Lennon, and he thought about this for a second and then said, "I ain't no fucking Russkie!" (Who thought who was stupider, I wonder?) Not content with these merely cosmetic accessories, he had also developed a stomach that made him look as if he were suffering from the world's worst case of gas.

And I told him what I thought about that, too, on the evening before he was due to fly to Miami. I said, "Holy shit, Chip, keep those knees together! I don't want you letting rip right across in my living room. Some of us value our personal environments, you know."

Prima had dropped by also, on one of her impromptu Feed-the-Impoverished-Author charity events. She had descended from above like some culinary angel to rustle up linguini in the kitchen. Hudson was purring around her ankles, driven crazy by the unusually gorgeous smells of good cooking. Chip was sitting in my director's chair cleaning that damned rifle of his.

"Kiss my ass," is what he said to me.

And I said, "Not while there are dogs on the streets."

The rifle on which Chip lavished such affection was a non-functioning replica of a 1903 Austrian Mannlicher Schoenauer .256—as used by the guide in "The Short Happy Life of Francis Macomber," by Harry Street in "The Snows of

Kilimanjaro," by Mr. Pop in *The Green Hills of Africa,* and by Thomas Hudson in *Islands in the Stream,* and by the great man himself hunting in Tanganyika in the thirties. Those were the days. The days before Hem learned to cover his drunkenness by looking smug. You stood up close to him toward the end, you could hear his liver wheezing water like a busted fan in the air-conditioning. But while he kept that quiet, knowing expression on his face, he was still (and always had been, and always would be) Papa.

"Sometimes," Chip said, peering down the barrel of the Mannlicher, "I wish this thing worked."

"You talking about the gun," I asked, "or your dick?"

"Boys, boys, boys," said Prima from beside the stove.

" 'S all right," said Chip. "We're just fooling."

"You might be," I told him.

I had only just started the new book. You could say I was tense. Tense? I was edgier than a dodecahedron. The first few pages had cranked themselves out relatively easily, but I was still waiting for the hysteria to take hold, for the plot to rise up of its own accord and sweep me along. Until that moment, I was a quivering bag of neuroses, a mass of jangling ganglions.

The meal arrived at the table, we pulled up our chairs, Prima served, and then she turned to me and asked how the book was going.

I told her it was going just fine.

She was glad.

Then Chip asked what it was about, and I said I couldn't tell him.

"Not even a tiny little clue?" he said.

"I don't know myself," I replied, offering him the cheese grater. "Parmesan?"

"Well, that's not much of a way to go about writing a goddamn book, is it, now?" boomed Chip, believing for one fateful moment that he was really Hemingway.

And that was that.

I told Chip he was going to lose the competition, and then I told Prima her linguini stank, and then I told both of them that with their chickenshit ambitions and their lack of talent they made a perfect pair. I don't know where these opinions came from. They sure as hell weren't mine. Suffice to say that we sat down to eat at eight o'clock, and by eight fifteen I was on my own, with a panful of cold linguini nobody wanted.

Chip left for Florida the following morning without saying good-bye.

I did not see either of them for two weeks. Then Prima came by and I handed her the first complete chapter of the book as a peace offering. By now I was altogether a happier human being. Things were going well, and if all was right with me, all was right with the world.

Prima sensed this, maybe. Sensed my need for forgiveness, certainly.

I made coffee, and then we sat facing each other, sipping in silence, while she thumbed through the opening pages. I tried to divine her expression. Was that a frown, or just the squinting of tired old eyes? Finally she looked up.

"You should know better than to expect me to pass judgment here and now," she said.

"But do you like it?"

"Does it really matter if I do?"

"It matters to me, yes!"

A sly smile. "Just keep going with it," she said.

"It's only a rough draft," I said quickly. "There's a lot of work needs to be done. Polishing and tweaking."

"It's horror, isn't it?"

"No!" I cried, horrified.

"Sci-fi, then."

"No!" I cried, curdling inside at the abbreviation, which seemed somehow contemptuous and dismissive. "If you *must* stick it in one of the genre ghettoes, try fantasy. But it's all just fiction, underneath. It's all just telling stories."

"You've not written anything like this before, though."

"I've never felt the urge before."

"The town," she said. "You realize it's a geographical miracle, don't you? To have somewhere with so much green in the middle of so much desert."

"Not really. There's a creek. The town's sort of sprung up

around that oasis. Besides, I don't think it matters. It just sharpens the allegorical aspect of the story."

"I'm reminded a lot of the way you describe the place you were brought up."

"Are you?" I shrugged. "I suppose it *is* a little bit like it. But it's also a little bit of every fictional small town I've ever lived in through books. It's Archie's Riverdale, and Scout's and Jem's Maycomb, and Doug Spalding's Greentown, Illinois, all rolled into one. It's Smallville without the flying boy, and Sac Prairie, and even Castle Rock as I imagine it might have been forty years ago."

"The sort of place where you wouldn't be surprised to see Andy Hardy and Pollyanna come waltzing hand in hand down the street."

"Exactly! A dreamscape drawn by Rockwell and animated by Disney, all grassy green lawns and white picket fences and blue, blue skies and endless, endless summers. Every town you've ever dreamed of or read about or hoped for or sometimes even in your wilder moods searched for, expecting to find. Every town that should have existed but never, couldn't possibly ever, have."

"Except in our collective nostalgia." She nodded her understanding. "And I'm reminded of you, too."

"How so?"

"The boy. There is a lot of you in the boy."

"There were a lot of boys like him where I was brought up. There were a lot of people like the townspeople. They're all from life. They're all memories. You see, there's an attic in my head full of all this stuff, and for some reason I've decided that now is the time to sort it all out, set it in order, put tags on things, arrange everything alphabetically."

"You have a compulsion to put the world right."   .

"Yes."

"Like the time you married me and Chip off."

Prima will never let me forget "No Man," a short story I wrote just over a year ago in which two characters, Chuck and Irma, whose apparent mutual loathing hides a deep and abiding affection, are stranded on a desert island and realize that their only hope of survival lies in working together, and as they struggle to stay alive each reluctantly acknowledges the other's virtues, and so they are reconciled and they fall in love, just before the rescue ship arrives. A short but pointed allegory that found a home in one of the more respected literary magazines, secured me a small amount of money, won me some fan mail, and saw to it that my two best friends didn't talk to me for a month.

All I'd been trying to do was get them to admit something they both felt. But as Prima said (when, eventually, we were on speaking terms again), "If people keep something to themselves, they usually have a reason for doing so." In other words, butt out, bozo.

"Talking of Chip, any news?" In a way, I was relieved to be able to change the subject. I had received no word from Chip, not even a postcard from the Everglades saying "Glad you aren't here." I was genuinely curious to know how he was getting on.

"He sent a longish letter," said Prima. "He's been hanging around Sloppy Joe's a lot, sizing up the opposition."

"Seeing who's fatter, you mean."

Prima scowled. "You're one to talk."

"Biggest part of me is my mouth," I countered.

"No argument there," she said. "He didn't mention you by name, but I could tell he's still smarting. Chip doesn't have many dreams, honey, and he doesn't need you dumping on the few he has."

"Yeah, I'm . . . sorry." I have always had trouble with that word, but I choked it out and felt a little better for it. "Maybe he *will* win this year. He deserves to."

"Are you going to leave this with me?" Prima asked, patting the thin manuscript.

"If you promise to treat it like each page was made of gold."

"Believe me, honey," Prima said, in the fading plushness of my apartment, "if this was gold, you'd never see it or me again."

I'd written six chapters by the time Chip returned from Florida. Prima had read them and returned them without comment. This was neither encouraging nor discouraging. But it was damn infuriating.

Chip waited a whole day before coming visiting. Prima—his first port of call—had told him that I had shown contrition, but even so, he was wary and I was wary. He stood in the doorway and we danced around one another like boxers in the ring, feinting little thrusts of conversation here and there. Then he asked how the writing was going, and I told him it was going okay. I asked how the competition had gone, and a look came over him as if a doctor had just told him he had three weeks to live.

"Don't ask," he said.

But it was too late. I already had.

"No go, huh?" I said.

"I said don't fucking ask, okay?" This drifted back over Chip's shoulder as he slouched into the room and flopped into the director's chair. Hudson trotted up to him, sniffed his leg, decided she remembered him, and asked to be picked up. Absentmindedly, Chip set her on his lap and ran a hand down her blissfully arched spine. The rhythm of stroking sent him staring off into space. For a moment, Papa was reincarnated in my apartment.

"But you made the final three," I said. "Surely."

Chip sighed wistfully.

"Jesus, have they *cloned* him or something?"

"A jury of fucking illiterates," he said. "Blind fucking illiterates. Do you know who won? Some guy who was a dead ringer for George C. Scott. George C. Scott, for Christ's sake! Anyway . . ." He tossed it away with an irritable shake of his head. "Prima tells me you're cooking."

"Huh?"

"The book. She says it's happening."

"Yeah. Well. Maybe." I took evasive action, gliding to the drinks cabinet.

"How much you done?"

"About forty, fifty thou."

"That's almost all of it!"

"No, it isn't." I brandished a bottle of Jim Beam. "Too early for you?"

"It's never too early."

"One finger?"

"Long as it's your thumb."

"I was about to make some sandwiches," I said.

"Make plenty, then," said Chip, patting his belly which, I noted, had deflated during his ten weeks in Key West. He had worked up a decent tan, too.

While I loaded cheese and pickle onto rye, Chip stroked Hudson some more and nursed his drink. Then he said, "Prima tells me it's different to what you usually write."

"Different *from,*" I corrected him.

"She says it's about you, about your childhood."

"Well, that's wrong for a start."

"I don't know. Prima's pretty sharp on these things."

"Almost anything a writer writes has got to be vaguely autobiographical," I countered.

"Small town in the Midwest. Young kid. Loves dinosaurs, comics, the movies . . ."

"Yeah, so what? There were lots of kids like that!" A pickle went skidding off the counter and onto the floor. I bent to rescue it, and when I straightened up Chip was grinning all over his face.

"I just don't like people making assumptions," I said. "And I don't like people jumping to conclusions, either. What I do is what I do. It stands there on the shelf and exists in its own right. What does it matter where it comes from? You might as well say it's significant that I had a cheese-and-pickle sandwich the day I wrote such and such a page, or that the reason this section makes no sense is because I'd just drunk a fifth of Jim Beam. God, I tell stories, is all! I start at the beginning, go through the middle, and finish at the end. They come to me and I set them down. There's nothing strange or sinister in that. Lots of people do it! All this theorizing, this bullshit psychoanalysis, really pisses me off!"

There was a short, panting pause, and then Chip said, "Touched a teensy-weensy little nerve there, have we? Someone scared to admit that some of his soul goes into his work?"

"Eat your sandwich," I said, thrusting a plate at him. Subject closed.

*   *   *

Your women," said Prima a few days later. The three of us were up on the roof, sheltering in the shade of the water tower from a fierce August sun, sharing a thermos of iced tea. The flat asphalt around us melted and stank in the heat, and down below the traffic sang its day-long droning song. New York simmered around us, stately, gray, and magnificent.

"What about them?"

"I have a problem with them."

"What kind of a problem?"

"Do you really want to know?"

"I really want to know."

"Well, they're either one of two things. They're either silky temptresses or they're frumpy homebodies. I don't think you're going to be winning any awards for political correctness."

"Thank Christ," muttered Chip.

"Is that so?" I said to Prima.

She nodded. "And the silky temptresses always have a weird streak. It's not just this book. I've noticed this in all your work, and I'm a little concerned. What could we have done to offend you so?"

"Nothing. It's just . . . Well, I don't seem to be able to get beneath the *skin* of female characters. But that's not my fault. Don't blame me. Blame my chromosomes."

"Hell, I don't think men should write about women at all," said the unplaced entrant in this year's Hemingway Look-alike Competition.

"Opinions like that," said Prima, "should never be spoken, even in jest."

"Who's joking?"

"What about the writer character?" I asked. "Isn't she more acceptable?"

"She's idealized," said Prima. "She's an image of femininity, but hardly realistic. She's more interesting for the fact that you made her a woman at all."

"What's so interesting about that?"

And Prima smiled that damnable secretive smile of hers, that tantalizing glimpse of the answers to a million Sphinxlike riddles. And Chip said it was some kind of fag thing: maybe

I dressed up in drag whenever I sat down to write, squirmed in lingerie at my desk chair. He'd always had his doubts.

Fall arrived. It had to, in the end. The slow-burn summer had lingered on like a boring party guest, staying way past its welcome.

Clouds unfurled over New York, and the first rain in weeks splashed down in huge warm drops, tackling the dust and grit with the gusto of an actress advertising kitchen cleanser. Within minutes, the gutters had filled and become raging torrents, and the sewers gurgled busily. Umbrellas floated along the sidewalks, covering huddled, laughing couples.

By the time it was all over, the trees in Central Park had raised their drooping heads and the parched grass had greened and the streets shone slick and fresh and life had returned to the sweltering city.

And I was stuck.

The heat had been acting as a catalyst. The close, sticky air had been bringing me nearer to what I was writing, enveloping me in the atmosphere of my little desert town. It was almost as if I actually were the magical writer lady in her beautiful home, finding joy and inspiration in all around me. And then, with the coming of the rain, I had suddenly fallen into a deep dark emptiness. I didn't know what was going to happen next. Had no idea.

I grappled with my Smith Corona. Shoulder to shoulder we fought it out, and the typewriter, as it usually did in these contests, won.

I should have been reasonable about this. I should have shrugged and walked off for a while, wandered the streets thinking positive thoughts, read other authors, gone on vacation, *something*. But that wasn't my nature. Instead, I sank into a haze of depression. Days melted past. Prima pretty much left me alone, and Chip kept dropping in to drink my alcohol and tell me he was ignoring me until I became better company.

The will to write was gone, and even the thought of writing seemed an effort. Slumped in my armchair, I watched the sun shift across the sky and followed the gradual browning of the leaves on distant branches. I took a perverse pleasure in weariness. I looked forward to the delivery of bills I couldn't pay. The highlight of my day was nightfall, when I could at least sleep without feeling guilty. I started to pay attention to the plots of the daytime soaps, although I never bothered to learn the names of the characters or who was screwing (in both senses of the word) whom, so that pretty soon all the serials merged into one afternoon-long orgy of sex and chicanery simulated by beautiful actors in ugly studio sets.

If I wasn't deadening my brain with television, I would sit and stare up at the framed Escher print on the wall above my desk: two hands holding pencils and drawing one another into life, each emerging from frail two-dimensionality into gloriously realized solidity, an everlasting cyclical act of creation. It should have inspired me. Instead, after long fruitless hours of absorption, I would reckon my talent up to Escher's and find it hopelessly wanting.

And I drank. Oh, yes, I drank. Haunted Bunyan's Bar. Talked to my martinis. Drank.

Then the Smith Corona started wheedling again. At first I resisted the summons of its scratchy steel voice. I was happy in my fog of booze and misery. But the little god that lurked between the keys was persistent.

What am I here for? it asked. *Why do I sit on this desk night and day, without pay? Is it for my health? I think not. Is it for my own gratification? I think not. Is it to indulge my fantastical whims? Get real! I'm here because* you *need me. I'm here because* you *have this selfish desire to inflict your dull little dreams on the rest of the world. As if the rest of the world gives a shit . . .*

Even muffled beneath the cover, the voice carried on.

So what are you going to do about it, pal? A hundred-odd pages in, and you run up against a wall. One tiny setback, and you feel like chucking the whole thing. What a wimp! What a total loser!

"Go away," I told it.

Screw you, blue! I haven't got legs. I got feet, but no legs. I'm not going anywhere.

"Except out the window."

Is this how it's always going to be? You blubbering and get-

ting all moody every time things stop going your way? Pissing your friends off, pouring money you can't afford to waste down your throat?

So I sat down in front of the typewriter, tore off the cover, rolled in the paper, hit some keys . . .

Words appeared.

Slowly at first, tapping themselves out letter by painful letter.

I sat back, looking over what had been written.

Leaning forward again, not knowing what to expect, I dipped my fingers once more into the typewriter's glittering mouth.

More words. Faster now. Whole sentences.

A sheet was covered. A fresh sheet was rolled in.

Surprise, surprise!

That's more like it, the typewriter said, chattering busily. *You see, a mist came down there for a while. But it's clearing now.*

Seven

1

A mist came down on Sunday morning.

Oblivious to the fact that it was high summer in Escardy Gap, a dense autumnal mist descended, covering everything upward of ten feet from the ground. It hid upper stories and roofs and treetops, wreathing them in a pure ethereal icy white.

Beneath the swathes and swirls of this unseasonable mist, toward the insistent tolling of an unseeable bell, devout members of the community made their way to morning service. Heads down low as if in anticipation of prayer, speaking in hushed respectful tones, some did and some did not notice the playbills that had sprung up overnight, like mushrooms, everywhere.

The playbills read like this:

**THE COMPANY
IS PLEASED TO ANNOUNCE:
THE SHOW TO END ALL SHOWS!
MARVELOUS!
MYSTIFYING!
MAGICAL!**

MOMENTOUS!
SEE IT ONCE!
SEE IT TWICE!
BRING YOUR FRIENDS!
BRING YOUR FAMILY!
ONCE WITNESSED ...
... NEVER FORGOTTEN!
SHOW COMMENCES 10 A.M.
SUNDAY!!!

There was one on the blackboard outside Billy's Bar &
Grill, right where the daily specials were usually announced,
and there were two at the Essoldo covering the posters for the
Freaks/I Led Two Lives double bill, and there were four on the
war memorial, one on each face of the obelisk where the roll
of the dead was called in stone, and there was one on the notice board by the stout bolt-studded door of the Reverend
King's chapel, and there were eight on the octagonal bandstand in Poacher's Park, and there was one in the window of
Wilbur Cohen's store (*inside* the window, much to Wilbur's
consternation), and there were sixteen—sixteen!—plastered
on the walls of the town hall. There was one masking the
Let's Get Cancer! information display in Doc Wheeler's waiting room, and one on the bulletin board in Walt Donaldson's
office. There was also one that made a nonsense of Miss Ohllson's neat copperplate school timetable, and another one hiding the list of overdue books in the library. There were many,
many more. In the dark interval between Saturday and Sunday, Escardy Gap found itself infested with, rashed with,
acned with, cankered with brittle-edged rectangles of blue on
yellow.

All below the level of the mist. None above.

2

The congregation at the Reverend King's nine o'clock service expected at least a passing reference to the new-
comers from the train, along with an acknowledgment of the
nocturnal bill posting. The weekly service was more than just

a pit stop for refueling with righteousness. It was a chance to catch up on the latest events in town, to find out who had been born, who was getting married, and who was dying, under the auspices of praying for them. Today, however, the worshipers were treated to a display of immaculate indifference from the town's holiest man, who stuck so rigidly to the order of service you might have thought it was a treasure map. Those who were of a mind to notice such things felt that the reverend's glass eye glittered a little more coldly than usual as he read the lesson, but they put it down to the thinned state of the congregation he saw before him: the absent eye was reflecting absences.

"And when the woman saw that the tree *was* good for food," Reverend King read, "and that it *was* pleasant to the eyes, and a tree to be *desired*"—he delivered this last word with such bass-laden spittle-speared determination that it raised a few murmured amens from the front pews—"to make one *wise,* she *took* the fruit thereof, and did *eat,* and gave also unto her husband with her; and *he* did eat. And the *eyes* of them *both* were opened, and they knew that they were *naked.*"

Finishing, the reverend looked up from his book and down on the congregation. To him, they appeared as chains of heads reaching to the doorway.

One of those heads was Bob Tremaine's. Seeing the reverend up in his pulpit put Bob in mind of Ike Swivven. But then he hadn't been thinking about much else all night long. Alice said it had been like trying to get to sleep beside a feeding alligator, what with Bob rolling over and over and gnawing at the pillow so. At one point—this must have been about three in the morning, the deadest hour of night—Bob had clambered out of bed, whisked back the drapes, and stared out into the shining dark. When Alice had gotten up to comfort her husband she had found tears rolling down his cheeks, and she had had to shush and soothe him as if he were a child, stroking his hair, blowing on his feverish brow. "They got him," Bob had kept saying. "They got him, they got him, the damn Russkies got him and turned him into a lousy Communist zombie. . . ." She had asked him if he was referring to Jeremiah Rackstraw and his troupe of traveling players (about whom she had conveyed to him all that she had witnessed at the station yesterday and all the rumors she had gleaned since), and in response he had said nothing, which she didn't take to mean yes but neither mistook as a no.

Bob was itching for the service to end so that he could call in at Doc Wheeler's to see Ike, but he decided that as long as he was there he would pray harder than he had ever prayed before. He prayed for strength and he prayed for guidance, and he prayed for America like no one had ever prayed for America before, he begged God to bless this fair land as he had never begged Him before, and Alice to his left and little Sandy to his right each held his hand whenever they were able and tried to feed him love.

Mayor was there, too, a couple of pews in front of the Tremaine family. He felt awkward in churches, mainly because he didn't like to sit in what was—let's be honest here—an *audience*. He didn't like someone other than him getting all the attention. Once, very early in his former career, when a reporter from one of the showbiz journals had asked this up-and-coming young hopeful whether he believed in God, Mayor had replied, with a Grouchoesque twitch of the eyebrows, "Certainly, ma'am. And one day I hope to play Him!" Such natural irreverence had to be put aside when he was actually beneath the chapel's vaulted roof, however. It wouldn't have been proper to have a mayor who didn't at least appear to be a God-fearing soul. If nothing else, Mayor enjoyed singing the hymns . . . usually as Mario Lanza, in effort if not in tone. So his motives for being there *were* pure (sort of), and if they weren't, hell, the Big Guy would forgive him, wouldn't He?

Josh was there, too, sole representative of the Knight clan: Grampa had declined to come along, claiming a bad headache. Josh, unfortunately, was not paying full attention to the proceedings. In the pulse-slowing sepulchral solemnity of the chapel, he was trying desperately hard to stay awake. His lids were heavy, his brain was turning to mush, and he kept singing the wrong verse of the hymn and giving the wrong response and fumbling with the amens, sometimes misplacing the darned things altogether.

Josh's night's sleep, like Bob Tremaine's, had been fitful.

In fact, when Grampa had pulled back the sheets and given Josh's butt the usual playful whack first thing this morning, Josh had felt as though he hadn't even been to bed at all. And then, over breakfast, Jeremiah Rackstraw had just sat there at the table, in *Josh's* chair, and gone on and on and on about Grampa's pancakes. "My, but these are *soooo* good!" he had crooned, with a sidelong glance at Josh and a smile that would have looked more at home on the face of a cat crunching the small bones of a still-struggling bird. Josh had been obliged to take up residence on the old chair with the broken seat, which every so often nipped a huge chunk of his bottom, and this had not improved his mood, or his manners.

"Will you be joining us in church this morning, Mr. Rackstraw?" he had asked, in a voice more laden with syrup than the hunk of pancake now poised to disappear into the man's mouth.

The reply had not been all that he had expected and hoped for. Jeremiah Rackstraw had not so much as blinked. "I don't think so, Joshua," he had said softly, and Grampa had swiveled around from the stove looking as if he was about to say something, but he must have thought better of it because he turned right 'round again, and Rackstraw had simply helped himself to another pancake and smiled some more of that bird-chewing grin at Josh before loading the slice into his mouth. And shortly after that Grampa's headache had set in.

Having been deprived of a large proportion of his breakfast, which had disappeared down Rackstraw's gullet, Josh had snatched up an apple from the fruit basket on his way out to church. The apple bulged solidly and promisingly in his jacket pocket. Josh couldn't wait for the service to be over.

Perhaps the real reason the Reverend King worked so hard at maintaining the illusion of business as usual was precisely because there was so much *un*usual going on in Escardy Gap at present. A sense of barely restrained excitement was running through the congregation like electric current through insulated cable. And what charged that current? Why, the prospect of the show. A show! A show of marvels and mystery and magic and moment, here in Escardy Gap, here in their little town in the heart of the big nowhere!

During the fourth verse of "Onward Christian Soldiers,"

the Reverend King slipped out his fob watch from a pocket
sewn into his vestments and when he thought no one was
looking glanced down to check the time. Just after half past
nine. The show was due to start in a little under thirty minutes. The service had just under half an hour to run. The tim-
ing couldn't have been better if it had been planned that way.

He returned the watch to the pocket and, lustily singing
"marching off to warrrr . . ." regarded his flock. For no reason he could fathom, he found himself thinking that they
would have been better off in battle fatigues than the Sunday
best they sported here; and feeling that, rather than spouting
sermons, he really ought to be conducting combat training.

3

Walt Donaldson had been knocking for a long time. It sure
seemed like a long time, at any rate. And standing out
there on Sara's porch, his specially polished left shoe propping open the screen door, Walt felt like every kind of fool
there ever was and some that hadn't been invented yet. Not
only that, but he was nursing a head somewhat thicker than
the hovering mist and twice as befuddling. Consequently, he
was having a hard time convincing himself that what he was
doing amounted to anything more than downright dumb.

An important man, he told himself. *I'm an important man
around town. That's it. Yes.*

He placed his hands firmly on his hips and, in so doing,
bent back most of the stems of a small freshly picked bouquet
of wildflowers against the flap of his tweed jacket. It had to
be said that in the slow and painful diminuendo of his hangover Walt felt considerably less important than he had yesterday evening during the free and easy crescendo of getting
drunk. He consoled himself with this thought: if he felt bad,
Clem Stimpson would almost certainly be feeling ten times
worse. The bottle of Jack Daniels that Clem had produced
after they had left the Bar & Grill had been full to the base of
the neck and Clem, he knew, would not leave that bottle alone
until it was bone dry.

When Miss Ohllson had shouted up to Walt at a quarter to

nine this morning, announcing that she was just about to leave for church and wanting to know if he was coming, he had popped his head around the bedroom door and claimed he was sick, a condition to which his pallid gray cheeks bore convincing testimony. Miss Ohllson had understood. She had said nothing, but her silence was significant.

Walt hated lying, particularly to his landlady—but what he had to do this morning was far more important than mere genuflection.

Now he took a step back, accidentally allowing the screen door to clash shut. When the echoes of detonation had stopped ringing around inside his skull, he frowned and addressed his throbbing mind to the matter at hand.

So where was she?

Being a writer type and too preoccupied with the mysteries within herself to care about mysteries elsewhere, Sara Sienkiewicz did not go to church. Clearly, then, she was at home, but somewhere where she couldn't hear his knocks. So, weighing up all the facts, Walt deduced that she must be out back in the garden. Ten to one, scribbling away.

Walt laid the kinked flowers down gently on the porch and set off 'round the side of the house, keeping his stride brisk and purposeful so that anyone watching would assume he knew what he was doing.

He stopped.

One section of the bed that rang along the side of Sara Sienkiewicz's house was like something out of a gardener's worst nightmare, a jumble of dead and wilted and trodden-down plants and flowers. Sweet williams had been flattened, roses were withered and shrunken in on themselves, stocks had been depetalled and slashed apart. No sign of life at all in that section of soil, while all around was lush and fertile.

With no pretense of self-assurance now, Walt ran back 'round to the front of the house, swung open the screen door and hammered and hammered for all he was worth on the main door, shouting, "Miss Sara! Miss Sara!"

The latch, loosely secured, gave way.

The door drifted open, inward.

And Walt saw her.

And standing out there on threshold of Sara Sienkiewicz's

neat, elegant home, Walt Donaldson suddenly felt tiny and humble and very unimportant indeed.

"Miss Sara?" He said it softly, in case using her name too loudly would shatter the fragile stillness within. "Miss Sara, are you . . . okay?"

Even as he said the words he realized how purely stupid they were. How could anyone be okay, lying like that, spread-eagled face down on the floor? How could anyone be okay, so unmoving, so still?

Walt hesitated before stepping over the threshold. He cleared his throat, because it seemed like the appropriate thing to do, and walked into the room as though he were an intruder, not a visitor; a thief, not a messenger of love.

He knelt down beside Sara Sienkiewicz. Not daring to touch her, he just looked. There was a bruise the size of a bird's-egg over her right eye, and her nose was all bloody and bent out of true, the blood brittle and dark as lies.

Walt lowered an ear to her lips and his joy at feeling a ghost of breath on his skin was as great as . . . well, as if Sara had just whispered "I love you, Walter Donaldson, important man around town. I *love* you."

4

Pity Clem Stimpson. Pity him his aching body, his pulsing skull, his heavy bladder. Pity him the night he had spent in a back alley beneath the cold stars, hugging the empty bottle of Jack Daniel's to his chest like a child would a favorite stuffed toy, and the morning that had come crashing down on him with a cascade of mist and icy dew. Pity him, above all, the sight that presented itself to his throbbing eyes as he staggered into the town square about five minutes before ten o'clock, heading for the public drinking fountain that would bring relief to a mouth dryer than the dust on a rattlesnake's belly.

The mist had lifted a little, and the great knotty mass of Century Cedar sure didn't look the way it used to anymore. It looked like some kind of big snail or slug had lifted itself up and slid around and around that old tree leaving a trail of dark slime all over its bole and branches.

All thoughts of water evaporated as Clem diverted toward the tree, running both trembling hands through his matted hair. What he would have given, or done, or sold, or said, or sworn to, for a shot of Wild Turkey right about then, with an Arctic-cold Schlitz to wash down the sting! That way he would have been able to make sense of this more easily, wouldn't have had to exert his sorely overtaxed brain so.

By the time he got right up close to the tree, Clem had figured out that the stuff wasn't snail trail or slug spit or some sort of branch sap. It wasn't string, either. Nor was it some kinda fancy decoration, though it almost *could* have been.

Pasted to the trunk he noticed a rectangle of yellow paper that said, in a curious mixture of bold blue letters and something that looked like clotted catsup:

```
                    COMPANY
        IS PLE        TO            CE:
                      D AL      WS!
                      LOUS!
                      FYI    !
                      ICA
                      TO  S          !
        SEE
        SEE
                      F  IENDS!
          G           F   ILY
                          D .
        . . .             T
          COM
                   D    !!
```

Given his condition it was surprising that Clem reached the solution to this conundrum as soon as he did, but then he had discovered another pretty large clue: the wetness soaking into his shoes.

The grass was too wet for dew, and it hadn't rained in weeks.

Clem looked down.

5

It was ten o'clock. It was ten by the town-hall clock. It was ten or as near as made no difference by the watches of everyone in the congregation at church (and you better believe they were glancing at them, again and again, trying not to, but they were). The hands on the alarm clock that Jeremiah Rackstraw gave Josh Knight probably showed ten, too, although there was no way of proving this. Definitely, assuredly, undeniably, incontrovertibly, it was ten o'clock in Escardy Gap, whatever time it was anywhere else in the world.

"Go forth in peace," said the Reverend King, and the congregation went forth, peacefully. They threaded out of the chapel, silently. Not a word. Only a feeling, shared by all. A fast-flowing, deep-running river of anticipation.

Ten o'clock, the posters promised. And here it was, ten o'clock.

Show us, they were all thinking. Some thought it expectantly, and some thought it as a challenge, and some thought it with not a little dread. *Show us*.

The mist was rising fast, unraveling upward to be burned off by the sun. It went up like a curtain, like an opaque veil, to reveal . . .

6

In the bright and blustery pages of the comic books treasured by Josh Knight and his peers, sandwiched in among the full-length strips and the all-too-brief one-pagers featuring such stalwarts as Varsity Vic, Professor Eureka, and Casey the Cop, alongside the advertisements (a whole trunkful of Civil War soldiers and horses and cannons for just ninety-nine cents), sat the occasional instructive item containing bizarre number-laden facts about everyday life in the vast cosmos. The titles of these pieces said it all: "Amazing Ratios," "Mysteries in Space," "Science Says You're Wrong If You Believe That . . ."

And here is one of the many astounding facts they contained.

"As the earth sweeps along in its orbit through space it 'collides' with eighty million meteors a day."

Wow!

And try this one for size.

"If the earth made a complete rotation in eighty-five minutes instead of the present twenty-four-hour rotation time, people living along the equator would become weightless!"

Jeepers!

And while you're still reeling from that one, how about this?

"An electron speeding around in its atomic orbit billions of times every second has as much space to move within its atom as a bee would have flying inside Madison Square Garden."

Jiminy Cricket!

And how about *this* one?

"The comparative weights of a dust mote in the atmosphere and the *Queen Mary* ocean liner is as the weight of the *Queen Mary* is to the weight of the earth." (This particular gem then went on to give the weights—81,335,000 tons for the *Queen Mary* and 6,570,000,000,000,000,000,000 tons for the earth. One to amaze and astound your friends with down at Fleischer's Creek on a Sunday afternoon, so long as you could remember the figures accurately.)

Whoever said comics rot the brain?

Now, facts about outer space and other planets are all very well, but even better are the facts about the human body. They kind of bring things home. (Not everyone has seen an electron or been on the *Queen Mary,* but everybody has a body, don't they?) This one's fairly typical: "The average-sized adult contains enough fat to make seven cakes of soap, enough phosphorus to make two thousand match heads, enough carbon to make eighty-five hundred pencils, enough iron to make one nail and enough water to fill a twelve-gallon barrel."

Think about it for a moment. With all that stuff jammed into a guy it's fair amazing there's room left for anything else. Like organs—lungs, liver, kidneys, heart. And blood, and veins, and arteries.

You wouldn't find it in any comic book sold in Wilbur Cohen's general store, you probably wouldn't be able to look it up in any dictionary or encyclopedia shelved in Hannah Marrs's library, and despite their medical expertise neither Doc Wheeler nor Nurse Sprocket would wish to hazard a guess about it, but if all the veins and arteries of an average-sized human body—one, say, twelve years old going on thirteen—were removed and wrapped around Century Cedar, they would circumvallate the biggest tree in Escardy Gap a grand total of 7,483 times. They would make that tree look like a wetter, redder version of the moth cocoons that Bob Tremaine and Carroll Evett rousted out of Hannah Marrs's attic spring before last.

Science says you're wrong if you don't believe *that*.

7

The scream was hoarse and ragged. It stretched up far beyond the power of mere human lungs, reaching for the stratosphere, for the planets that whirled beyond the limits of the sky. It was a pained and painful sound, filled with horror and grief and an overbearing sense of futility.

All eyes turned.

The figure over by Century Cedar was hopping around like a hillbilly at a hoedown, clutching the sides of his head and staring down at the ground. Whoever he was, he appeared to be standing in the middle of a huge dark puddle, trapped there as though stuck in tar.

Before he went to see what was the matter, Reverend King took a last glance back through the doorway of his chapel and saw the pews stretching solidly off toward the sanctuary of his pulpit, his monocular vision showing them piled on top of each other like a scale model of a ziggurat. He wished he could just make an excuse and slip back inside, close the door behind him, shut out whatever was going on in the town square, and not just in the square but throughout the town.

But he was the reverend, he reminded himself, and these people were his flock.

"All right, everyone, all right," he said to the crowd in as calming a voice as he could muster. He raised his arms in an attempt to hush the rattling bluster of gabble. "Please. *Please*. Please, everyone just wait here and I'll go see what all the commotion's about."

And with that, the reverend picked his way carefully down the wooden steps onto Main Street. Manfully—for he was feeling very much man at that moment and very little priest— he crossed the grass.

Turned out it was Clem Stimpson making all that noise. The old boozehound! A bad case of the DTs, that was all it was.

And so the reverend was relieved to think, until he set one foot in the wet darkness that covered the grass around the base of the tree like a liquid shadow, and his foot made a sucking squelch and something spattered over the gleaming liquorice leather of his shoes.

Then he saw the head.

Not since the childhood accident with a firecracker that had stolen one eye and his perception of depth had the Reverend experienced so sudden, crushing, overwhelming a sense of injustice and despair, such injustice as the death of a loved one impresses on the bereaved friends and relatives, such despair as men feel in lonely beds on nights when the wolf howls around the house and the wind runs cold fingers over the roof slates, and dawn and hope both seem a very long way away indeed.

Tom, thought Reverend King. *It's Tom Finkelbaum. My God, my God, it's Tom!*

And fell to his knees.

8

Clem Stimpson just kept right on screaming. He was aware of Reverend King coming up behind him, but he rightly figured there was nothing the man of God, or for that matter the God of man, could do here. It was better just to let rip from his lungs and blot out everything with noise.

Because not even Jesus Christ himself could have put up a hand and healed the parts of boy that were torn and strewn from here to heaven, or brought life to the emptied, flattened, deflated body, or connected the bones together again, or rekindled the spark in the eyes of the head that rested on the ground, horribly intact, passing stern judgment on Clem Stimpson's crazy, tormented jig.

9

"Doc! Doc!"
Walt Donaldson. Running fit to burst, breathless, legs pumping like flabby pistons, tearing up the old dirt track leading out of town, dust billowing out behind him.

"Doc! Doc!"
Even though he felt sure Doc Wheeler would not be able to hear him yet, Walt kept shouting nonetheless. A thumping thudding had started behind his eyes and there was an unreal clarity to his vision. Doc's place, the hospital, cool mint green, fresh snow white, loomed up ahead.

"Doc! Doc!"
A figure rose up from behind the picket fence. It was Doc.
The mad-running-clammy-sweating Walt pulled up to a halt and gaped and gasped at Doc Wheeler, who stared back patiently but curiously, a mug of coffee steaming in one hand, the funny pages of the Sunday newspaper folded in the other. Behind him Nurse Sprocket, equally patient but curious, sat with a pulp romance perched on her thighs.

"Walt," Doc said, when it became obvious that Walt would need a little more time to recover.

"Morning, Walt," said Nurse Sprocket.
Walt propped himself against the fence and hauled in air, his eyeballs bigger and whiter than peeled hardboiled eggs.

Doc set his coffee down on the grass, opened the small gate, and stepped out into the roadway, giving Nurse Sprocket a covert nod. "I think Walt here could do with a cup of your special Sunday morning medicinal coffee, nurse."

"Is that a professional opinion or just a layman's observation?" Nurse Sprocket muttered, getting to her feet.

"Both," replied Doc, without cracking a smile.

Walt Donaldson shook his head. "No time," he managed to blurt out. "Sara."

"Sara?" said Nurse Sprocket.

"I'll get my bag," said Doc, turning.

10

The Reverend King's congregation was at a loss. Surely the reverend had had enough of praying for one morning? And yet there he was, genuflecting on the grass as though the voice of God had just issued forth from the creviced bark of the great tree. Whispered comments and abortive conversations and puzzled asides drifted in and out and around. What was going on? What was wrong with Century Cedar? Why did it look so weird? What in tarnation *was* that stuff? Was that Clem Stimpson screaming? Why was Clem screaming? Why wouldn't Clem *stop* screaming? And though all the answers seemed to lie less than a hundred yards away, no one was in any hurry to go over and find out for themselves.

No one, that is, except two.

Josh Knight was halfway across the grass before anyone even thought to stop him, a kid, just a kid, from attending to what seemed to be adult business. The people of Escardy Gap were very particular about what constituted child's play and what games were the province of grown-ups. They drew a very firm line between the two, one that Josh by his very nature trespassed across regularly, as he was doing now.

Then Mayor, tendering "Just a moment here" and "May I get by here?" and "Excuse me, please" left, right, and center, set out after Josh. As he strode along, he loosened his tie.

Josh glanced around, saw Mayor, and halted. "Are you going to try to stop me, Mayor?"

"Heck, no," said Mayor, "but only if you're sure you don't want to wait on the steps."

Josh did have to think before replying, "I guess not."

"Good," said Mayor. "Because I think I'm going to need some moral support."

Josh sensed a gentleness in Mayor, a stern and authoritative gentleness not always to be found in Escardy Gap's thespian official. *Spencer Tracy,* he thought. *Mayor's gone into Spencer Tracy.*

They set off together over the grass toward the kneeling reverend and the screaming Clem Stimpson. Coming beneath the great umbrella of the tree, what they were walking on stopped looking like grass. It was reddish black and glistened. It no longer felt like grass, either. Lumps of gristle and fragments of bone crunched underfoot.

Mayor said nothing. Josh said nothing.

The Reverend King was murmuring a prayer under his breath, eyes fastened shut, rocking to and fro with his hands across his belly as if he were in pain from a stomach cramp. Clem Stimpson was still dancing and screaming, screaming and dancing. Tom Finkelbaum's head looked on at the proceedings with casual distaste, disgust almost.

Mayor and Josh still said nothing. There was nothing to say.

A shout came from over back at the chapel. The word was all but unintelligible. It sounded like *"Reds!"* The person who had shouted broke away from the crowd. It was Bob Tremaine. Bob ran, not toward Century Cedar, but in the opposite direction, past the Merrie Malted, out of the town square. Alice and Sandy were calling after him to come back, come back, please come back, wife and daughter, alto and soprano in unison. Hubbub from the crowd floated across the square like birdsong over a battlefield after the fighting has ended.

But the show had only just begun.

Eight

1

There were two things uppermost in Walt Donaldson's mind as he and Doc Wheeler and Nurse Sprocket raced toward Sara Sienkiewicz's house. One was that he felt sharp, painfully sharp, his brain zinging like lemon peel, all trace of last night's excessive intake of beer no more than a dull throbbing memory. The other was that he felt stupid, painfully stupid, all dressed up like this, as if he were some city boy going out for a night at the opera, not a fat stationmaster rushing to the aid of a sick woman. Whereas before Walt had thought he had looked rather fine in his combination of English tweed, Italian leather, and plain old Yankee denim, now he felt like a dummy in a toupee, one of those bizarre faceless living-dead dandies in wide lapels, padded shoulders, and two-tone wing tips that Wilbur Cohen sometimes put on parade in the window of his general store. Okay, so Walt's attire was considerably more sedate than that sported by Wilbur's sartorial mannequins, and it *was* Sunday morning, when almost everyone was to be seen out and about in their very best, but still he felt overdressed and overobvious. He felt like a kid caught red-handed passing notes in class. The doc didn't say anything about it. Nurse Sprocket didn't say anything about it. In fact, neither of them said *any*thing about *any*thing during the run over from Doc's place. But Walt had a pretty shrewd idea they were laughing at him on the inside.

Onward they ran, Doc (pounding) and Nurse Sprocket (sprinting lightly) and Escardy Gap's stationmaster (merely marking time), all of them wishing there was some more convenient way of getting where they wanted to go. Regrettably, Doc's beat-up old Ford had died on him a couple of days back, and Earl Evett had been promising to come over and take a look under the hood but hadn't quite gotten 'round to it yet, despite Doc's repeated phone calls and entreaties. The first thing Doc had said to Walt and Nurse Sprocket as he had come hurrying out of the hospital was, "I hope neither of you's had a big breakfast, 'cause thanks to that danged Earl Evett we don't have any other means of transportation but our legs!"

At Doc's insistence, the three of them paused for a rest outside Jack and Cora-May Chisholm's place on Furnival Street, with its ever-present wooden board creaking in the gentle breeze, announcing to the world:

ROOMS AND FOOD
YOU NEED 'EM?
WE GOT 'EM!

Inside the house, on the radio, a preacher was leading a choir into the opening bars of "Nearer My God to Thee."

As Doc and Walt caught their wind and Nurse Sprocket adjusted a lock of hair that had fallen out of place, a loud murmur of voices echoed across the rooftops, coming from the town square. They didn't notice the sound, preoccupied as they were with the matter at hand, these frantic Samaritans bound on their mission of mercy. They just straightened up and set off again along the dusty street, and so missed out on the opportunity to witness at first hand the sight of young Tom Finkelbaum's body wound around the oldest tree in Escardy Gap like cotton candy around a stick.

As he ran Doc kept an inner ear peeled to the racket his heart trundled out in his chest, a thick clopping noise bereft of any discernible rhythm, like the hooves of a drunken horse in a three-legged race. His heart had seen better days and he knew it. Nurse Sprocket knew it, too, but she would never have let on. Instead, she would sometimes let slip vaguely medical generalizations about people in their "golden years" taking life "a little easier," but nothing more specific than that. In fact, she worried about him all the time. His health was her constant concern, and she watched him tote that bulky body around with something like a maternal eye, the same eye with which she watched him construct multistoried architectural fantasies out of playing cards on the kitchen table, his fat pink tongue jammed out of the side of his mouth like a two-day-old stogie. Pride and anger are the twin poles of motherhood, with a longitude of justified concern between, and as Nurse Sprocket was beyond the possibility of becoming a real mother, she was content to be mother as well as lover to this whiskery, rotund, drink-happy baby of a man. She would never have dared try to slow Doc down. That would have been more than her life was worth. She understood, for instance, that right now they had to get to Sara's as quickly as they could. She had realized right away that things were dangerously wrong with Sara from Walt's breathless and far-from-succinct account of the situation. Doc's ticker would simply have to grin and bear it. She prayed that it could.

She sneaked a sidelong glance at him. His face had gone a blotchy red, and his jaw was set in grim, jowly determination. His trusty battered medical bag swung at his side. She felt pride for him right now, but anger, too. The old fool would leave her one of these days. It might be tomorrow, might be next week, maybe next year, almost certainly in the year or two that followed. Or at any rate, he would try. Just let him try. If this old fool went and died on her, why . . . she'd *murder* him!

Finally they made it, in a bluster of dust, to the gate that gave on to the path that led up to Sara Sienkiewicz's front porch, trammeled between two neat lines of white picket fence and bordered with peonies.

Nurse Sprocket and Doc Wheeler waited for Walt Donaldson to open the gate. It seemed only right that Walt should perform this function. Walt, however, could not unglue his hand from the gatepost. He regarded the house with an almost holy terror. His heels planted themselves in the dust and refused to budge.

With an impatient cry of "Out of the danged way, Walt!" Doc thundered past him and up the path to the door, Nurse Sprocket following close behind. Walt hung back a moment more, and then, with a tread as heavy as the Frankenstein monster's, he moved forward. Up the path. Up the steps. Across the porch where the discarded posy of broken-stemmed flowers he had brought for Sara lay, growing limp and dry in the sunlight. Through the screen door.

A quarter of an hour ago, Walt thought, *I was standing here with my heart in my mouth. Now it feels like it's somewhere down in my shoes.*

Within, Doc and Nurse Sprocket had hunkered down and were turning Sara gently over, the doc cradling Sara's head in his hand.

"She's breathing," Walt heard Doc say, and Walt found *himself* at liberty to breathe again.

"Shallow, though," Nurse Sprocket observed.

"I can see that for myself, Nurse."

"I was just confirming the fact, Doctor."

Doc Wheeler grated his teeth. He felt Sara's wrist and then her neck at the angle of her jaw. "Pulse slow. Very weak. Carotid's hardly there at all."

Walt forced himself to look at his beloved and instantly regretted it. Her skin was Halloween white and shiny with sweat. Her lips held the faintest trace of turquoise, the color of the prized lupines that, along with several other species of flower, now lay trampled in the bed along the side of Sara's house. And of course there was the vomit, a thick tacky puddle of the stuff on the floor with a crusty hole where her mouth had been resting.

Nurse Sprocket took each of Sara's hands in hers, left then right, and then Sara's feet, the same way. "Cold."

"Give me a bulletin when you've got some *real* news," said Doc. He rubbed his index finger over Sara's lips and then inserted it in between. As they parted, the lips made a dry rasping sound like paper being torn. He shook his head and reached a hand up to Sara's eyes, lifting the lids briefly. Walt couldn't help looking, couldn't stop his mouth from dropping open. Her eyes were wrong. They were big, black, empty, not Sara's eyes at all.

Doc stood up, stretched, and moaned, flashing his hands to the small of his back.

"Doc," said Walt, barely a whisper.

Doc twitched his head on his neck, working out a small crick.

"Doc," said Walt, his voice growing slightly stronger, "tell me, is she going to be all right?"

The doc shrugged and cast a short but meaningful glance at Nurse Sprocket. "Can't rightly say, Walt. Not so soon."

Nurse Sprocket squatted down on her haunches like a weightlifter and raised Sara Sienkiewicz up bodily and laid her down on the couch. "I'll get some warm water and a cloth," she said, and bustled out of the room in the direction of the kitchen.

"Is she going to . . . is she going to die, Doc?" It seemed to Walt right then that the universe must hold him in appalling contempt, to want to steal away the woman of his dreams just when he was about to make those dreams a reality. With this in mind, he steeled himself for the worst, crossed his fingers, and *hoped*.

Doc Wheeler faced Walt full on. "You can see for yourself she's not well, Walt, old pal, and I'm not about to lie to you and tell you otherwise. She's not well at all. Now tell me straight. You found her here like this?"

Walt nodded. "Just like this."

"And there wasn't anything near her? Like a bottle or a pillbox or anything?"

Walt shook his head. "No, nothing at all." Confronted with these questions and Doc's unflinching stare, Walt was beginning to feel guilty, as though it were he that had caused this terrible thing to happen; as though, if he had only stayed at home and not come out here to declare his love for Sara, Escardy Gap's noted authoress might now be sitting at her desk deep into another of her stories.

Had Walt been a little quicker in the intellect department—this was, after all, someone who listened to and took advice from *Clem Stimpson* of all people—he might have deduced a connection between the arrival of the Company and what had happened to Sara. Had he been Big Ben Burden, say, or Josh Knight, who was generally acknowledged to be smarter than most adults, Walt might have spotted a common denominator. Had he been a real detective or private eye, and not just an avid devourer of crime fiction, he might have smelled a rat and played a hunch. But he didn't. Doc, however, was not so concerned about the patient and did therefore notice certain similarities between Sara's condition and that of Ike Swivven.

"So what's wrong with her?" Walt asked.

Doc removed his glasses and pulled a handkerchief out of his pants pocket, which he used first to wipe the lenses and then his own forehead.

"Well, a heart attack seems out of the question."

Relief sighed into Walt, inflating him like a balloon.

"However, it could be a brain hemorrhage."

The air hissed out of Walt again.

Nurse Sprocket returned with a large ball of cotton wool and a saucepan full of lukewarm water from the faucet, to which she had added disinfectant from Sara's medicine cabinet. She set about swabbing the blood and vomit from Sara's face.

"Then again, could be an aneurism."

"Wh-what's ananyourism?" It crossed Walt's mind that ananyourism might be contagious and that he should have nothing further to do with Sara Sienkiewicz, but then he almost immediately cursed himself for entertaining such a notion. A *real* lover would be only too glad to die of the same disease that had taken his paramour.

"An . . . an-eur-ism," said Nurse Sprocket without looking up from her task. "It's like a little weak spot on the inner tube of a bicycle tire. It balloons out and then either leaks or bursts, bleeding into the brain and making everything stop."

"Thank you, Nurse," said Doc Wheeler.

"My pleasure, Doctor."

"Is that what she's got, then? Can you tell that just by looking at her?"

"We're not going to be able to tell anything, Walt," said Doc in a kindly but tired voice, "until we get Sara back to the examination room and run some tests."

"Oh," said Walt. "Tests?"

"Nothing to fret yourself about, Walt." One of the best methods Doc knew to calm a friend or relative of the patient on the verge of panic was to treat them like a fellow doctor, pretend they had some say in the making of medical decisions. Even if they didn't understand a word he said, at least they felt they were involved in the process, not helpless bystanders. "First, we gotta examine Sara's blood sugar, see if she's diabetic and we didn't know about it. It's a slim chance, but it's a chance. Diabetes can strike at any stage in life. Then we'll look for signs of motor aphasia, see if she's had a stroke. We'll put her on a saline drip, make sure she don't come to any more trouble while we sort this out. Examine her heart and respiratory system, urea and electrolytes, biochemical screen, check for common poisons—"

"Poisons!" Walt's panic began to brew. "You think someone *poisoned* Sara?"

Doc looked down, shifted his feet.

"There's a possibility that Sara poisoned herself, Walt," said Nurse Sprocket.

Walt shook his head, looking from doctor to nurse and back again. "Nah. Sara'd never do something like that to herself." Another shake. "Never."

"No one's saying she did," said Doc. "There's a possibility, is all. Tell me, Walt, you knew her pretty well." Walt almost blushed. "Was she unhappy about anything? Anything at all?"

"Don't think so. Don't imagine Sara would be unhappy about *anything*. What's she got to be unhappy about?"

"Just wondering, thinking out loud," said Doc.

Chewing his bottom lip to keep himself from crying, Walt blinked hard, twice, to refocus his vision. "She *is* going to be all right, isn't she, Doc?"

"How long is a piece of string?" replied Doc. Anyone could see it wasn't the answer Walt wanted to hear. "Now, listen, Walt, you sit and rest awhile and gather your strength, because we're going to need it shortly to help carry this little lady to the surgery."

"I'm your man," Walt told Doc Wheeler, and Doc shot a smile at him.

Walt moved off, leaving the medical twosome to attend to Sara. "First Ike, now Sara," Walt overheard Doc say. "I don't think we're looking at coincidence here."

At the desk, Walt began rummaging idly around, lifting papers and poking among the pens and ink bottles and pencils and notebooks that sat in a large, faded blue tin, all carefully sharpened and ready for use. The tin bore the legend Kentucky Club for Pipe Lovers above a picture of a man on a horse leaping a two-bar gate. Walt remembered the old slogan:

For Uncle Jim and brother Will,
For Grandpa, Dad and postman Hill,
For every man that you rate high—
Kentucky Club's the gift to buy.

He wondered, with a faint twinge of envy, who of Sara's acquaintance used smoking tobacco. He realized, with a faint twinge of regret, how little he knew about her. He picked up the notebook that lay on the desk. He ran a finger over the cover, the cover that Sara's hands had held and caressed.

"What you got there, Walt?" said Doc.

"Story of Sara's, I guess."

"Ain't polite to poke around a lady's belongings, you know."

"Why not, Doctor?" said Nurse Sprocket, with as much of a leer as circumstances permitted. *"You* do it all the time."

"That ain't what I meant, Nurse. I was talking about private property."

"So was I."

"I'm only looking," said Walt. "No harm in looking," he added, putting the notebook down again as if he had never intended to touch it in the first place.

"All right," said Nurse Sprocket, bunching up the stained clump of cotton wool and plopping it into the bucket. "It's time we moved our patient."

"Yep," said Doc. "Walt, will you come and help me look for something to carry her on? There'll be a board or something we can use out back."

"Sure thing, Doc."

Walt glanced over at the supine Sara Sienkiewicz, now restored to something of her former beauty with the cleansing of her face. He couldn't believe she had inflicted this on herself. He didn't dare believe it. Had she gone crazy? Was the whole world going crazy?

2

"Mr. Rackstraw."

"Ah, Grampa." Jeremiah Rackstraw looked up from the Sunday newspaper. "How is your poor head?"

"Better, thank you."

"I always say headaches are a sign of intellect. I suffer from them myself."

"Well—" said Grampa.

"Is it a constant throbbing, or more of a dull nagging?"

"Well, I wouldn't say—"

"A great spike being hammered into your forehead, or just a clench-clench-clench at the back of your jawbone?"

"I'm not sure—"

"An iron band tightening around each of your eyeballs, or a—"

"*Mr. Rackstraw!* Would you please, just for one time in your life, be quiet?"

Startled by the sudden vehemence in Grampa's voice, Rackstraw put down the newspaper and gave every indication of attentiveness. Grampa seemed to have forgotten what it was he had been going to say, so Rackstraw prompted him. "What would you like to know, Grampa?"

"I'd prefer if you didn't call me by that name," said Grampa. "Only family and people I like get to call me that, and much as I'd like to like you, Mr. Rackstraw, because I'm the kind of guy who likes to like people, I'm afraid I just can't."

"I'm very sorry to hear that. I'm not sure what I've done to offend. Please tell me. Perhaps I can make amends."

"Frankly, Mr. Rackstraw, I don't know *why* I don't like you, and that bothers me. If there was some reason, like maybe you'd insulted me or Josh or anyone else I *do* like, that'd be fine. As it is, it's something I can't put my finger on, something about you that just rubs me the wrong way. Maybe it's just because you talk too damn much and too damn fancy. Maybe it's those weird folk Josh says you brought along with you. I don't know."

Rackstraw rose from the most comfortable chair in the Knight household, Grampa's very own favorite armchair, to bring him eye level with Grampa. (Jeremiah Rackstraw did not like to be looked down on.) The two men held one another's gaze for a breathless, blinkless minute. They *comprehended* one another. Somehow the room didn't seem big enough for both of them. The whole town didn't seem big enough.

"I can't imagine what I've done to deserve such hostility," said Rackstraw. "Is there something intrinsically wrong about accepting hospitality from hospitable people? Is there a law against giving gifts?"

"Some gifts, there ought to be. Since he got that clock from you, I ain't never seen Josh so spooked. Boy looks like he didn't sleep a wink last night."

"I hardly see how that can be my fault. A touch of indigestion, perhaps? He is a sensitive young man."

"Oh, you think you're so sly, Mr. Rackstraw, so gosh-darned snake slippery. You think no one's seen through you, you and your friends, the whole . . . *goddamn* lot of you."

"What is there to see that we haven't already shown you, Mr. Knight? We're traveling performers. We travel, we perform. What could be simpler?"

"Yeah, but what exactly is it that you perform? That's what I want to know."

Rackstraw was suddenly elated, like a teacher who discovers a hitherto hidden glimmer of intelligence in one of the dullest pupils lurking at the back of the class. "What indeed, Mr. Knight!" he exclaimed. "An excellent question! I've been wondering how long it would be before someone got around to asking that. I would say the answer was Wonders, Mysteries, and Marvels, but that's just carny pitch and I don't think that'll satisfy you, not now, not anymore. So instead I'll tell you the truth, the truth unhindered by patter or illusion or circumlocution."

"I'd like to hear *that* from *you*," muttered Grampa Knight.

"My colleagues and I are here to *perform* a duty," said Rackstraw.

"And what duty is that?"

"Do you really want to know?"

"I really want to know," said Grampa Knight, resting his fists on his hips.

In the last instants of his life Grampa glimpsed Rackstraw's right hand flashing out, forefinger extended, and felt the fingertip touch his forehead and move across it from right to left in a jagged up-and-down and sideways motion, tickling as it went, and he had time to wonder what the heck the fellow was up to, and he even had time to make a grab—ineffectual—for Rackstraw's arm. But that was all.

Rackstraw watched as the old man crumpled in a heap at his feet. He sucked in a breath and tutted. "You had to ask, didn't you, *Grampa?*" he said. "Well, there. You got your answer, you wrinkled old fart."

Rackstraw had written a word on Grampa's forehead in finger-thick capitals that stood proud of the skin like bruises.

The word on Grampa's forehead was "DEAD."

And so was Grampa.

Nine

1

Standing in front of Mayor, in the narrow penumbra of his shadow, was suddenly a very comforting and reassuring place to be, and Josh was glad he was there as he stared at the gray-pink and glistening ribbons tethered around the sagging, tired-looking branches of Century Cedar, the remains of the boy who used to sit three desks in front of him in class (with Andy Gallagher and Stan Kirby in between). He forced himself to believe it was true. It wasn't easy. Things like this didn't happen even in the outer-space movies shown at the Essoldo, at least not on-screen. Some of the stories in comic books touched occasionally on the blacker side of retribution and punishment. He thought of the one that ended with a baseball game, when parts of an over-ambitious and ruthless player were taken and used for bases by his disgruntled teammates: his heart for the plate, his head for the ball. . . .

Josh found his gaze drawn remorselessly to the spherical shape sitting in the lee of the old tree and, for one heart-stoppingly horrible moment, the eyes of the living met the eyes of the dead and they regarded each other with grave solemnity. (At about this moment, Grampa Knight and Jeremiah Rackstraw were regarding one another in pretty much the same manner, with pretty much the same eyes.)

Tom, Josh's mind cried out, *who did this to you?*

The awful part was, the head reminded him of one of those masks from the back pages of *Famous Monsters* magazine, which he liked to pore over in the eerie half-light of late-night bedroom solitude, to the accompaniment of the basso profundo snore that emanated from Grampa's bedroom, reverberating along the lamplit landing. In these pages lay all manner of available wonders, from mad-doctor hypodermic syringes, 3-D comic books (which Josh knew weren't really three-dimensional because he had seen *Adventures into the Unknown* and it was a cheat but fun anyways), twelve-inch-high skeletons that glowed in the dark, and masks, masks, and more masks: teenage werewolves, cyclopes (with cunning, near-invisible slits for the benefit of two-eyed wearers), vampires, ghouls, gorillas. . . . For almost two years now Josh had coveted the scratchily drawn picture of the Frankenstein-monster full-head latex rubber mask advertised in the back pages of his magazines. For just three ninety-eight—plus the inevitable twenty-five cents for postage and packing—he could have had that mask, if Grampa hadn't put his foot down, saying (in that pleasant but firm tone adults use when there ain't going to be *no* argument) that he wasn't having monster heads in his house and that was final. Josh didn't know exactly how realistic those masks were but he figured they must be pretty realistic—and right now he figured they probably looked like Tom Finkelbaum's head, except maybe they were a little neater around the neck and maybe didn't have all those tiny shreds and raggedy rips in the skin, hanging down like a curtain frill.

"Best not to look, lad," said a gentle voice.

For a second Josh thought it was Errol Flynn and that he had somehow fallen into *The Adventures of Robin Hood.* But it wasn't and he hadn't. It was just Mayor. Good old Mayor. Josh felt the strength of Mayor's hand through his shirt, gripping his shoulder.

"Mayor," he said, "how could anyone *do* that?"

Before Mayor could answer—assuming he *had* an answer —the Reverend King staggered to his feet, his face scrunched up as though he had just eaten a lemon, a chili pepper, and a wasp all in one go. His eyes, wet with tears and craving forgiveness, were like red craters. His lips were speckled with saliva. He came toward Josh and Mayor, staggering slightly, shoulders hunched against an unseen storm, shaking his head, blubbering, sobbing. A man and yet (Josh thought uncharitably) not a man, less than a man. Something had been stolen from him, reducing him in stature, hollowing him out.

Mayor reached out to him as if to a child. "Okay, now, John," he said to the reverend. "We must try to keep calm, think this thing through."

"Oh, Mayor, how could *He* do this?" The emphasis on the "He" left no one in any doubt whom the reverend was referring to. "How could He allow this to happen here? In Escardy Gap? In His green acre?"

Mayor threw his arm around the reverend's shoulders like a magic blanket of reassurance. Feeling like an intruder, Josh turned away from them, just in time to see Mr. Burden and Mr. Connors lay a black shroud gently over Tom Finkelbaum's head. (It wasn't actually a shroud, it was someone's Sunday jacket, but it served the same purpose as a shroud and it would never be worn again as an item of clothing.) Over by the church steps people were moving, as though the invisible shield that had kept them away from the grass had suddenly come down. They drifted in ones and twos and threes, whispering together, shaking heads and pointing, disbelieving.

2

Big Ben Burden took command. Moose Rollins was ordered to fetch a ladder to lean against the sturdy lower branches of Century Cedar. Jed the barber got hold of a saw and climbed the ladder, the teeth of the saw blade glinting in the sunlight in sharp dazzle bursts. Earl and Carroll Evett attached a hose to the fire hydrant outside of the Merrie Malted.

Big Ben, looking over at Old Joe Dolan's ice cream emporium, recalled his son, Jim, making some remark about Old Joe closing up early last night. Then it hadn't seemed significant. Now it seemed a grim piece of news. He went over and hammered on the door for a full two minutes, but there was no response from within. "Joe," he called. "Hey, Joe!" No reply.

3

The shades were drawn and in the day-darkened gloom inside the Merrie Malted Soda Shoppe someone stirred, turning toward the sound of knocking and gazing blankly. When the noise eventually ceased, he turned back and moved a slow fat hand to raise a spoon to his lips. He slurped melted ice cream into his mouth, dribbling a thick foamy spume of it down his chin. He moaned. He belched. He heaved. He was violently sick. The vomit splashed across the counter, sweeping a sugar shaker off its feet, washing a napkin dispenser along like a silvery surfer catching a wave. This wasn't the only vomit currently adorning the furniture, fixtures, and fittings of the Merrie Malted. There were several puddles of it around the feet of the stool on which Old Joe Dolan sat. They were blueberry blue and gooseberry green and raspberry red, a bright rainbow of food colorings, and here and there was a half-chewed glacé cherry, or a smattering of candy sprinkles, or more hot fudge sauce than the average person could eat and regurgitate in a month. Some of the puddles were older and dryer than others, but the flies weren't picky. They darted from one to the next, gorging themselves and filling the air with their contented drone.

Old Joe reached across the counter and prized another carton of ice cream from the glass-fronted freezing cabinet. The lid was off and his spoon digging in before he had even had time to register the flavor (Boysenberry Ripple). He set his elbow in the puke on the counter and began to eat, his arm working like a machine, piling in, piling in the ice cream. His skull and jawbone ached from the coldness. His eyes rolled glassily.

"A consuming passion, Joe?" remarked the big-headed man half-hidden in the shadows.

Old Joe's reply bubbled thickly and incoherently through pink-lathered lips.

"You know, Joe, like that, you remind me of Moose Rollins, Jr., the time he filled up his cheeks with ice cream and blew it all over your shop. You won't remind *you* of that occasion, of course. Far as you're concerned, Moose Rollins, Jr. hasn't been born yet, and Moose Rollins, *Sr.* is just a pudgy little pal in shorts." Felcher held up a small green bottle the size of a liquor miniature, letting it twinkle in the dull light. The bottle was full to the base of the neck with a cloudy liquid looking like one of those stomach-turning medicines for colic or constipation. "There's still a little room in here, Joe," he leered. "Where are we with you now? Early youth, I'd say, barely out of diapers. No wonder you got so fat, Joe. You weren't just a milk baby, you were a goddamn *ice-cream* baby. And no wonder women like Hannah Marrs won't go near you. Face it, you are and you have always been a pig. Hannah must take one look at you and think, *Uh-oh, grade-A porker here!* Am I right, Joe? Am I?"

Old Joe tilted the carton and scraped at the bottom, spooning the last of the pint into his mouth. There was a momentous borborygmic rumble, a horrendous gagging choke, and then an arc of pink vomit sprayed out across the room, slapping against seat backs, splashing across tabletops, and partially refilling the empty carton in front of him. Old Joe looked down into that carton and, without hesitation, without qualm, set to shoveling warm, barely digested Boysenberry Ripple back down his throat. Much to the delight of his companion.

"God, your life was so disgustingly happy and simple, Old Joe," said Felcher. "I think it's going to be too sickly for *my* palate. I think you're going to stick to my teeth. Now, take that Ike Swivven fella. Now *there's* a life with some kick to it. A hint of melancholy, a soupçon of suffering, and just enough sourness to make the tastebuds tingle. He had real vintage, that fella. Real class. Real juice. The longer you leave 'em, the better they are, I always say. You, Joe, you dedicated your life to sweetness. You made yourself and hundreds of children happy the only way you knew how. Ice cream was your only pleasure in life, wasn't it? The making, the fixing, the mixing, the eating—that was your substitute for sex, wasn't it, Joe? Must have been. Because you sure as hell never got much of the real thing, did you?"

Groaning, Joe reached for a fresh carton: Watermelon Fizz.

"It's funny how memories and fantasies can get confused," said the big man, peering at the contents of the bottle intently. "In here, you're convinced you smothered Hannah Marrs in whipped cream and chocolate chips and licked it all off. That would have been one hell of a knickerbocker glory! But you never did, Joe, you never did. It was all in your sweaty-old-man's dirty-little-boy mind. If you had lived anywhere else but here, you could have become a baby raper, Joe. Stuck it up schoolboys till they screamed and left little girls out in the woods bleeding to death from between their legs. And you'd have gone on doing that till they caught you and stuck you away in prison and let the other cons cut tattoos in your skin with their razor blades and buttfuck you till your asshole hung down to your ankles. But not here, Joe. Here in Escardy Gap, you're some kind of folk hero. To every damn kid here you're the father who never says no. You're goddamn *God*. They come here to worship you, Joe. You work Miracles. You dance Fandangos. You send Rockets shooting up into the sky."

Old Joe gave another superlative display of projectile vomiting. When he was finished and done, the color blossomed in his cheeks and forehead, turning them redder than any watermelon flesh, and his chest heaved as though trying to restrain a heart that had swelled to twice its natural size and was hurling itself against the bars of his rib cage. He slumped face first over the counter, panting, blowing bubbles in the puke, snot oozing from his nostrils.

"Hey, *God*," said Felcher, "you've got your wish, haven't you? All you've ever wanted since you were a kid is to eat ice cream until you explode. All I've done is take away the years of self-control from you, the denial, the adult restraint, your conscience. So, come on, Joe. One for Mommy. One for Daddy . . ."

Old Joe's hand crawled through the puke and wrestled a tub of Strawberries-and-Cream from the freezer case. He began to eat again, the spoon trembling and slopping globs of ice cream down his apron front and into his lap.

There were twenty-eight empty cartons lying on the floor and counter. There were nine full ones in the freezing cabinet and another seventy-six in the freezer chest in back of the shop. Add to this the pots of hot fudge sauce waiting to be melted, and all the wafers and the whipped cream and the chocolate chips and the glacé cherries, and Old Joe Dolan was going to be pretty busy for the next few hours.

4

Through the tiny grimy window in the attic of the house the sun shone, probing as only the true shine of day can probe, drifting and fingering and searching through a mausoleum of memories preserved in cobweb by industrious spider keepers, brushing the boards so as not to disturb the stifled dusty hush; and sifting and shuffling also through the windows of the floor below, settling on carpets, cloth, and clothes in the unwalked and dust-layered rooms and corridors of the upper story where the literate Miss Hannah Marrs, custodian of a thousand and one storytelling nights, had not ventured in more than a decade, confining herself instead to the lower reaches of a house far too large for one person, dwelling contented and sublimely blissful in two second-floor rooms—bedroom and bathroom—and two more rooms on street level, one of which was the reading room and the other the kitchen. (Even a librarian must eat.)

In Hannah Marrs's bedroom the sunlight spread, picking its way across and between the piles of stacked books and magazines to caress the carefully made twin beds with their pristine pink sheets and plumped-up pillows. Books were everywhere in this room, as they were in all four rooms of this annex to the fusty aisles and shelves of knowledge, mystery, and imagination, of the library itself. Books thronged ledges and windowsills, their bindings slick with mildew, their pages bloated with dampness. Books were propped against tables and chairs and cupboards. Books lay forgotten beneath plants and clocks, and books assisted the equilibrium of unstable furniture by nosing obediently between floor and elegantly carved and varnished leg.

Specks of dust traveled along the light beams in a flurry of dance, never settling, never calming. No one had slept in either of the meticulously laid-out and turned-back beds over the previous night. No one had lain in this room, resting to wake refreshed. But the bedroom *had* received a visitor. The drawers in the large wooden chest were open, carelessly yawning their contents in a jumble of cream hose and pastel silks and elastic, a frozen waterfall that reached the floor and collected there in a kaleidoscopic pool of softness and color. Over on the other side of the room, the towering wardrobe stood with its cantilevered doors agape, almost in horror, its fastidiously folded and painstakingly placed garmentry now adrift and courting crease and fold in a manner to which each lovingly pressed and folded item was entirely unused.

On the floor just inside the door, as further evidence—had any been needed—of nocturnal investigation and illicit examination, lay a curious bundle of coverings. (Few in the immediate vicinity would have referred to this raiment as "clothes," yet that is what they had once been, though they had been used primarily to conceal rather than in any way to adorn.) Here were thick stockings and plaid woollen skirt; here were wedge-heeled shoes sporting overlarge piratical buckles and a linen shirt; here, too, was a green-flecked buttoned sweater with deep, baggy pockets that crinkled and hid, curling coarse material over and over; here was a large-cupped brassiere, each conical container brimming with rags; and here were some voluminous panties, distended and strained around the crotch as though once home to a family of warring rodents or a collection of rotting and rancid sweet potatoes dripping exotic syrups into the fine stitching.

And these were not the only stains to mar the sanctity of this room.

Two wide splashes had laid ruinous claim to Hannah Marrs's soft Axminster carpet, disturbing the autumnal greens and beiges like a pair of creamy white Rorschach blots. Three more had caught the chest of drawers, thick globs that had eaten into the age-polished grain with a casual indifference. Yet more had speckled the wardrobe door, like toothpaste foam sprayed there by an angry infant trying to prevent a parent cleaning its teeth. It was the stains that caused the smell that filled the air here, a rooty mix of camphor, stagnant ponds, and the damp black residue that lies between the toes of the infrequently washed.

Outside the room, in the hallway on the bedroom floor, more of these marks were visible, though less abundant. Down the stairs, too, and into the kitchen. Here, more books filled the shelves, although few were of the recipe variety. A haphazard array of coverless, dog-eared tomes tottered drunkenly beside the wood-burning stove into which, in moments of logless desperation, the word-besotted resident was wont to thrust a volume or two to bring a brief show of crackling cheer and some light relief to cold wintry evenings. (What are logs anyway but prototype books? And what are books but former logs?)

And through the kitchen, into the heart, the kernel, the very epicenter of this literary labyrinth: the reading room. Here, the casual visitor—though, in truth, few ever called unannounced on Hannah Marrs, while fewer still were invited—would, of necessity, have to negotiate piles and piles of books simply to find a suitable surface on which to sit; a surface which, all too often, would turn out to be a secondary or even tertiary construction of board and leaf, jacket and marker, foreword and epilogue.

Once satisfactorily seated, such a visitor might pause to take in the magnitude of the room, to register the racks of books that seemed to support the very ceiling itself, and to show due jaw-breaking astonishment when apprised of the fact that Hannah Marrs had read every word, perused every punctuation mark, considered every consonant and verified every verb on every page of every book in her household.

On that particular Sunday morning of sunshine and distant birdsong, a visitor *did* sit there in Hannah Marrs's reading room, hands clasped in her lap, eyes twinkling behind the smoked glass of her spectacles, ankles demurely crossed in mute anticipation. Almost dutifully she listened, though her general demeanor and her quietly frenetic rocking, the feigned attentiveness achieved by the rhythmic staccato motion of her upper body pivoting on her hipbones, betrayed an ulterior interest.

Opposite her, in a large chair on the other side of the room, sat Hannah Marrs, the town librarian, a woman whose beauty was largely inner but who nevertheless exuded a certain self-possessed charm—enough to rouse latent loin passion in the greatly girthed Old Joe Dolan and to stir a blind-eyed maggot of lust from beneath that huge ice-cream scoop of a belly. She was reading.

"'I now approach an event in my life, so indelible, so awful, so bound by an infinite variety of ties to all that has preceded it, in these pages,' " said Hannah, eyes red rimmed and sore, throat rasping and hoarse, " 'that, from the very beginning of my narrative, I have seen it growing larger and larger as I advanced, like a great tower in a plain, and throwing its fore-cast shadow even on the incidents—' " A cough erupted, a strangled dog bark that peppered the hallowed pages of *David Copperfield* like a spray of sea spume. "Oh, excuse *me,* please forgive me, Agnes, my throat is parched. I've been reading all night." She looked across at the blind woman, whose face hardened visibly, eyebrows knitting in freckled folds of forehead. "Could I please have just a *little* rest?"

Agnes shook her head slightly and let out a sigh before getting to her feet. Hannah still felt strangely uncomfortable seeing her own clothes hanging so loosely, so ill-fittingly, around the blind woman's figure. Agnes Destiny had explained that her own clothes had felt tired and soiled and that, bereft of suitable alternatives, she had ventured into the librarian's inner sanctum to find fresh ones. Hannah had not had the heart to say, when asked for an opinion on the presentability of the garments, that they looked ridiculous. No, worse than simply ridiculous: they looked obscene. (Hannah could not have explained why that word had so readily sprung to her mind, save that it was the *correct* word.) Instead, she had muttered something about "Oh, those old things!"—though they were, in fact, among her best and most treasured items of apparel. She had added, "I'm sure I can find you something a bit more comfortable," and made to go up to her room. But the blind woman would not hear of it, would not even hear of Hannah leaving the room. Hannah had been obliged to begin reading, and it was only when, some hours after she had arrived home, Hannah had begged Miss Destiny for her leave to use the bathroom, that the woman reluctantly granted a recess, accompanying Hannah to the bathroom door, where she held a patient vigil until Hannah emerged and then escorted her back downstairs again. "I've been so lonely all by myself," Agnes had explained, "that I just can't bear to be alone for a minute more."

"I suppose you are entitled to a brief respite now," said Agnes Destiny. She adjusted those ebony-lensed frames on her nose and snorted the words out as though dislodging an intrusive mote of dust.

Hannah tented the book on her chair and walked toward the kitchen, her eyes staring thirstily at the waiting faucets. "Most kind, Agnes," she said, reaching for a glass from the shelf beside the sink. "And really, I think I ought to be going to bed. Lord knows what the time is. I haven't stayed up all night since I was in my teens and discovered Jane Austen for the first time."

From the room she had left came the unmistakable swish of curtains being drawn. Hannah filled the glass and drank, staring through the window at the unfurled day outside. In her mind's eye she saw Agnes pulling the huge reading-room drapes closed, and this caused a spark of apprehension to ignite deep in her stomach. Then she imagined she saw the blind woman turn from the covered window to face back into the room, and through the room toward the kitchen. She saw, in this vision, her own unprotected back. Then she realized she had not received an answer to her tentative request. "I said, I think I ought to be going to bed, Agnes. And you, too." At the same time a particularly observant brain cell fired off a tiny question: Why would a blind woman close curtains?

"Why don't you—?" The sentence, begun in a tone uncharacteristic of Hannah's houseguest, was interrupted and hastily restarted, this time in her normal voice, a voice altogether more . . . more feminine. "Why don't you come back here and finish the chapter? You can manage a chapter, can't you? And it's such a vital one, too."

Hannah spun around to face the reading room. Agnes Destiny was nowhere to be seen and the room was dark, forbiddingly dark. From somewhere out of sight came the distinct *drrrrt* of a zipper being pulled and the rustle of falling clothes.

"Agnes?"

No answer. Then a soft *plat,* like a heavy bead of dew tumbling from the porch guttering onto the step.

"Agnes? Is anything the matter?" Hannah placed the glass gently, almost tenderly, on the drain board and took one hesitant step toward the darkness.

The blind woman appeared wraithlike from the black emptiness of the reading room, partially removed clothing hanging in a parody of a tattered peasant-woman's garb, billowing about her as she strode determinedly into the kitchen.

"Hannah, dear heart," said a voice. The words matched the movements of Agnes's mouth but the timbre of the voice had changed utterly. Now it was a man's voice. And the black spectacles were gone, replaced by eyes, fierce, slightly swollen, and resembling for all the world the button-head orbs stitched into teddy bears and cuddly stuffed rabbits.

Hannah's favorite blouse, torn open to reveal Hannah's best brassiere, sagging sideways and grotesquely stuffed with pads of stockings. The hem of Hannah's long green skirt dragging along the carpet, the skirt itself inching its way inexorably to the floor until Agnes could step effortlessly out of it . . .

The scream was stopped somewhere down at the bottom of her throat as the small hand of Agnes Destiny, so feminine and delicate, grasped the face of Hannah Marrs and squeezed tightly and with a ferocious strength. Hannah shook her head and fought to keep her eyes in their sockets, unable to turn her gaze from the things that even now were nuzzling from the side of Agnes's panties, hardening and stiffening and lengthening by the second, trailing along the floor to leave a slightly steaming stain of snail spit in their wake. With the other hand, Hannah's houseguest gathered up the dribbling appendages and gripped them as a bowman grips his arrows.

"Let us repair to the reading room, my dear, there to partake of further delights." So saying, Agnes Destiny hauled the hapless Hannah unceremoniously into the waiting darkness.

It has to be admitted that Hannah—her head aflame with

the earthy pungency emitted by that multitude of veiny, weepy-eyed erections—did begin to harbor some distinctly unseemly thoughts, especially when Agnes threw her down on to the couch, scattering books left, right, and center, toppling towers of fiction, laying waste to citadels of dreams, and grasped her wrists in one suddenly hairy hand and pinned the infinitely more delicate appendages trapped therein against the antimacassar. But these thoughts were easily swamped by her terror and shame and disgust.

There was the briefest fumble of skirt, the shortest clawing of blouse, before, in a tearing, rending rip of cotton, off came Hannah Marrs's skirt, garter belt, and panties in one swoop of destruction. Hannah fixed her eyes on just one of the many cyclopean faces that salivated before her. Saw its sluggish stirrings. Watched in perverse fascination its hollow empty eye winking and glistening. Marveled as it slowly shrugged its head from its collar of skin, gorging itself and growing fatter and fatter on borrowed blood and then standing tall and twitching like a drunken soldier on parade. To its side came others, pushing against one another like piglets at teats. Agnes Destiny wrapped his/her free arm around the pack and, bridling the ever-thickening monsters before Hannah, whispered to them as a doting owner whispers to his collection of feeding fish, "Now, now, my dears, my darlings. One at a time!"

5

Bob Tremaine clung to the crossbar of the uneven fence that staggered alongside the road leading east out of town. He squinched his eyes shut, refusing to look again at the impossibility confronting him, hoping against hope that it would go away.

He hadn't intended to come this far out at all. He had only started running out of the town square because that had seemed like the right thing to do at the time. He hadn't had any plan. He had just wanted to get away from the horror of Century Cedar. Why? He couldn't rightly say why. On this wild and weird Sunday morning, when something from hell had broken loose and taken up residence in the town square, finding a reason or a purpose for anything seemed a futile exercise.

And now this. It was too much. Way too much.

As the myriad infinitesimal cogs and wheels, conduits and canals, cells and synapses that went to make up Bob Tremaine's brain began to grind slowly and inexorably toward systems breakdown, the hapless Bob could only allow himself one question.

What *was* this?

He didn't dare look again. Not yet. If he kept his eyes shut hard and tight, maybe it would go away.

He had run from the church steps where almost everyone who had attended the service had been standing, and he had heard his Alice calling out after him and little Sandy calling out after him. *"Bob! Dad!"* they had cried. *"Come back! Come back! Please, Dad! Please, Bob!"* Like leading ladies in a movie, when the hero sets out to do what a man's gotta do.

But no one had given chase. No one had pursued him. He had just run and they had just let him run. He had run and run through the empty streets, soon reaching the signpost that marked the town limits:

YOU ARE NOW LEAVING
ESCARDY GAP
CALL AGAIN SOON!

and out beyond the edge of town and past the turnoff that led up to Boundary Hill and Ike's place, all the way to where he was standing now, facing the unknown, the unknowable.

A savage and irresistible curiosity finally got the better of Bob's fear, and he opened his eyes and looked straight ahead.

And it was still there. Or rather, it still *wasn't* there.

In front of him, about one long stride away, the world ended. About one long stride away there was only whiteness. Absolute, perfect whiteness. No road, no trees, no desert, no horizon, no sky, no sun, no clouds. Nothing.

Beside and immediately behind Bob, the fence traveled alongside the road—a little rickety maybe, but unbroken nevertheless, uninterrupted. Then, right in front of him, it stopped.

Just like that, with the horizontal bar reaching out from the last of the uprights and hanging suspended, incomplete, attached to nothing. The crossbar couldn't make it to the next upright because the next upright wasn't there. Simply *not there*. There was nowhere for it to exist. There was just whiteness, and by the way the whiteness curved to the left and to the right, Bob was almost certain that it surrounded the entire town. He knew he was looking at just an arc, a section of an enclosing circle.

Overhead, a dense fluffy cloud hung in the sky, half of it sunk into the whiteness. Coaxed by stratospheric winds, the cloud slowly hauled itself free of the wall of whiteness and floated out fully formed across the serene blue. Behind it, another cloud was already being born, a nub swelling outward from the whiteness and taking shape.

You couldn't see it from town. Unless you got up close to it, real close, the whiteness was invisible.

To reassure himself that this was the case, Bob took a few faltering steps backward. Sure enough, when he was about three feet away, desert suddenly appeared where the whiteness had been, a vista filling in that empty space as though God had switched on His projector and was shining an image onto a blank screen. Good old familiar sagebrush and sand, good old familiar globe-spanning blue sky stretching all the way to the horizon. Look! There was even an eagle soaring across the sky. (It sure looked like an eagle, at any rate, but Bob was fast learning to question the evidence of his own eyes.)

Bob stepped forward again and the scene whited out, eagle and all, to be replaced by that awful, unarguable blankness. One step back, and there was the eagle again. It had spotted prey and was swooping in for the kill. Step back, step forward again. Now the eagle was rising up, a small mammal squirming in its talons.

Bob spent a while stepping back and forth across that unseen line that divided the mundane from the just plain insane, watching desert and sky and flora and fauna switch in and out of existence.

He felt an urge to sit right down and laugh like a loon, and fought it, and thought he won. He rubbed a hand hard across his perspiring face. *Why?* and *how?* hurtled around one another in his head like two dogs chasing each other's backsides.

And then suddenly he understood. He knew.

It had finally happened.

They had finally done it.

The Reds.

The Reds had finally dropped the Bomb!

It was crazy, but it was so crazy it had to be true. It was insane, but it was the only explanation that made any sense.

Bob's mind pitched and rolled and yawned with the enormity of this deduction. The last of his sanity—the few columns left standing, the broken pillars, the lucky cornices—came tumbling down. An astonishing collapse. An Atlantean cataclysm. All gone in a single annihilating mushroom cloud of realization.

The Reds had dropped the Bomb and laid waste to America (and Europe, too, most likely). But somehow, through some freak of geography, the prevailing wind or something, Escardy Gap had survived. Of all of the free world, just this tiny, innocent corner had survived.

And then the Russians had seen this and had set up a kind of screen, no, a force field around the town, a force field that looked from a distance exactly like the desert. The Russians had manufactured an exact copy of the entire area, a 3-D illusion using some kind of advanced Red technology. (The *Post* was forever going on about how the Russians were ahead in the Space Race and had all the best rocket scientists and bomb scientists and everything.) And they had decided to claim the last remaining corner of the Free World for themselves. And they had infiltrated it, and they meant to enslave the populace and take down the Stars and Stripes and raise the Hammer and Sickle over the town hall and give Escardy Gap a new name like New Moscow or Khrushchevgrad or something like that.

What a fool! He should have known! He should have realized yesterday when he found Ike out by his fence all drooling and empty eyed. *The Reds had got to Ike.* They had taken him and they had attempted to brainwash him with their propaganda, and Ike had fought them, of that Bob had absolutely no doubt. Ike had fought their mind probes and brain rays and evil serums with every ounce of strength in his old body, and Bob was quite convinced that Ike had won, but at a price. The struggle had wiped the slate of Ike's brain clean.

Bob cursed himself for not having realized this earlier. It wouldn't have done Ike any good, but at least Tom Finkelbaum might have been saved. He cursed himself for not cottoning on sooner that the Company were nothing more than a bunch of low-down, dirt-sucking, yellow-bellied, knock-kneed, Lenin-loving Reds. Hell, the words Company and Communist weren't *so* far apart. It was almost as if they *wanted* their cover blown. They had conquered the world, after all, so there wasn't that much to gain by passing themselves off as a troupe of traveling players. Force of habit. Deception was second nature to a Russian. Once a sneaky, two-faced Red, always a sneaky, two-faced Red.

Oh, what a joke! What a grand, terrible, appalling, monumental shitkicker of a gag!

Bob laughed, and the laughter sounded like a fart at a Mormon prayer meeting in the awful, silent, pure, perfect stillness out there at the edge of town where everything all of a sudden stopped, without warning; where fence and road and desert and sky all disappeared into sudden nothingness; at the end of the world.

After a while the laughter died down to a few dry giggles, and then a series of loud heaving gasps that sounded like sobs.

Doc Wheeler, Mayor, Big Ben Burden, all of them were under the illusion that the Company were just a bunch of performers. They were blissfully unaware that the End of Civilization As We Know It had arrived, and that Escardy Gap was the last remaining pocket of decency and democracy. Only Bob knew. And even now the Company of Communists, under the leadership of Jeremiah Rackstraw—and if that was his real name, Bob was Harry S-for-nothing Truman!—even now the Company were preparing to strike at the very heart of everything he held dear and true.

Home.

Hearth.

Family.

Alice . . .

Sandy . . .

Bob sprang up and shook his fists at the white force field. "You . . . you goddamn Commie pinko *bastards!*" he snarled out in a mouthful of spittle and fury, and the invective flew into the whiteness and was lost without an echo.

Then he turned and set off back into town at a fast lick, a man with a mission.

Ten

1

So much to do, so little time to do it in.

Jeremiah Rackstraw rested Grampa's corpse against the wall, and, supporting the body with one arm, bent down, laid his hand on his knee, and caught his breath. He was not cut out for this kind of work.

"I'm not cut out for this kind of work," he told Grampa's corpse. "I'm a man of words, not deeds."

No, indeed. Deeds Jeremiah Rackstraw was only too happy to leave to others. Deeds were for those not blessed with intellect and eloquence. Deeds were the province of his monstrous foot soldiers who were currently springing their snares on the unsuspecting innocents of Escardy Gap. This was one of the very few occasions that Rackstraw had taken a personal hand in matters. As a rule, he much preferred to delegate.

The reason for his haste was simple. The boy would be back soon. Rackstraw didn't know how soon but he did know that the good people of Escardy Gap had had their first taste of what was available and would be trooping back to their homes very shortly, to learn what other treats and delights lay in store for them—although some, of course, like naughty children sneaking downstairs before dawn on Christmas morning, had already found out. So the boy would be back soon, and the boy was dangerous. How dangerous not even the boy himself was aware. Oh, he was smart and he was shrewd, but that wasn't nearly enough. Rackstraw was a dozen times smarter and shrewder. What Josh had was the gift of apartness. He didn't *belong* to Escardy Gap the way all the other residents did, all buddies and pals and families crowding down together at the trough like a litter of piglets—no, like a flock of *lambs*. (Altogether a more apt farmyard metaphor, thought Rackstraw.) Josh kept his distance. He loved his grandfather and he liked his friends, but that was about as far as it went with relationships. If anyone was going to turn and break away from the herd, pose a threat to Rackstraw and his people, it was Josh Knight. Still, plans were afoot, and the countdown was ticking (and tocking).

With a creaking and unknotting of neckbones, Grampa's chin lolled down onto his chest and a fat dry tongue sagged out from between his lips. The word "DEAD" on his forehead had turned a faint lilac and would be gone within the hour. What was it Bacon had said? "We write in sand. . . ."

Rackstraw was reminded of the writer woman. Like a bottle of fine wine she had been laid down and set aside for his later delectation, a gratification deferred and therefore enhanced, to be sampled at leisure, the best saved for last. Neville Nolan had seen to her, delivering the letter that he had insisted on calling, in his naive alliterative way, the Coma Communiqué. Coma. Comma. A misspelled pause. Rackstraw's own invention, of course. Ah, the subtle invisible might of words! Words to bring low the wordsmith.

"Okay, Gramps," said Rackstraw to the stiffening corpse, "let's get you tucked away before the brat comes crawling home."

There was a closet beneath the staircase in the Knight household where Grampa kept brushes and brooms and dusters and mops and buckets and cloths. The door was held shut by a peg, which Rackstraw now released, allowing the door to swing open and a smell of scouring powder to come wafting out.

"Come on, old fart."

Rackstraw wrestled and manhandled and shoved and

pulled and pushed Grampa's slack corpse in a sick parody of
a couple at the tail end of a three-day dance marathon, the one
struggling to keep the other upright and moving. Again,
Rackstraw wished someone else could carry out this undig-
nified function on his behalf, but time was short. He propped
the heads of two long-handled brooms up beneath Grampa's
armpits, then brought the old man gently forward, closing
the closet door at the same time until Grampa's forehead was
resting against it. Shutting the door completely, Rackstraw inserted the restraining peg and grinned. It was little touches
like these that gave Rackstraw the greatest satisfaction, and
confirmed, for him at least, the superiority of his intellect. Always planning, always thinking, always looking out for op-
portunities.

   Just one thing remained to be dealt with.

   It was upstairs.

   Waiting.

2

Josh was troubled by the way the townsfolk recovered so
swiftly from the shock of Tom Finkelbaum's murder and
set about the business of reestablishing order, restoring the
town square to the way it used to be. It was almost as if they
had been half expecting an event like this, and now that it was
out of the way, finished, dealt with, over, done, life could go
on, as if disposing of the remnants were no more than an
unwelcome task to be completed, an obligation to be discharged. Maybe this was the natural way of dealing with out-
of-the-ordinary occurrences, this was how people coped after
earthquakes and hurricanes had devastated their homes and
their lives, in which case there must be something not quite
right about *him* that he was still feeling sickened and stunned
and angry, that he wanted nothing more than to get hold of
whoever was responsible by the throat and shake the life out
of them. Maybe he lacked the resilience everyone else
seemed to be exhibiting. Somehow, though, he didn't think
that was it.

   Watching the folk of Escardy Gap tidying the square up,

sorting things out, Josh felt the first stirrings of an emotion he hardly recognized.

That emotion was contempt.

And so Josh spun on his heel and walked away, putting as much distance as possible between himself and the town square before the feeling could get any stronger, the contempt take root and flourish deep in his soul.

Although he wasn't aware of heading in any particular direction, he soon found himself on Delacy Street, approaching the Evett brothers' grain and feed store. Here he stopped. He breathed in deep: the usual familiar smells of spruce and pine and desert dust. The reek he had detected yesterday was gone. Or perhaps it was still there but he had become accustomed to it.

There was a sudden rustle nearby. Josh whirled around, a couple of heart valves jostling in his chest.

It was only a squirrel.

Josh gave a high little nervous laugh and swallowed hard to clear a mysterious obstruction in the back of his throat. Jumping at the tiniest noise. There was nothing to be scared of.

The squirrel dropped from a low-hung sycamore branch, scampered all stop-go motion across the hood of Earl Evett's 1948 Kaiser sedan (a dead ringer, or so Grampa said, for the car that veteran traveler Lowell Thomas reckoned to have made his ten-thousand mile tour in) and leapt down onto the narrow path that ran up the side of the Evetts' place down toward the train tracks.

Toward the train tracks.

Now that he was here, Josh sensed that his subconscious had been goading him, prodding, pushing him in this direction all along, for a specific purpose. A secret part of him had known what he really wanted.

He really wanted to get a closer look at that train.

The path would get him down to the tracks, and then he could cross over and clamber along the embankment overlooking the station. That way he could observe the train unseen, just like a G-man or an FBI agent on a stakeout.

With a quick glance around, Josh squared his shoulders and set off down the path. The quick glance failed to spot the figure lurking behind a tree beside Doc Wheeler's place. That was because the figure didn't want to be seen. Because being seen would have endangered his mission. Which was to seek out and eradicate the enemy that had taken over this town.

3

With considerable relief Bob Tremaine watched the Knight boy go. Right now he didn't think it wise to make his presence back in town felt. He had to move secretly, employ guerrilla tactics, if he was to have any chance of succeeding. The Reds mustn't know he was onto them. He must move like a wraith among them, a shadow among shadow people.

Bob waited until he felt sure that the boy wouldn't reappear just as he was sneaking across the road, and then he sneaked across the road. He eased down the handle of the front door of the hospital, peered through the gap, saw the coast was clear, and crept in.

First things first. Before he saved the town, he was going to rescue Ike.

4

Mr. Macready was having a small problem.

Until now, Buzz Beaumont, the man in the solenoid suit, had been the model lodger: polite, humorous, extremely concerned to be the least possible inconvenience to his host, a solid appreciator of Mr. Macready's solid home cooking, an early-to-bed heavy sleeper and, praise the Lord, no dawn riser. Couldn't have been less trouble if he tried. In fact, the only slight complaint Mr. Macready had about Buzz Beaumont was the way light fittings in the ceiling flickered and fizzled whenever he stood beneath one, and the icebox hum stuttered before starting again whenever he was in the kitchen, and the record-player needle skipped a groove several times while they had been listening to Duke Ellington, whose voice, between stutters, kept drowning and resurfacing in a sea of static. Clearly it had something to do with that unusual suit, and Mr. Macready wondered if Buzz encountered this problem wherever he went. But Mr. Macready didn't mention anything about it to Buzz, and he didn't dwell on the matter. What a man wore was his own business.

This morning, though, shambling down to the kitchen to prepare a hearty repast of bacon, eggs, and hash browns, Mr. Macready had been more than startled to discover a pool of water around the base of the icebox. A quick investigation revealed the source. The ice had thawed. The light didn't come on inside the icebox. The icebox wasn't working.

Mr. Macready checked the plug, and the plug was plugged in. He changed the fuse. No joy.

"Damn!" he cried. "Darn thing's not supposed to break down. A lifetime's faithful service, that's what it said on the guarantee. A lifetime or your money back. Damn! Can't trust anything if you can't trust a guarantee."

He salvaged what he could from the refrigerator, running a sink full of cold water to keep the bottles of milk fresh. Then, on an impulse, he tried a light switch. Nothing happened. He went through the house, trying light switch after light switch. He turned on the radio and waited for it to warm up, but the backlit wave-band display stayed dark. He went to the fuse box and examined each fuse in turn, and the wires were good and it was all very frustrating and perplexing. He went out to the sidewalk and looked both ways up Carnegie Drive, hoping for some sign that his house wasn't the only one affected—a porch light still burning, perhaps. But it was a bright morning. The sun ridiculed any artificial light. Mr. Macready ventured out into the middle of the street. Dust, silence, stillness.

Damn!

Back in the house he called up the stairs. "Mr. Beaumont! Buzz! Would you mind coming down here? I seem to be having a little problem."

There was no reply. Buzz, it seemed, was even more of a slugabed than himself, because it was getting on for half past ten and the man wasn't even dozing, he was still sleeping soundly. Recharging his batteries, as the late Ma Macready used to say.

Up on the landing, Mr. Macready raised a knuckle to knock at the door to his guest room, but stayed his hand when he heard the sound emanating from within. Then Mr. Macready chuckled. Lord, he hadn't heard snoring like that since his pappy passed away. Old Bandsaw Nose, Ma Macready used to call his father, to which Pa Macready would retort, "I don't snore, woman, and I know that's so because I sure as heck ain't never *heard* myself snore."

It was, indeed, a snore of some magnitude, and constant, as if Buzz Beaumont weren't even pausing for breath, just sucking the air in through hog's nostrils and forgetting to breathe it out again.

Mr. Macready stifled his amusement and knocked. The snoring didn't stop, so he knocked harder. The snore droned on. Mr. Macready gave the door the good old military tattoo treatment, yelling, "Buzz! Rise and shine, Buzz! Day's awasting."

Finally he turned the handle and went in.

Buzz Beaumont was lying on the bed, on top of the covers, still wearing his solenoid suit, the bed beneath him still made, one corner tucked back just as Mr. Macready had left it, as if the man had simply gone and laid himself down and fallen fast asleep. That would have been all right, Mr. Macready would have been able to deal with that, but there was more. All over the supine body of his houseguest, from his head to his feet, sparks were playing. Blue flashes of electricity were rippling and writhing like neon elvers, leaping between buttons and fingertips, chin and lapels, tiepin and toe caps, sometimes swelling up into great flaring arcs that crackled and popped all the way up to the ceiling. Buzz's hair was as stiff as a brush and teemed with tiny fireflies of light that whizzed along the erect strands and whirled and spun and whirligigged. His teeth were all dazzle, quivering tendrils of blue light poking up between them like weeds in the cracks between paving stones growing in fast motion. Behind his serenely closed eyelids a yellowy glow shimmered, showing up the capillaries in red relief.

The source of the current wasn't difficult to find. A length of cloth-bound electric cord led from Buzz's breast pocket to the outlet just above the baseboard. Somehow he had diverted the entire supply of the house into his solenoid suit and there he was, like some kind of mad sunbather, basking in a couple of hundred volts of electrical juice.

It struck Mr. Macready that he no longer had a little problem. He had a very, very big one.

Tentatively he reached out a hand to shake the volt-charged man awake, and then thought better and drew the hand back. He wasn't quite quick enough, however. A spark detached itself from Buzz Beaumont's shoulder and leapt the gap to the tip of Mr. Macready's middle finger. There was a loud snap and Mr. Macready's world was filled with searing bright blue light.

Smoke blustered around the bedroom, taking the smell of charred meat with it wherever it went.

Buzz Beaumont slept on, peaceful as a baby.

5

Josh crouched behind a small tuft of bushes at the top of the embankment, watching the huge metal monstrosity parked in the siding a hundred yards from the railway station, and tried not to think what Grampa would have to say about the tear in his pants, inflicted during a particularly difficult hands-and-knees scramble for cover across open space that put him in sight of the train. He had made it, anyway. More importantly, he thought that he had made it without anyone seeing him. The rip in the knee of his right pants leg was surely a small price to pay for continued cover.

The view his perch afforded him of the locomotive, and pair of attendant carriages was good, but he cupped his hands around his eyes because, although this did not magnify the object of his scrutiny, it helped cut out any peripheral distractions. He moved his head slowly to take in the locomotive a section at a time. First the viciously toothsome cowcatcher, two fixed five-rung ladders and a circular steel plate sporting two straight handles (rather like the hands on a clockface at one o'clock), this situated just below the enormous, bulbous funnel, on top of which was mounted a swinging bell like a grisly figurehead; then back along the cylindrical boiler with its silver whistle and wide running boards to the small cabin with its tiny round black windows tacked on like a grim afterthought.

There was something wrong about the cabin. Something he couldn't quite put his finger on . . .

To help his starved brain think and to keep his stomach from rumbling—which it was in danger of doing, so loud it might reveal his whereabouts to anyone with a remotely sharp pair of ears—Josh took out the apple from his pocket. He ate it slowly, taking care to keep the scrunch of teeth penetrating red skin and pale flesh to the bare minimum. When the apple was no more than a core, he tossed it away.

The ruminative device worked. Josh suddenly realized what it was about the train, that was so weird.

There was no way into the cabin. No door.

How this piece of information would profit him, he had no idea. It seemed to offer him only deeper confusion. If there was no way to get into the cabin, how did anyone drive the train? Did *anyone* drive the train at all?

Josh cast his mind back to the day of the train's arrival and watched the mental moving image unspool. The platform, the women, the passengers, Mr. Rackstraw and . . .

No engineer. No Casey Jones. No blue-bibbed engineer with sooty face and striped bandanna, wiping his hands on a permanently oily rag that he kept in his pants pocket.

So then what kind of a train was it?

Before Josh could apply himself to answering his own question, a head popped out between the tender and the first carriage, long dark tresses swinging as it jerked side to side, apparently sniffing the air. Josh caught his breath and snuck down behind the shrubs, peering gingerly through their leaves.

The woman pulled herself through the gap, stepping over the couplings in her bare feet, and dropped to the ground beside the locomotive. A second woman quickly followed, this the one with the wild red hair. Then a third, the blond. All three stood momentarily by the side of the train, heads back, tongues poking out as if tasting the breeze. Josh could hear loud sniffs clearly above the soft and gentle singing of the midday heat. And he could hear something else, too. A clacking, chittering sound, a cross between the sound a spun penny makes as it nears the end of its revolutions on Old Joe's countertop and the staccato rapping of a woodpecker hard at work on tree bark.

Something had obviously disturbed the women from whatever it was they had been doing. Josh tried hard to believe it hadn't been him, it had been maybe a rat or a prairie dog or a gopher or *some* kind of critter snuffling down the tracks. But he knew deep down that this might well not be so. He knew it might well be Josh Knight, casting his presence before him the way he cast his shadow along the sidewalk when the afternoon sun lit his body from behind, that had drawn them out.

He watched apprehensively as the first woman, the brunette, moved slowly, catlike, toward the rear of the train. At the same time the blond walked in a similar crouched fashion toward the front. The redhead, meanwhile, simply stood her ground, poised for pursuit, staring, wary, scanning for signs of motion in the shrubland immediately in front of her. The scant clumps of grass at the foot of the slope afforded little in the way of concealment. Josh hoped she was just being thorough. And then something else occurred to him: maybe the redhead was only *pretending* not to be able to see him. Maybe she was just waiting for him to dart out of hiding, patient as a cat waiting at a mousehole.

While her two companions checked up and down the train, the chitter-clack separating into three distinct sources as they did so, the redhead concentrated her attention farther afield. She moved cautiously forward, turning her head this way and that, inching her way closer to the incline. Soon she would be at the bottom, and then she would look up the slope. If she hadn't seen Josh already—and she was moving with a caution that suggested she had not—she undoubtedly would then. But if she was just pretending, toying with him, then she sure as heck knew how to go about scaring him out from his hidey-hole.

Josh pulled his body into a small ball, sinking his head as far into his neck as he could. He looked to either side, slowly, careful not to make any sudden movement. A twitch, a tic, might reveal him. He entertained the notion of just upping and running, then dismissed it, because he had a pretty shrewd idea that if he tried, the redhead would be upon him before he had gone a dozen yards, overhauling and bringing him down with unearthly grace and speed. And he felt, with a prickling dreadful certainty in the pit of his belly, that being caught by these girls was the last thing he wanted to do, and would quite probably be the last thing he ever did.

Suddenly the redhead pounced, launching herself into the air and landing with a soft *phlap* of dust on a thick clump of brush and, standing once more erect at the denouement of that same fluid motion, she lifted a frantically struggling and squealing prairie dog up in her fist. Brandishing the spoils of her victory aloft, she glanced both ways. The others, though they had had their backs to her, visibly relaxed and turned and smiled at her, their huntresses' frowns gone. Then, with a quick flick, the redhead raised the hem of her long skirt and thrust the animal beneath the material, tucking it up and out of sight. There followed a frightened and agonized squeal, a soft crunching noise, and then silence. A brief silence. Then the sound, perfectly pitched across the small distance to the woman's solitary audience, of someone chewing and munching on a large mouthful of meat. Then the chitter-clacking resumed, slower, muted, sated.

The redhead withdrew her hand and let her skirt hem fall. Her hand and forearm were covered in a dark, oily substance that Josh recognized only too well from the grass around the base of Century Cedar. Josh wanted to close his eyes, but he couldn't. He *had* to watch. The redhead lifted the gooey arm to her lips and, laughing, licked it. The other two rushed over to her and started to push and pull at her, craning their heads close so that they, too, could get a taste, but the redhead wasn't in the mood for sharing. With a playfully angry shriek, a mixture of hiss and giggle, she broke free of their grasp and ran back to the train, leaping effortlessly over the couplings between the tender and the front carriage. The blond and the brunette, clacking madly, gave chase. A few seconds later they were all gone, disappeared through the same gap, their strange urgent wails settling into the dust behind them.

Josh waited for what seemed like long enough and then

jumped to his feet and dashed back along the incline to a small gathering of trees, and past that, along the track to the Evett brothers' grain and feed and the safety and security and sanity of town.

Eleven

1

As morning pivoted around midday and turned into afternoon, Mayor stood at his office window nursing an old, chipped "I Like Ike" mug in his hands and watched figures flitting through the streets of Escardy Gap. The majority were townsfolk, no doubt heading for neighbors' houses to join them for lunch, although, if the atrocity that had been found at the Finkelbaum residence was anything to go by, there was every chance that something less appetizing than a three-course meal would be waiting for them. The rest were members of the Company.

Good guys and bad guys.

If, like Mayor, you drew your inspiration and metaphors from the silver screen, you would have been aware of the code that distinguished the one from the other. Simple, really. White hats and black hats. Randolph Scott and Audie Murphy, for instance, wouldn't ever possess a single item of dark headgear. Lyle Bettger, Jack Elam, and James Cagney, on the other hand, were the men in black. Mean as all get-out, and proud of it.

Mayor, gazing down at the figures passing to and fro across the town square, started giving out hats.

There went Earl Evett and Big Ben Burden down by the town hall steps, making for Ben's house. Wearers of whiter-than-white hats the pair of them. Bearers of whiter-than-white faces as well.

Someone had had to go round to the Finkelbaums' to break the bad news about Tom to his parents. Big Ben had volunteered, and had taken Earl along for moral support, leaving Earl's brother, Carroll, to hose down the grass beneath Century Cedar.

The front door to the Finkelbaum residence had been locked, which was in itself unusual, and Big Ben and Earl had been obliged to break in through a downstairs bathroom window. Inside, they had found Harry and Frieda Finkelbaum seated at their kitchen table, quite dead.

The smell, Earl had confessed to Mayor just a few minutes earlier in this very room, was the worst he had ever encountered—like bad eggs, old poultry, and soft cheese all left out in the sun for too long.

"Me'n Ben found them bodies right away," Earl had continued. "You could say we just followed our noses. But I tell you, Mayor, no way could we have gone into that room without wrapping our shirts around our faces first. And then, when we noticed that the oven was on, well, we kinda hoped it might be a Sunday pot roast, but somehow we both knew that that wasn't what we were going to find in there. We knew that like you always know when something's not going to be the way you want it to be." Earl had sounded unnaturally calm just then, as though he realized that if he didn't keep a very tight rein on himself, he was going to burst with the horror of it.

"The most horrible thing about it," Big Ben had added, "was that although those things in the oven were human eyes and hearts, they looked for all the world like boiled eggs and hefty half-pound steaks, laid out on one of Frieda Finkelbaum's best baking pants and cooking away on a low heat in her oven."

Earl and Big Ben planned to go back to the Finkelbaums' this afternoon with a burial party to remove the bodies and inter them alongside their son in a nondenominational corner of the churchyard. Neither of the two men was much looking forward to the task.

Mayor took a long sip of coffee and exhaled, his hot breath misting up a pane of the window. He was vaguely keeping an eye out for the tall, pale lad, the one the town kids had taken to calling the Boy. There was a strong likelihood that *he* knew something about Tom Finkelbaum's grisly demise, might even be the one responsible. A grim-faced Jim Burden had come forward and informed Mayor that he had been with Tom and the Boy last night and had left them around half past seven to go home for dinner with his parents and the seriously *weird* fella who was their houseguest. Jim had added that around about then he had seen Old Joe Dolan close up the Merrie Malted. So, Mayor reflected, the Boy had had plenty of time to murder Tom, string him up, and then go back to the Finkelbaums' house, where he could have then killed Harry and Frieda, removed their eyes and hearts, and popped them into the oven to bake. That line of reasoning seemed straightforward enough, and at the same time hideously plausible.

Mayor shuddered, unhappy that he could think so calmly and reasonably about things that ought to have had him screaming and swinging from the light fixtures.

Okay, he told himself, try *this* one out for size: Why was the Reverend King, of all people, so distraught? Sure, the sight of the thing at Century Cedar would have been enough to send anyone nuts, but with most folk a kind of circuit breaker seemed to have kicked in and had prevented the enormity of the horror from engulfing them——the mental equivalent of the little Dutch boy with his finger in the dike holding back the flood. In John King's case this faculty seemed to have failed. Maybe men of God possessed it to a lesser degree than others, relying instead on their faith and their unimpeachable standing within the community to shield them from harm. Whatever the reason, the reverend had fled to his chapel and had locked himself inside, unable to offer anything in the way of assistance when faced with the sort of crisis that didn't crop up too often in the Holy Scriptures (except, perhaps, right at the very end of the New Testament). What color hat did the reverend wear? Well, a light gray——the gray of one of the everyday shirts he wore along with his throttling white dog collar.

Fine. Now, what about Old Joe Dolan? Old Joe had never before closed down the Merrie Malted so early on a Saturday night, except once in winter when he caught the virulent flu bug that was making the rounds and that carried off, to everyone's regret, Emily Swivven. Unless he was sick, Old Joe was unlikely to have voluntarily passed up the opportunity to refresh the palates of the church congregation in their best bibs and tuckers with a few of his Sunday Sundaes and Peach Floats. White hat. Assuming Old Joe was still alive to wear one.

Cora-May Chisholm and her husband, Jack, also had to be taken into consideration. Cora-May never missed a Sunday sermon.

Mayor drained the last of his coffee and stared down at the grotesquely disfigured man hobbling along the sidewalk with a carpetbag swinging heavily at his side. Mayor didn't recognize the face. Therefore he had to be another of the Company. (Was there no end to them?) Therefore, by definition, he had to be wearing a black hat. Everyone who came out of that train: black hats. Black, black, blacker-than-black hats.

Mayor went over to his desk and settled down into the scroll-footed chair whose padded seat and back had, over the years, adapted and molded to suit his bony contours. Escardy Gap's mayor behind his desk. To his right, an empty in-tray. To his left, an equally empty out-tray. By his hand, a chunky black Bakelite telephone. On the blotter in front of him, nothing. Not even a blot.

Mayor contemplated this empty prospect, this barren plain of officialdom before him, and was still contemplating it an hour later when Jeremiah Rackstraw arrived, sporting a hat as black as night.

2

Bob Tremaine moved cautiously through Doc Wheeler's parlor, a room resplendent with colonial sofa and comfortable wing chairs. He spent several minutes at the inner door making sure that nothing could be heard from the other side. Upon opening the door, he discovered a long corridor leading from the frosted-paned double doors on the left— this was the entrance regular callers used—to a staircase about thirty yards to the right. Along the corridor were four more doors, all closed.

Bob held his breath and listened. From somewhere far off he could hear voices mumbling. He kept listening, straining to hear what was being said, but couldn't make out the words distinctly enough. One thing was certain, though: the voices did not originate from this floor. He looked up at the ceiling. The voices were coming from up there. Each sentence buzzed down through the floorboards, sounding like a fly taking off from the capital letter, buzzing around a bit, and then landing at the period.

Bob started to walk toward the staircase, placing one foot delicately in front of the other, testing the carpeted floorboards for squeaks before bringing his full weight to bear on them. At each door he paused and placed an ear against the wood. On each occasion, having satisfied himself that a room was empty, he would move on.

The carpet beneath Bob's feet was a frenetic kaleidoscope of swirls and lines in stark contrast to the corridor's plain lime green walls. In the dust-thick interior gloom, it seemed to Bob that he was wading through brackish water that was alive with plankton and other microscopic organisms. So real was this impression that Bob's legs and feet began to feel sluggish, as though dragging through imaginary ooze and slime. He began to find breathing difficult. The air was glutinous, soupy. He leaned one hand against the wall. The stairs seemed both near and far away, shimmering through a greenish haze. The whole world seemed to be pulsing as though it possessed a heartbeat. There was an identical pounding behind his eyes. His head, his brain, every part of him seemed to be saying, *This is wrong, this cannot be, this is all so very wrong.*

Mind tricks. Brain beams. Artificially induced hallucinations.

Softly Bob began to chant beneath his breath, "O-o-oh say can you see . . ."

Straightening up, he put his best foot forward, bracing himself against the wall as he walked.

". . . by the dawn's early light . . ."

The stairs swam into focus again, solidifying.

". . . at the twilight's last gleaming . . ."

As Bob reached the foot of the staircase, a sense of triumph welled in his belly.

"And the rocket's red glare . . ."

Grasping the handrail, he lifted one foot from the eddying waters of the carpet and stepped onto the first stair. It gave slightly, and he stopped singing and bit his lip, waiting for an ominous creak to sound . . . but none came. He lifted his other foot and set it down next to its twin. Reasoning that the stairs would be securest—and so less inclined to betray his presence—at their edges, he hooked an arm over the handrail and proceeded to climb the stairs by placing his feet as close as possible to the joins. Two steps farther on he realized that, because the carpet went only up the center of the stairs, this exposed wooden area was acting like a sounding board for the soles of his shoes. He paused to remove his shoes and, tying the laces together, hung them around his neck.

That was better. He made good time on the final few stairs of this first flight, and within moments had reached the landing. The staircase turned a hundred-and-eighty-degree corner, rising another six steps before reaching the next floor. Bob leaned round the partition and looked, using his head like a periscope. He saw another corridor, more doors.

Then there was a voice, coming from the only door that was half-open, some fifteen feet away from him. The voice was Doc Wheeler's. "Have you fixed up that IV yet?" Doc said.

"You're rushing me," Nurse Sprocket replied. "Stop rushing me."

IV? thought Bob. What the hell was that? Code for something, surely. IV, IV, IV . . . Turn it around: V. I. Lenin's initials! Vladimir Ilyich. Of course. That was it. They were establishing a radio link with their bosses in the Kremlin, in order to tell them that Escardy Gap was secure, the covert operation had been successfully completed and the invasion-proper could begin. And "IV," Lenin's initials reversed, was their code word.

This left Bob in no doubt that it wasn't Doc Wheeler up there. It was someone who walked and talked like Escardy Gap's one and only physician, a master of disguise who had the gait and the diction of the good doctor down to perfection, but who was an impostor all the same. A crummy Commie counterfeit. The same was true of Nurse Sprocket. She had told Doc he was "Russian" her. They were making jokes about it. They were making jokes to each other about their Commie-ness!

Nurse Sprocket then asked Doc to fetch her something. Bob didn't catch the word, but it sounded like the name of a drug. Something-amine. Had to be a truth serum. They were going to extract information out of somebody. And the only somebody Bob knew to be here was Ike Swivven. He had brought Ike in himself. He had carried the old guy straight into the lion's den—into the *bear's* den.

Bob slumped back against the wall. There was the sound of footsteps. He sneaked a glance round the corner just in time to catch sight of a pair of legs, feet shod in heavy Oxfords, emerging from the half-open doorway. The legs turned and came clumping along the corridor in the direction of the stairs.

Bob spun and raced back down to the first floor on sock-softened tiptoes. At the bottom of the staircase he wrenched open the first door he came to and threw himself through.

Easing the door shut behind him, Bob found himself in a large, long closet. The walls were lined with shelves and the shelves were laden with bottles. There were big bottles and little bottles, blue bottles and green bottles, bottles with long necks and bottles with short, stubby necks, bottles containing pills and capsules (visible through the colored glass), and bottles of liquid, some full to the brim, some only half-full. Beside a sink set into the long worktable that ran down the middle of the room all the way to the window were jars and glasses, beakers and vials, tubes and yet more damn bottles.

Big mistake. Oh, big mistake, Bob. This was where they kept the drugs. This was where the Russky was heading.

But it was too late for Bob to back out. The footsteps had

reached the stairs and were clumping down, down, down with the steady, regular tread of someone accustomed to marching across Red Square. Bob cast around for something with which to protect himself, but there were only bottles, bottles, and more bottles. Then he spotted a piece of wood leaning against the frame of the sash window at the far end of the closet. An old chair leg.

The footsteps reached the bottom of the stairs.

Bob darted over to the window and hefted the chair leg. Heavier than it looked. Good solid American wood.

Behind him the door opened. He turned to see the face of Doc Wheeler peering in, scanning the shelves, frowning.

When Doc Wheeler's gaze fell on Bob, his eyes narrowed behind his little round glasses.

"Bob?" he said, incredulously. "Bob Tremaine? Is that you? Now just what in tarnation are you doing in here?"

"None of your business," replied Bob with a snarl and a sneer.

"You bet it's my damn business what you're doing when you're in my medicine room! Come on out, right now!"

"Come in and get me, Commie!"

" 'Commie'?" said Doc, puzzled. "Am I hearing you right, Bob? Did you just call me a Commie?"

"Yeah," said Bob. "A lousy dirty *Commie.* I know what you're up to. I've unraveled your little plot, see. And I'm going to stop you. You may have destroyed the Free World, pinko, but the spirit of America will never die. Huff and puff all you like, but you can never snuff out the flame of freedom."

"*What?*" Doc exclaimed. "Bob, have you been drinking? Have you swallowed something from here?" He scanned around, looking for an open bottle, a scattering of pills, spilled medicine.

"I've seen your force field," Bob went on. "You won't be able to keep it a secret much longer. And when everyone knows, you and your comrades are going to learn that as long as the last American draws breath, the spirit of America still lives."

"Bob, put down the chair leg. Now. Before someone gets hurt."

"Make me."

"Bob, I know you've been under a lot of strain. Don't think you're the only one. What's happening affects all of us, and we can only face up to it and survive if we stand together, don't crack up, stay strong."

"Don't try any of that Marxist shinola on me, Ivan. It just won't wash."

"The chair leg, Bob." Doc held out his hand. "Pass it over. Come on. Before you do something we both regret."

"No way. You come and get it, and get what's coming to you."

From overhead came Nurse Sprocket's dulcet growl: "Doctor, are we going to have that medication sometime before 1960?"

"We have a slight problem here, Nurse. Would you mind coming down?" Doc turned back to Bob. Bob could tell the phony was scared of him. He was trembling. It was only to be expected. All Reds were yellow at heart.

"The chair leg, Bob. Please. Give it to me." Doc waved his hand in a supplicatory gesture.

"I'll give it to you, all right," said Bob, and he lunged forward, swinging the chair leg with every ounce of righteousness in his body. This was for Ike. This was for Escardy Gap. For the Free World. For America!

The chair leg caught Doc upside of the head and sent his spectacles flying against the doorjamb. A thin spray of blood spattered over the door and the floor and the end of the central table. Doc Wheeler went down like a sack of cement.

Bob stared down at the body. It was still breathing. Seeing the blood and the gash in Doc's head, Bob fought the urge to vomit.

"Doctor? Is everything all right?"

Nurse Sprocket.

Without a second thought Bob bounded over the supine Doc and hurtled up the stairs. He couldn't allow the woman who looked and sounded exactly like Nurse Sprocket to be ready for him. Surprise, and the chair leg, were his only weapons. God alone knew what the Russian was capable of if cornered. Visions of cyanide cigarettes, poison darts, and stiletto knives flashed through his head.

As Bob reached the top of the stairs, he and Nurse Sprocket

lurched into one another, narrowly avoiding a collision. The nurse backed away when she saw Bob's expression and the piece of wood he brandished. Instinctively she raised an arm to protect herself.

Bob showed no mercy.

The first swing struck Nurse Sprocket on the temple, bending her head sideways. There was a pop of fracturing vertebrae. Bob hit her again, this time on the crown, saw her graying hair glisten redly, even saw some yellow bits and pieces swimming around in there. . . .

As Nurse Sprocket started to crumple Bob leapt at her, whisking the chair leg again and again into her face. Beneath the onslaught her jaw folded inward, her nose splintered obliquely, and one eye socket ruptured and flung out its passenger orb, which skittered across the floor, fetching up against the baseboard.

Nurse Sprocket slumped in her blood-spattered uniform, spread-eagling indecorously over the floor, and lay still, except for one arm that twitched galvanically.

Nimbly Bob jumped astride her, pinning her shoulders beneath his knees. He didn't think she had much fight left in her, to be honest, but it paid to be sure. You never knew. She might be faking. He then proceeded to pound at her head with his makeshift weapon until there was nothing recognizably human about it, until it resembled a piece of raw steak—and what a size! Moose Rollins size!—salted with granules of broken tooth and peppered here and there with tufts of coarse hair.

A short while later, panting, arms aching, Bob clambered off the corpse. Remembering the eye, he strolled over to where it lay in a small pool of sticky fluid, the optic nerve trailing away from it like a comet's tail. He took his shoes from around his neck and put them back on (an operation that took longer than he might have wished because the laces had become entangled). Then he raised one leg.

It took two attempts to destroy the eye. His first stamp sent it scuttling toward the head of the stairs, almost as if it were trying to escape. The second stamp got it, though. No problem. *Squish-pop!*

Bob scraped the sole of his shoe on the edge of the top

stair and surveyed his handiwork. He permitted himself a small smile. So far, so good.

What was that? A rustle? A cough?

Bob tightened his grip on the chair leg and moved down the corridor, stepping cautiously around the remains of Nurse Sprocket. He was dimly aware that a small tic had started up in his right eyelid, but he did his best to ignore it.

He passed a closed door, behind which, unbeknownst to him, Sara Sienkiewicz lay in a freshly made up bed, and, coming to a door that was slightly ajar, painstakingly slowly edged his face around the frame and looked in.

Ike Swivven stared back, utterly expressionless. He was sitting hunchbacked on the side of a large white bed, a thin web line of saliva dangling from his chin to his lap.

"Ike," Bob whispered.

Ike didn't bat an eyelid when Bob started to cry.

Showed no sign of fear when Bob stalked tearfully into the room.

Made no attempt to defend himself when Bob lifted the chair leg.

Made not a single sound except *squachshwuludge* when Bob embedded the edge of the chair leg right in the middle of his skull.

And all the time Bob sobbed.

And Bob kept sobbing until he heard . . .

Clump, clump.

Unsteady, certainly, but the same footsteps. The footsteps of Doc Wheeler's double.

Bob had been intending to go back downstairs and finish Doc off before heading into town, but now it was too late for that.

The Russian would be armed. The Russian would shoot him, hoping to wing him and capture him and inflict hideous tortures on him; failing that, kill him outright.

Bob couldn't allow that. He was Escardy Gap's last, best hope. The Free World's last, best hope. He had to escape.

Clump . . .

Clump . . .

Bob burst into the corridor and sprinted toward the window

at the far end. With a loud, desperate yell he hurled himself through. Glass bristled and splintered glintingly around him.

And he flew.

And he flew.

And he landed, miraculously, in the waiting arms of the old walnut tree that stood a few feet away from the side of the building.

The branches hurt him, ripped him, and scratched him as they pinballed him down to the ground. He bumped and rolled and rocked and yawed down through the foliage, grunting at each scrape, slap, and puncture. He hit the earth with a whump. No time for lying around. He staggered to his feet. He was bruised and he was bleeding, but the pain invigorated him. It was almost refreshing.

As Bob brushed a number of small twigs out of his hair (realizing, with some astonishment, that he was still holding his weapon, his lucky piece of wood), he heard the Russian give vent to his anger. He heard inarticulate epithets voiced in a bearlike growl.

With the raucous, heady laugh of a free man, Bob turned and headed off into town.

3

In the wonderful, weird, and wacky world of Neville N. Nolan there were certain occasions that stood out as the apogees, the acmes, indeed the apexes of his existence, shining spars, proud peaks, when the rigid rules that bound his behavior suddenly proved their purpose and justified their jurisdiction over his journey through life, leading him to believe that a being of preternatural power—a genie, a god even—guided his footsteps and flights flawlessly, secretly steering him toward a goal, a greater glory that he could only guess at.

This was one of them.

"*Earl* Evett?" he cried, clapping his hands together, then striving for self-control. "No, I can barely believe it. Surely it's spelled differently. U-R-L, maybe?"

"Nope," said Earl Evett, more than a mite confused. "It's Earl, as in 'Duke of.' "

"Oh, the sheer serendipitous supremacy of it! My toes and tit tips are all atingle."

"Ben," said Earl to his host, who was sitting at the other end of the kitchen table and looking sullen and weary and puzzled all at once, "am I missing something here?"

"There's only one person here who's missing anything," replied Big Ben Burden, tapping his temple and nodding in the direction of Neville N. Nolan.

"Neville, I take it you'll be joining us for lunch," said Janey Burden, gathering a handful of cutlery from a drawer.

Before Neville could launch into an egregious encomium to the joys of Janey's culinary capabilities—the excellent smells emanating from the stove were turning his taste buds to taffy—Big Ben stopped him with a stern stare and a confrontational clearing of the throat.

"*Ahem.* Janey, my love, Earl and I would like to have a word with Mr. Nolan by ourselves. In private. Would you mind letting us alone for a moment?"

"You mean, Ben, would I mind getting out of my kitchen while I'm in the middle of preparing lunch for you and Earl?" replied the long-suffering Mrs. Burden, who could never understand why her husband insisted on keeping the low company he did and who considered it a terrible hypocrisy that he should be so unwilling to tolerate a friend of *hers*.

"We won't be long, honey. Why don't you go call Jim in from the yard?"

"Why don't *you?*" Janey replied huffily.

"I got other business."

"Well!" Turning on her heel, Janey stomped out of the kitchen. Just before the door slammed she said this: "If the beef's burnt by the time I get back, Ben Burden, don't blame me!"

Her parting remark drew a smile of profound satisfaction from Neville N. Nolan. "Do you know," he said, "I couldn't have phrased it more finely myself."

"Don't sit down, Mr. Nolan," said Big Ben, getting up, going to the door and turning the key in the lock. "Don't even think about making yourself comfortable. I'm going to keep this short and I'm going to keep this sweet."

"Short and sweet," said Neville. "I can surely sympathize with that."

"I don't know what kind of fools you people take us for," said Big Ben, "but rest assured, we're nowhere near as dumb as you think. It doesn't take a genius to figure out that you and your kin had something to do with what happened to the Finkelbaums. Hell, I don't know for sure that it wasn't you personally that did for them. So I'll say this only once. Get out of my house. Get out of this town. Don't come back. Ever. Understood?"

Neville rested his hands on the back of a chair as if he were just itching to pull it out, sit himself down, and tuck into the mouthwatering meal that was mere minutes from manifesting itself on the tablecloth. "Big Ben," he said beseechingly, "won't this wait until our appetites are assuaged?"

"Like heck it won't! When I say I want you out of my house, Mr. Nolan, I mean now. I mean *right* now. I mean, git!"

"And if you ain't prepared to go under your own steam," said Earl, rising to his feet, "then Ben and I are just going to have to evict you."

"Evicted by Earl!" exclaimed Neville. "Banished by Ben! Why, even jettisoned by Janey! I'm starting to perceive that you're none too pleased with my presence. A perennial problem for a peripatetic. And casting aside for a moment the question of whether or not I *can* leave through a locked door—which I can, by the way, if the keyhole is capacious enough—I would much rather we sorted this out sensibly, like rational men, rather than like rapacious, marauding monkeys."

"That all depends," said Big Ben. "If you go quietly, then no one gets hurt."

"Ah," said Neville. "I perceive a paradox in your plan. I foresee a failing. This is Escardy Gap here. Everyone gets hurt."

Earl frowned. "What're you talking about?" he said with a growl. "Are you threatening us?"

"Simply framing a statement of fact. Your deaths are as inevitable and ineluctable as the setting of the sun."

"I'm not a physical man, Mr. Nolan. . . ." warned Big Ben, brandishing his fists in a decidedly physical manner.

"We could spend months," replied Neville equably, "we could mount seminars, we could set up debates discussing details and forming philosophical theories around that remark, Big Ben. We could—"

"Ah, the heck with it!" said Big Ben, and swung his fist at Neville's jaw.

The blow would have connected, too, and sent his humorous houseguest hurtling heavenward, had Neville Nolan remained where he was. But, fast as a fly, he darted deftly out of range, sidestepping to the sink and from there skipping smartly up onto the sideboard, which shivered and shook and rattled and redistributed several of its racked dishes onto the floor with a catastrophic crash of crockery.

Big Ben whirled around, saw Neville crouched on the sideboard, and, strangely, began to chuckle.

"You ain't going to go easy, are you?" he said, and rolled up first one, then the other sleeve of his plaid shirt. Like this, with his thick beard and barrel chest, Big Ben bore a more than passing resemblance to Popeye's perennial foe, Bluto.

"I *ain't*," said Neville, delivering the vernacular verb with decided distaste, "going to go in any way except the manner of my own making."

"Earl," said Big Ben, "you go 'round the other side of the table. He may be quick, but he can't get by both of us."

"Ben?" came Janey's tremulous voice through the kitchen door. She tried the handle. "Ben, what's going on in there?"

"Nothing, honey. Mr. Nolan and I are just sorting out a few differences of opinion."

"Was that my best plate I heard just now?"

"No," said Ben, surveying the shattered wreckage of some pieces of very expensive and paranoiacally well-tended china. "Nope, it was just some old pie dish."

"You'll burn in hell for that one, Ben," whispered Earl.

"Then," said Big Ben, gesturing at Neville Nolan, "let's hope I have some company down there."

Neville grinned "The winsome wife wonders, and the hapless husband hands her half-truths. Lordy Lord! Love makes liars of us all."

"Ready, Earl?"

"Ready, Ben."

The two old friends moved menacingly toward the man perched precariously close to the edge of the sideboard, balancing on the balls of his feet. Ben's and Earl's expressions were deadly serious, but to look at Neville you would have thought they were all of them just playing a schoolyard game.

"Now!" yelled Ben. "Get the guy!"

He and Earl lunged.

"This guy," said Neville, "will not gladly be gotten."

As Ben and Earl converged on the sideboard, with a leap and a flip and a somersault Neville transported himself to the other end of the kitchen, ending up delicately balanced on one leg on the corner of the stove. Ben's bearded chin butted Earl's ear with a squidgy clomp and their heads recoiled, dragging their bodies after them by the neck. More crockery avalanched from the sideboard shelves, adding to the rubble of china littering the terra-cotta tiles that Janey liked to keep scrupulously swept. Ben ended up on his backside; Earl cracked an elbow against the wall. Both men's oral orifices opened up to emit oaths. Curses clouded the kitchen air.

"Ben!!!" came Janey's voice again, this time with an unmistakable note of reproof. "Whatever's going on in there, there's never any call for that kind of gutter language."

"Nothing's going on, honey," said Big Ben, rubbing his bruised jaw tenderly.

"Well, if it *is* nothing, it's a pretty noisy nothing, is all I can say."

"Nothings don't come noisier," Neville N. Nolan called out, evidently delighted at the dialogistic development of his unwitting disciple. So lightly and easily was he balancing on the one foot that it appeared that he weighed next to nothing and that he was hovering in midair, only touching the stovetop with one toe so that the illusion would not seem entirely incredible.

"And you can mind your own business, Mr. Nolan," Janey replied. *"You're* the cause of all this!"

"You make me miserable, ma'am, blaming me for the bullishness of Big Ben and the overenthusiasm of Earl."

"Will you stop your prattling for a moment!" bellowed Big Ben, his cheeks flushing to an apoplectic, apocalyptic scarlet. "I'm sick to death of it! I'm sick of your loony language and your terrible tongue-twisters and your aggravating alliteration and your . . ." Big Ben's hand flew to his mouth and his eyes bulged halfway out of their sockets. "Oh, my God."

The wounded look on Neville's face slowly softened, becoming a broad and genial grin. "It's infinitely infectious, is it not? I find I can influence whole households within hours of my auspicious arrival. I can have people dreaming in similar-sounding syllables, searching for suitable synonyms in their sleep."

"Just go," said Big Ben, all the determination drained out of him, his hands hanging hopelessly by his hips. "Please. Just get out of my house."

Neville shook his head. "Why should I, when I'm finding this such fun?"

"Because . . ." said Earl, and he was holding a sharp steak knife by its tip between thumb and index finger of his right hand.

Now, it should be pointed out that while Earl was the most skilled with a throwing knife of anyone in Escardy Gap—the annual contest in Poacher's Park had in recent years become something of a one-horse race—he had never before wielded a blade in anger or aimed one at a living creature. Fixed, inanimate targets were just fine because they didn't move and they didn't squeal and they didn't bleed when struck. But Earl had never killed, or ever intended to kill, any living thing, not so much as a gopher or a rattlesnake. Somehow, Neville sensed this.

"You don't dare," he said. "You can't kill."

"Maybe not," said Earl, with a reasonable man's shrug, "but I can see to it that you walk with a limp for the rest of your natural life."

"Or unnatural," murmured Big Ben into his beard.

"Is this a simple standoff," Neville wondered aloud, "or an excellent endgame?"

"Tell you what," said Earl, angling the knife by the side of his head and closing one eye, "why don't we find out?"

"Do it, Earl," urged Big Ben. "The world'll thank you for it."

Earl braced himself on his back foot. The knife stayed in his hand. Janey asked through the door what was happening now, and tried the handle again, to no avail. A saucepan full of potatoes bubbled away on the burner by Neville's toes.

"Evidently, Earl," he said, "your balls aren't big enough. Your testicles are too tiny. Your *cojones* lack the capacity. Your scrotum is too scraw—"

The knife *thwipped* across the room. Big Ben watched it go, knowing instantly that its trajectory was taking it to a point right between Neville Nolan's eyes, and knowing also that God would forgive Earl for breaking the Ninth Commandment just as surely as He would consign a dead Neville Nolan's soul to the deepest, darkest regions of hell (assuming Neville Nolan *had* a soul).

The knife struck home with a resounding thunk.

Thunk?

People's heads didn't go thunk, did they?

Walls, however, did. The knife stood quivering, embedded a couple of inches into the woodwork behind the wallpaper above the hob. Of Neville Nolan there was not a sign.

Earl gaped at Big Ben, who gaped back at Earl. Big Ben was just about to say something—what, he wasn't sure, but he felt he ought at least move his lips to show that he wasn't dumbfounded—when a low drone filled their ears, and the largest fly either man had ever seen swooped out of nowhere, buzzing over the kitchen table to alight on the draining board, where it nonchalantly began washing its head with its forelegs.

"I don't believe it," said Earl.

"I do," said Big Ben. "Where this Company is concerned, I'll believe anything."

"A fly. He turned himself into a goddamn fly."

"That ain't just a fly, Earl. Look at it."

Earl looked at the creature apparently made of metal and precious stones, diamond and jet and ruby and emerald and opal and a wealth of others.

"Look at its *wings.*"

Not for this fly the veined gossamer of its lesser brethren. Nothing less than paper-thin crystal, refracting the sunlight into prismatic rainbow arcs, would do for *its* aviational apparatus.

So there they were, Big Ben Burden, Earl Evett, and

Neville N. Nolan in fly form, eyeing one another in Janey's kitchen like a trio of itchy-fingered gunslingers, waiting, not wanting to be the first man (or fly) to fire.

Seconds passed.

Ticked by.

One by one.

And were those potatoes bubbling? And was that joint of beef sizzling away in its roasting pan? And was lunch late? And was Janey, locked out of her own kitchen, starting to fret? Why, yes. Yes is the answer to all those questions.

And then the werefly launched himself from the drainboard and bulleted across the table, heading straight for Earl. There was a sound like an ax chopping a log, and Earl turned to Ben, and at first Ben thought Earl had grown a third eye, but then he realized that he could see the pattern of the wallpaper through the hole in Earl's forehead, and then Earl's knees buckled and his face said he knew something was the matter here, he just couldn't quite put his finger on it, and as Earl collapsed Big Ben heard the fly-whine change pitch like a distant car shifting gears, and he glimpsed the glittering winged shape hurtling toward him, and he saw the crimson compound eyes and the flicking, fluttering proboscis, and then a hammer crashed into his head—it *felt* like a hammer. . . .

And on the other side of the door Janey listened to the sound of a second body falling to the floor, crushing cracked crockery beneath it, and she covered her face with her hands and started to scream.

4

Sometime later, Neville N. Nolan took flight from the Burden household, delighted by the successful resolution of another amazing alliterative adventure. His proboscis unfurled and flickered as he flew, tasting tantalizing temptations on the air, and his wings whirred wildly, shining silver in the midday sun. His rubicund eyes flashed ferociously.

His journey was looping and circuitous, the muscid alternative to a beeline. He rode the whim of the winds, diverting toward any interesting smells they blew him. Above the town square, he swerved downward to inspect the still-bloodstained branches of Century Cedar (and what a joyfully named juniper *that* was!), circling three times and inhaling the fine lingering bouquet of Finkelbaum flesh and blood. Then he veered away again, up into the brilliant blue sky.

If a fly can grin, then Neville N. Nolan in fly form was grinning like a death's head.

Twelve

1

"The Merrie Malted," said Jeremiah Rackstraw, and he was there.

"Oh, it's you," said Felcher, and turned back to resume what he had been doing.

Rackstraw doffed the rather fine broad-brimmed hat he had put on just before leaving the Knight house (a split second earlier) and sleeked his dark hair into place. "Don't mind me," he said. "Carry on as if I'm not here."

The instruction was superfluous. Felcher was as absorbed in the task at hand as only a true artist could be. Rackstraw stepped delicately between and over and around the dried puddles of regurgitated ice cream that were spattered all over the floor, an archipelago of red and blue and green and brown islands gradually being colonized by flies. He found himself an unsullied stool a few yards along the counter from Felcher and Old Joe Dolan and sat and observed a craftsman at work.

As if Felcher hadn't humiliated Old Joe sufficiently already, the same used-diaper smell that now was Ike Swivven's constant companion also hovered around the Merrie Malted's obese proprietor. This, coupled with the stench of vomit, made the air in the ice-cream parlor hot, ripe, and rank, where once it had been a haven of peppermint and vanilla and lime coolness even on simmering midsummer afternoons. Old Joe's breaths were coming in a series of ragged spurts interspersed with long silent pauses. A patient dying of lung cancer might breathe like that, or an old, old man slowly forgetting *how* to breathe.

Standing beside the corpulent figure of Old Joe, Felcher held one of his small bottles canted just below the chin of Escardy Gap's sundaemaker extraordinaire to catch a milky white liquid that rolled in fat droplets from his mouth. He was prizing the earliest memories from Old Joe, the ones embedded so deeply in his psyche not even Old Joe was aware of them: nights in his cradle staring up at the road map of hairline cracks in the ceiling; days in his baby carriage; the cold clinging sensation of a wet diaper; crying, yelling, bawling; a brightly colored wooden toy sheep that delighted him; the cooing and gurgling of adult faces looming large and absurdly wrinkled in his field of vision; the warm security of his mother's nipple between his lips as he drank deep of creamy lifestuff; and almost constant enveloping love and kindness. These last lingering recollections Felcher now pricked out of Joe with interrogative needles. (Remember when? . . . What about? . . . And do you recall? . . . And didn't . . . ?) They accumulated on Old Joe's lower lip, balling into great fat pearls that rolled into the waiting bottle when they were full and ripe and ready.

Crude though he was in speech and manner, Felcher had to be admired. Like a master vintner he took the utmost care and professional pride in both the cultivation and consumption of his produce, refusing to be hurried except when, as in the case of Ike Swivven, circumstances demanded it. With his strangely hypnotic voice he coaxed and wheedled the memories out of hiding, be they bitter, be they sweet, delving deeper into the past, further and further into the mind until it was scoured clean of all experience. He gathered whole lives into his bottles, which he wore as a badge of his trade and sometimes sipped from to savor the taste of misery mingled with happiness, joy salted with despair, pain sweetened with ecstasy.

Rackstraw could have watched Felcher at work all day, but there were other demands on his time. "Felcher," he said, softly so as not to break the spell.

Felcher nodded, not taking his eyes off Old Joe.

"Our Angel wishes to see us tonight. Just after sundown, as usual."

Again, Felcher inclined his big head forward.

"Good." Rackstraw put Grampa's hat back on, tipped the brim, and said, "Carnegie Drive," leaving Felcher to his work.

2

Rackstraw appeared smack dab in the middle of Carnegie Drive, exactly halfway along the street, right on the ridge of the dusty cambered hardtop. A glance this way, a glance that, and he had identified Mr. Macready's homestead by its telltale lightning rod, old Father Time with his turquoise scythe shouldered against the deep blue sky. He strolled to the house amiably slowly with his hands in his pockets.

The door was not locked, naturally, so Rackstraw pushed it open and wandered in unannounced. Fizzing, sizzling, crackling sounds led him upstairs to the guest room where he found Buzz abed and a miniature lightning storm darting along the wires of the solenoid suit and playing over the exposed skin of the suit's wearer. The air reeked of scorch and ozone. Buzz was still fast asleep, content as a kitten.

On the floor beside the bed lay a pair of shoes, side by side. They couldn't have been Buzz's—for a start, they were several sizes too large, and more to the point, Buzz still had on his own pair of stout brogues (the soles rubber and the uppers decorated with skillful leather filigree and further adorned with an intricate living webwork of blue sparks). The shoes on the floor were filled to overflowing with ashes. More ashes surrounded them in a neat, crisp circle. It looked like someone in their socks had had an accident with a very large pepper shaker.

Rather than disturb Buzz Beaumont's slumber, Rackstraw

jotted down a note reminding him that the Angel wished to meet them at sundown as usual. He propped the note up against the bedside lamp.

Then he said, "Hannah Marrs's house."

3

In Hannah Marrs's reading room Agnes Destiny was kneeling beside the librarian, who at some point during her terrible ordeal had managed to curl herself up into the fetal position, as if this would somehow ward off the indignities and obscenities and atrocities being committed upon her person. Rackstraw appeared in the doorway behind Agnes. Agnes didn't see him and blithely carried on what she was doing over Hannah's body. Rackstraw stood and watched. Agnes had not a stitch on, unless you counted the wig. Both her arms were working furiously, her hands hidden in front of her. Her body juddered and her spine arched and straightened, arched and straightened. All that could be heard in the book-baffled stillness and shelf-soundproofed silence of the reading room were her quick panting breaths, an occasional moan, and repetitive slick squelching sounds.

Distaste and amusement met on Rackstraw's face, arching an eyebrow, curling a lip and flaring a nostril or two. It occurred to him that to catch someone in the act of masturbation was to witness them at their most naked (whatever their sartorial situation); to see them as they really were: self-absorbed beyond the reach of basic human contact, a pleasure-obsessed machine, as if this was all they ever did, and relentlessly. Thus Rackstraw, disgusted as he was, as propriety told him he ought to be, was also strangely delighted, for to him Agnes Destiny had always been something of a closed book, a confection of skirts and girdles, rouge and pancake, padding and corsetry, capped off by those blind-man's spectacles that made her eyes unreadable and her motivations, consequently, indefinable. Seeing Agnes bereft of spectacles, clothes, and falsetto voice, Rackstraw knew him for what he was: a man so stupendously and superfluously overendowed that he yearned for the clean lines and tucked-away tidiness of femininity, wanting nothing to do with manhood, or manhoods.

With her collection of penises bunched in both hands like a double fistful of cables, Agnes pushed and pulled and unrolled and rolled and finally brought herself to multiple, dewy orgasm over the lifeless body of Hannah Marrs. For half a minute or so Rackstraw was obliged to avert his gaze. The noises were displeasing enough. He drew out his handkerchief again and masked his offended nose.

When it was all over he removed the handkerchief and said, "Well, well, well."

Agnes gave a high-pitched squeak and clutched for the clothes that were strewn all over the floor, gathering them around her waist and lap. She groped for her smoked-glass spectacles which were on the arm of one of the chairs and jammed them onto the bridge of her nose, though not so fast that Rackstraw didn't catch a glimpse of shamed, horrified eyes.

"What *would* your mother have said, Angus?"

"Agnes! Agnes!" screamed the not-blind not-lady, still on her knees and now struggling to get her braless torso into the pleated blouse she had borrowed from Hannah Marrs.

"Apologies, Agnes, but under the circumstances a pardonable error, don't you think? Without your costume, you're quite a different person."

Agnes, grappling with the blouse, huffed. She tried to fit her head through an inappropriate hole and succeeded in ripping a seam. One of her penises snaked out from beneath the loose jumble of clothing around her waist and lolled down onto the floor, glistening whitely and wetly like an albino eel.

"Is the woman dead?" Rackstraw asked.

"I gave her the ride of her life," Agnes snarled, at last triumphing with the blouse.

Rackstraw looked over at the librarian's corpse wrapped in shreds and tatters like a mummy. There was blood, bone, and a twist of bowel. All seemed to his satisfaction. He waited until Agnes had done up a few buttons on the blouse before he spoke again.

"You were right," he said. "She *does* look like your mother." He couldn't resist adding, "Especially now."

"Don't mention my mother ever again, Jeremiah," Agnes hissed, turning her face up to him so that Rackstraw could see himself reflected twice over in the glasses, darkly. "Mention my mother again and I'll turn you inside out."

"It was a slip of the tongue, Agnes."

"Your tongue doesn't slip, Jeremiah. Not unless it means to."

"The occasional pratfall . . ."

"By definition, deliberate."

"I can never fool you, Agnes, can I?"

"You can never fool any of us, Jeremiah, and you're a fool if you believe you can. We tolerate you, but it's never anything more than that. You have your uses."

"As do you, Agnes. As do we all. We can all be useful to one another and at the same time retain our independence. That's what makes us better, that's what raises us above idiots like this." Rackstraw indicated Hannah Marrs but the gesture was sweeping enough to take in the entire town. "You'd have to be blind not to see that."

"Is that a joke?" asked Agnes.

"Of course not. You only *pretend* to be blind, Agnes. I was speaking as one fully sighted man to another."

"Man?"

Rackstraw sighed. "Human being, then."

"You habitually tread on thin ice, Jeremiah. It is not, I would suggest, the best way of ensuring a long and healthy existence."

"Perhaps not, but it *is* much more fun," said Rackstraw. "Now, my dear, I must be off. I only came to see how things were progressing and to remind you that our usual meeting is on for this evening, after sunset. Don't be late."

"I won't be late," said Agnes. "And you don't have to speak to me as if I'm a naughty child."

"You're so right. I mustn't *mother* you."

"*RACKSTRAW!!!*" shrieked Agnes, launching herself across the room in a flurry of falling skirts and flying gingham and bare boyish limbs, but Rackstraw merely said, "The Chisholms' guest house," and wasn't there anymore, and Agnes collided with a bookshelf and brought a flock of novels crashing down onto her bewigged head.

4

"This habit will be the death of you, Mr. Olesqui," said Rackstraw, fanning his face against the thick smoke that filled the Chisholms' living room.

"It's all that makes life worth living," replied the diminutive tobaccophile, "and if it kills me, then at least I will have died in a worthy cause. Eh, Jack?" The pile of gray sludge on the sofa beside him emitted a faint, all but inaudible "Mmm-mmmmmmmm" by way of response.

"Cora-May?" Rackstraw inquired, pointing to a second pile that lay on the floor like a concrete cowpat. Mr. Olesqui nodded, and the pile gave a small agreeable sigh that spoke of contentment and satisfaction beyond imagining, as if it had just unlocked the secret of the universe and was basking in the glory of the discovery.

"Well done, Mr. Olesqui," said Rackstraw. "A task elegantly and efficiently completed."

"Don't patronize me," said the midget, tapping the bowl of his pipe irritably on the heel of his child-sized shoe. "Just because you have a few more inches than I do doesn't make you superior. Only taller. And as we all know, size isn't everything. It's a medical fact that small people are more intelligent. The small person's brain is closer to the ground and the blood doesn't have to struggle so hard against gravity to reach it."

"But then the brain itself is so much smaller."

"Not smaller—more compact. Like a car. It runs faster with less weight to hold it back."

"A specious and, if I may say, solipsistic, metaphor."

"Long words. But again, size isn't everything."

"I beg to differ. The longer the word, the greater its potential. Polysyllables are rife with meaning."

"Nonsense," said Mr. Olesqui. "Longer words are fixed, pinned down by their own weight and size and self-importance. Shorter words are quicker, nimbler. There's less room for manipulation or misinterpretation."

"I could go on like this for hours," said Rackstraw, sounding genuinely aggrieved that duty called him elsewhere. He delivered his message, and Mr. Olesqui replied that he would duly be at the station by dusk although, he pointed out, there was much smoking to be done before then.

"And who are you off to see next?" the little man inquired. "Where will the Traveling Tongue take you?"

"I must say, I'd like to pay a visit to Neville Nolan, but the trouble with him is that you can never tell where he's going to be. So it's Clarence, I suppose."

"Give my regards to the big lug."

"I think you'll find at this precise moment Clarence is a very small lug. Until later, Mr. Olesqui."

"Mr. Rackstraw."

Rackstraw said, "The Evett brothers' grain and feed store," and the smoke rushed to fill the man-shaped space he vacated.

The pile of sludge on the sofa beside Mr. Olesqui said, "Mmmmmmmmmmmmm."

Mr. Olesqui said, "I couldn't agree with you more, Jack," and solemnly refilled his pipe.

5

No one witnessed Rackstraw's arrival at the Evett brothers' grain and feed store except the squirrel crouching on the hood of Earl Evett's Kaiser sedan. The squirrel, bright as a button and perky as a cup of black coffee, blinked twice, hopped down to the ground, and scurried over to Rackstraw's feet, its body and tail undulating sinuously as if the creature was sliding on its belly over a series of invisible bumps. Rackstraw peered down at the little animal and smiled without humor.

"As you really are, Clarence, if you please."

Suddenly the squirrel's shiny little eyes ballooned up to the size of large mushrooms. One tiny paw suddenly became a lobster claw the size of a spade and tentacles began to sprout from the squirrel's body, whipping out in all directions, red and purple and yellow and fleshy and covered in suckers, flailing around like fronds of a windblown willow. Then, as though it had let off a cylinder of compressed air inside itself, the squirrel inflated and inflated and inflated until it was as tall as Rackstraw and twice as wide, its tentacles correspondingly thicker and longer and its lobster claw now joined by another six or more of similar dimensions, all of them clicking and clacking and big enough to snip a man's leg in two. Several dozen sets of teeth appeared in the erstwhile squirrel's skin (which was now the color and texture of chopped liver) and gnashed and chomped a few inches from Rackstraw's face, unleashing gusts of meaty bad breath that would surely have turned an ordinary man bilious green—one more unpleasant stink to add to today's array of vomit and shit and semen. Evil is a malodorous business.

The clawful, lobsterous, tentacular thing that had just now been a fuzzy-furred little squirrel loomed huge over Rackstraw, dwarfing him and doing its best to intimidate him with the formidable array of weapons at its disposal. But Rackstraw's arsenal was altogether mightier. Dictionaries were his ordnance, grammar his cannon, sentences his slings and arrows.

He merely said, "I command you to adopt a more acceptable form, Clarence."

Whoomph.

Suddenly there were two Jeremiah Rackstraws standing in the street at the outskirts of Escardy Gap where a sign welcomed travelers from outside and bade a fond farewell to refugees from within. To look at, the two Rackstraws were identical in every detail except Grampa's hat, which distinguished the real from the ersatz. Only one of them could talk. He examined his doppelgänger and nodded his approval. "I cannot imagine a more acceptable form than that."

Clarence returned an unctuous and decidedly Rackstrawesque smile.

"Now listen carefully, my mutable friend," said the genuine article. He spoke in slow, measured tones so that Clarence would be able to follow. "Has no one gone past?"

Clarence (as Rackstraw) shook his noble head, but then a frown creased his fine patrician brow.

"Someone has?"

Laboriously, Clarence nodded.

"A boy?" Rackstraw held his hand up at chest level.

Clarence shook his Rackstraw head and sucked on his Rackstraw lip. A boy *had* come this way but he hadn't crossed the boundary, and Clarence's orders were only to stop the boy if he crossed the boundary, stop him in such a way that he never crossed anything ever again.

"A man?" Rackstraw's hand came up to just below his own height.

Clarence nodded.

"Fat?" Rackstraw stretched out his arms like a fisherman telling the story about the one that got away.

Clarence shook his head.

"Thin?" Rackstraw brought his palms almost together like a fisherman telling the *truth* about the one that got away.

Clarence indicated that it was somewhere in between.

Rackstraw chose his next question carefully. "Running?"

Clarence beamed from ear to Rackstraw ear.

"Tremaine," Rackstraw muttered. "I trust you let him go."

Clarence nodded, a trifle warily.

"No, don't worry. I told you not to stop anyone from leaving except the boy and the actor."

At once Clarence displayed uninhibited happiness. "Nnnnnkkkk . . . oooooo . . . unnggghhh . . . urrrrrrrr . . . muuuuhhhhh . . . urrrrhhhhh."

"Not at all, Clarence. Thank *you.*" Rackstraw gave Clarence a pat on the head. A blush came to Clarence's cheeks. As he was the spitting image of Rackstraw, the sight was remarkable and not a little disconcerting. The real Rackstraw would never have blushed, not even if there was something to be gained by it.

"Now, I have a little job for you, Clarence. A special errand. One I think you're going to enjoy."

He explained to Clarence what he had to do, and when he was sure the changeling understood, he smiled, and said, "Poacher's Park."

And then there was only one Rackstraw out at the edge of town, hatless in the heat of midday.

6

Blinkless black eyes—rather like Agnes Destiny's spectacles, but more like two jet orbs embedded in the face of a plaster-of-Paris bust—observed Rackstraw's abrupt arrival with an unwavering stare. The Boy was in Poacher's Park, at the scene of yesterday's ballgame (marked by the scuffs and divots torn out of the grass). He was sitting cross-legged in the shade of an elm, humming to himself. He was not wearing his gloves. When the Boy wore his gloves it appeared, and indeed to all intents and purposes it *was*, as if he had a pair of perfectly ordinary, jointed, articulated, dexterous (if a touch sinister) hands. These gloved hands had shaken Harry and Frieda Finkelbaum's hands yesterday as any pair of hands would. They had held a knife and fork to cut and eat his supper last night as any pair of hands would. They had looked and *felt* to Harry and Frieda like any pair of hands. Without his gloves, however . . .

The Boy's arms ended at the wrist, as though neatly severed and cauterized without having been burnt. You could see the two white ovals of bone, packed around with dark meat and a layer of skin. The meat had holes like Swiss cheese where the blood vessels pumped into nothingness. You could see the vein at the base of the wrist fluttering.

But he had no hands. Without the gloves, he had only stumps.

With these stumps he had plucked out the hearts of Harry and Frieda Finkelbaum. With his invisible, intangible fingers he had distributed parts of Tom Finkelbaum all over the oldest tree in Escardy Gap, and in so doing had announced to the citizens of that pleasant burg that their lives of ease and innocence were well and truly over.

"You want?" The Boy inquired languidly, passing one stump over a patch of grass and mowing an arc through it, leaving no clippings behind.

"A moment of your time, if I may," said Rackstraw, removing Grampa's hat once again and clasping it beseechingly over his chest. "I know you must be busy," he added, even though the Boy was clearly doing nothing.

"A moment of my time, yes."

"I don't mean to presume to suggest to imply for even a second that you might have forgotten," Rackstraw oozed, "but a busy young man such as yourself has many things to occupy his mind and so it is possible—highly improbable but possible nonetheless—that you might need reminding about this evening's rendezvous with our Angel. And of course, if you have a prior engagement then your nonattendance will be understood. Your presence will no doubt be sorely missed, but your own obligations must surely take precedence."

The Boy was puzzled by the complexity of Rackstraw's speech and the oleaginous delivery of same, but such was the humility of the man's attitude, like a courtier in the presence of a great king, that the Boy thought he ought to be flattered. So he bestowed an approving glance on Rackstraw and said, "I attend."

"Furthermore, may I say that your handling of the Finkel-baum situation has been exemplary."

"It is good, no?"

"Good? *Good?*" exclaimed Rackstraw. "It was nothing short of inspired!" He neglected to mention that it had also been his idea.

"Thank you, Mr. Rackstraw."

"No, no, thank *you.*"

With further contortions, convolutions, and circumlocutions Rackstraw took his leave of the Boy, who dismissed him with a wave of one truncated arm.

Rackstraw said, "Boundary Hill."

7

The Swivven place waited. What was it waiting for? Ike's return? Some hope of *that.* The house might as well wait for dear departed Emily and Rufus to come back, too. A new occupant, then? The prospect seemed very dim, given that Rackstraw and Company had begun their systematic extermination of the denizens of Escardy Gap and would carry on methodically and relentlessly until not a single member of the populace remained alive. No, all the Swivven place had to look forward to was a life of emptiness, dust, and dreams. (Oh, yes, houses can dream, too.) Up there on Boundary Hill it would stand, a haven of memories, bearing the impressions of happier times like a photographic plate imprinted with the ghost images of laughter and long conversations: Ike and Bob sharing beers and swapping mildly blue jokes, Emily and Alice giggling as they prepared pumpkin pie, little Sandy tugging big dumb old Rufus's ears and big dumb old Rufus, meek as a lamb, just letting her. Good times, family times, loving times, trapped forever in the paneled corridors and the dadoed stairwells and the abandoned oak-floored rooms.

"God, what a place," said Rackstraw with a shudder, and he moved out of the house's shadow, going toward the wire fence that Ike had not been allowed to finish renovating. Here he stood gazing out over the ten-acre field where a couple of dozen cows gently grazed or else lay in the shade of a small copse flapping their ears and tails. This amused him. He was also amused by the vista of desert and sky beyond. What a masterful illusion! He tried to make out the hooks from which the sky was hung. He tried to spot the join where the painted desert met the real. A theatrical backdrop hung around the entire town, from a distance so perfect in execution that not even the keenest eye could have discerned the fakery. Only up close did the illusion fail. It was trompe l'oeil, after all, not true magic.

Things were going well. But of course they were. Rackstraw planned his operations with the precision of a Swiss watchmaker. The world turned, the sun and moon went around and around, and Jeremiah Rackstraw's schemes went well.

He took this moment to relish the sense of achievement, like an artist stepping back from the execution of a painting and seeing that all the correct elements are falling into place and that another masterpiece is soon to be finished.

He derived further satisfaction from the knowledge that he had set aside a little treat for himself, to be enjoyed when the work was done, a *bonne bouche*. He knew of writers who kept a bottle of something nice on hand with which to celebrate the completion of their latest book (and with which to dull that peculiar pang of regret that accompanies the typing of the words "The End"). He was going to go one better than that. His treat *was* a writer.

To be specific, he was going to celebrate by taking Sara Sienkiewicz's virginity. Breaking the seal of her magical perfection and drinking deep of her intoxicating power. Popping her cork and flooding himself with the woman's fizzing imagination. Ah, yes!

He licked his lips in anticipation. It would be a deliciously sordid and sordidly delicious moment, sullying such beauty.

He could hardly wait.

Who to visit next, he wondered.

And then, singing out bright and clear across the rooftops, through the still summer air, came a single peal of a bell.

A summoning. An invitation.

"The chapel," said Rackstraw, with grim delight.

8

The hush that filled the chapel was broken only by the weak echoes of scuffles and gasps that batted back and forth among the rafters. These soon lost impetus and faded. Then there was only Jeremiah Rackstraw's breathing and the faint creak of taut rope, both all but inaudible.

Rackstraw cocked his head until its angle matched that of the Reverend King's. Leaning forward, Rackstraw inhaled the reverend's odor, then, drawing back, he inspected the floor at the reverend's feet. There he found a few spatters of semen that had dribbled out from the inside of the reverend's pants leg and down the uppers of the reverend's shoes to form swirling white hieroglyphs on the dusty boards.

"What a crude sense of symbolism the Creator has, to draw the comparison between sex and death so obviously, so unsubtly," Rackstraw murmured.

The reverend's swollen purple tongue said nothing.

"And what did you think of our little sacrificial lamb, Reverend?" he asked softly. "Is this how it made you feel?"

The reverend's left eye had rolled up in its socket, pointing to the chapel's vaulted roof and the hereafter. The right stared dead ahead.

"And tell me, Reverend, what is it like over there? Is it everything you hoped for? Does it match up to your expectations? Did they greet you with open arms? Did they hand you a harp and fix wings on your back and tell you to pick a cloud, any cloud?" Rackstraw's eyes twinkled hellishly. "Or did they prod your backside with pitchforks and shepherd you straight into the eternal flame?"

No answer.

Rackstraw reached out and popped the protruding purple tongue back into the reverend's mouth and drew the reverend's eyelids down like Venetian blinds to cover the eyes, the real one bloodshot and dull, the glass one bright porcelain white and gleaming. Now the Reverend King appeared not to be dead, but rather sleeping. The bell rope knotted around his neck seemed no more than some ghastly accoutrement, as though he were playing a practical joke on his parishioners, dangling there to scare the living daylights out of them.

"It's a pity," Rackstraw said. "I was rather hoping we would be able to have a little chat about . . . well, about everything. The whys and wherefores of Being. The nature of Good and Evil. The meaning of Life. All the *easy* subjects. But it appears you've taken matters into your own hands, Reverend, exercising your free will just as the Good Lord intended. Perhaps later." He shrugged. "Who else, I wonder, might I share these thoughts with?"

Then he smiled, and said, "The office of Mayor Douglas B. Raymond."

9

By rights, Mayor should have jumped out of his seat with terror when Rackstraw manifested in his office. By rights, Mayor's suit should have been sitting in his chair and Mayor himself should have been squatting at the top of the tallest cabinet in the room, naked but for his ankle socks and BVDs. At the very least, Mayor ought to have yelped and spilled coffee all over the desktop. In fact, all he did was glance up and nod grimly to himself, as if he had been expecting something like this to happen.

And suddenly he was no one. He floundered for a moment in characterlessness. He didn't know what to say or do. It felt like drowning.

And then . . .

Ladies and gentlemen, please give a big hand for the one, the only . . .

(What was that name again? Oh, yes.)

Douglas B. Raymond!

"Afternoon," said Mayor. Warily.

"Good afternoon to you," replied Rackstraw. "May I sit down?"

"Don't see why not."

"Thank you." Rackstraw drew up a chair and eased himself into it. He removed the black hat from his head and laid it neatly on his lap, but not before Mayor spotted the name stenciled into the sweatband in gold lettering: David Knight. Mayor did not comment on the hat, but he felt the fingers of a cold hand creep across his heart.

"Coffee?" he said.

"Don't mind if I do."

"Milk?"

"Please."

"Sugar?"

"No, thank you."

"Whisky?"

A perfunctory wave of the hand, an almost imperceptible blink of the eyes. "I abstain."

Mayor filled two mugs from the percolator, not neglecting to add a tot of the hard stuff to his own, and set Rackstraw's down on the desk before him. As he took a sip, Rackstraw's eyes strayed to a framed poster on the wall behind Mayor's head.

"Curse of the Rat Folk," he said. "That was never distributed, was it? The studios couldn't even persuade the drive-ins to take it."

"I believe it was shown once," said Mayor. "In Wichita," he added.

"You played? . . ."

"Uncle Bill. Not a vital role." He stirred the alcohol into the coffee and then laid the spoon on the polished table. "The rat folk got me in the first reel," he said. "But I gave it my best. It called for a lot of screaming."

"Perhaps it will be rediscovered one of these days. Maybe it will be hailed as a classic. Your career could be reevaluated. You might even be acknowledged as one of the greats."

"I should be so lucky."

"Stranger things have happened. Look at Johnny Weissmuller."

"That talentless muscle-bound meathead!"

"Exactly. Excellent coffee, by the way."

"My pleasure."

"Where does it come from?"

"Wilbur Cohen's, of course. Where else?" Mayor rested his beloved "I Like Ike" mug on the desk. "I have a feeling we ought to be talking about something more important than coffee, Mr. Rackstraw."

"Escardy Gap seems to be very fortunate in that respect, don't you think?" Rackstraw replied, as if Mayor hadn't spoken. "It has plenty of everything you could want and nothing you wouldn't want."

Mayor gave a weary smile. "We like to think we're lucky. Good weather, good people, and always enough on the table to keep a body fed and comfortable."

"Comfortable. Doesn't that imply something else to you?"

"Such as?"

"Complacency. Softness. Stagnation."

"I appreciate that we're not perfect here, if that's what you're driving at, Mr. Rackstraw." Mayor, suddenly finding himself on the defensive, groped for and found a surge of pride. "I appreciate that to outsiders we might, just *might,* seem a tad complacent. But we like it here. We like our lives. And yes, we're content. Is there anything wrong with that?"

"Nothing at all." Rackstraw smiled.

"Then why," said Mayor, spreading his hands flat on the desktop and staring at his fingernails, "why in God's name are you people trying to destroy us?"

Briefly, *very* briefly, Rackstraw considered denying the accusation—deceit being second nature to him (and first and third as well)—but the atmosphere in Mayor's office was one of cards-on-the-table honesty, and besides, there was little to be gained from hiding anything. Not now. There was nothing the old has-been, or indeed anyone, could do to divert the course events had taken. Rackstraw and Company were a flash flood sweeping through the town, washing away everything in their path, purging, ridding. No one could achieve anything by standing in the way except the hastening of their own deaths.

So Rackstraw settled back in his chair and brought his hands together, tenting his fingers, feeling better now, more confident, more relaxed. He was the calm and collected Spencer Tracy to Mayor's bumblingly righteous Frederick March; the cool and calculating Edward G. Robinson to Mayor's indecisive and vulnerable Fred MacMurray.

Mayor had asked why they were trying to destroy Escardy Gap. Now Rackstraw answered him. And he told him the truth.

"Because we must. Because that's all we do. Because that's all we ever do."

The words hit Mayor's face like bird excrement spattering into a bowl of vanilla ice cream.

"Because," Rackstraw went on, "when we see Goodness and Wholesomeness and Innocence and Integrity we know we have to stamp them out. Because we are the people of the shadows. Because we are the cynics who lurk in the dark corners, muttering doubts. Because our smiles are unsmiling, our laughs are unlovely, and our eyes never gleam with anything but malice. Because we are dead people in living clothes, dead hearts in heaving chests, dead souls in breathing bodies. Because we are walking contradictions, incarnate perversities, dying lives, living deaths. Because we are the insects of society, cold and inimical and unknowable, the locusts, the yellowjackets, the scorpions, the fire ants, the praying mantises, the black widows, the cockroaches, the tsetse flies—we are all these, and more. Because we eat, we frighten, we bite, we sting, we kill, without compunction. Because we are impervious, impenetrable, deadly, and you cannot argue with us and you cannot plead with us and you cannot compete with us. And because we hold true to only one thing: our own natures."

Mayor felt a distinct reduction in the room temperature

and looked out of the window, half expecting to see the sun dimmed by a cloud. The sun burned on over Escardy Gap.

"I see," he said.

"I think you do." It was Rackstraw's turn to look out of the window. The street was deserted, but he knew it belied the frantic activities taking place up those little paths, behind those little painted doors, inside those little wooden homes. He smiled. It was going so well.

"But why us? What have we done wrong?"

" 'Wrong' is a qualitative term, Douglas. It is your term, not mine. It suggests a *re*action to an action. A punishment in response to a crime. I may call you Douglas, by the way?"

Mayor shrugged. "I suppose."

"And as I said yesterday, you must call me Jeremiah. Understand this, Douglas. You aren't special. Escardy Gap isn't the first or the last place we will ever visit. There are as many Escardy Gaps as there are motes of dust in the universe. When our time here is up, we'll take our leave and move on to the next town down the line."

"Jackson Vale?"

"I'm not necessarily speaking geographically." Rackstraw gave a brief, sly smile. "We do what we do. It's as simple as that." With the thumb of his left hand he began to rotate his clown-face ring around his fourth finger, around and around and around, its gold setting glinting in the Saturday afternoon sun.

Mayor watched the clown face appear and disappear a few times, orbiting the finger like some gaudy moon, and then shook his head and blinked hard.

"That's what I don't understand. What *is* it that you do?"

A smile. Jeremiah Rackstraw in control. "I thought you'd have got it by now, Douglas. What we do is destroy. And what *you* do is be destroyed. That's how it is. That's how it's always been. 'As it was in the beginning, is now and ever shall be. World without end.' " He stopped rotating the ring.

"Amen," Mayor murmured automatically. He sensed he should be appalled at himself for compounding Rackstraw's blasphemy, but for some reason he was not.

"You see, this isn't *Our Town* anymore, Mayor. This isn't some naive Thornton Wilder fantasy. This is *my* town, and I will do with it as I please." Rackstraw's laugh was tight and merciless.

Mayor deliberated for a moment, then said, "Is there no way I can convince you people to leave Escardy Gap alone, Jeremiah?"

"Absolutely none."

"Money?"

"Do I look as if I need money?"

"Food?"

"Do I look hungry?"

"Not for food, you don't. How about an appeal to your better nature?"

Rackstraw shook his head wearily. "My colleagues and I have only one kind of nature, and 'better' isn't the relevant comparative adjective."

"But, for God's sake, we've done nothing to deserve this!"

"And if you had, we wouldn't be interested in you. The very fact of your guiltlessness condemns you. Does the cow deserve to be turned into beef? Of course not. Nor does it stand there fretting about its fate. It carries on grazing, breathing, being, dumb but happy, until the time comes and the dinner table beckons."

"Well, what hope does that give us?"

"None whatsoever."

"No get-out? No escape clause?"

"Not in this contract."

"But that's just so goddamn . . . *unreasonable!*"

"Precisely. Were there a reason, it would make our job ten times harder, not to mention ten times less enjoyable."

"At least you admit you take pleasure in this."

"Perhaps pleasure isn't the correct word. 'Job satisfaction' I think encapsulates it. There's nothing wrong with taking delight in the only thing you do. It would be rather sad if there was. What if the shark hated eating? What if the politician loathed power? What if the writer suddenly threw away his pen and declared he couldn't stand books?"

"So, argument fails," said Mayor. "What's to stop me leaping across this desk and throttling the life out of you with my bare hands?" He was trying to sound brave, but without John Wayne's drawl or Jimmy Cagney's slur to back him up, with only Douglas B. Raymond's cracked, somewhat slightly frail voice, it wasn't easy.

"Three things," said Rackstraw. "First, I doubt you'd have the courage. Second, killing me wouldn't divert my colleagues from their labors one inch. And the third and perhaps the most practical consideration is that before you got to within a yard of me, your entrails would be dangling from the ceiling like Christmas streamers."

"Heh." Mayor laughed in spite of himself. "Well, you can't blame a man for asking."

"I would have been surprised if you hadn't. Basically you're not a weak man, Douglas, just a man without conviction in himself. A common complaint among actors, I'm told. They're only as good as the part they're playing, and between parts, waiting for the script writer to come along and put words into their mouths, they're ciphers—inadequate in themselves, and unable and unwilling to take responsibility for others."

"Not like you, I suppose," said Mayor with as much sarcasm as he dared.

"Me? I'm all script. I freely admit it. There's nothing beneath." Rackstraw hit his chest with both hands, the hollow thump echoing through Mayor's office like a hammer on a vault door. "I'm as thin as letters on paper. I'll exist for as long as there are lines on the page, just as you'll exist until the stage directions say 'Exit Mayor'—which, I may add, is only a few short scenes away. Sad, isn't it, don't you think? Fulfilling roles and having no idea why we're playing them, other than because we have no choice. This, of course, is the main drawback in the possession of an intellect: the misguided belief that we have any say in what we do."

"At least we have the ability to believe."

"Oh, do tell me the use of that. I'd be delighted to know."

"Well . . . It means we can look for some kind of plan."

"Some kind of divine plan?"

"Yes."

"Ah. Ha ha. Excuse me. Ha. Oh, Douglas, don't be so ridiculously shallow. Faith is such a minuscule, empty thing. A tiny whisper in a huge and echoing vault." He finished his coffee and held out his cup above the floor. "Have faith,

Mayor, that God will prevent this cup from smashing, that He will show you a sign and reward your goodness. And if the cup does smash, then believe, why don't you, that it was His will, that it was some tiny imponderable part of a greater scheme that the cup be dashed, smashed, and crashed. And then do that with every cup, and with every breakage believe, *dear* Douglas, that it does not prove there is *not* a God, but merely that this God likes broken crockery. And"— Rackstraw lowered his voice, eyes darting left and right—"on that single inexplicable occasion when the cup bounces and rolls unhurt, then sing out, 'Lord! Hosanna to You in the highest! You have saved my cup! You have *not* forsaken me!' " The last few shouted words reverberated around the room on something that, to the increasingly apprehensive Escardy Gap town official, seemed for all the world like a wind, cold and mean, aloof and sarcastic and spiked with more than the simple promise of harsh weather.

And the cup fell.

It fell through the void betwixt hand and floor slowly, dreamily slowly. And both men watched it descend, the one white haired, the other black hatted, the one pinning upon the fate of a discarded cup all the hopes, dreams, and beliefs of a right-on-the-side-of-good, and the other set to prove the perverse and obtuse credo that was the staple element of his own existence.

And, lo . . .

. . : the cup bounced, turning over and over on itself, a small pirouetting cartwheel, end upon end, lip upon handle upon base, to bounce again, and then once more, meeting its shadow before rolling and spinning on its tiny axis to a clattering, echoing stop.

Mayor looked at Rackstraw.

Rackstraw looked at Mayor.

"Plastic," Mayor said.

And he smiled.

Mayor would never have believed that such a thing as black light could exist, but there it was, in two balls of burning ebony glow, one in each of Jeremiah Rackstraw's eyes.

"Your God . . ." Rackstraw seemed to be finding it difficult to speak. "Your God is rewarded by a trick. You knew the cup would not break." A clear fluid seeped from the corners of his mouth, and bubbling noises came from somewhere out of sight.

"I had faith," said Mayor calmly.

Perhaps the sound was a laugh. "You only *think* you have faith, Douglas, because that's what it says in the character outline. 'Mayor is a God-fearing soul, a devout man of Baptist extraction.' Father Mendacious in *The Priest and the Parrot*—he didn't have faith. Uncle Bill in *Curse of the Rat Folk*—he didn't have faith, or if he did, he wasn't on-screen long enough for it to be of any importance. You have so immersed yourself in this part, little man, that you've begun to lose sight of who you really are: an insignificant blemish by the name of Douglas B. Random."

"Raymond," Mayor corrected him, firmly enough.

"Yes. Silly me."

"Well, Mr. Rackstraw, you've made your position pretty clear. All I can say is, don't expect us just to roll over and die. We'll put up a fight. You can count on that."

"Oh, I am counting on it, I am."

"There's fire in these people's bellies. You just keep stoking it and you see if you don't get burned."

"I'd expect no less. Although I have to say, soft living hardly breeds great soldiers, does it?"

"Maybe not, but we'll surely do our best to defend our own. Families, friends, and homes are all that have any meaning here. Threaten those and you just see how we respond."

"I look forward to it."

"We'll go down guns blazing."

"I have other things to attend to," said Rackstraw with a bored yawn. "More important things. And you"—he gestured at Mayor (as if there were anyone else in the room he could have been talking about)—"you will have to wait. Showdown isn't until tomorrow. The first act is almost finished. The curtain will go down with the sun and rise, after the interval, at dawn tomorrow." He stood up. "We probably won't meet again, not on these terms, so it's best we say our good-byes now. Many thanks for the coffee." He held out a hand.

Mayor shook his head and kept his hands firmly beneath the desk. He recalled his first encounter with Rackstraw yesterday and the bogus reciprocal warmth of their greeting. This parting called for none of that. This parting was solemn and sober and forthright, two men who could never under any circumstances be friends showing a kind of fractured respect for one another but at the same time, like boxers just before the bell rings for the first round, signaling that from now on it was every man for himself.

"As you wish," came the reply and a curt nod of Rackstraw's head. "I, or one of my colleagues, will return for you. I suggest you be ready." He made to walk away and then, catching sight of the discarded cup, turned back. "Oh, one more thing," he said. "Please bear in mind, it's nothing personal."

"God forbid it should be," replied Mayor.

Rackstraw smiled, turned, and, in a single fluid motion, lifted his foot and brought it back down, grinding the cup into a pile of powder. Then, in a voice that had a strange echoing quality to it, as though it had to be summoned up from a deep cavern, he said, "The station," and disappeared, leaving Mayor with the afterimage of his naked, tooth-baring grin hovering in the air, like the Cheshire Cat.

Mayor looked down at the telephone perching on the corner of his desk, its black Bakelite gleaming dully, digits peering out from the holes in its chrome-plated dial, its black cord connecting here to the outside world.

It was time to call for help.

Thirteen

1

Things might fall apart, the center might not hold, but one thing you could always count on in Escardy Gap was Sunday lunch.

Come hell or high water, those checked tablecloths would be spread out and all manner of culinary delights would grace the dining rooms of the sun-washed houses up and down Muldavey Street, Carmichael Avenue, and Carnegie Drive, or sit steaming on weathered trestles erected in the shade of oaks and cottonwoods in a hundred or more backyards a stone's throw away from Main Street.

It was truly an immovable feast. And despite all that was happening in their once-tranquil burg, the townsfolk still went about preparing huge plates of hams and yams, dishes of glistening creamed onions, trays of immaculately sliced meatloaf, deep dishes of chicken pie and large pots of potatoes. There was much to be discussed. There was news to share and rumor to spread. But this was not allowed to hamper the important business of eating.

Walt Donaldson would have been looking forward to just such a meal, prepared with consummate skill by his landlady, the homely Miss Ingrid Ohllson. Walt would have been all but drooling at the thought of a plateload of makkarat sausages followed by a healthy helping of her Karjalanpaisti hotpot (even though he couldn't get his tongue around the name, he sure liked to get his teeth into the reality), and then some blini pancakes, washed down with a glass or three of Miss Ohllson's home-pressed lemonade. Walt would have been rubbing his swelling midriff at the prospect of all this . . . had Sara Sienkiewicz not gone and ruined his appetite.

When Walt had returned home from Doc Wheeler's, where he had been kindly but firmly assured he couldn't be of any further help, the last thing on his mind had been eating. He had headed straight upstairs, offering Miss Ohllson only the most cursory of greetings.

"Walter? Walter? You are wanting some lunch? It will be on the table in just a few minutes."

Walt had paused halfway across the landing and rested a hand gently on the rail. "Oh. Not for me, thank you, Miss Ohllson."

A deep crease had appeared across the schoolmistress's forehead, and her bushy brows had crouched down over her eyes. "Walter, are you still not well?" She had never known a hangover to affect Walt's appetite before. Something else must be wrong.

"Uh, yeah, that's right," Walt had said. "Not well." And he had disappeared into his room, and Ingrid Ohllson had stood there watching the (large) space Walt had just occupied, and then returned to her kitchen and stirred the Karjalanpaisti, glumly thinking, *Walter is upset, and whatever upsets Walter upsets me.*

Walt had divested himself of his fancy jacket and constricting necktie and pinching shoes and lowered himself down onto his bed. Arms behind his head, he had stared up at the cracks in the ceiling, tracing their erratic paths over and over again. They ran in nearly straight lines, roughly parallel, almost but not quite touching. Not even the delicious smells drifting up from downstairs could convince Walt there was any point in moving from here.

Now, an hour later, there came a knock at the front door.

Walt heard Miss Ohllson down below mutter something in her native tongue. He heard her cross the kitchen floor and go out into the hallway, tsking and tutting to herself ("On a Sunday, too!"). He heard her open the front door. It had to be one of her friends. All of *his* friends knew better than to visit him here, with the Scandinavian Cerberus guarding the gates, ready to bite off the head of anyone trying to enter her kingdom who didn't belong there.

He waited for the mutual caws of two women greeting.

They didn't come.

Instead, Miss Ohllson said something Walt didn't catch, although he recognized the tone of the words all right enough. Frosty formality. Then he heard her heels clacking across the hallway.

"Walter!" she called up. "Someone to see you. Walter? Are you awake? He is not at all well, you know," she said to the visitor. "It may be better if you come back another time. Walter?"

"Yeah?" said Walt wearily.

"You have a guest here."

"Send 'em up," Walt said. "Please."

"Wouldn't you like to come down instead?"

"I don't think I'm really up to it." He wasn't about to go downstairs just to see Clem or Big Ben or whoever.

"Please go up, then," said Miss Ohllson to the visitor.

There was a pause. Miss Ohllson muttered, "Well, and I am pleased to see you, too!" Then she said something else, another thing Walt didn't catch. A soft cry, perhaps. A gasp of outraged decency. The visitor must be Clem. Miss Ohllson had probably just caught wind of him.

Somebody, Walt thought, closed a door rather too hard. And it seemed an awfully long time before he heard footsteps coming up the stairs and a light, polite knock at his bedroom door.

"Come in. It's not locked."

The door opened.

After some moments of lying there on the bed, gaping like a goldfish, Walt finally managed to utter his visitor's name: "Miss Sara!" And then: "Golly, aren't you? . . . I mean, weren't you? . . . I mean, how are? . . . I mean . . . Come in! Please! Come right in!"

Escardy Gap's famous lady author and the object of Walt's adoration, that paragon of pulchritude Miss Sara Sienkiewicz, passed graciously and gracefully through the doorway to Walt's humble living quarters, moving straight to the chaise longue and seating herself, smoothing down her skirt and then smiling up at Walt prettily.

A single exclamatory sentence flashed through Walt's head, repeating itself over and over, each time with fresh emphasis:

She *has come to see me!*
She has *come to see me!*
She has come to see *me!*
She has come to see me!

Finally Walt came to his senses, and offered up a brief prayer of thanks to the god of modesty that he hadn't removed any more of his clothing than jacket, tie, and shoes. He scrambled over the side of the bed, thrust his feet into his shoes, and struggled to fit them in. As he fumbled with the laces he thought the shoes felt oddly constricting, as though his feet had grown several sizes in the past hour. He stood up. Boy, they were squeezing! It was only then that he realized he had put the shoes on the wrong feet. But it was too late to do anything about this, not without looking like a *complete* idiot.

He turned to his guest. Sara had clearly made a full recovery from her collapse, and it was on this that he first commented. "I guess you must be feeling better."

Sara did not reply, and so the remark hovered between them for half a minute and then dropped to the floor like a swatted fly.

"Well," said Walt, "anyway, it's a relief to see you up and about. You gave us quite a fright, you know."

Again, Sara didn't favor Walt with a reply, although she continued to smile sweetly and benignly at him, which to Walt spoke volumes. No denying it, that Doc Wheeler was a miracle worker. Walt looked down again, feeling suddenly self-conscious. Nervous. Weak in the presence of such beauty.

"Can I get you something to drink?" he asked, remembering his manners but forgetting that he had nothing of his own to offer her. Fortunately, Sara declined with a gentle shake of her head. "To eat?" Again, Sara declined.

"Well, it sure is an honor to see you, to have you come and visit, I mean, for you to drop by like this when you can't be feeling your best, it's a . . . I'm privileged. Sorry the place is such a mess, well, it's not a mess, but if I'd known you were coming I'd have done something about the mess, not that it's *that* messy. . . ."

Aware that he was gibbering, Walt took a firm grip on himself. He was an important man around town. He should say something nice to her.

"I liked your story." Yes! A compliment! That was good. Women loved compliments. "The one in the latest *Weird Tales*. 'The Plane Tree's Plaint.' Read it yesterday. Didn't get to finish it, but what I did read was great. Of course." He tittered like a silly girl. "Because everything you write is great."

Sara seemed to agree, although a tiny pucker of bemusement besmirched her otherwise flawless forehead.

"Are you comfortable enough? Can I get you a cushion or a pillow maybe?"

She didn't say yes, she didn't say no, so Walt tottered over to the other chair in the room and grabbed a flattened cushion that had wedged itself down between the seat and the back, flipping it over quickly to hide a coffee stain. He plumped the cushion into life, then plopped it back down on the chair, forgetting why he had picked it up in the first place.

Sara Sienkiewicz was staring at him. Her head had swiveled around and she was watching him intently, trying to divine some meaning to his actions, trying to fathom if this rotund, pink-cheeked man was anything more than the hapless clown he gave every impression of being.

Then she grunted.

It seemed that the grunt came right up from her shoes. It was like a concrete slab being dragged across a stone floor, long and rasping, a sound of strength and weight.

On her neck, a lump appeared.

"I guess Doc felt you should get out, huh?" Walt said.

The lump moved. Or something *inside* the lump moved.

"Well," said Walt hoarsely, "I'm glad he did. Glad *you* did."

He watched the lump deflate, disappear. "You know, from the way Doc was going on, I thought you were, you know, *real* ill. Dying. Ha ha."

Then the lump was back, larger. It moved around her lily white neck, then disappeared again.

The aftereffects of aneurysm were many and strange, Walt decided, wishing he had paid closer attention to Nurse Sprocket's explanation of the condition. Had odd grunts and moving goiters fallen under the nurse's inventory of symptoms?

"But then I've got too much imagination, that's what my pa used to tell me," Walt went on. "Too much imagination for my own good. You'd know all about that, of course, wouldn't you, Miss Sara? 'Cept you don't have too much for your own good. You've got just enough, just the right amount of . . ."

Sara straightened her head. One of her eyes was tightly closed. It looked almost sunken.

"So, what *has* happened to your voice?"

Sara shook her head.

"Lost it?"

She sort of nodded.

"Shame."

Then it occurred to him. Her lost voice presented him with a golden opportunity, a chance to say what he had been longing to say to her, a chance to reveal what he had been yearning to reveal to her—without fear of interruption or contradiction or, God help him, rejection. And *she* had come to visit *him,* remember. She must have had a purpose. She must be expecting him to say or do *something*.

And so . . .

"Miss Sara," Walt began, and then his mouth dried up and he was left stranded.

Sara Sienkiewicz arched her eyebrow in a quizzical fashion. Walt took this as a cue to continue.

"Miss Sara," he began again, more forcefully this time. He was still watching her neck, watching for the lump to reappear. He couldn't concentrate. His eyes scanned that soft swanlike swoop of skin for the spasming goiter to show itself.

Frustrated, Walt turned and paced up and down the length of the room until he felt he had restored calm to the turmoil within him. (His feet, imprisoned in the wrong shoes, sang out in protest.) He plucked up the courage to face Sara again. As he did so, he noticed a peculiarity about her hands, which had been clenched tightly on her lap. The hands were slowly coming apart. Her fingers were growing, thickening out like sausage balloons. Then they returned to their usual slender size (the size that held pencils delicately in order to shape the words that transported Walt to worlds of wonder).

Her brow and forehead were moist, beaded with tiny droplets of perspiration, a rash of finely sprayed water. Immediately, Walt felt guilty. There she was, recently arisen from her sickbed, and here he was, subjecting her to this outpouring of emotion, this passionate tirade of feelings. . . . Well, as a matter of fact, he had yet to make his true feelings known, but he was sure he was communicating with her, the way people truly in love can talk to one another without a word actually passing between them (or so Walt had heard).

"Miss Sara," he said, and because he wasn't trying to say anything crucially important he was able to continue, "are you all right?" He knelt before her, and saw her pull her head back in surprise as he lowered his voice to the most attentive of whispers. "Do you think you should be up? I mean, oughtn't you to be resting? I'm not trying to get rid of you or anything, but, well, Doc seemed to think it was pretty serious, what you had. Maybe you should lie down." At the thought of Sara lying on a bed, desire surged through his body. "You . . . you could even use my bed, if you wanted," he added, the words scrawking off his dehydrated tongue.

He stood up to give her room, to make her feel less pressured. His shoes were killing him now. He reckoned at least three of his toes were turning black.

From this vantage point, his gaze dropped involuntarily to Sara's bosom, to the magical spot where material gave way to the soft pliancy of smooth skin. But it wasn't there. There was a point, of course, where the colors changed, from the gray-blue of a fine cotton blouse to the peachy pale white of Sara's neck and clavicle. But even without touching it, even without reaching out and allowing his coarse hand to trail across the snowy slopes of that fabulous domain, Walt Donaldson could see there was no *tactile* change between body and clothing.

With immaculate elegance Sara lifted herself from the chaise longue and walked toward Walt. The certainty that she was coming to kiss him overwhelmed Walt with both fierce sensuality and morbid terror. He took a few flustered steps backward, his inverted shoes taking him in the wrong direction so that he bumped against an ornament table, which toppled sideways, spilling a hubcap ashtray and a jar of mustard—strange bedfellows if ever there were any—onto the carpet.

"Oh . . ." said Walt. Miss Ohllson would not be happy. He considered bending over to right the table, but then Sara was standing directly in front of him. The tip of her nose was almost touching his.

"Miss Sar—" But before Walt could say any more, Sara Sienkiewicz spoke.

"Nnnnnnhhhh . . . uvvvvvv . . . oooooo . . . orrrrrt . . . onnnhhhhh . . . unnnnnnh . . . ssssssnnnnnn."

The voice was neither soft nor feminine. It was a far cry from the bell-like trilling that could so enchant and allure Walt even when all it was saying was "Good morning" or "A return to Jackson Vale, please." It was a monstrous distortion of a voice, mangling language into protracted nonsense syllables, gargling on words as if they were broken glass. Issuing from the sleek throat and the sensuous lips of Sara Sienkiewicz, it was as shocking to Walt as if it had been a gush of steaming vomit.

This wasn't Sara.

He knew that, and he had known it all along, but he had just been too startled and too stupid to accept the evidence of his senses.

But if it was not Sara . . . *what was it?*

Walt watched, appalled, as the woman he had adored from afar for years began to change before his very eyes.

Her flesh writhed. Great blisters, similar to the lump he had glimpsed earlier, distended her features. Her eyeballs bloomed to the size of lightbulbs, bulging from their sockets. Her silken hair vanished, to be replaced by bald scalp that boiled and bubbled like molten lava.

The clothes had gone. Vanished. They had folded in on themselves, to be replaced by that which lay on the other side, the *in*side. It looked like fresh liver. Tentacles lashed this way and that. The body swelled to more and more grotesque proportions until it no longer displayed any trace of the shapely form Walt had only ever dreamed of caressing.

It grew tall, and taller, and taller still, looming up above Walt, towering over him, peering down with her huge eyes and opening and closing a vast misshapen mouth in which teeth poked out at irregular intervals and crooked angles, like tombstones in a neglected cemetery. And the smell! All the rot and reeking putrefaction in the world heaped together in a fetid, steaming pile surely could not smell as bad.

The noise that accompanied these changes was a veritable symphony of pops and cracks, squelches and twangs, some dull and low, some sharp and falsetto.

Walt's head drained of all thought. There was nothing in his world except the sheer spectacle of the transformation in front of him. Escape seemed a remote notion, something beamed down from another planet. He was vaguely aware of the existence of a door, somewhere in this universe. It didn't seem to matter.

When he did at last move, he moved like a frightened animal, whimpering, shivering. He groped his way along the wall, but the thing that had once resembled Sara Sienkiewicz advanced, kept pace with him, uttering more of its guttural nonsense.

Walt reached the corner of the room, where a big bay window looked out over Miss Ohllson's garden. The backs of his knees struck the lip of the seat, and he collapsed backward. Into the window. Through the window.

If the picket fence had not been directly beneath Walt when he fell in a shower of glass shards, flailing his arms, he might have survived the ten-foot drop, well padded as he was. He might well have bounced and rolled and fetched up, bruised but alive, in one of his landlady's flower beds.

But the picket fence was there, and broke his fall, and broke him. Three of its stout wooden stakes penetrated his back, forcing themselves in between his ribs, thrusting up through fat and muscle, one of them passing through his heart and spiking the left ventricle.

In the penultimate minute of his life, Walt gazed up at the sky above Escardy Gap and saw that it was serene and aquamarine and beautiful. Then, as his vision began to fade, he lowered his gaze from the sky to the house.

From the blue to the gray of shingles.

From the roof to the smashed frame of his window, through which he dimly made out the shambling hulk of the thing roaming his room, wrecking, rending, furious.

He knew why it was furious. He had stolen its moment. By falling through the window he had ruined the finale to its act.

He would have laughed, had it not been too painful.

Then he heard Miss Ohllson's voice, and the final minute of his life began.

By craning his head upward and looking over the hillock of his belly, gritting his teeth so hard that two bicuspids split in half, he saw her. "Walter," she was saying, lifting the word up at the end so that it sounded like a question. There was no energy in her voice, no spirit, no strength.

Ingrid Ohllson was hanging inside a first-floor window, suspended by a floral valance that usually covered the curtain rod, but now drooped lazily, wrapped around Miss Ohllson's chest and neck and looped beneath her arms. She was unable to move any part of her body except her shoulders. All the other bones were shattered. She hung limply, a twisted wreck of woman.

It was as though Walt were looking through a misted-up pane of glass that had suddenly been cleared by a cool breeze, to reveal the truth.

"Ingrid!" he said, and a fine spray of blood flecked his lips.

She smiled. Despite her agony, she managed to smile.

In the window above her something large and monstrous stopped what it was doing, paused from its senseless destruction. It turned to face the window, then shambled nearer, out of the shadows, to peer through the shattered casement, poking one eyeball on the end of bright red stalk that dangled from its head.

Walt wanted to tell Miss Ohllson that he was sorry, he never realized, he was sorry, oh, so sorry. What emerged from his mouth instead was a sigh, a hiss of air and life departing, leaving on a long journey with a one-way ticket and bags packed full of hope.

Miss Ohllson watched Walt's head loll back onto the grass. Then she rolled her eyeballs to follow the sound of the thing upstairs that was not the Sienkiewicz woman as it moved quickly across the floor above, heading for the stairs.

Miss Ohllson looked back at Walt. "Wait for me, Walter," she said softly.

2

Quincy Hogan opened the doors of the Essoldo Motion Picture Palace at three o'clock precisely. There was a larger crowd than usual queuing outside, a couple of dozen at least. The thin ranks of the Sunday-afternoon diehards (loners, like Quincy himself) had been swelled by the presence of several members of the Company, all of whom made it clear—some by sign language—that they were carrying no money on them and expected to be allowed to enter without paying. Quincy initially objected, but then he remembered Jeremiah Rackstraw claiming how poverty-stricken he and his colleagues were, and he remembered how Jack Chisholm had been so ready with his offer of free board and lodging on the station platform yesterday afternoon, and so he relented and let the strangers in for nothing. He grumbled, but he let them in for nothing. He reckoned you could take hospitality too far, but he let them in for nothing.

Quincy was one of the few people in Escardy Gap who had still not heard about the events at Century Cedar. This was because he had spent most of the morning asleep in bed, and had eaten a hearty lunch on his own, cooked by himself for himself—the habits of a single man happy in his solitude.

At a quarter past three, Quincy shut the till drawer on his takings, closed up the ticket booth, and headed inside to run the coming-attractions reel and advertise the refreshments that could be bought from the kiosk. Luckily, none of the members of the Company wanted refreshment. Quincy would have definitely drawn the line at handing out free sodas and popcorn.

It struck him as odd that the Company had decided not to sit in a bunch, all pals together, but instead had spaced themselves evenly throughout the auditorium, each with at least three seats between them and the nearest neighbor. All that traveling cooped up in that train, Quincy supposed, and he recalled Jeremiah Rackstraw saying to Mayor, "How quickly we tire of our own company. . . ."

At three-twenty, Quincy started *Freaks*.

While the film ran, Quincy stationed himself in a collapsible director's chair in the corner of the stuffy projection booth. He inhaled the familiar dense smells of hot machinery, film stock, Wynn's friction-proofing oil and his own Palmolive aftershave lotion. Wafting in from the auditorium came a variety of fainter scents: the Pine Sol he used every other day to clean the seat backs and the narrow stage; the warm and welcoming nasal throb of brushed-velour seat coverings; several years of crushed Jolly Time popcorn, melted candies and spilled sodas; the slick and greasy hum of Wildroot hair tonic and Brylcreem; sweaty armpits and cheap perfume and high-tar cigarettes and the faint tang of discarded pheromones that lingered around the back three rows. Breathing in this delicious multiplicity of odors was, to Quincy, like luxuriating in a hot bath. He settled back and let the smells wash over him in invisible waves.

The reel of memory unspooled.

Quincy's earliest recollections were of his father, G. W. Hogan, operating the projector, way back when the Essoldo Motion Picture Palace was known as the Essoldo Picture Hall. Crouching in the darkness of this very room, he used to watch his father run quick, expert fingers over the machinery to keep the reels running as smoothly as possible, clucking over the tiniest hitch or slip of the throat sprockets. Even then, Quincy knew that he never wanted to do anything else when he grew up except follow in his father's footsteps.

In those days, the main attraction at the Essoldo had been not so much the movies as the nightly appearance of Quincy's older sister Abby, a fine-looking girl with long braided strawberry blond hair and a smile that could charm a hog out of a hollow. Abby played the piano accompaniment to the silent films that G. W. screened while Betty, his wife, Quincy's and Abby's mother, took the money: a dime for a place on a bench seat, plus a nickel for a blanket or a fan, depending on whether it was winter or summer. Betty also came around with freshly made popcorn, lemonade, and coffee in the intervals.

Abby was not a strong girl. Unbeknownst to anyone, she had been born with a heart defect, and one night she just slumped over her piano keyboard midmelody, played an almighty crashing last chord with her forehead, and passed away. It was a Wednesday, and the evening's bill comprised a Chaplin short and *The Kinsmen,* with Henry Edwards, Chrissie White, James Carew, and John McAndrew. In the audience was the young town doctor, a heavyset fellow with salt-and-pepper sideburns who looked like he would be more at home logging trees in Maine than tending the sick in the middle of nowhere. He did all he could for Abby, which was not a lot, and the performance ended prematurely with the girl being removed from the auditorium by three strong men with a jacket over her face. The rest of the main feature was not shown.

It was the first death that Dr. Victor William Wheeler, then twenty-eight, had encountered in Escardy Gap, and he cried his own tears when they carried Abby Hogan out into the street, followed by her sobbing mother.

Later that night, after Doc Wheeler had sedated Betty Hogan, G. W. sneaked back into the Essoldo and ran *The Kinsmen* to an empty house. Up to that point he had not shed so much as one tear, and he never shed one afterward. But during that showing he let out a flood of grief. And sixteen-year-old Quincy, huddled down between the seats over by the Muldavey Street exit light, watched both performances, the one on the screen and the one in the seats, with a heavy heart.

The Essoldo was closed for business the following day, then opened again the day after that as though nothing had happened. From then on, right through to the end of the silent era, there was never any music at the Essoldo. Movies were shown with nothing but the chatter of the projector and the audience's stifled coughs and mutters for accompaniment. Izzy Cohen came and took back the piano, which G. W. had been paying for in monthly installments. Izzy even gave G. W. three crisp ten-dollar bills, which he was not legally or contractually obliged to do, but he knew the Hogans had little spare cash for burials and suchlike.

There was another change in the way the Essoldo was run,

one so slight you would have to have been a particularly acute observer of human nature to spot it; but if you did spot it, you'd wonder how you ever could have missed it.

Neither G. W. nor his wife ever smiled again. Not to their customers. Not to their friends. Not to anyone. Not even to each other.

So the remainder of Quincy Hogan's upbringing was a somber affair. It wasn't that his parents felt no love for him. It was just that they no longer felt they could show it. G. W. had been hurt once, and that was once too many. When Betty Hogan died of bronchitis during a particularly bad winter when the snow had covered the ground from mid-October until the first thaws of spring the following March, G. W. and Quincy ran the Essoldo together without so much as a word passed between them—at least not one that anybody could vouch for.

The movies became G. W.'s life. He ordered books and magazines from Izzy's store—which was increasingly being run by Izzy's eldest son, Wilbur—and spent the time when he was not running the projector sitting up in his booth leafing through page after page of news and gossip from Hollywood.

With the dawning of the decade, the movie industry reached its golden age. In 1950 the Essoldo ran no fewer than two hundred and eleven different movies. The last film that G. W. screened was *Captain Blood, Fugitive*. He died in his sleep later that night, aged seventy-three. Quincy didn't miss a performance. The heart of the Essoldo didn't skip a beat.

When they buried G. W. Hogan in the graveyard 'round back of the church in the town square, the new vicar, the Reverend John King, performed the ceremony, the first ever funeral he had officiated over. Quincy himself gave a short speech at the end.

"This is for everyone who has ever had a dream," he said. "But more than that, it is for anyone who has ever let their dreams grow so big that there is no place for anything else. Particularly, it is for a foolish old man too scared to love; for a woman too scared to grieve; and for a girl whose heart was just too big and too frail. Amen."

That afternoon, one of those impossibly beautiful fall afternoons that only seem to happen once in a lifetime, making the rest seem pale imitations, Quincy Hogan broke down and cried for the father he had lost and for the love that he had never been given. And that night, at a special showing of an Abbott and Costello double feature, the new full-time resident projectionist/owner of the Essoldo Motion Picture Palace drank in the sound of laughter as he had never done before. It was a sound of life and of caring and of belonging.

And around the back of the Essoldo Motion Picture Palace, a thick muddle of unraveled film could be found hanging limply from one of the bent and beveled trashcans into which Quincy Hogan usually jammed rolled posters and armfuls of lobby cards, all lovingly tinted and textured in all the technicolors of cinematography. That film was *Captain Blood, Fugitive.*

(Over the years, deep in those same aluminum treasure troves, Alan Ladd rubbed diminutive shoulders with the wiry Douglas Fairbanks, Myrna Loy with Loretta Young, Laurel and Hardy with Huntz Hall and Leo Gorsey.)

The year that G. W. Hogan picked to bow out was also the year of great innovations in the movie business. Fox's *The Robe* was the first CinemaScope release and, before he showed it, Quincy Hogan spent $1,685.75 having the Essoldo's screen widened. It was a timely investment, because it meant he could also show the new 3-D releases.

Three-D lasted a year and then it was finished, over, a faded fad. RKO's *Cattle Queen of Montana* and UA's *Vera Cruz* introduced SuperScope, which then gave way to Todd-AO, in the shape of *Oklahoma*. Economic necessity forced seat prices up to fifty cents but Quincy's projector still played to packed houses every day. Which was just as well. Central heating and air-conditioning had set him back a small fortune, especially the Trane Unit Ventilator System, with its "exclusive Kinetic Barrier action," and he needed a full auditorium in order to recoup the expense. Which he did, as they say, in spades. By the time *Around the World In Eighty Days, Carousel,* and *The King and I* were playing in Escardy Gap, Quincy Hogan was a rich man. This meant that he could afford to become a little eclectic, and he decided that for every "big" picture he showed at the Essoldo, there would be a dozen "small" ones. He decided that these would be run on

Sunday afternoons, because experience had taught him that after church and Sunday lunch most people were too stuffed to move and just about the last thing on their minds was a trip to the cinema. So at the end of a week of *South Pacific,* for instance, he showed *Terror in a Texas Town* coupled with *My Gun Is Quick.* At the end of a week of Elia Kazan's *A Face in the Crowd: The Halliday Brand* with *Hell Island.* After *Tennessee's Partner: Machine-Gun Kelly* with *Baby Face Nelson.* After Sam Goldwyn's *Porgy and Bess: High School Confidential* with *Untamed Youth.* After *No Time for Sergeants: Rock All Night* with *The Cool and the Crazy.* After *The Vikings: Hot Car Girl* with *Motorcycle Gang.*

One noteworthy Sunday saw the first appearance of a swivel-hipped singer (of sorts) going by the name of Elvis Presley in *Jailhouse Rock.* Quincy, now in his forty-eighth year, didn't think much of that rock and roll music, but the kids just lapped it up.

It was by this means, and by a judicious sprinkling of the worthy old among the spanking brand-new, that Quincy kept packing them in. Adults would turn out in their droves for the occasional George Raft movie, the odd Humphrey Bogart, and the once-in-a-while Audie Murphy/Randolph Scott double bill, and the kids were all in favor of George Reeves, bulging alarmingly beneath his skintight costume, Fess Parker and his coonskin cap, and Michael Landon complete with hairy face, foaming mouth, and baseball jacket.

Now, that was an important factor in the Essoldo's longevity and continuing appeal right there: monster movies.

The patrons of the Essoldo were already familiar with the creature features put out by Universal over the previous three decades. Ever since *Frankenstein* and *Dracula,* the theater had rocked to the delighted screams of mouths filled with popcorn and Dr. Pepper. But things had moved on from those days. The old scaremongers with bolts in their necks and capes on their backs had been replaced with tinglers, mole men, alligator people, and an entomologist's paradise of giant insects. Then *those* had become passé. There were new creatures to be scared of, new nightmares to prowl the dark and the shadows. There were Ymirs and Xenomorphs and star creatures and crab monsters and pod people, Its and Thems and beasts from beneath the sea, from outer space, and even from beyond space—they had attempted to conquer or destroy mankind (and had failed or been foiled in the last few moments of the final reel). There had been silent invaders, invisible invaders, and invaders from Mars, teenagers from outer space and space children, saucermen and flying saucers, Klaatu and Gort, and planets angry, forbidden, and red—and the Essoldo had shown them all.

Considering this, Quincy in his director's chair allowed himself a small smile. He loved movies, period. Even if they were as dumb as a beaver chewing a telegraph pole, he loved them, and he loved the fact that other people loved them, too. Not that anyone who was even remotely acquainted with Quincy would have realized this, because Quincy had spent his life cultivating the appearance of constant moroseness. It was something he had learned from his father. He showed movies, but not emotions.

Freaks rolled on smoothly until it reached the part where the human skeleton and the bearded lady have a child. Then the projector stopped whirring and the big screen went blank.

Quincy leapt to his feet and checked the projector cord, bending down to tap the wall socket. Everything seemed to be okay there. He inspected the indicators on the covered panel of the projector housing. Again, okay. Then he unfastened the clasp on the input spool. No problem there. Output pulley? Fine. Maybe he had threaded the film incorrectly. If he had it would be a first, but then there was a first time for everything. He switched off the power supply on the housing and unbuckled the tension brace. The output reel obliged by going slack.

He had prepared himself for foot stamping and catcalling from the auditorium, and was surprised when it did not come. The strangers who made up most of the audience obviously understood that a fault in the system was nobody's fault. Quincy began to feel a little more kindly disposed toward the Company. They might be freeloaders but they were at least *polite* freeloaders. Mind you, people who were getting something for nothing were really in no position to complain.

As Quincy was winding the input spool backward, spinning it with his left hand while holding the output spool tightly with his right, the silence in the auditorium began to prey upon his mind. It was all very well that nobody was complaining, but surely some of the regulars must have felt moved to turn to their neighbors and remark on this unusual event: a hitch in the projection, the first such hitch, in fact, since *The Kinsmen* all those years ago, when Abby Hogan had collapsed over her keyboard.

Quincy stood up from the projector and walked to the window.

The house lights were way down but he could make out the backs of the seats, row upon row of them ranked down toward the screen. He leaned closer to the window, careful to breathe through his nose so that the glass would not mist up.

Now that was queer. Whereas before the audience had been composed of single, separate heads, now it seemed to be made up almost entirely of couples, with the occasional threesome.

Getting friendly, thought Quincy, uneasily.

And still not a sound from down there. Not a hint of a breath of a whisper of a conversation.

Then arms came up, all at once, as if on cue, as if a dozen nervous would-be lovers had decided simultaneously to dare to embrace the would-be beloved in the next seat. Hands glowed luminously in the subdued light like giant moths.

Getting real *friendly,* thought Quincy, his unease shifting toward alarm.

And the arms came down, descending casually onto shoulders and necks and heads in a graceful, vicious parody of teenage romance.

Quincy could do nothing but watch. Even if he had wanted to do something, he wouldn't have been able to. He wouldn't have had time. It all happened too fast. One moment there was absolute silence, the next the auditorium resounded to a series of hideously loud cracks, as though a firing squad had loosed off a volley of pistol shots at their target.

Quincy saw heads loll on rubbery necks, nuzzling against neighbors' shoulders. Dread settled in his belly, heavy as a medicine ball. He was dimly aware of a low whine coming from his mouth. He stumbled back from the window and clutched the metal edge of the projector table for support.

The noises he then heard from the auditorium reminded him of nothing so much as a roomful of diners snacking on heaped-high plates of oysters. Slurps, slobbers, lip smacks, and the occasional creak and snap of something being prized apart. Quincy, in his tiny projection booth, listened to this feast and to the blood thumping in his ears, and he prayed that they would forget about him; that the Company would finish what they were doing to the other moviegoers and leave by the clearly marked exits and forget anyone called Quincy Hogan had ever existed.

But then there were footsteps at the bottom of the stairs leading up to the projection booth and Quincy knew he was out of luck.

There was no lock on the door, not even a bolt. G. W. Hogan had always maintained that there should be as few barriers as possible between the projectionist and the audience. The projectionist, he had told Quincy with unsmiling severity, should never lose sight of the fact that he is just a moviegoer who happens to be in charge of threading the reels through the machine. G. W. had sounded just like a preacher then, one of the humbler, more honest variety who insist there is no difference between themselves and ordinary people in the eyes of God.

Quincy threw a panicked glance at that unlocked door, and then at the steel table on which the projector rested. Without a further thought he bent down, braced his shoulder against the table's edge, and *shoved.*

Nothing happened. The table didn't budge.

Quincy shoved again with all his might, and there was a high-pitched squeal from the table's feet. The projector rocked on its base for a moment. Quincy felt a brief surge of triumph. A few more pushes and the door would be solidly blockaded and he would be safe. Trapped inside, yes, but safe. And once he was safe, he could figure out what to do, how to get out. . . .

There was a light tap at the door.

"Mr. Ho-o-oga-a-an," someone said in a merry, singsong voice.

"No!" cried Quincy breathlessly. "Not here!"

"Oh, Mr. Hogan, *really.*"

"There's no one in here!"

"Please, we just want to know what's happened to the film. We were so enjoying it. Can you tell us what's gone wrong?"

As Quincy desperately cast about for some kind of weapon, a detail from the many vampire movies he had screened flashed into his head. "Don't come in," he said. "I refuse to let you in. You may *not* enter freely and of your own will."

"How very quaint, Mr. Hogan. How very charming." The door handle was tried, and the door inched out from its frame. A hand came through the gap. It was caked in dark liquid, and a smell of dew and iron filings crept into the projection booth, overpowering all others.

"Get out!" Quincy yelled. "You're not allowed in here!" He picked up an empty reel can and hurled it at the bloody hand, missing by a good yard. "Leave me alone! I want to be alone!"

"You vont to be a lawn," mimicked the voice in a bad German accent.

"Go away!" Quincy yelled. He was beginning to weep now, hot tears of shame and terror. "I haven't done anything to you. What have I done? Tell me! What?"

There were more footsteps on the stairs.

And the voice said, "Absolutely nothing."

3

The last thing the Essoldo screened in its forty-year history was perhaps the most unusual feature ever committed to celluloid. It was long, silent and monochrome, a study in scarlet, with only one actor and no discernible direction. Even the most eclectic or pretentious of critics would have been hard-pressed to claim a shred of artistic merit for the production, unless they were prepared to describe it as an exercise in meaninglessness and futility.

Such audience as there was loved every minute of the movie. They loved the differing shades of red that flickered across the silver screen. They bathed in the ruddy glow that lit up their faces and shone reflected in their gleaming eyes and off their blood-smeared skin. They clapped and clamored and craved for more, more, more.

Up in the projection booth, deeply gratified by the appreciation of the audience, a member of Jeremiah Rackstraw's Company giggled as he fed Quincy Hogan through the projector of the Essoldo Motion Picture Palace, inch by bloody ribboning inch.

4

Honey, you're home!"

Alice Tremaine rushed down the hallway to greet her errant husband, Bob, and smother him in kisses and shower him with questions.

"Are you all right? Where have you been? Whatever did you think you were up to, running off like that? Oh, Bob, it's so good to have you back. Sandy! Sandy, Daddy's home! Oh, my sweet Lord, look at the state you're in, Bob! How did you get those scratches? You've ruined your shirt. Have you been in a fight? Sit down and let me fetch you some coffee. Sandy! Oh, I was so worried. We both were. It was all so sudden. Never mind, never mind. Come through. Sandy!"

Young, pretty Sandy Tremaine appeared at the top of the stairs, took one look at the reunion below and flew down in a flurry to meet her father and encircle his waist with her arms and lay her face against his chest. Tears were glistening in both her and her mother's eyes. It was a moment of tenderness and gladness and joy for all.

Except Bob. He patted Sandy's head and he returned his wife's kisses with all the affection he could muster, which wasn't much. He succumbed stiffly to their embraces and let their hands crawl over him, shuddering inwardly at their touch as though their fingers were the hairy legs of tarantulas. He allowed himself to be led through to the living room and seated with all pomp and ceremony in his personal armchair, and as Alice went to the kitchen to make the coffee he fondled the hair of his daughter, who had curled up on his lap. God, it sure as hell felt the way her hair usually felt. It sure as hell slipped through his fingers like spun gold, like fairy gossamer, like silk. She sure as hell *smelled* the way Sandy did, that sweet little-girl musk of milk and sweat and freshly laundered clothes. Oh, God, it was almost possible to believe this really was his family, and not the pair of Russian impersonators he knew them to be.

He buried his nose in Sandy's hair and his heart was cold.

Alice returned with the coffee. "Would you like some lunch, honey? I'm afraid it's been sitting around in the kitchen for a while. . . ."

"No. No thank you. I'm kinda exhausted."

"So I should think, charging around in this heat like that. Like you were ten years old again! Really!"

"Daddy," lisped little Sandy, "I'm glad you're back. I love you."

Bob regarded his daughter carefully. He looked straight into her deep blue eyes, eyes that were full of nothing but trust and adoration.

"I love you, too, darling," he said, his stomach turning.

Fourteen

1

One of the women who were known to the Company as the Man-eaters, the brunette, started up the incline, moving unerringly toward the spot where Josh had crouched and wished he was elsewhere. The redhead and the blond were close behind. The brunette sank to her knees beside the clump of bushes and lowered her nose to the ground where Josh's buttocks had imprinted two neat dimples. She smelled boy-sweat and boy-fear and a three-hour-old fart. The collected odors of a *boy* who had the nerve to consider himself a man when a nosy, bratty little *boy* was all he really was. The women giggled. Their teeth chitter-clacked. Down on the track, the locomotive with its attendant carriages sat and ticked to itself in the heat of the day. And then—ha! The brunette caught sight of the apple core. She snatched it up. She showed it to her sort-of sisters. All three cackled and clacked with glee. Boy-teeth had gnawed through the red skin and the pale soft flesh, nibbling through to the seeds in their shiny cases. Boy-saliva speckled the ridges of the bites where the white had rotted to brown. Boy-fingerprints marked the base and the stalk of the apple.

The blond gave a triumphant yelp. There! There! She gesticulated. Look! A shoe print! And there, another! And another! And a dozen others! Right, then left. Right, then left. Their edges soft. Soil scattered. The ghosts of running feet. Frightened boy. Terrified boy. And what had he seen? How much had he seen? The Man-eaters didn't need any further prompting. Whatever the boy had seen, it was too much.

The women ran. With their heads of hair rippling out behind them, they ran, bent double with their noses near the ground like hounds on the scent. Leaping, loping, sometimes going down on all fours, they followed the spoor along the top of the embankment to the path that led past the Evett brothers' grain and feed store and out into the deserted street. The hood of Earl's Kaiser sedan clicked loudly, ticking off seconds of sunshine.

The redhead pointed along Delacy Street, and the others agreed with her wordlessly (unless the chitter-clack of unseen teeth spelled out a kind of Morse code that only these three could understand). They came together, joined hands, and walked down the street as one, not hurrying now, sensing that their quarry had gone to earth and would not move from his hole until they disturbed him. No urgency. There was plenty of time.

The streets were empty. The whole town was empty. The wind whistled through hollow windows and slammed screen doors: Bang, *bang*. Bang, *bang*. The houses were shabbier than good homes had any right to be. Paint flaked away from picket fences. Rust had formed on guttering. Weeds were staking their claim on once-impeccable front gardens. Who would have thought that a whole town could so rapidly go to seed? The only movement, the only sign of life: the three women. They passed into the town square, tracing the route Josh had taken in his panicked headlong flight from the station. Century Cedar looked as it had always done, a proud guardian, head held high, branches raised in salute and welcome. The shades were up in the Merrie Malted. Inside was all chrome-and-marble cleanliness, but fresh cobwebs hung in the corners and busy spiders were already working their way down to the counter and stools. A shutter had come loose on the town hall and was slapping open and shut with peculiar insistence, as though counting.

The three Man-eaters, still hand in hand in hand, turned up Muldavey Street. How horrible the elegance, how savage the unearthly loveliness of these three huntresses moving in for the kill. Lissome limbs, clinging dresses—could a Christian God ever have created these beauties? Surely they were every *man's* dream of untamed pagan womanhood made flesh. And what flesh!

Soon they were outside the Knight house, pausing where Josh had paused to recapture his breath. Here drips of his sweat had made minute craters in the dust, spelling out the name of Josh over and over to the women's hyperkeen senses. Josh relieved. Josh daring to believe he was safe. Josh looking forward to seeing his grandfather again. Josh wondering how he was going to explain to his grandfather what he had seen, what he wished he had never seen. Josh longing to ask the old man what they were going to do.

He had gone up the steps. The women went up the steps. He had gone inside. The women went inside. He had called out *"Grampa!"* The women said nothing, only chitter-clacked the teeth in their nether mouths. He had called out, more tentatively, *"Grampa?"* The women said nothing, still chitter-clacked the teeth in their nether mouths. He had even called Rackstraw's name, hesitantly. The women still said nothing, but the teeth in their nether mouths chitter-clacked a little harder. He had headed for the stairs and shouted up, *"Grampa? Grampa?"* The women gathered at the foot of the stairs. He had scented, *sensed* something not quite right here. The women breathed deep of sweet corruption, sugary decay. He had yawned. The women grinned horribly.

They knew that the *boy* was upstairs. The *boy* was lying fast asleep in his bed. Exhausted by his fear, by all the awful and incomprehensible things that had piled on top of one another yesterday and today, drained and weary, he had tottered upstairs to bed, barely managing to pull off his jacket, pants, and shoes before crawling beneath the counterpane, closing his eyes, and leaping into Slumberland like Little Nemo. Upstairs he lay. Victim. Prey.

One after the other the Man-eaters made their way up the staircase, leading themselves by their noses.

Blond: the color of corn ripe to be scythed.

Brunette: the color of a chestnut tree ready for the ax.

Redhead: the color of a swollen blood-orange begging to be sucked dry.

At the door to Josh's room each of the women raised a hand, the fingers crooked into claws. One tapped, then another tapped, then the third tapped. Again: a tap, another tap, a third tap. And again: tap, tap, tap. Tap, tap, tap. Tap, tap, tap. Flowing seamlessly. Tap after tap after tap. Evenly. Tap, tap, tap. Regular as clockwork.

Tap, *tap,* tap . . .

Tap, tap, *tap* . . .

2

Josh sprang awake, dislodging the several copies of *Tales from the Crypt, Vault of Evil,* and *Haunt of Fear* that had formed an irregular four-color patchwork quilt on top of his bedspread. He barely noticed as he sent that unholy trinity of Crypt-Keeper, Vault-Keeper, and Old Witch slithering and sliding to a messy end on the floor. His eyes were riveted on the door to his bedroom. His whole being was focused on that door, and on what lay beyond. He listened intently. He had forgotten what sound it was he was supposed to be listening out for until he heard it, sure and steady and unmistakable.

Tap, *tap,* tap . . .

Tap, tap, *tap* . . .

No, not tap, *tap.*

Something else.

Tick, tock.

Tick, tock.

Tick, tock.

The clock.

Just a dream.

But try telling *that* to a body that was as supercharged as a dynamo, its tendons wire taut and the blood breaking world speed records through its veins. There's no such thing as *just* a dream, not where the dreamer is concerned. While he is asleep the dream is everything—world, experience, truth.

And when he wakes the dream is still there, especially if, as in Josh's case, it is a particularly realistic and unpleasant dream.

So three hands crooked like claws were still tapping on his bedroom door, although the taps had shifted pitch and timbre and now sounded remarkably similar to the ticking and tocking of that awful leering clock which Josh had secured, or *believed* he had secured, beneath that laundry bundle of shirts, socks, and rags last night to muffle the noise and (more importantly) hide the face. The very bundle he could see from here. It was on his desk. It was still doing its stuff.

Wasn't it?

Because he could *hear* that darn ticking and tocking, large as life, loud as day. He could hear it even though the clock had that extraordinary habit of falling silent when it was out of sight. (Out of sight, out of mind, Grampa liked to say, usually with reference to his nasal hair or a plate of food he was about to clear.) In fact, thinking about it, he had heard it as he was falling asleep a few hours ago; he had been too tired to realize what was wrong with that.

Tick, tock.

There.

Cautiously (and Josh didn't know *why* he should be cautious, but he was. Still tired, he guessed. *And* still scared.) he swung one leg out of bed and then the other. He was mildly surprised to discover he was wearing his socks *and* his underpants *and* his very best shirt. He must have been tired, all right. Bushwhacked.

He drew himself upright. Slowly. Quietly.

Tick, tock.

First things first. Josh padded over to the door and clasped the handle . . .

. . . and didn't turn it. Who could begrudge him an attack of nerves? The three women, so vivid in both his dream and his memory, *could* have been waiting behind; *could* have smelled him coming; *could* have been standing there in deadly silence.

For some reason he remembered the Greek musician guy Miss Ohllson had told the class about, Orpheus, who got himself ripped to shreds by a crazy bunch of ladies called maenads because he stumbled onto one of their orgies. Some of the backsliders in class had thought this story was tops and had suddenly shown a renewed (if brief) interest in Ancient Mythology and Classical Civilization, until the lure of gazing out of the window or at Sandy Tremaine's pigtails had led them back into their bad old ways. Josh, of course, had felt profoundly sorry for Orpheus. The guy had had a big talent and it was a waste of a life. Wasn't that often the way? And no one deserved to get pulled to pieces, not even by crazy ladies.

And those three crazy ladies at the train had crazy Greek names. Were they by any chance related to the Bacchanals? Direct descendants, even? Josh was of the considered opinion that they were. And he, like Orpheus, had unwittingly observed one of their secret rituals. . . .

Well, there was no point dithering. If he was going to be shredded limb from limb, better to get it over and done with.

He whisked the door open.

No one.

Of course.

Just a dream.

Tick, tock.

"All right!" said Josh, turning to face the bundle on the desk with a determined set of jaw and eyes blazing like brush fire. Gift or no gift, he had had just about as much as he could take of Rackstraw's clock. *Just what he'd always wanted*—huh! All Josh wanted right now was the clock out of his life. Likewise, Rackstraw. And the three women. And all the Company. And the train itself (ugly iron monstrosity). He wanted the world back to normal. He wanted Grampa in the house, now, where he could see him and know he was safe and well. He wanted the past twenty-four hours to be a dream. He was ready to wake up now, ready to wake up, ready for Grampa to come in and wrestle the blankets off his bed: "Move that butt, soldier! In a hurry, Murray! Look alive, Clive!"

Framed in the window the sky was still bright, but Josh could tell that the best of the day was done. The sun was shining with less enthusiasm, as if exhausted. Josh wondered what time it was.

Tick, tock.

He would find out in a moment. And then he would pick up the telltale timepiece and hurl it out of the window, like the man who wanted to see time fly. He would watch it spin and tumble all the way down, that grinning loon face with its brass-bell Mickey Mouse ears, until it hit the street and shattered in a sparkle of cog, coil, and spring. And he would cheer. Boy, would he cheer!

As warily as he had opened the box containing the clock yesterday, Josh began to peel away the layers of cloth in which he had rewrapped it. He knew almost right away that the clock wasn't inside. The bundle fell apart. Like the crust of tatters encasing an ancient, crumbled mummy, it unfurled flat on the desktop. Empty.

Josh stared for a moment in disbelief. Disbelief jumped the central reservation and became fear. Fear propelled Josh around to face the room.

Tick, tock.

It could have been coming from anywhere. Each deep sonorous tick, each stalwart pursuing tock. Anywhere. Underneath the bed. Inside the closet. Behind the wardrobe. From any one of the shelves where books slumped against loose-leafed piles of comics. From the cavern in the Neverseen Era . . .

Yes.

Tick . . .

Because there was a slight echo.

Tock . . .

As though the sounds had to bounce once before they could emerge.

Josh didn't need to ask who had moved the clock. He vaguely wanted to know *why,* what purpose this action could possibly serve. But he didn't care that much. Within ten seconds, ten more ticks, ten more tocks, the question would be academic, and the answers would be strewn all over the street, spilled cogs like so many brass snowflakes. He stalked over to that wondrous work of history-defying prehistoric art, the product of dozens of eye-straining, back-breaking hours of gluing, painting, and crafting. His world, a world where everything was exactly as he wished it to be, perfect, just so.

He stopped at the edge. He gazed down.

Within the cavern where several tiny plastic families were supposed to dwell he caught a glimpse of brass, a cartoon eye, the corner of a dumb grinning clown mouth.

Tick, tock.

He knelt down and laid one hand on a barren patch of green sawdust grass, between a stegosaurus and a squat, armadillo-like anklyosaurus, spreading his fingers out so that there would be less danger of breaking through the fragile papier-mâché and chicken-wire shell braced over the wooden armature. He leaned forward, reaching for the cavern with his other arm.

Tiiick, tooock.

It seemed to take an awfully long time for his hand to travel over two yards of prehistoric landscape, almost as if those two yards really were the two miles they were intended to represent.

Tiiiiick, tooooock.

An awfully long time, indeed. Though Josh kept stretching and stretching, the cavern didn't seem to be coming within his grasp.

Tiiiiiiick, toooooooock.

What was this? Was there something wrong with the clock? From the sound of it, it appeared to be winding down. Well, good. Because then he would feel less guilty about destroying it. *It stopped working, Mr. Rackstraw, and since there's no key . . .*

Tiiiiiiiick . . .

Still not quite within his grasp, although his fingers had just entered the cavern.

Tooooooooock . . .

Almost there. Almost made it.

BBBBBBBBBBBBBBBBBBBBBBBBBBBBBBBBBBBBB
BBBBBBBBBBBBRRRRRRRRRRRRRRRRRRRRRRRR-
RRRRRRRRRRRRRRRRRRRRRRRRRRRRIIIIIIIIIIIIIIIIIIIIII-
IIIIIIIIIIIIIIIIIIIIIIIIIIIIIIIIIIIIIIIIIIIIIIIIIIIIIIIIIIIIIIIIIIIINN
NNNNNNNNNNNNNNNNNNNNNNNNNNNNNNNNNNNN
NNGGGGGGGGGGGGGGGGGGGGGGGGGGGGGGGGGG
GGGG!!!!!

The force of the ring, the sheer weight of decibels, hurled Josh backward, clean across the room, to land flat-bang-slam against the closet door. The noise didn't simply deafen him. It dazzled him. It thumped like a mallet blow against his sternum. His insides felt as if they had been mushed to jelly. Winded, his lungs groped for breath. The effect couldn't have been more devastating if someone had detonated a stick of dynamite, a concussion grenade, and a magnesium flare all at once in the confines of young Joshua Knight's bedroom.

Stunned, Josh rode the sickening aftershocks, helpless as a yacht in a typhoon. Walls and ceiling and floor played musical chairs, 'round and 'round and 'round, suddenly stopping, then 'round and 'round again. Objects came into focus—the bedstead, the desk, the bedside lamp—only to slip out again, blurring, doubling. His ears registered an appalling silence, as if too damaged ever to hear anything again, like a blown radio speaker. He tried to speak, but whether he said something and couldn't hear it or he couldn't work his voice box, it didn't make much difference. He had to all intents and purposes been struck dumb.

Gradually the world settled back on its axis and resumed its usual rate of spin. The silence howled on. From where he sat, silent and helpless, Josh had a clear and uninterrupted view into the scale-model cavern. He could see the whole face of the clock. The clock, likewise, could see all of him. Its comical mouth said so. Its laughing-lunatic eyes *knew* so. There was a vengeful tilt to its wavy eyebrows. Its expression was a clear manifestation of intent: *You thought* that *was bad, buster? Wait'll you get a load of* this. . . .

The hands stood at a quarter after four. Josh had no reason to believe that this wasn't the correct time. Then the minute hand started to move. Slowly at first, clocking up the five-minute segments as a second hand might, with the hour hand moving obediently after (but never managing to catch up—such is the hour-hand's lot). The light from the window began to dim. The clock said eight. Abruptly it was night. The clock carried on, the hands gathering speed. Blessed with luminosity, they stood out boldly bright in the darkness. There was no way Josh could not see them hurry past midnight and into the wee small hours. By the time dawn broke—and it was really that sudden, it really *broke*—the hour hand was traveling as fast as any second hand. And getting faster. The minute hand was a mad whirl. The sun beamed brightly through the window, and then it was past lunchtime and the light lost its harshness and paled. Then it was dusk again. The clock whirled on.

Josh couldn't do anything but sit and watch. A whole day had passed, and he had just sat there with his back propped against the closet door. He marveled idly at this. His brain shrugged a mental *So what?* Deep down and distant inside him a little voice told him he ought to be afraid, because this, this thing that was happening, was not natural. Not natural at all. But bell-shocked Josh was too dazed to care.

Night fell like a black velvet blind suddenly unrolled in front of the window. Then it was day again.

That made it Tuesday, didn't it? Sure as heck still felt like Sunday.

The hands spun faster and faster. Day dimmed—*whap!* Night again. Day again. The hands were a blur, a white veil suspended over the clock's clown face. Night again. Two luminous concentric circles, the larger superimposed on the smaller. Day. Veil. Night. Circles. And so on. And so on. Light. Dark. Light. Dark. Hypnotically. A strobe flicker. His room. Nothing. His room. Nothing. Wild shadows streaking from left to right. Pitch blackness. The wild shadows again, retracing yesterday's paths. Pitch blackness once more. And so on. And so on. And on. And on.

Josh began to feel weird. Disoriented by the stop-go flash of days passing impossibly fast, certainly, but the weird feeling went deeper than that. Weird inside. Weird in his bones. His shirt had started to constrict his chest, and looking down at his legs he saw that they had sprouted hairs. The hairs were growing quickly and thickly, hastening out of their follicles like toothpaste squirts from a host of tubes. Pretty soon his legs were covered in an even pubic mat, and his knees were nobblier than he remembered. Something else was taking place down there. The pouch of his underpants was swollen, stuffed with unfamiliar baggage.

Day became night became day.

Josh brought one oddly hirsute hand up to prod the new acquisition at his crotch. Definitely flesh, definitely part of him. Lord, his stub of a penis had grown as fat as a plump tuber.

"Well done, boy," he felt like saying. "At last!" And no doubt, had he been able to speak or hear himself speak, his voice would have rumbled out bassily broken.

Day, night, day.

Ping! A button flew from his shirtfront, and *ping! ping!* There went two more. A manly chest peered through the strained opening, replete with curly hairs. Josh lifted a hand to his chin, and sure enough, a beard had appeared there, thicker (to his touch) than Big Ben Burden's, and horribly itchy. How did Mr. Burden put up with the itching all the time? How, for that matter, could *Mrs.* Burden bear to bring her soft womanly lips to kiss this scratchy mat?

Day, night, day.

His insides were not as they used to be. They felt harder and tighter, almost as if callused by constant use and abuse. He was alarmed to see his belly swell and *ping!* the remaining buttons from the front of his shirt. He had kind of hoped he would never develop a belly. So many men of a certain age in Escardy Gap seemed to carry a basketball strapped around their waists, but Josh had always believed it wouldn't happen to him. It had.

Time flickered by. Weeks were seconds. Years were minutes.

Getting old, Josh, he told himself. *Sitting here and your life is flashing by.*

Getting old—just what he'd always wanted.

How come Rackstraw had known that?

Josh's legs were spindly white sticks now, spotted with moles and tiny inexplicable red spots. A tracery of large veins loomed up beneath the skin. The backs of his hands—well, what was a few liver spots between friends? And the raised coarsened knuckles were sort of appealing, in a lived-in kind of way.

Getting old.

The racing clock. The on-off days.

Strange pains were afflicting him: sharp little darts up and down his shins, sudden twinges in and around his heart, and an ache in his hands that settled in to become a deep-rooted throb. He opened his mouth to moan, and without warning a hail shower of teeth rattled out, collecting in his lap. The hairs on his legs turned white, as though someone had stroked a brushload of whitewash over them.

Getting *real* old. Exactly how old was he going to get? He felt almost the same age as Grampa. He was beginning to feel *ancient*. When was it going to stop?

And then he realized that it wasn't going to stop, or rather that it was only going to stop at the inevitable conclusion, at the red light at which every life braked. He was hurtling a thousand times too fast toward death. The clock was hastening him on his way. He had to stop it. He had to kill the clock before it killed him.

Time's wingèd chariot was racing so swiftly that the interchange between night and day had blurred into one long twilight gray. Josh didn't know how much time he had left but he didn't think it was a lot. He had a whole room to cross in this recalcitrant, protesting almost-corpse of a body. It looked like a mile to the cavern, across a plain of carpet. And he would have to crawl every inch of the way.

With a supreme effort of will Josh forced himself to move. Limbs creaked like rusty doors and shrieked in arthritic anger, in rheumatic rage. It would have been easier to bend iron bars than draw in those bony legs, but Josh gritted his few remaining teeth and grunted against the agony. He flopped forward in an approximation of a crouch. His hands and his knees contained red-hot coals that found a new way to flare every time he thought they were about to cool. Like this he shuffled two, maybe three feet, before collapsing in agony. No use. He wasn't going to make it. The clock was just too damn far away. He would be dead before he got there.

No! That was precisely what Rackstraw intended. And Josh wasn't going to give him the satisfaction—that cuckoo, that stealer of places at tables, that word bender and trust twister and abuser of kindness. Josh wasn't going to grant Jeremiah Rackstraw, of all people, the privilege of ending *his* life.

These thoughts flashed through Josh's brain in the space of a second—or, if you prefer, a week. Sheer contrariness, sheer stubborn perversity galvanized him. One gnarled hand grabbed a chunk of carpet, growling with pain. The attached arm hauled his body a few inches forward. The other hand came up. Digging into the dusty Axminster, one of its brittle nails splintered and broke off. Blood beaded and blossomed. Josh felt the pain, but at one remove. It was a pain among many pains, all screaming, all vying for his attention. He had to ignore them all. His eyes were fixed on the prize, the clock in the cavern with the bezel of brass around its loathsome, hilarious face.

Getting older than old. He could feel it. In the marrow of his bones he could tell he was dying. So much carpet to cross! So much ground to cover! All that way . . .

Hand over hand he dragged his frail body. The muscles in his forearms looked like strips of bacon wrapped around a stick. His long, white beard brushed the floor. The tips of his hoary mustache tickled his lips.

Hand over hand.

Over hand.

Over hand.

And then he was near. The edge of the Neverseen Era was less than an arm's reach away . . . but he was so tired, so dog-tired, so life-tired. Pain, his bosom buddy for the last couple of decades, was advising him to give it all up, let it all go. What was there left to live for? He had a weak, wasted body that didn't see and hear and smell and taste and feel anything as sharply as it had done when he was twelve going on thirteen. Its senses had been sanded down, nerve endings blunted to nubs. What the heck was he hanging around for? Death was so much better, warmer, kinder.

No!

Weeping with the effort Josh levered himself up onto the Neverseen Era, dimly hearing a creak beneath him. A diplodocus rolled stiffly down onto the floor, where it lay on its back with its flat feet in the air, looking for all the world like a dumb plastic toy. Josh slithered on. God moved across the face of His creation. Trees crashed. Ferns fell and mighty oaks were toppled. A tyrannosaurus rex, realizing it was outclassed, tumbled over on its side and played dead. The cave people were surprisingly calm as imminent apocalypse crawled toward them. One or two keeled over, perhaps fainting from fright, but the majority just stood or sat and carried on what they had been doing, for there was little point in fleeing. This great crashing angry deity, old and snow bearded as a deity should be, had decided for his own reasons that it was time for the world to end. Thus, the world ended.

Vast cracks appeared in the ground as Josh struggled up the slope toward the cavern, felling forests as he went, crushing men and dinosaurs beneath him. One almighty hand broke through the earth's crust as though clutching for a fistful of molten core to scatter like red-hot cannonballs in his path, but in the event finding only chicken wire. He withdrew his arm from the crater with a roar of rage and pain that shook the very mountaintops.

He was close now, so very close. One withered arm reached into the cavern. The clock. The whirring clock. His fingertips brushed its brass rim. He lunged again and caught hold of the tiny hammer between the bells. The clock tumbled from the cavern and landed with a splash and a *ting!* in the shallow lake where the toothy ichthyosaur was wont to float. Josh reached down. His eyesight was failing. Blackness encroached from all sides, clouds of it like squid ink in water billowing across his vision. He seized the clock. He had one chance only. He had to smash it. He didn't think he had the strength. The clock looked too sturdy. Besides, how could he be sure that if he smashed it he would return to normal? He might be left like this, at death's door. Then it would only be a matter of minutes, real minutes, before he stumbled over the threshold into death's house. So what did he have to gain? Nothing . . .

. . . except showing Rackstraw that he had been defiant to the last.

Yes!

With the dregs of his strength, with the lees of his life-force, with the last ergs of electrical energy that sputtered and sparked along his nerves and synapses, Josh raised the clock, drew back his arm . . . and pitched. A perfect curve ball. The clock flew. Its face, turning over and over, was nothing short of furious. Its mouth was screaming, not laughing.

It struck the bedroom wall.

But it didn't break.

It bounced.

And rolled.

And fetched up face down at Josh's feet. Unharmed. Except that the tiny door in its back had fallen off, popped from its rivets by the force of impact.

Josh half crawled, half rolled down the papier-mâché slope, hearing a brittle bone snap in his left leg as he hit the floor and realizing, with mild amazement, that he couldn't feel a thing. One clawlike hand groped for the clock. If he couldn't shatter the thing, he could surely stop its workings, snap the mainspring or something.

One finger thin as a stick of asparagus prodded into the square hole where the door had been.

And found not flywheel and mainspring and cog, but softness and stickiness and slipperiness.

Hooking the finger, Josh drew his hand back, and the finger brought with it a twist of something that looked like tagliatelli lathered in tomato sauce. Josh's ancient face pulled into a grimace, but he plunged his finger in again and this time fished out a slimy wet organ a little like a kidney and a little like a liver, those nutritious foodstuffs a growing boy just loathes to eat. The finger, now coated to the second knuckle in dark ooze, disappeared into the clock again, and emerged, and disappeared, and emerged, and disappeared, and emerged, each time winkling out something fleshy and repugnant, which it added to a small but growing pile on the floor.

Josh watched, revolted and triumphant, as his finger, almost of its own accord, disemboweled that terrible timepiece morsel by vile morsel.

And time stopped.

3

It was a while before he felt capable of moving, and then he was almost too frightened to do so in case a great gout of pain flooded up one or all of his limbs, announcing that he was still old Josh: bearded, brittle, broken boned, and ripe for the Grim Reaper. There was one simple but sure test to determine whether he was fully restored to youth. That was to move his tongue and feel for teeth. If his teeth were back, then the rest of him was back, too. If they weren't if the tip of his tongue wandered over hard ridges of gum . . .

It was perhaps the hardest thing Josh had ever had to do. No mathematical problem, no passage of Shakespeare, no white of a model dinosaur's eye had ever presented him with such a challenge. And when his tongue encountered its first obstacle, a smooth and perfectly formed upper incisor, Josh yelped for joy. And as the tongue discovered an adjacent canine, and then a clutch of molars, and finally a full set of teeth, Josh's yelps grew in magnitude until he was all but screaming.

He held up a hand to his face. It was a hand he knew. He knew it like the back of his hand.

He looked down at his legs. There were hairs there, but few and downy, not a coarse profusion.

He checked inside his underpants. He was a bit sorry about losing *that,* but . . . well, give it time.

He was lying beside the wreckage of his world. Everywhere was chaos, calamity, and cataclysm. It was the end of an era. As he struggled to his feet he stumbled, and more of the papier-mâché broke, more white cracks were riven in the verdant surface of his perfect creation. He realized then, kneeling there, that he would never rebuild it. It wasn't that he lacked the determination or the will, but he knew that however well he put together a second Neverseen Era, it would never be as good as the first. Certain minute details would be missing. The craftsmanship, the *love* would not be there. He could do it, but his heart wouldn't be in it.

He didn't shed a tear. Later, there would be time for crying. Now there were matters of greater importance.

Brushing sand and sawdust from his legs, Josh bent down and gingerly turned over the eviscerated clock. The mad eyes glared up balefully at Josh, its murderer. There was a stench in the room like a butcher's shop.

"I won," Josh told that erstwhile union of organic and inorganic. "I beat you."

One of the clock's hemispherical bells gave a faint, sad *ting.*

4

Downstairs and dressed, Josh took his rightful place in his chair at the kitchen table and sat and thought things through. The elation of victory was surging through him, sweeping minor considerations like terror and exhaustion to one side. His brain was uncannily clear, working to the very best of its abilities. He knew he had no right to be feeling so good, but he had never felt better.

So Rackstraw and his cronies, who for reasons unknowable had set their sights on destroying the whole town, wanted Josh dead, neutralized, out of the way. Why? Because he had spied on the train? No, Rackstraw had given him the clock yesterday, when Josh had had only suspicions but no definite proof that the Company weren't kosher. Why, then? Because they were vindictive and vicious? Possibly. But the clock was a considered plot, a carefully laid trap, malice aforethought rather than a malicious afterthought. Which meant they regarded Josh as a threat. Had Tom Finkelbaum been a threat, too? Or had he just been in the wrong place at the wrong time? Josh suspected the latter, because Tom was only a kid, whereas he—pardon his arrogance—was a whole lot more.

In fact, he was quite flattered to be perceived as a threat. And more than a little scared. Because when it became clear that the trap hadn't killed him, that he had beaten the clock, the Company would undoubtedly want to try again. And again. Until Josh Knight was no more.

And where *was* Grampa?

The almost inescapable conclusion was that Rackstraw had done something to him. What? An answer presented itself all too readily and pertly, but Josh wasn't prepared to give it head space, not so soon after his brush with mortality. He chose to think that Rackstraw had kidnapped Grampa and was keeping him somewhere. Where?

Where else? The train.

He would have to go back there and free Grampa. But he wasn't going to do that on his own, no sir. Two close shaves in one day was two too many. It was time to call in reinforcements. It was time to summon the cavalry.

The closest thing Escardy Gap had to a cavalry was none other than its redoubtable mayor. Mayor alone would not provide sufficient support, but with his status and his authority—and he *could* be authoritative, as Josh recalled from this morning in the town square, when something had taken charge of that thin old body and brought to the fore a strength and wisdom Mayor did not usually choose to display—he would be able to rustle up a posse and they would descend on that train and sort everything out once and for all. Yes. To the town hall, then.

Josh was making to leave when he remembered the mess he had left up in his bedroom (destroyed world, gutted clock). If Grampa came home and saw that . . .

But Grampa wasn't able to come home. . . .

But assuming he was able. Assuming Josh was just jumping to conclusions, fearing the worst.

He was a conscientious kid. Best to keep things tidy. Just in case.

He went to the broom closet beneath the stairs.

He reached for the restraining peg.

His nostrils started twitching.

He began to pull the peg from its socket.

A loud knock at the front door stayed his hand. It also sent his heart leaping up into his throat. His first thought, his immediate instinct, was that Rackstraw had returned to check whether the clock had done its stuff. Who else could it be? Josh took two steps back and pressed himself hard against the hallway wall. He scarcely dared look at the door.

The knocking came again, and his eyes slid left.

Half the door was mottled yellow glass, framed with small leaded rectangles of red glass. It showed the silhouette of a caller but rarely gave a clue to his or her identity. However, from what he could see, Josh was pretty sure it was not Rackstraw. The silhouette looked more like that of someone his own age. A kid.

"Josh? You in there?"

Jim Burden.

"Hey, Josh? Grampa Knight? *Anyone?*"

"I'm here," said Josh at last. He went slowly to the front door and, equally slowly, opened it.

"Boy, Josh, am I glad to see you!" said Jim, rushing in. He was carrying his Louisville Slugger. He looked on the verge of tears. "I came 'round earlier, but you weren't in."

"What is it? What's the matter?"

"You gotta help. Something's happened to my pop and Mr. Evett."

"What?"

"I don't know. I'm not sure. Mom's gone half-crazy, screaming and yelling fit to burst. Something went on in the kitchen. A fight, I think. There was a lot of crashing around. That weird Nolan guy . . ."

The tears were brimming at Jim's eyelids. "The door's locked. I couldn't get in. But I think they're . . . I think he . . ."

The dam broke. The tears came. Josh slipped an arm around his friend, a comforting, paternal arm. He let Jim sob against his shoulder and waited for the storm of emotion to abate.

"Listen, Jim."

Jim looked up, red-eyed, sniffing hard. "I want to kill them all," he said grimly. "I was kind of hoping to see the Boy on the way over here. I'd have shown him."

"I know how you feel, Jim, but you can't take them on like that. They're too dangerous. They can snuff you out like that"—Josh snapped his fingers—"if they feel like it."

"Then what do we do?"

"*You,*" said Josh, "have to go back home and get your mom and shut yourselves both in a room somewhere, draw the blinds, bolt the windows. Stay there and don't move. Don't, whatever you do, break into the kitchen. They leave traps, these people. And keep that bat by your side."

Jim gave his friend an imploring look. "Will you come with me?"

Josh hesitated. "I can't."

"You can't? What do you mean, you can't?"

"I just can't. I've got stuff to do."

"Such as what?"

"Stuff. Go home, Jim. Please. Do as I say."

"You too *proud* to come with me? Is that it? Huh?"

"No, Jim."

"You are my *friend*, aren't you? Or have you just been pretending all these years?"

"It's not like that, Jim."

"'Cause a friend would help another friend if he came asking, wouldn't he?"

Josh let a sudden surge of irrational rage simmer down before replying. "Jim, I want to help you. I want to help everyone. But I have to do it my own way. You understand that, don't you?"

"All I understand is that you're refusing me, Josh, you're turning me down. You've always thought you were too good for us, haven't you? You only hang around with us 'cause we're your own age and you can't hang around with anyone else. Looking down your nose at us. *Tolerating* us."

"That's not true!"

"Is so! Just because you get better grades and play baseball better and make models better than anyone else. Well, okay, Joshua Knight, I can take a hint. You go off and save the world. *I'm* going home to look after my mom."

"That's the best thing, Jim. Go and look after her."

Jim's anger was a frail construction, built from shoddy materials such as fear and hurt, so it didn't last long and the tears were soon back, welling from his eyes. When this second spate of crying was past, he turned and glumly set off down the porch steps. At the bottom he looked back up at his friend, and said, "Is it going to be all right, Josh? I mean, everything? The town, everything?"

"Sure," said Josh with a little shrug of his shoulders. But he didn't sound very sure, and added, "I think so," because he didn't want Jim to get his hopes up too high. The higher hopes went, the more painful it was when they came crashing down.

"Every cloud has a silver lining," Jim intoned.

"That's not always true," said Josh. "That's just something people say about bad things because they don't want to believe that bad things happen. They want to believe that everything's good, even the things that kill you."

"I know. But you're supposed to say it, aren't you? When things go wrong?"

"Yeah," said Josh, thinking, *For all the good it does.*

"I sure hope you're right. About all this. About everything."

"So do I, Jim."

"See you around." Jim shouldered the baseball bat and headed off down the street, looking for all the world like the home team's last hope going out to bat at the bottom of the ninth, with the score tied, the bases loaded, runner on the first, everything to play for.

Josh watched Jim turn the corner and disappear. His nostrils started twitching again. He could smell something new in the air, new and yet familiar: a faint tang of burning, an electric quiver of anticipation. He glanced up. Over to the east, evening was amassing itself, long purple fingers of cloud stretching out over the town. There was a distant rumble like a drumroll. Josh raised a hand and shielded his eyes. Within the dark depths of the clouds he could just make out mercurial flickerings of light, quick and sinuous like eels writhing in a skybound Sargasso. The first chilly, whispering winds from the coming storm wound their way down Muldavey Street, driving the road dust before them in tiny skittering swirls. A loose shutter blap-blapped against the side of a house, reminding Josh disturbingly of his dream of the three women. The owner of the house opened the window, reached out, and secured both shutters. All along the street, other people began doing the same. Josh would have done so, too, had he thought it was really worth it, had he thought wooden shutters would be able to protect his home from the real storm, the storm that had started with the arrival of a black-and-silver locomotive and wouldn't end until it had destroyed everything.

Another dim rumble reverberated from the horizon, ever so slightly louder now, ever so slightly nearer.

Fifteen

1

With his coat collar up around his face, Josh entered the town square, furtive as a thief.

Faced with the prospect of crossing that wide expanse of civic amenity, he suddenly felt exposed and vulnerable. He lingered in the shadow cast by the high side of the library, scanning the square for signs of life. Catching sight of Century Cedar—which was stirring its blood-caked branches languidly, as if waking up from a long sleep—a trickle of grief sprang up from deep within him. Poor Tom.

The coast was clear, not a soul about, but that didn't rid Josh of the creepy sensation that he was being watched, his every move scrutinized. He wished he could he get into the town hall by the back entrance, but he knew that door was bolted from the inside. The front doors, on the other hand, were never locked during the daytime.

Drawing a deep breath, Josh set out across the square.

He hugged the shadows. He made the gathering gloom work for him, stealing from doorway to doorway, from storefront to chapel, from shelter to shelter in a chain of quick, flurrying dashes.

In less time than he expected, he was at the foot of the

broad flight of stone steps that led up to the town hall's main doors.

He was about to ascend when a chittering, skittering sound froze him in his sneakers. The sound was coming from behind him. It was speeding toward him. He could only think of the three women and their sinister, toothy chitter-clack, and he saw them in his mind's eye swooping toward him across the square, their toes barely touching the ground, their hair and their dresses rippling out behind them, their faces pulled into rapacious, elaborate sneers.

Something cold slapped against his ankles, and it was all Josh could do to hold back a huge yelp.

Reluctantly, fearing the absolute very worst, he peered down.

One of the ominous playbills promising marvels and mystery had flapped and cartwheeled its way across the square in the wind and had hooked itself up around his ankles, and was clinging and shuddering there like an amorous poodle.

Josh bent down and prized the piece of paper off, crumpled it up into a ball and dropped it discreetly into a nearby trash can. Dusting off his palms and laughing quietly at himself, he turned back to the town hall.

It was an imposing piece of architecture, fronted by a colonnade of scrolled and fluted pillars that made it look vaguely like a Greek temple, and also like a smaller version of that more famous seat of power in Washington, D. C. Josh couldn't see light in any of the windows behind the pillars, but that didn't mean anything. The day was not so defeated yet that electrical illumination was necessary. Besides, Mayor might have his curtains closed.

He prayed Mayor was in. He didn't relish the prospect of having to go on to the old man's house from here. The thunder was getting nearer. Each rumble was preceded by a lightning flash that briefly flooded the eastern sky with pure whiteness, and the gap between flash and rumble was narrowing. Rain was on its way. The taste of it hung thickly, the feel of it clung damply in the air. Josh didn't want to have to run through the rain and dark, not with the Company out there waiting for him. He had risked enough already simply coming here.

If Mayor wasn't in, Josh decided, he would wait for him at the town hall. He would wait the whole night if need be. Mayor would surely come back at some point. Unless, of course . . .

No. They couldn't have gotten Mayor. No way. Uh-uh. Impossible. Mayor was far too wily a coyote for that.

But then Grampa was a wily coyote, too, and they had gotten *him*.

The large double doors were never locked, but they did require a good deal of shoving and shouldering to open. Josh slipped through the gap into the dusty hollow hush of the great vestibule, leaning the doors shut behind him. The lights were not on. Gloom hung everywhere. The high, vaulted ceiling collected shadows the way lepidopterists collect moths.

Josh moved across the marble chessboard floor. Ahead loomed the sweeping main staircase, a pale ziggurat in the semidarkness. The stairs led up to the next floor where Mayor's office was. Josh wondered whether he should call out Mayor's name, but the silence seemed far too hungry and greedy for that. The vestibule's corners and lofty alcoves would swallow the sound of his voice and giggle for more. His shuffling footfalls were dogged by echoes from above.

Josh was halfway across the floor when he heard the hiss of a caught breath.

He stopped. He listened. His eyes, not yet completely adapted to the dark, stared.

And he knew he couldn't have imagined the sound. He knew he was not alone here. He could sense the presence of another human being disturbing the very molecules of the air, sending out ripples of its presence like a stone cast in a pool.

Far off, the thunder complained.

There! A movement in the darkness. Over there, to his left. A head was peering out from the rectangle of an open doorway. Eyes glittered—big eyes, as big as golf balls, perfect circles of malevolent emptiness. Looking at him. Straight at him.

Terror pure and absolute filled Josh from crown to sole. The hairs at the nape of his neck prickled as though an army of ants were marching up his vertebrae. What *thing* was this? Which of the Company's many bizarre variations on a theme was lurking in that doorway, ready to attack? The midget? No, the lurker's head was too high off the floor. One of the women? No, there was none of the chitter-clack that accompanied them wherever they went. The Boy? The eyes were too bright, not those black, light-trapping, soulless pools.

Jeremiah Rackstraw himself?

No, thought Josh with an inward laugh that bordered on the hysterical. No, Jeremiah Rackstraw could never lurk in silence. It wasn't in his nature to keep his tongue still for any length of time.

Weak as it was, the joke untapped something inside Josh, opened some floodgate. Out rushed mad, reckless courage. Forcing every ounce of that courage into his throat, Josh addressed the lurker in the shadows. His voice surprised him with its strength.

"Who's that?" he said.

"Who's *that?*" came the reply.

"I asked you first."

"And I'm asking you."

"Are you on our side?"

"I can't tell you that until you tell me which side it is you're on."

Josh thought he recognized the voice, but it was so distorted by the echoes he couldn't be completely sure. "I know which side I'm on, sir," he said. "You have to prove to me that you're on the same one."

"And how am I supposed to do that? Right now, I'm not sure which side *anyone's* on."

"I'm carrying a knife," Josh said. "If you're an enemy, I'm not afraid to use it."

"And if you're who I think you are," said the other, "then you're bluffing. You wouldn't dream of using a knife, let alone carrying one."

"So who do you think I am?"

"Even if I told you, I might not be right. I'm not sure about anything at the moment. Seems like the whole dad-blamed town's gone to hell. Black's white, day's night. . . ." There was a pause, then, "Oh, damn it, what difference does it make? Here I am. If you want to kill me, kill me. Get it over and done with."

The lurker emerged from the doorway with his arms spread out in a pacifying gesture, and Josh saw that the voice did indeed belong to Doc Wheeler. Or at any rate, something that resembled Escardy Gap's medical practitioner. Correct down to the protruding belly and the short narrow tie and the round spectacles (which, reflecting what little light there was in the vestibule, had given the impression of the large white eyes), it was a perfect simulacrum of Doc Wheeler, with a few minor modifications. There was a small dressing on his left temple, clumsily applied, with a dark spot where blood had seeped through, and his walk was no longer the breezy, all-embracing walk of a confident, successful professional. It was more of a stooping shuffle, suggesting bitter resignation, the world-weariness of a broken man.

Josh didn't know what to make of this, but he did know one thing: he wasn't about to take any chances.

"Don't come too close," he warned the approaching figure.

Doc halted a few yards off, lowering his arms. "I'm the real McCoy, Josh—that is, assuming you *are* Josh. If you aren't Josh, why don't you show me who you really are, and let's get this farce over and done with."

"If you're Doc Wheeler, Doc Wheeler, tell me something only you could know about me."

Doc sighed. "Heck, Josh, you can't expect me to remember anything like that right off the top of my head. Why don't you just take my word that I am who I am, and I'll take yours."

"I can't risk it. Come on, Doc. You must be able to remember *something.*"

"Well, let me see, now. . . . You're twelve years old, or maybe thirteen now. I lose track of you kids. You grow up so damn fast. What else? Your mom and pop were killed in an automobile accident on the way over to Grant's Crossing. Came off the road. The brakes failed."

"That's not enough, sir. Everyone's heard about that. It's common knowledge. I want you to tell me something only *you* could know. Something personal."

"I performed the autopsy, son. That's pretty damn personal, don't you think?"

"No, personal to me."

"Oh, Lord, oh, Lord," said Doc Wheeler. "Is this what those people have reduced us to? Challenging one another in darkened hallways? Jumping at shadows? Josh, if you knew what I'd been through today . . ."

"I've been through it, too, sir. In a manner of speaking. Please, will you do as I ask?"

"Very well," said Doc. There was a moment's silence as his brain ransacked its shelves, its repositories and dusty vaults of memory. Thunder filled the vacancy. Then Doc said, "I was present at your birth. It wasn't a difficult birth, but you did wait until about four o'clock in the morning to emerge, which was pretty inconsiderate, really. Kept us up most of the night. Right then and there your mom decided to call you Joshua. Your daddy added David because it's your grand-pappy's name. So there you are. Oh, yes. At age five you came down with a bad case of the whooping cough. And you were about eight when you fell outta that tree and sprained your knee. Or was that the Gallagher kid? Lord, I can't re-member. It's not my job to remember. That's what Nurse Sprocket's there for. Oh, God . . ."

Doc broke down into a series of heaving sobs, and Josh, al-though not understanding the cause of Doc's grief, felt moved to go over and comfort him . . . but couldn't. Not yet. He let Doc weep. The loudest peal of thunder yet rippled through the sky. The town hall's twin doors shuddered in their frames. The storm was still some way away, but it was covering the ground fast, eager to get its paws on Escardy Gap.

After a while Doc was all cried out. He removed his glasses, ran a cuff around the steamed-up lenses, and put them back on.

"Blubbering like a baby," he said, and sniffed miserably. "Look, son. Frankly I don't give a damn anymore whether you believe me or not. I'm here to see Mayor. I'm going to turn around now and go up those stairs, and if you do have a knife and want to stab me in the back, go right ahead. Feel free. Reckon you'll be doing me a favor."

With that, Doc about-turned and marched off toward the staircase. His shoulders were hunched up around his ears. It was clear he was expecting the death blow to come at any second.

It was a bold move, and it served to dispel any lingering doubts Josh might have had. He called out softly, "Doc! Doc!"

Doc looked round.

"I believe it's you," Josh said.

Doc thought about this and seemed satisfied. "Well, I believe it's you, too, son. Come here." He held out his right hand. "Let's shake on it."

Josh hesitated, then overcame his reluctance. But even as he covered the distance between them, his every nerve was tingling and his every sense was alert for the slightest hint of deception or betrayal. He extended his arm. His hand met Doc's, his fingers pressing into Doc's dry, pudgy palm. He clasped Doc's hand. Clasped it more firmly. Gripped it. Shook it hard.

Josh and Doc beamed at one another, two moon-crescent grins shining out in the darkness.

"Boy, am I glad it *is* you," said Doc.

"The feeling's mutual."

"You forgive me for doubting?"

"You should forgive *me.*"

"Nothing to forgive."

"But you can understand, can't you, Doc? I mean, you *were* hiding."

"I was hiding from you. Heard someone come in and assumed it was one of them—"

CRACK THERRUMP!!!

Both Josh and Doc ducked reflexively as the thunder exploded overhead. Both then offered up nervous laughs.

"Gonna be a doozy," Doc muttered. "The giants are out walking tonight."

Josh nodded grimly. "Feels like it's the end of the world," he said.

"Let me tell you, son. Unless we do something about it, it is. At least, as far as this town is concerned."

"But what? What do we do?"

"I was kinda hoping Mayor'd have the answer to that."

"Me, too."

"Come on, then," said Doc Wheeler, clapping Josh on the

back. "Let's go up and see if that crazy actor's in and receiving visitors."

2

The crazy actor was in, but whether he was in a mood for visitors was open to debate.

"Goddamn thing!!!" Josh and Doc heard him yell from the far end of the corridor that led to his office. The cry was followed by the unmistakable thunk-clunk of a telephone receiver being none too gently returned to its cradle. "Least you can goddamn do is work when I goddamn need you! Goddamn it! You sing out all the time when I don't want you to, and now you can't even *hum.*"

Doc knocked on the half-opened door and poked his head 'round. Mayor leapt up from his seat, not so much startled as embarrassed to have been caught in an off-moment, backstage, out of camera, venting his spleen on an inanimate object.

"Doc," he said. Catching sight of Doc's smaller, slenderer companion: "Josh."

"I would ask if this was a bad time, Mayor," said Doc, "but the question seems a mite ridiculous."

Mayor ran a hand over his face, rubbing at an imaginary beard. "Tell me about it, Doc. I've been trying to get through to the authorities at Grant's Crossing, at Jackson Vale, at just about every damn town in the county. Do you know how long I've been trying? How many numbers I've dialed? And not a damn thing. Not a squeak, so much as a whisper. Can you believe it? Not a single operator's answering. Ma Bell seems to have decided to call Sunday off."

"The storm?" Josh suggested. "It might have downed the cables."

"Don't think so, son," said Mayor. "I've had my ear to that thing for the past four hours, give or take. Long before—"

Right on cue there was a short flare of lightning quickly followed by an almighty *CRACK THERRUMP!!!* that shook windows throughout the entire building, making them rattle like a boxer's teeth when a perfect roundhouse hits him squarely in the jaw.

Mayor pointed upward. "Long before there was any of that. My guess is the lines have been cut. Wouldn't surprise me. Nothing much surprises me anymore."

The first silvery droplets of rain appeared on the darkened panes of the window, each landing with a tiny tick and slithering down the glass.

"Sit down, you two, sit down," said Mayor, ushering them to seats. "Unless you're going someplace."

"I ain't going *any*place till this storm lets up," said Doc.

"Then we better get comfortable, 'cause I reckon we're going to be here all night."

Mayor switched on the lights and immediately noticed the haggardness of Doc's face and the small, self-administered bandage on his left temple. "Good Lord," said Mayor with a whistle. "Doc, you look like you've just been to hell and back and forgot to take any pictures for the folks at home. What happened? Where'd you get that cut?"

"You won't believe me if I tell you."

"Try me."

"Bob Tremaine."

"Bob Tremaine did that to you?" Mayor exclaimed.

"That's not all he did." Doc removed his spectacles and pressed a thumb and forefinger into his eyes.

Mayor, sensing that roles had been reversed from yesterday and that now it was his turn to dispense the medicine, went to the drinks cabinet in the corner of the room and fetched out a quart bottle of Wild Turkey and two small tumblers. He glanced at Josh and took out a third tumbler. He winked at the boy. Josh smiled back, a little apprehensively.

"Won't kill you," Mayor reassured him.

Mayor poured out the whisky and handed a glass to Josh and to Doc. Although Josh's was only a finger full, it seemed to him to be loaded to the brim. He sniffed the amber liquid tentatively, wrinkling his nose at the mixture of sickly sweetness and burning sourness. He put his lips to the rim of the tumbler and regarded the two older men who, without hesitation, upended their glasses and downed their drinks in a single shot. Josh tipped a trickle of the whisky into his mouth. It seared his tongue. It scorched several layers of skin off his palate. It melted his teeth down to nubs. His mouth expanded to a vast hollow cavern filled with molten magma. Heat flooded up his sinal cavities. Tears sprang to his eyes. Bracing himself for the impact, he swallowed. For a second he felt nothing. Then his belly exploded with warmth. The warmth suffused through him, and every organ it touched started to glow like gold. Alchemical alcohol.

For no earthly reason a smile came to Josh's lips.

Seeing the smile, Mayor grinned to himself. He watched Josh raise his tumbler again and take a second, less conservative, more confident sip. *Perverting the young and innocent,* he thought to himself, a little reproachfully. Not that it *was* perverting, and not that Josh was especially young or especially innocent. No, he was merely introducing the lad to the less innocuous pleasures of adulthood, something that Josh would no doubt have discovered of his own volition sooner or later. Mayor was merely speeding progress along.

He turned back to Doc Wheeler. "Ready to talk about it?" he asked.

Doc nodded weakly, and he began to tell them about his encounter with Bob Tremaine; about the way Bob had attacked him, spouting all those crazy threats and warnings; about finding the mutilated corpse of Nurse Sprocket and then that of Ike Swivven. . . .

The rain started to attack the window with a sudden, savage fury, swooping in so hard the panes seemed in danger of shattering. The storm was not content to rage impotently around buildings. It wanted in. It wanted to pierce and penetrate and damage beyond repair. The lightning wanted to crack the sky in town with its forks. The thunder wanted to dismantle the world.

3

Twice during his account Doc dissolved into tears. Twice Mayor recharged Doc's and his own glasses. Then, when Doc had said everything he had to say, Mayor dispensed a third shot of whisky for the two of them, and then returned to the chair behind his desk and laid his head in his hands and stayed like that for the next ten minutes. If he was weeping, he was doing so privately, soundlessly.

Josh's abiding mental image of Nurse Sprocket was of a fearsome, forbidding apparition in gingham and white linen whom he had only visited when he was unwell, which understandably colored his perception of her; but he could see how much Doc had loved her, and still loved her, and this got him wondering how he himself would cope with such a loss. If, say, Grampa . . .

No. Best not to think it. Best to leave that thought in the back of a drawer, somewhere hard to find. Out of sight, out of mind—as Grampa was fond of saying.

Josh fumbled with his not-quite-empty tumbler, not quite knowing where to look. The whisky had set off a pleasant buzzing in his skull and made his vision slightly hazy, reminding him of how aging, once-beautiful actresses were shown in close-up in the movies, the gauzed lens masking the evidence of hard lives and a multitude of sins. He knew now why adults enjoyed their drinking so much. It put circumstances, no matter how dire, into perspective. Drink—with a maturity that belied the few years it spent in the distillery—said that nothing mattered in the long run, nothing at all. It reinforced a sense of the Now as opposed to the Then or the May Be. It substituted Living with Existing. He looked out of the window at treetops raging in the wind. Lightning split the sky. Then came the *CRACK THERRUMP!!!*

At last Mayor looked up, looked evenly at Doc and then at Josh. His expression was without a trace of anything that could be called benevolence. There was no twinkle in his eye, no dimple in his cheek. He was Cagney, he was Raft, he was every tough guy who had ever fired a gun on-screen at an innocent victim, murdered in cold blood; every blank-eyed killer who had ever left a trail of corpses across reel after reel before his final, fatal encounter with Nemesis.

"Way I see it," he said, his voice sighing out like a soul from the grave, "we've two choices. Either we stay and fight, or we get out and go for help. If we stay and fight, we have to get everybody together, we have to mobilize the whole town, we have to arm ourselves with everything we've got, every hunting rifle, every shotgun, every shovel, every pitchfork, every pocket knife, and we have to take these devils out. We outnumber them twenty to one. You might think those are good odds. Me, I'm not so sure. And even if we do manage to organize ourselves in the time we have left, which isn't much, I still don't rate our chances very high. If I were a betting man, I'd keep my wallet firmly in my pocket."

Neither Josh nor Doc felt inclined to disagree.

"The alternative, then," Mayor went on, "is to get out and go for help. A few of us, maybe, could manage it. It's just over twenty miles to Grant's Crossing. About five hours on foot."

"Less than an hour by car," Josh pointed out.

"Perhaps, but I think we have to consider stealth over speed. A car engine the Company would almost certainly hear. I shudder to think what kind of ways they'd have of stopping us, but no doubt they've taken that into account. I agree it's quicker, but it's too much of a risk."

" 'Sides, my old Ford's as dead as a dodo," said Doc, "and you don't own a car, Mayor."

"All we'd have to do is find Mr. Cohen or one of the Evett brothers," Josh said. "Any of them could drive us."

"I said I ain't prepared to risk it." Mayor was Public Enemy Number One again.

"If we walk, we'll be sitting ducks."

"Not necessarily, kid," said Mayor. "I'll let you in on a little secret. This afternoon I was privileged to receive a visit from Mr. Jeremiah Rackstraw."

Josh's jaw dropped. A visit from Rackstraw, and Mayor was still alive to tell the tale.

CRACK THERRUMP!!!

Mayor gave a short, mirthless laugh. "Yeah. No one's as surprised as me to be sitting here and still breathing. But he didn't come for that. He came to crow. He came to tell me about how he had everything sewn up and how no one was going to escape and how goddamn marvelous he was and how goddamn stupid we were. Well, I just sat here and let him babble on. A lot of it made no sense at all, but he was having such a good time I didn't think it polite to interrupt. But then he got careless. He let me in on something I don't think he should have. He told me that the Company have ceased operations for the day. They're taking the night off. That gives us a chance to get out of here."

"Run away?" exclaimed Josh.

"Go and get help."

"You mean save our own skins."

"Son, we can't face up to him. That won't work. Rackstraw is expecting at least some of us to put up some kind of resistance, but we can't possibly win a fight with these people. The only course of action that's going to do us any good is to do the unexpected, and the unexpected thing to do is get out of town, head for the hills, hole up somewhere, lie low until the heat dies down, then make a break for the border. I know this place down in Mexico, just south of Tijuana—" Abruptly Mayor realized that he was getting carried away with the part of the killer and was in danger of losing the thread of the conversation. He became Douglas B. Raymond again, shedding the killer's snaky skin. "Well, not exactly that, but you get my drift."

"I've another idea," said Josh.

Mayor leaned back in his chair and folded his arms behind his head. "Shoot."

"My Grampa's gone, disappeared somewhere, and I've every reason to believe Mr. Rackstraw took him. The only place I can think of that he might have taken him is the Company's train. I say we go there and rescue him."

"Gone?" said Doc warily.

"They've got him. They've kidnapped him."

"Why would they do that?" Mayor inquired, allowing as little inflection as possible to enter his voice, not wanting to alarm the boy.

"I don't know. Maybe they're holding him hostage."

Mayor and Doc sneaked a glance at each other, and their expressions said the same thing. There was a slim chance that Grampa Knight *was* in the clutches of the Company, but knowing how these people operated, the greater likelihood was that Grampa was no longer around to draw breath or a pension. This afternoon, Mayor recalled, Jeremiah Rackstraw had been wearing Grampa's hat when he had appeared in this office. Mayor didn't think David Knight would have willingly surrendered his hat to anyone, no matter how much they were in need of one, no matter how politely they asked, least of all Jeremiah Rackstraw.

But he didn't tell Josh this. If Josh needed to believe that his Grampa was still alive, then so be it. It was not for Mayor to try to disabuse him of the notion. A time would surely come when Josh would have to acknowledge the truth, but that time was not now.

An immense *CRACK THERRUUUUUUUMMMMMM-MMP!!!* caught them all by surprise.

When his heartbeat had returned to normal, Doc spoke. "Son, the three of us wouldn't stand a snowball's chance in hell of rescuing your Grampa."

"It doesn't have to be just us. We could get others along. Mr. Burden, the Evett . . ." Then Josh remembered Jim Burden telling him that something dreadful had happened in his mom's kitchen. Jim hadn't been clear exactly what, but Josh suspected neither Big Ben nor Earl Evett were going to be of much help, not now, perhaps not ever.

And what about Grampa? said a tiny voice at the back of his head. *If they killed Mr. Burden and Mr. Evett, do you seriously believe they haven't done the same to old Grampa?*

CRACK THERRUMP!!!

"For the time being," said Mayor, "we have to assume that there *isn't* safety in numbers, but that there is safety in sticking with who you know."

"We can trust each other," said Doc.

"Exactly. But we can't trust anyone else. And like you say, Doc, it would be insane for the three of us to launch an attack on the train just to get Grampa back. No offense, Josh."

Josh shook his head: none taken.

"Chances are we'd all of us end up vulture meat," Mayor went on. "And even if we did get him out safe and sound, what then? We'd be in the exact same position we started from, only there would be one more of us to worry about. You see where I'm coming from, don't you, Josh?"

Josh nodded.

"The only thing that makes any sense is to wait for this storm to blow over and then head for Grant's Crossing using back alleys and side streets so's we won't be so visible while we're going through town."

Doc nodded in agreement.

"Then, when we come back with the police and the National Guard and, God knows, maybe even the army, *then* we free your Grampa. You see the logic of that, don't you, Josh? That way, all of the bad guys get rounded up and are made to stand trial. Believe me, as God is my witness, I'll make sure Jeremiah Rackstraw and his buddies pay for every single crime they've committed. I'll see to it personally that they feel the full force of American justice. That goes for Bob Tremaine, too."

Doc remained impassive, but a zealous light came on in his eyes and blazed away.

Assuming it was *Bob,* Mayor thought to himself. He was having trouble believing that Bob Tremaine could really have turned mad-dog murderer. Though Bob had always been a little short on common sense, and his obsession with all things Communist could get a mite wearisome after a while, Mayor still remembered him as a good man, a good husband and father, a hard worker, a devout churchgoer, a stalwart member of the community.

CRACK THERRUMP!!!

Then again, a tiny spot of rot can infect the whole fruit in no time at all, if the conditions are right.

"So we're agreed?" he said. "When the storm's over, we go out by the back door."

It was agreed, although Josh was slightly slower in his assent than Doc.

"Then, gentlemen, I suggest we make ourselves comfortable. It looks like it's going to be a long night."

Mayor reached for the bottle of Wild Turkey.

4

Clem Stimpson reached for his bottle of Jack Daniel's. Numbly he unscrewed the cap and brought the neck of the bottle up to his mouth. The whites of his eyes were crazed with blood vessels and flecked with chips of yellow. The scrub of stubble around his jaw and chin glistened with raindrops, spittle, and spilled whisky. His wet clothes sagged limply off of him, as if his body had shrunk dramatically overnight. He stank like an outhouse in high summer. The rain had tried to wash away the smell, but it had its work cut out for it, what with the booze breath, the body odor ingrained into the fabric of his clothing, and the dried boy-gore spattering his boots.

"Oh, yeah!" said Clem as the liquor hit his belly and danced a soft-shoe shuffle all around his innards. "Oh, boy, that's better."

Clem was sheltering in the waiting room of the railway station. The entire day had passed in a garish, phantasmagorical haze, images of blood and trees and severed heads flitting madly batlike through his head as he staggered from street to street beneath the beating heat of the sun. In Poacher's Park he had briefly come to his senses, enough to recover from his secret hiding place in the bandstand the two emergency bottles he had purchased with the last of his week's welfare money, and then he had sat there and he had drunk and drunk until he was drunker than drunk, so drunk he was in danger of going right through to the other side and becoming sober again.

When the storm had started to brew, his first instinct had been to find shelter and warmth. He had tried the Bar & Grill (closed), then the Merrie Malted (also closed), then the library (closed on Sundays), then the Reverend King's chapel (locked). Then, beginning to panic, he had hurried over to Belvedere Way, where his one and perhaps only friend, Walt Donaldson, lived. But there had been nobody home. Clem had swung and swung the knocker as though he meant to smash a hole in the door. Not a peep from inside. Not even a tirade from Miss Ohllson. He had tried the handle. Locked. Just his luck that the Ohllson woman was the only person in Escardy Gap who locked the damn front door.

Clem had been getting pretty desperate by the time he reached the station. The first fat raindrops had been splashing down, darkening the road dust. The thunder had been cackling and crackling right overhead. Casting a last glance up at the glowering sky, he had darted inside like a hunted animal going to earth.

It was dark in here, and drafty because there were no doors, only wide-open entrances, and Clem was hunkered down on one of the benches, shivering, hugging his legs to his chest for warmth and cuddling the bottle at his crotch. It had just turned six, according to the clock that he could see through the window that gave onto the platform. The hands divided the face into two semicircles. Beyond the platform awning the rain streamed down in a shimmering curtain, the overflowing gullies spilling their loads in long trickles and loud spatters.

Tonight, it seemed, the whole world was trying to drown its sorrows along with him.

Clem had an abhorrence of water in any shape or form: water in baths, water in drinks, water from the sky—he particularly loathed water from the sky. When you didn't have a roof regularly over your head, the last thing you wanted was Mother Nature reminding you of that fact, soaking you to the skin, trying to give you pneumonia and bronchitis and God knows what else.

He sneered and cursed the rain, and took another slug of Jack Daniel's. Then, in a rare fit of self-denial, he screwed the cap back on. The bottle was two-thirds empty and would have to last the whole night—

CRACK THERRUMP!!!

"Jesus H. Christ!" Clem hissed, flinching. There hadn't been a storm like this since longer than he could remember. Which wasn't all that long, owing to the parlous state of his memory cells. All over Escardy Gap, however, people with better memories than Clem Stimpson were coming to the same conclusion. These people—good people, concerned people, worried people, even frightened people, people cowering in their living rooms and dens, people huddling in loved ones' embraces and people soothing alarmed toddlers—kept casting upward glances and wondering out loud if anyone could recall a storm quite like this one, lightning quite so bright, thunder quite so terrible. The suddenness and ferocity of it had caught everyone by surprise. This, coupled with the suspicions and rumors that were flying around, the reports of peculiar disappearances, the firsthand and secondhand accounts of murders, the silence in certain neighboring houses, and the presence of the strangers who had threaded themselves into the community, latching on like some kind of parasitic virus, led these people to fear not just for their lives but for the continued existence of everything they held dear and true.

From the platform entrance to the waiting room there came a loud throat-clearing, a voluble and peremptory "Harrumph!"

Clem nearly redecorated the interior of his pants.

The figure standing there was tall and lean and silhouetted in black. He had his hands on his hips and from the angle of his hatted head Clem could tell the man was looking right at him. Clem lost his grip on the bottle. It slithered from his grasp, down his chest, to land unbroken on the bench. From there—cruel irony—it rolled onto the floor, where it shattered.

Clem didn't notice, didn't care, didn't think he would ever have need for a bottle of anything ever again.

For Death was standing in the doorway.

Death had come for him.

A split-second blitz of lightning lit up the angular contours of Death's face, throwing knife-shaped nose and sickle smile into sharp relief. Then the face was lost in darkness again, and from the aftermath of the ensuing *CRACK THERRUMP!!!* Death's voice emerged, low and precise and ringing out as clear as a knell.

"You're not supposed to be here," Death said. "No one's supposed to be here. Haven't you a home to go to?"

"N-n-no," said Clem.

"Ah, it's Stimpson, isn't it?" said Death. "Very much the wild rover you are, Clem, old fellow. Here one moment, somewhere else the next. Such an irritating habit. I like to know where people are. It makes everything so much less complicated. I like people to be in places and stay there."

"P-please leave me alone. I ain't done nothing."

"A common cry," said Death. " 'I ain't done nothing so I don't deserve nothing to be done to me.' Of course 'I ain't done nothing' means quite the opposite from what you intend it mean. Those double negatives can be so-o-o tricky, can't they?"

"But I ain't ready yet. Please don't take me."

"Take you? What would I want to take you *for,* Clem? And *where* would I take you?"

"Please. I don't want to die."

"Naturally you don't. Few of us do. But Death comes for all of us in the end, Clem. Whether we like it or not, he swoops down and plucks us up from the ground in his talons and carries us off to the Forever Hereafter. You should learn not to fear him. Learn to appreciate him. Learn to *love* him. That way, when he comes for you, it won't be a parting, but a meeting."

Death strode into the waiting room, the swish of his clothing like a scythe cropping through good corn. Clem scuttled backward along the bench until his shoulder blades met wall and he could go no farther. Death came to a halt. Lightning fluttered in his eyes, two tiny flames dancing in the abyss.

CRACK THERRUMP!!!

"Oh, good God, oh, sweet Jesus . . ." murmured Clem.

"Don't ask *them* for help, Clem," Death advised. "They've got better things to do than waste time on a miserable sinner like you. They've got holy men and saints and nuns and monks to look after. Do you fall into any of those categories? Heavens, no, Clem. You're a disgrace. You're a walking, shambling pile of shame. You're Escardy Gap's greatest embarrassment. All those fine upstanding people just look the other way when they see you come staggering toward them, don't they? Just turn up their noses and pretend you don't exist. But you do! Oh, you do! And how marvelous that you *do*! You've spent your life reminding them that this is what they could become, these are the depths to which they could descend, should things go wrong, should the Good Lord turn a blind eye for a moment, should His grip on them slacken. In a way, you know, I admire you, Clem Stimpson."

Through the fog, understanding dawned. "You . . . you ain't Death!" Clem exclaimed. Then, less sure: "Are you?"

"In a sense, yes. In a sense, no," said Jeremiah Rackstraw (for it was he). "Death and I have what you might call an arrangement. I'm certainly a major contributor to Death's fund. However, I can assure you I didn't come here to kill you, Clem."

"Oh, praise be." Relief came over Clem in cooling waves,

and he offered up a short vote of thanks to whichever lucky star had smiled on him today.

"No," said Rackstraw, "that sordid little task I will leave to others." He found a switch and illuminated the two overhead bulbs that hung unshaded from the ceiling on lengths of cord. Clem was dazzled.

Hitching up his pants so as not to ruin the creases, Rackstraw sat down on the bench beside Clem. He doffed Grampa's hat and smoothed his dark hair into place. "Honestly, Clem," he said, "I meant it just now when I told you I admired you. I do. You've been a perpetual thorn in Escardy Gap's side, a permanent blot on the landscape. Some say that beauty can be gauged only by contrasting it with ugliness. You are the imperfection, Clem, that makes Escardy Gap all the more beautiful. The mole on Marie Antoinette's cheek. It's not a desirable role by any means, not one anybody would willingly have played, but you took it on nevertheless, Clem, and you have played it to the hilt. For that, I think, you deserve some kind of reward."

"Reward?"

"Reward. Clem Stimpson, what you are about to see is a rare behind-the-scenes glimpse of the Company. It will also be the last thing you ever see, but, honestly, what a way to go!" A thrill shivered through the last five words. "I hope you appreciate the honor I am conferring on you, Clem. I hope you will be properly grateful, and show that gratitude by not struggling or resisting when the time of your death comes."

Dumbly, Clem Stimpson nodded.

"Then sit back!" said Jeremiah Rackstraw cheerfully. "Relax! Make yourself comfortable! And let this little sideshow commence."

5

A few minutes later, they began to arrive.

Mr. Olesqui was first, coming through the entrance in a whirl of pipe smoke. This smoke cloud had surrounded him all the way across town from the Chisholms' residence on

Furnival Street. It had kept him completely dry, deflecting the rain as efficiently as any umbrella.

Mr. Olesqui bowed to Rackstraw and passed through to the platform. Rackstraw turned to Clem and told him the midget's name and described his penchant for a particular kind of tobacco grown only on the slopes of a certain remote mountain in Peru, the soil of which local tribesmen fertilized once a month with semen and menstrual blood, thereby imbuing it with magical properties. Clem nodded his head without taking any of this in.

Then came the Boy. He was not wearing his gloves. Where his hands should have been there was a lambent glow that sometimes took the shape of hands and sometimes transformed into hideous malformities. The Boy fascinated himself with these creations. Without even acknowledging the presence or existence of anyone else, he passed through the waiting room.

"A princeling," Rackstraw explained. "Although his ancestry is not entirely clear, it is believed that his grandfather or great-grandfather is none other than the Count of the Undead."

"Um, yeah," said Clem.

"He was born without hands. In their place there are two fields of eldritch energy. No one is exactly sure how they work, but it seems they have the ability to twist and alter reality. They can make new the old, make old the new, bring chaos to order."

Zzzzzap!

Thus did Buzz Beaumont signal his arrival, accompanied by an almighty flash, a hail of sparks, and the smell of ozone. He stood there, blue fireballs whizzing up and down the length of his solenoid suit, a halo of flickering blue sizzling around him like St. Elmo's fire. When he spoke, Clem saw miniature arcs of blue light leaping across the back of his mouth from molar to molar.

"My kinda weather!" Buzz informed Rackstraw.

"I'm very happy for you," replied Rackstraw. "A showman born and bred," he whispered aside to Clem. "His act was banned in several states after spectators began to be killed accidentally. Accidentally!" he repeated with a wink and a nudge.

After Buzz came Agnes Destiny, clad shambolically in items of clothing pilfered from Hannah Marrs's closets and chests of drawers. She threw Rackstraw a contemptuous look and waltzed haughtily past, trailing several limp phalli along the floor behind her.

Rackstraw nudged Clem and said, "The lady is a tramp."

Next up was Walt Donaldson.

Clem gasped. "Walt?" he said. "Walt, old buddy, what are *you* doing here?"

Walt didn't even glance at Clem. He crossed the waiting room, and as he did so his body began to thin. He began to shrink. He began to change. Clothing, hair, eyes, nose, mouth, all shifted fluently, until, by the time he had reached the entrance to the platform, Walt Donaldson was no more and in his place strode Ingrid Ohllson.

Clem gulped hard, then turned to Rackstraw. "That wasn't Walt, was it?" he said, and an amused Rackstraw gently shook his head.

"There aren't many of Clarence's kind left in the world," he said. "Most of his race have made one change too many and have forgotten who they really are. Now they lead lives as boring animals or ordinary humans, in forests and towns, working and playing, melding in with their surroundings. It's really rather tragic."

Now Felcher ran in, dripping wet, puffing and panting, his bottles glittering and chinking around him. He stood there shaking the water from his hair, cursing the weather and cursing God and cursing Escardy Gap hardest of all. He uncapped one of his little bottles and took a restorative sip.

"Felcher," said Rackstraw, and indicated Clem. "Our friend here is also something of a connoisseur of intoxicating beverages. Perhaps? . . ."

Felcher regarded Clem with what can only be described as naked contempt and reluctantly proffered him the bottle. Clem hesitated before accepting. He sniffed the chalky white liquid inside. It smelled of things he vaguely remembered, things from distant days, faded souvenirs from the far-flung country of the past: a hint of aniseed, a tinge of sarsaparilla, a touch of vanilla, a notion of bubblegum, a wisp of cotton candy, a suggestion of peppermint, a proposition of popcorn, a soupçon of buttermilk, a shade of chocolate, a tincture of cough linctus, a breath of lemonade, and much more besides.

Clem only pretended to take a sip, then handed the bottle back. He vowed right there and then that if he ever got out of this alive, he would never touch a drop of the hard stuff again. Oh, no. From this day on—should the Lord see fit to preserve him—it would be milk and orange juice for Clem Stimpson.

Felcher grouched and grumbled off, joining the others on the platform beneath the awning.

"Memories are the grape and grain," said Rackstraw, "from which he distills his exotic concoctions."

A large fly came fizzing through the open doorway, swerved sideways and buffeted against the bulletin board with a mildly metallic clonk. Before Clem's very, very startled eyes, the fly assumed human shape, its jeweled joints lengthening into limbs, its muscid body becoming muscle and bone, its fly features flowering forth into a face.

"Jeremiah Rackstraw!" cried Neville N. Nolan. "Joyous rapture! Genial regards! Genuine respect!"

"Nice of you to notice me, Neville."

"Notice? Nothing is nimble enough to evade my eye."

"And you've done your job right, I trust."

"Job right, Jeremiah Rackstraw? How arrogant of you to ask! Big Ben is a burden no more. Earl Evett has entered the eternal ever-after. Both men have met their Maker."

"Brilliant. Excellent."

Neville N. Nolan and Jeremiah Rackstraw exchanged a few more purple pleasantries, and then the werefly walked through to the platform.

Clem hadn't followed a word that was said, and figured these guys were talking in some kind of fancy code known only to members of the Company. "Is that it?" he asked Rackstraw.

"Oh, no," came the reply.

Clem didn't know whether to be glad or worried.

And on and on they came, the storm announcing each new arrival with a thunderous drumroll.

Most of them Clem recognized. He had seen them come out of the carriages of the train yesterday. He did not know their names or anything about them, but Rackstraw conscientiously filled him in.

Here was Mort Carroway, a cadaverous anatomy of a man with a fondness for creeping through small holes, penetrating crevices, lurking in crawl spaces, and lingering in crannies, watching through knotholes, spying through cracks, and seeing everything.

CRACK THERRUMP!!!

Here was Gypsy Zelda, headscarved and hoop-earringed, who made predictions of imminent mortality which, strangely enough, always proved true.

CRACK THERRUMP!!!

Here was a man known only as the Mayfly, who had over the past twenty-four hours forcibly impregnated three of Escardy Gap's youngest and prettiest females. The seed of his loins, Rackstraw explained to Clem with a zestful smacking of lips, had the unusual characteristic of growing to full size within a matter of minutes, and then eating its way out, and then, alas, dying on contact with air. The Mayfly was in many ways a tragic figure, a desperate philoprogenitive who could never father any offspring that lasted for more than a few precious moments. The Mayfly's eyes were red and swollen from crying.

CRACK THERRUMP!!!

And this was the diabolical Nick St. Nicholas, who wasn't interested in bargaining for your soul as long as he could control your body for an hour or so and have you perform acts of self-mutilation, which he watched with childish, demonic, cackling glee.

CRACK THERRUMP!!!

And the Crone, an awesomely wrinkled hag who always carried a spare set of lovingly tooled and sharpened dentures for those awkward meals, the ones that involved biting through living flesh and bone.

CRACK THERRUMP!!!

And Dr. Canker, who had once been a real doctor, and still made housecalls, leaving each home with the heavy slopping carpetbag he toted a few growths and tumors lighter.

CRACK THERRUMP!!!

And Titus Nonesuch, an expert with pencil and ink brush, the artist responsible for the playbills all over town, who had drawn Andy Gallagher into his own version of an EC Comics horror anthology and had flipped the young fellow from story to story, making sure he met with a grisly end in the closing panel of each.

And on and on they came.

And Clem watched this parade of human and not-so-human monsters pass by, and he listened to Rackstraw's brief descriptions of their needs and deeds, and he grew numb, and number, and number still.

"And that," Rackstraw said finally, dusting off his palms, "is everybody. Come on, Clem. There's one last thing you ought to see."

Clem let himself be helped to his feet and ushered out onto the platform, pliable as an etherized patient.

The gathered Company were chatting idly to one another, comparing notes. Through the plummet of rain and ripples of thunder Clem caught snatches of their conversations.

". . . their screams, music to my ears . . ."

". . . down and down, like a shower of red petals . . ."

". . . and he said to me, 'That's a funny pouch you've got yourself there' . . ."

". . . tasted good, if a little too sweet for my palate . . ."

". . . job's worth doing, it's worth doing well . . ."

". . . was, I may say, a moment of egregious ecstasy and eternal embarrassment . . ."

". . . David Copperfield . . ."

". . . made 'em sing, made 'em dance, made 'em pop their fingernails back one by one . . ."

". . . boiled his eyeballs in their sockets like hard-boiled eggs . . ."

". . . baked a fine pecan pie, though . . ."

". . . heh heh heh . . ."

". . . my sweet children, my poor little babies . . ."

". . . lamb to the slaughter . . ."

". . . blood . . ."

". . . vomit . . ."

". . . strings of intestine . . ."

". . . Freaks . . ."

". . . waited for them to die before I closed them up again . . ."

". . . there's nothing nasty about cancer cells, they're just cells that grow too well . . ."

". . . *lead* the way, ho ho! . . ."

Leading Clem away from the hubbub, Rackstraw said, "Our Angel should be arriving shortly. Really, Clem, you are the most privileged man I know. I can't remember when was the last time that one of our victims actually got to meet our Angel."

Angel? Was he saying something about an angel? It didn't make any sense to Clem. He thought these people must be in league with the devil, not with an angel. It must be said, though, that right then nothing much was making any sense to Clem.

Rackstraw led him right to the edge of the platform. He turned and peered along the track, trying to discern movement through the rain. Finally he said, "Ah. Here we are."

There was a short, shrill scream. The tracks began to whine on their ties. Clem heard a huffing and puffing, a laborious clanking and churning. Then he became aware of a huge shape moving through the air toward them, silhouetted in the rain. Gradually it came closer, the huffing and puffing and clanking and churning grew louder, and the air was filled with a fizzing noise—the sound of raindrops striking piping-hot metal and turning to steam.

The train drew up to the platform and squealed to a halt. The three women Clem remembered from yesterday danced over the boiler, their hair plastered down in tangled rattails and their gossamer gowns clinging wetly to their bodies to reveal everything beneath—*everything*—in pornographic detail, from the pink concentric Os of their nipples to the dark pubic triangles at the base of their taut bellies. Their triple chitter-clack was audible above the rain, above even the thunder.

The carriage doors flew open, but nobody made a move to climb in. Clem became aware that a hush had fallen over the assembled Company. They were no longer talking to each other. A quick look over his shoulder confirmed his worst suspicions. They were watching him. Every pair of eyes was trained on him.

"Uh, Mr. Rackstraw . . . What happens now?"

"Now, Clem," said Rackstraw, laying a gentle hand on Clem's neck, "you die."

"Oh, p-please, Mr. Rackstraw! Please! I ain't ready. I ain't ready to die. I've got a few good years left in me. A *lotta* good years. I swear I'll be a better person from now on. I swear it! Won't drink, won't cuss, won't look at ladies in a bad way—"

"Clem," said Rackstraw, shaking his head sadly. "Clem, if I had a heart, it would be touched. It might even be moved to forgiveness. If I had a merciful bone in my body, I'd let you go, let you run out into the street as free as a bird. But of course, the quality of mercy is something I find a bit of a strain."

Tears spilled down from Clem's yellowy red eyes, seeping into his scrubby beard. He clutched the lapels of Rackstraw's jacket and he begged, he implored the leader of the Company to spare him. Rackstraw merely regarded Clem's grubby mitts with disdain and then plucked them, left, then right, from his lapels.

"It's no use, Clem. Save your tears. Use the last few moments of your life wisely. Make your peace with God, if you have to."

"Ohhhhhh . . ." Clem groaned, and slumped against Rackstraw, a sack of a man. Rackstraw pushed him brusquely away.

Between blubbering sobs Clem managed to ask, "Will it hurt?" Not wanting to hear the reply, he stared miserably down at his boots.

"Yes, it'll hurt, Clem," said Rackstraw. "I cannot tell a lie. It will hurt like hell."

"Can't you make it quick?"

"No, Clem. All the same, I think you'll find your particular death a not altogether unpleasant experience. In fact, the pain will be so intense and dizzying as to be all but indistinguishable from an orgasm."

So saying, Rackstraw stepped back. The Company had formed a tight circle around Clem. Clem's back was to the locomotive, from which were coming deep murmurs and gurgles like the sounds of a digestive system working hard in anticipation of a meal. Clem had always thought he would die alone, silently slip away in the night in an alley somewhere. He didn't think his last moments would be so public, with a ring of onlookers around him, watching, waiting.

Clem glared at them all with his rheumy eyes, a mad dog, a cornered fox. He snarled and spat at them defiantly.

The chitter-clack was coming from right behind his head. With an air of desperate resignation, Clem turned to meet his fate.

As if obeying some unspoken cue, the Man-eaters raised their gowns and pulled them neatly over their heads, baring their pale bodies to the rain. The gowns fell in three crumpling piles around Clem's feet.

Clem gawked up at the naked beauty before him. He ran his eyes over each and every inch of those smooth-skinned, tight-fleshed frames, his gaze coming to rest at each well-sprung pair of breasts, each scooped navel, each matted pubic thatch—honey brown, bear black, fire red. Clem felt the first stirrings of the lust worm that nestled at his crotch, dormant all these years but welcoming resurrection like a soul on Judgment Day and swelling, steepening, stretching its neck.

"Oh, my sweet Lord . . ." Clem sighed.

He barely listened as Rackstraw spoke to him, telling him about the Man-eaters with the air of a museum curator explaining an exhibit to a gaggle of eager schoolchildren. "Predators since before the dawn of history, men—and I refer directly to the male of the species here—have given women such as these three names like Furies, Fates, Hesperides, maenads, succubae, and many other things besides. Men have always regarded them as the foe and have always been afraid of them, for they represent everything that the masculine sex do not and cannot know, and they wield an influence that holds sway over the very root of a man's being. These three are among perhaps the most fearsomely rapacious examples of the breed, and have been our Angel's guardians and fellow travelers since before even I joined the Company. They are, in a literal sense, Man-eaters."

The women descended from the engine, portions of their

flesh jouncing resiliently, exquisitely, and Clem watched them in awe and rapture. They approached him, still chitter-clacking madly, and ran their hands over him, fondling his sodden clothing, stroking his bristly cheeks, gazing at him adoringly, avariciously.

Before Clem realized what they were doing, they had stripped him bare—quickly, dexterously, in fewer movements than he would have thought possible. Gooseflesh puckered all over his bare skin, arching the lank hairs on his chest and forearms. He shivered. He shivered with cold and delight and cold delight. How absurd that he had mistaken the man in the waiting room entrance for Death. Death was quite clearly a lady. Three ladies. Death was a beauty and a delight and a joy.

The Man-eaters caressed him. They brought his penis to twitching tumescence until it felt bigger than a flagpole, bigger than a grain silo, bigger than the whole damn Empire State Building. It felt like a nuclear missile, primed and ready to explode.

Then the three women joined hands and came together, giggling and chitter-clacking. It was then that Clem noticed the way their navels seemed to be moving around, dilating and contracting like . . . well, for all the world like *nostrils*.

Then their nipples opened.

Blinked.

Glistening eyeballs shone.

Three pairs, matching the blue, brown, and green of the eyes of the blond, brunette and redhead.

Eyes, nose . . .

And Clem knew now where that dental chitter-clack was coming from, but somehow that knowledge didn't instill terror in his heart or cause his rivet-hard cock to droop so much as a degree from vertical. Somehow that knowledge filled him with a deeper yearning, a profounder need for the touch and caress and, oh, yes, the sweet sinking into the warmth of these three women. If the Man-eaters had been shallow lagoons with jagged rocks lurking just beneath the surface, Clem would still have wanted nothing on earth so much as to dive into them from a great height.

He spread out his arms. He gave them his body. He surrendered to them willingly.

Some time later—he didn't know how much later—Clem died writhing, his spine arching and his jaw clenched in agony and bliss.

6

Safe and snug in their parlor, the Tremaine family weathered out the storm. Sandy had refused to go to bed, and so Bob was sitting with her on his lap, hugged to his chest. In another chair Alice busied herself with her needlepoint, glancing occasionally at her husband and daughter and thinking to herself, *Maybe it's all going to be all right, maybe everything is going to turn out just fine after all.* Bob had been acting normally this evening—a little tense perhaps, but almost his old self again. Alice couldn't ask for much more than that. She was grateful just to have Bob alive and home again. When the right moment came, she would winkle out of him what was troubling him so, and she would take his worries and soothe them away as a good wife should.

CRACK THERRUMP!!!

"Can anyone remember a storm like this?" Alice wondered aloud. "I know I surely can't."

"Daddy," said Sandy's Russian impersonator in a gut-wrenchingly perfect imitation of her voice.

"Yeah, honey?"

"Daddy, I'm scared."

"No need to be scared. It's just a storm."

"Well, not *scared,* not scared like I was that time I saw the snake in the backyard, all rolled up and looking at me and flicking its tongue at me, and you said it was only a grass snake so I needn't be scared, and you frightened it away with the shovel."

"And do you remember what I told you then?"

"You told me the snake was probably scareder of me than I was of it."

"That's right."

"Why does God make storms and snakes and things like that, Daddy? He can't be a very nice God if He likes frightening people, can He?"

"God doesn't frighten people, honey. People frighten themselves."

"Only if they're silly."

"And you're not silly, are you?"

"No!"

"So there's no reason why you should be scared of the storm, or of anything."

"I'm not scared of anything," Sandy decided, "not while you're here, Daddy."

Steeling himself, Bob brought his face down and kissed the impostor-daughter's head.

CRACK THERRUMP!!!

"Right now, honey, you're going to have to get off."

"Where are you going, Daddy?"

"Bathroom."

"Can I come with you? Please? That way, I won't be scared."

"Sandy," said her mother.

"Um, no, not really, honey," said Bob. "But don't worry, I won't be long. I'll be back before you can count to a hundred."

"Okay, then." And Sandy began counting. "One, two, three . . ."

Bob turned to Alice. "Look after her a moment, won't you?"

"Four, five . . ."

"Of course," Alice replied.

"Six, seven . . ."

Bob left the parlor, easing the door shut behind him. Instead of turning left for the stairs and the bathroom, he turned right and padded down the hallway toward the front door. There, he waited for a flicker of lightning, and when the inevitable *CRACK THERRUMP!!!* came, he unlatched the door and snuck out onto the porch.

The chair leg from Doc Wheeler's place was where he had left it earlier, when he had come home, down behind the porch swing, which the wind was swaying like a pendulum. Bob drew the chair leg out and hefted it in his hand. There was blood and hair stuck to one end of it, and what looked like a splinter of bone. Who would have thought that a simple piece of wood could be turned into such an effective instrument of vengeance?

Bob waited for another thunderclap, and slipped back indoors.

Sandy had reached fifty and, taking a deep hoarse gulp of air, she carried on. "Fifty-one, fifty-two . . ."

The snake. How could the Russians have known about the grass snake in the backyard?

That stopped Bob in his tracks. Sandy had come across the snake, what, a year ago? A year and a half? For several months afterward she had been wary of going out into the yard, even though he had managed to convince her that the snake wouldn't come near the Tremaine house again, not since it had seen his shovel. He had assured her that that snake had slithered halfway to Nebraska by now and wouldn't stop going until it reached the coast.

But how could they have known?

"Sixty-one, sixty-two, sixty-three . . ."

They must have captured her. They must be holding her somewhere in order to extract certain facts out of her that the impostor could then use in conversation to fool Bob into believing this was his real daughter. He didn't like to think of the methods they might have employed to gain this information. He hoped that they had used the latest truth serums and brain machines, and not plain old-fashioned torture.

"Seventy-eight, seventy-nine . . ."

Bob realized there was only one place in Escardy Gap where the Reds could be keeping the real Alice and Sandy: the train. First thing tomorrow, Bob would pay a visit to Mr. Rackstraw and Company. And he wouldn't be going empty-handed.

"Eighty-five, eighty-six . . ."

Resolved once again that he was doing the right thing, Bob moved on down the hallway. He entered the parlor. Sandy stopped counting at ninety-four. Moments later, the screaming began.

7

The Company watched Clem Stimpson's protracted death agonies with enraptured delight. With every twist and contortion of his body, they twisted and contorted themselves, too, and as the Man-eaters moved over him, squatting and ministering to him with their nether teeth, consuming him in bite-sized portions—now a finger, now an eyeball, now a strip of flesh torn from the flaccid muscles of one thigh—picking him clean like vultures, it was hard for many of the assembled artistes to keep themselves from leaping over and joining in. Even those that didn't have a taste for human meat found themselves licking their lips and eyeing the feast greedily. Not one of them, however, would have been mad enough to interrupt the Man-eaters during a meal. Not unless they wanted to become an entrée themselves.

Rackstraw himself affected a weary disdain for the proceedings, sitting on a bench some way along the platform from the rest of the Company with one leg crossed over the other, every so often glancing at his watch and stifling a yawn. The storm continued to rage overhead unabated, and the rain drummed on the roofs of the carriages and on the locomotive, individual droplets hissing as they struck the boiler's iron hide.

The Angel was waiting. Though it was relishing every second of Clem's mutilation, the Angel did not simply want its hunger for suffering satisfied. As ever, the Angel wanted some recognition for what it had done on the Company's behalf: finding this town, isolating it from the rest of the world, providing the Company with a stage to work on, a theater in which to operate, above all for giving them the means and the wherewithal to fulfill their dark desires and indulge their perverted pleasures. The Angel was waiting for the Company to renew their pledge to it.

Though Rackstraw, in the pit of pits that was his heart of hearts, bore a deep resentment that he had to be beholden to anyone or anything, nonetheless he was practical minded enough to realize that even he needed the Angel, and if all he had to do was pay it homage every so often and give its ego a good massage, well, he could swallow his pride and do that. He could tell it all the things it wanted to hear. He didn't have to *mean* them.

When there was nothing left of Clem but bones and clinging shreds of sinew and gristle, Rackstraw rose to his feet and clapped his hands once, twice, three times.

Even over the storm and through the haze of their prurient bloodlust, the Company heard him and came to attention— they knew what those claps signified.

As Rackstraw strode toward the crowd, the Man-eaters broke off from their repast and hurriedly slipped on their gowns again, then stooped and picked up Clem's remains. Clutching armfuls of bloody bones to their chests, the women scampered up onto the locomotive and over. Their movements were not as graceful as usual because their bellies were full and they were beginning to experience the sluggishness that comes after a good meal, and perhaps also because their food had been positively marinated in alcohol. Indeed, the brunette lost her footing as she leapt down onto the ground on the other side of the locomotive, and stumbled and started giggling like a nun who has stolen and imbibed a bottle of communion wine.

Bearing their armloads of human remains—snacks for later—the three Man-eaters ran alongside the first carriage, ducked one after another into the gap between it and the second, and disappeared.

Meanwhile, Rackstraw took center stage.

"Friends, fellow artistes," he began.

The majority of the Company did not consider themselves Rackstraw's friend, and it was debatable whether he was an artiste of their caliber. Really all he was was a jumped-up carny barker with delusions of grandeur. But they stifled their murmurs and grumbles. At this juncture, a certain solemnity was required.

"You, like I," Rackstraw continued, "have known what it is to be out of work, to be—hateful word—'resting.' Have we not all of us, at some time or other, wondered if we would ever find employment and despaired of ever meeting anyone who would have a use for our particular talents and predilections?"

There were nods and general rumblings of assent.

"Have we not, in fact, felt that our artistic abilities have often been misunderstood or underappreciated? Have we not feared that nobody would ever sponsor us or provide a home for us? For public taste is fickle, is it not? Worse, the public rejects that which disturbs or appalls them, even though these are as honest emotions as sentiment or nostalgia, and far harder to evoke. And so we individualists, we iconoclasts, we distinctive voices, we have had to seek whatever backing we can find. We have been prepared to make a deal with whomsoever would patronize us, accept their generosity unquestioningly, and accept, too, the terms of any contract they might offer us."

His oratory rose above the racket of the storm and resounded along the platform with preternatural clarity.

"How fortunate, then, that we have found ourselves our very own Angel. And how fortunate that our Angel had the wit to spot our peculiar talents and seek us out and offer us its protection."

And here he turned toward the locomotive, and the rest of the Company turned also, and Rackstraw raised his hands and held the forward in supplication, and said, "Your kindness is our salvation. Your sponsorship is our shelter. Your satisfaction is the highest compliment we can be paid."

And the Company repeated his words, intoning them in voices that ranged from a falsetto screech to a gravelly, all but incoherent growl.

"We pledge to bring you pain. We pledge to show you human suffering in all its myriad forms. We pledge to hurt and harm and maim and mutilate until you have had your fill and the plate is wiped clean. We pledge to bring you good souls screaming, to sate your craving and replenish your power. This we do in the full knowledge that without you we are lowlier than dirt. Without you we are nothing but dust."

Over and over Rackstraw repeated this unholy litany, and over and over the Company echoed him, until the call and response settled into a rhythmic chant.

"Without you we are lowlier than dirt. Without you we are nothing but dust."

Over and over, while the clouds clashed up above and sent

down shotgun blasts of rain, and the Company swayed from side to side as one, like stalks in a wind-lashed field of corn, their mouths working in unison, their gazes fixed on the locomotive.

"Without you we are lowlier than dirt. Without you we are nothing but dust."

And from inside the locomotive there came gurglings and deep sighs, and an almost palpable aura of contentment radiated out over the Company from the boiler as their Angel basked in their praise and gloried in their obeisance.

"Without you we are lowlier than dirt. Without you we are nothing but dust."

The ceremony continued long into the night.

Sixteen

1

Sunup," said Mayor.

Josh turned around from the three-tier house of cards he was constructing on Mayor's desk, his umpteenth such edifice. Doc, who was lying on a narrow couch in the corner, made waking-up noises, snuffles, and babyish grunts. He stretched his arms, and the empty bottle of Wild Turkey slid from his stomach onto the carpet, rolled with a hollow rattle and came to a stop against the couch's leg.

Behind Mayor, the window framed silhouettes of houses beneath a swathe of bruised sky. Between sky and houses a tiny sliver of bright orange had appeared, an aperture that was gradually widening, allowing more light to creep across rooftops and treetops. The light touched everything with a subtle, gilding hand. Birdsong twittered near and far. It seemed as if every bird in the state had opened its throat and was sending forth song, as if the reluctant sun actually needed enticing to come out and shine today.

"Thought I'd never see you," said Mayor to the sunrise.

"What time is it?" Josh asked.

"Just past five."

Five? How could twelve hours have gone by so fast? Josh had expected them to crawl, limp along like lepers. Instead, they had cruised past in smooth-running hot rods. That was one of the terrible perversities of Time. When you wanted it to pass, it dawdled. When you wanted it to stay, it sprinted. Time was the contrary guest, never doing anything you asked of it.

The storm had abated just after midnight, but the wind, clearly not aware that the party was over, had howled on through the small hours. Doc had dozed off around two-thirty, an event that had absolutely no connection whatsoever with the emptying of the bottle of whisky. Mayor and Josh had then played a few hands of gin rummy, Mayor winning the majority of the games. Then, leaving Josh to amuse himself with solitaire and house building, Mayor had stationed himself at the window and waited and watched for dawn.

Josh wished he had been able to sleep like Doc, but his concern for Grampa wouldn't let him. The combination of a lack of sleep with a lack of food left a rusty-tin taste in the back of his mouth. Swallow as he might, he just couldn't get rid of it. One wakeful night following another had put his rhythms all out of kilter. He felt dreamily detached from himself, a stranger inhabiting a strange body.

Doc swung his legs from the couch and, groaning, rubbed the backs of his knees, then touched the bandage on his forehead. He disappeared into the small rest room that connected to Mayor's office, and about a minute later there came the sound of trickling water as Doc's bladder leaked out a few drops.

Mayor lifted his vest from the back of the chair. His jaw was set in stone. Exhaustion bags hung heavy beneath his eyes. He tightened up his necktie, thrusting his chin out, craning his head back. "Time to get going," he said.

Josh stood up, deliberately jogging the desk so that the cards collapsed in a landslide of hearts and clubs, kings and queens, aces and numbers.

Shrugging, he said, "I'll build it again. Later."

2

Dawn saw Bob Tremaine dragging the smaller of the two
Communist infiltrators into the bathroom. The larger
one, the spitting image of his wife, already lay in the tub,
naked. Bob had intended to deal with them separately, phony
wife then phony daughter, but the more he thought about it,
the more it seemed like a waste of time and energy. It made
far better sense to do them both together. How much effort
did anyone want to put into disposing of a pair of lousy Commie corpses?

He hauled the Sandy impostor up by her armpits and tossed
her down onto the Alice impostor. The two bodies met in a
gangle of limbs, almost as if they were mother and daughter
embracing. Sandy's forehead cracked against the lip of the
tub, and the impact echoed hollowly through the porcelain.

It was unnerving, the way they looked. So damn realistic,
even in death. Damn, what those Commies could do!

After he had killed the impostors, Bob had spent long minutes looking for makeup, mask marks, tuck ties behind the
ears and beneath the jaw. Nothing. Obviously their whole
faces had been altered by surgery—surgery so flawlessly executed you couldn't find a join or a seam anywhere, and accurate even down to the chicken-pox scar on little Sandy's
right cheek.

Bob could almost have believed that these were indeed
replicas grown from pods, like the outer-space people in that
movie with Kevin McCarthy. He recalled Quincy Hogan rec-
ommending *Invasion of the Bodysnatchers* to him a week before it was due to be screened at the Essoldo. "You'll like
this one, Bob," Quincy had said with a wink. "It's what you
might call a parable. Kevin McCarthy, Joe McCarthy . . ."

Parable nothing. It was just a dumb movie about pod people from outer space—although Alice had had difficulty getting to sleep that night.

Before they had died Bob had tried to get the infiltrators to
speak to him in Russian but, deceitful to the last, the woman
who had taken Alice's place had begged and screamed in per-

fect English. "Come on, *comrade,*" Bob had yelled at her, swinging and swinging the chair leg. "Let's have a few prayers to the mother country and the great god Marx. Hey? *Da? Nyet? Da?*"

As for the doppelgänger daughter, she had just bawled and bawled and bawled in no language at all, until one last thwack from the chair leg had struck her dumb.

Their blood was red.

Naturally.

3

The back entrance to the town hall was located at the far end of the main vestibule, along a narrow corridor that smelled of mildew, down a short and unprepossessing flight of stone steps. The door opened onto a paved strip of yard where the trash cans were kept, a favorite haunt of the town's cats since it offered free food along with an ideal setting for fighting and fornication.

It was agreed that, once they were out in the open, not a word would pass between Mayor, Josh, and Doc unless it was absolutely vital. ("Like, for instance, 'Look out, it's Mr. Rackstraw!' " Mayor had joked just before they had left his office. He hadn't anticipated any laughter in response, and that was just as well, because he didn't get any.) And so the three of them passed through the yard in silence, their faces taut and ghostly in the early light.

The yard gave onto a back alley that ran parallel with Washington Street, then jogged left to come out in Hampton Boulevard, Escardy Gap's smartest residential area, where each house sprawled in a two-acre lot. It was often said, with more than a smidgen of blue-collar pride, that if you could afford a house in Hampton Boulevard, you had no right to be living in Escardy Gap. This was unfair. The Lieber family lived here, and Kevin's pop was Mr. Average Income. (It should be borne in mind, though, that Al Lieber had inherited the place from his father, who had inherited it from *his* father, who had been a big wheel in the barbed-wire industry way back when there *was* a barbed-wire industry.) Wilbur Cohen owned another of the palisaded, mansionesque residences, and while no one would describe the proprietor of Escardy Gap's only general store as poor exactly, neither would you classify him as stinking rich.

Some of the houses on Hampton Boulevard lay empty, their whitewash yellowed, their windows boarded up and their lawns grown long, thick and straggly, still choked with dead leaves from the previous fall. A real estate prospector passing through town would have spotted several bargains straight away, but real estate prospectors rarely troubled Escardy Gap; it was too far off the beaten track for all but the most adventurous outsiders to find.

The stealthy trio passed Wilbur Cohen's lime green Hudson Hornet Hollywood hardtop, which was sitting in the driveway outside the Cohen house, its bodywork beaded with drops of rainwater. The car crouched low on its whitewalls, but none of the three noticed this. There was a light in one of the upstairs windows. This did not strike any of them as unusual. They simply assumed Wilbur was up early, preparing to go down to the rail yard to take delivery of another batch of milk and newspapers. For Wilbur this no doubt seemed like just another Monday morning. Another day, another bunch of other people's dollars.

They stalked on.

4

But it was not just another Monday morning for Wilbur. It was, he fervently hoped, the last Monday morning he would see in Escardy Gap for some time to come.

Wilbur was not what you might call a sensitive man, but even he had realized all was not well with the town. He likened the sudden shift in the atmosphere to a shelf full of fruit rotting overnight: fine and ripe one moment, pustulent and crawling the next. An infection had struck right to the heart of the town, and the town was turning sour. So yesterday evening, Wilbur had loaded up his Hudson Hornet with luggage and supplies. Then he had stood, or more accurately sat, on guard behind the front door all night long, armed with a brass poker.

Now first light had come, and just as the fugitive trio passed his house, Wilbur was rousing his wife and daughter.

Rebecca dressed bleary-eyed Josie and carried her downstairs. Yawning, Josie crawled into the car, and Rebecca slid in beside her, her backside squeaking on the Naugahyde upholstery.

"Where are we going?" Josie demanded.

"On a trip," her mother replied. "We're going to visit Uncle Harry in Wayneville."

"I don't like Uncle Harry. Well, I do. But I don't like Cousin Jacob."

"Cousin Jacob adores you, Josie."

"He's a little brat. He always wants to play with me."

"That's enough, Josie," snapped Wilbur, fitting himself behind the wheel (lime green, to match the car's bodywork, and equipped with the very latest in power steering). "Here." He extracted a bright red lollipop from his pocket and unwrapped it. Josie stabbed it eagerly into her mouth, and there was silence.

Wilbur fitted on a pair of kid driving gloves, planted a Havana between his lips, and turned the ignition. The motor caught first time, its growl swiftly dropping to a purr, and Wilbur praised the Lord for American engineering.

Then, abruptly, a backfire.

In the serenity of early morning, the sound rang out as loud as a pistol shot.

5

If sweat from hard work was a measure of a man's honesty, then Bob Tremaine, dripping from every pore, was well on his way to sainthood.

He paused from his labors, resting the hacksaw against the side of the bathtub, and mopped his face with one of the small towels arranged neatly along the rail by the sink. Spots of blood smeared off on the fabric along with perspiration. The blood was not Bob's.

In the tub the corpses had lost all humanity. They were meat soup: skin, hair, bone, and gristle, tubular lengths of purple and yellowish green, sheets of transparent membrane, all swimming in red juice.

The hacksaw was ribbed with congealing blood, as were Bob's hands. Blood bedecked the shower curtain and spotted the pink wall tiles. Blood everywhere. Bob could not help but be reminded of Tom Finkelbaum, and he drew a grim satisfaction from the fact that these Reds had met a similar fate to the one inflicted on that poor kid. Poetic justice.

Looking up, Bob caught a glimpse of himself in the mirror over the basin, and he wondered when it had happened, when precisely he had become the haggard, mad-eyed creature that glared back at him. Was it when he discovered the awful truth, the whiteness at the end of the world? Or was it before that, when he had found Ike out on Boundary Hill? Or had it begun even earlier than that? Had this transformation been brewing as long as his doubts about his own fatherhood, his marriage, his fears of the Red Menace? It couldn't be coincidence, could it, that little Sandy was born on the same day that the Russians tested their first A-bomb, September 23, 1949, the day the pendulum started to swing the other way. The news from Doc Wheeler's hospital that afternoon could not have been more shocking to Bob than the news he heard over Billy Connors's radio set just after Alice had gone in labor. One child's birth into the capable hands of Nurse Sprocket weighed up against several megatons of atomic death now in the hands of brainwashed madmen—there was, in Bob's mind, no contest.

That had marked the beginning of the end for Bob: the realization that this squalling, squirming, purple-faced little innocent was not going to be brought up in a world safe for democracy, where the good guys had the edge over the bad guys, but rather had emerged at a time when the peril, the immediacy of chaos, was never greater. Oh, how Bob had wanted to shield his baby then. How he had wanted to hug her to his chest and whisper to her and squeeze and squeeze her until she choked for air, until she could no longer draw breath, until she was released from this terrible enslavement to fear.

Instead, he had simply held her and let her live. He regretted the decision now, regretted it bitterly. It was his biggest mistake.

Sudden racking sobs convulsed him. Bob bent over and wept into the towel that smelled of fresh laundering and Alice's care.

Some time later, he picked up the hacksaw and set to work again. There was no trace of tears or despair on his face. There was just the grim determination of a man proud of his convictions.

6

The three fugitives cut down a path that threaded its way along a gully between two of Hampton Boulevard's yards. Trees overshadowed them, and brambles sprang at their faces. The undergrowth rustled with unseen animal life, and the air smelled thickly of earth and dust. Scrawny Mayor went in front, followed by supple, slender Josh, with corpulent Doc taking the rear. Their breath came out in wispy plumes, and the sweat on their skin chilled the instant it came into contact with the air.

The sun, however, was beginning to instill some heat into the day, and encouraging the birds to increase the volume and complexity of their songs. The fugitives were glad of the chorus, because it masked the crash of their footsteps, the roar of their breathing, the triple-time thump of their heartbeats. They were acutely aware that someone might be watching and listening. None of the three was more conscious of this than Josh, whose close encounter with the women at the train was still painfully fresh in his memory.

The backfire startled them all to differing degrees. Mayor practically jumped out of his skin, Josh whirled in the direction the sound had come from, while Doc merely twitched as though a mosquito had just buzzed his ear.

"What was that?" Mayor whispered, clutching his neck.

"I don't know," said Josh, voice quavering. "A door slamming?"

"That weren't no door."

The boy's anxious face peered up at him, the whites of his eyes almost luminous in the early light.

"Well," said Mayor with great resolve, "whatever it was, there's nothing we can do about it. We're just going to have to be even quieter and more careful. Onward, ever onward."

Mayor had never had to be brave for anyone else's sake before. It was a strange feeling, but not completely unpleasant.

7

Neville N. Nolan blinked a bleary compound eye. His proboscis slowly uncurled and tested and tasted the morning air. Then a foreleg came 'round and slid along the length of that long ebony organ, wiping it clean. He cocked his head. A pulse of life passed along his jet black thorax and through his abdomen. Metallic plates shifted and jostled. His wings flexed in two shimmering prismatic arcs.

What had woken him? How had his rest been ruined?

From his perch beneath the moldering eaves of one of the abandoned homes on Hampton Boulevard, it didn't take Neville long to locate the source of the sound that had sundered his slumber.

A large, grand automobile like a lime green armadillo was rolling resplendently down the road. Its motor murmured, its chrome finish flashed crisply in the low light, the tread of its tires sang in a soft wheel whine.

Neville sighed for joy.

It wasn't just that the car was a beauty, although its automotive allure appealed abundantly to his appreciation of the aesthetic. More than anything, it looked like a large insect making its stately way through a miniature model town, and this filled the fly-man with a sincere sense of sympathy. His curiosity was also kindled. Where was this captivating car carrying its passengers? Jeremiah Rackstraw would be genuinely, rightfully indignant if he wasn't informed.

With a leaping lunge, Neville launched himself from the eaves, and corkscrewed down toward the crawling car. He flew around it three times in shrinking circles.

The first time he read the word on the lip of the hood: Hudson.

The second time he read the word on the wing just behind the headlight: Hornet.

The third time he read the word near the driver's side door: Hollywood.

Hudson Hornet Hollywood.

Plain, pure, perfect rapture!

8

Bob loaded the remains of the replicas of his wife and daughter into burlap sacks. He could only find four of the sacks in his basement, and they weren't as capacious as he might have wished, so that much of the ersatz Alice and Sandy had to be washed down the drain of the bathtub. What wouldn't go down of its own accord Bob had to mash up and shove down by hand. He then spent the best part of ten minutes at the sink scrubbing gummy Commie ooze from beneath his fingernails.

The limbs and the heads went into two of the sacks, the other two sacks took the torsos. Bob realized he wouldn't be able to carry all four, and so he selected the head-and-limb sacks and hefted one up in each arm. Bob was a powerful man. He knew he was a powerful man. Heavy as they were, he was pretty sure he would be able to carry those two sacks where he wanted to take them. It wasn't far. Just along South Street, then 'round the corner and down Washington to the station.

Bob set down the sacks and went to the bedroom, where he stripped to his underwear and put on a clean shirt and his dungarees. He took his soiled shirt and pants back to the bathroom and stuffed them into the laundry basket, more from force of habit than from any belief that Alice would be coming back to wash and starch and iron them and make them as good as new.

At the sink, Bob lathered his face and shaved, then brushed his hair and teeth. He bared his sparkling incisors at the mirror.

Back in the bedroom, he rooted around in the drawer of

one of the bedside tables. He found his Colt revolver easily enough, but of the bullets there were no sign. Then he remembered that Alice had insisted on bullets and gun being kept in separate places, in case Sandy happened upon them one day and there was a terrible accident. Bob, reluctantly, had seen the sense in this. The bullets were kept on the top shelf of the wardrobe. He fetched them down. He took six from the box and snugged them into the cylinder. The box, which contained another dozen and a half bullets, went into the pocket of his jeans. He looped a leather holster-belt around his waist and sheathed the gun.

Then he spun around to face the full-length wall mirror, and in one swift motion drew, cocked, and aimed at his reflection's head. The hollow end of the gun barrel obscured one of the reflection's eyes.

"Okay, Comrade Rackstraw," he snarled. "Time to parley."

9

The path petered out, giving way to lawn. The three fugitives had reached the backyard of the home of Miss Ingrid Ohllson. Even if they hadn't known this for a fact, they might have guessed from the rigid mathematical neatness of the flower beds, the clipped precision of the privet hedges, and the ruled straightness of the gravel paths. Who else but Escardy Gap's stern Scandinavian schoolmarm could correct and neaten nature as if it were a messy midterm math paper?

This spotless horticultural copybook had, however, been blotted.

The little Clarence the changeling had left of either Walt Donaldson or Miss Ohllson was nevertheless enough to enable Doc to identify both bodies with a fair degree of certainty. The cavernousness of Walt's rib cage was that corpse's distinctive feature, and what remained of a severe and restrictive girdle could not have belonged to any other woman in Escardy Gap except, perhaps, Hannah Marrs.

The position in which the mutilated bodies were lying

caused Doc some consternation. Miss Ohllson was on her back, legs spread in a shameless V. Walt Donaldson was on top, his pelvis thrusting into hers. The absence of genitalia on either body suggested to Doc that the positioning had taken place after death rather than during or before. It was as if the murderer or murderers had wanted to cause maximum outrage to whoever had the misfortune to discover the bodies. A sick sense of humor was at play here, and Doc was more angry than distraught. Righteous indignation filled that bulky frame of his. He turned to Mayor and Josh. Ashen faced, the two of them returned his gaze.

"There'll come a reckoning, you mark my words," muttered Doc. "Hanging's too good for these people."

"In time, Doc, in time," said Mayor.

"Damn 'in time'!" Doc rejoined. "The longer we leave it, the more people die."

"Doc, I thought we'd been through all this."

"So did I, Mayor, but I'm beginning to wonder if this plan of yours is really the best thing. I'm beginning to wonder if young Josh here isn't right and we shouldn't just rustle up a posse and move in on that train and burn those bastards to kingdom come."

Mayor stepped toward Doc. Suddenly, the situation had become precarious. Everything was at risk. If Doc backed out of the plan to walk to Grant's Crossing, then Josh would probably go along with him. That would leave Mayor on his own. He could manage the distance, that wasn't the problem. The problem was that when he got to Grant's Crossing he would be alone. Alone, he would have to persuade the authorities that his town was under siege. Alone, he would have to convince them that Jeremiah Rackstraw and his cronies amounted to a significant threat. That wouldn't be easy. People who didn't know Mayor well reckoned he was a few bricks short of a load. People who did know him well thought pretty much the same, but they were willing to overlook his eccentricities because, apart from anything else, he was a damn fine mayor. Over at Grant's Crossing they didn't know him well. They just knew of his reputation. They might be inclined to think that this sad figure of an ex-actor who had walked twenty miles across scorching desert to spout some crazy story about a train and a bunch of homicidal maniacs (which sounded like something out of one of the very bad movies he used to appear in) had finally flipped. They might be inclined just to lock him up and forget about him, or send him off to rot his last days in a rest home for the terminally bewildered.

He needed Doc, one of the most trustworthy and dependable people in Escardy Gap. Without him, it would be hopeless. Without him, he might as well just go back to his office and wait for the arrival of Rackstraw or whichever of the Company had been assigned to deal with him.

"Doc," he said. "Victor."

Doc just looked at him.

Josh looked at both of them. Although Mayor was speaking softly, Josh sensed the anxiety in his voice.

"Everyone knew how close and Regina were." Mayor couldn't recall when it was he had last used either Doc's or Nurse Sprocket's Christian names. Maybe this was the first time ever. "You tried to hide it, arguing and bickering the way you did, but even an old dog like me can tell when two people love and respect one another. But she's gone now, Victor. She's gone. And there's two things you can do about that. You can throw yourself away. You can go after Rackstraw and Bob Tremaine and all of them, and you can get yourself killed, and what good will that have done? What will you have done for the memory of Nurse Sprocket? Nothing. And people'll say, 'That Doc Wheeler, he sure was a good doctor, but he sure was a fool, too. He gave up when he should have carried on. He didn't follow his own advice. He didn't heal himself.' Is that what you want them to say about you, Victor?"

Doc didn't reply.

"Or," Mayor went on, "you can do something worthwhile. You can help bring the Company to justice. You can see to it that they stand trial and you can see that justice is served. And then people'll say, 'Doc Wheeler—a great man. He didn't let his grief overwhelm him. He didn't let despair get the better of him. He stood up to the very worst that life can throw at a person and he made the best of it.' Now, isn't that what you want?"

"What you're saying," Doc replied, slowly and evenly, "is that you don't want me to act like a human being. You want me to act like some tough guy in a movie. No grieving, no crying."

"No, that's not—"

"That's how it damn well sounds, Douglas!"

"Keep your voice down."

Quieter: "That's how it sounds."

"Look, Victor, I *need* you. I really do. I need you to come with me. I can't do this on my own. That's the honest truth. How long have we been friends?"

"I don't know. A long time. Longer than I can remember. That's a cheap card to play, Douglas."

"It's all I've got. So I'm asking you, in the name of that friendship, to stick with me, Victor. Trust me like I trust you. Let's see this through together, you and me, me and you. Hey? Just like old times."

There was a silence that went on longer than Josh could have held his breath. He looked from Doc to Mayor, Mayor to Doc. Their gazes were locked on one another, unwavering, unflinching.

Finally Doc said, "Okay. Okay, okay, okay."

Mayor reached out and hugged him. After a moment, Doc reciprocated, patting Mayor's bony back.

"Guess like everyone else I just want to be a hero," Doc said.

"You'll get your chance," said Mayor.

"God, I loved that woman."

"I know."

"Ornery old harpy she could be, but I loved her."

"I know, Doc."

Flies had begun to descend on Walt Donaldson and Miss Ingrid Ohllson and set to laying their eggs in the few remaining shreds of skin and flesh still attached to the chalk-white skeletons. In the heat of summer, it wouldn't be long before the eggs hatched and the corpses were writhing in a squelching sea of soft white maggots. Soon the bones would be picked clean, and a cloud of young fattened flies would arise and disperse all over the town, searching for fresh flesh, new putrefaction . . . of which there would be no lack.

10

The burlap sacks were leaking. It would have been better if they had been plastic, but Alice had never liked that stuff and didn't want it in the house. "It's a Great American Invention," Bob had told her, although he didn't know this for sure. Plastic certainly *ought* to have been a Great American Invention.

The sacks were dark and slick at the bottom, and squelched as he lifted them from the floor. He slung one over either shoulder, and by the time he reached the front door the backs of his thighs were soaked. He had left a trail of blood spatters down the stairs. He would leave a trail of blood spatters all the way to the station. Somehow, this seemed fitting and symbolic.

Burdened with parts of his family, Bob stepped out into a brilliant morning. The air was so clear and fresh it made him feel giddy. He stood for a while on the porch sucking in that air, breathing out the stink of blood and death, purifying his lungs. He raised his face to the low sun. The Colt was a solid, reassuring weight against his hip. It was a great day to be alive. It was a great day to be one of the last free Americans in the world.

11

Even as one crisis passed, another reared its ugly head. Mayor was beginning to think that some supernatural force was against him, some evil spirit was dogging him with bad luck, doing all it could to make him stay in town and accept his fate meekly.

Because as the three fugitives reached the end of a narrow back alley that connected Belvedere Way with South Street, who should Mayor catch sight of sneaking out from his house but Bob Tremaine?

Mayor pulled up sharply, and the parade of two—somber Doc, wary Josh—came to a halt behind him.

"What is it?" Josh whispered.

Mayor held a hand up to indicate silence, then motioned for them to press themselves back against the fence. They did so. The fence was high and tightly slatted so that there was no way anyone could see down the street without poking their head around the corner. Mayor poked his head around, then drew it back and turned to his companions and said, "It's one of them."

A lie, sort of. If Doc was to be believed, Bob had switched sides or else one of the Company had hypnotized him, or was maybe even masquerading as him. The Bob Tremaine that Mayor had just seen was up to *something,* anyway, lugging two mysteriously heavy sacks down South Street toward Washington Street. Mayor didn't know what those sacks contained, but they sure looked suspicious. The weight and shape of them, the discolorations . . .

"Coming this way?" Josh said, not caring that his voice was trembling.

Mayor shook his head and pointed in the other direction.

Bob Tremaine had reached the end of South Street and was adjusting the weight of the sacks on his shoulders. Mayor squinted hard. There was . . . some kind of stain all down Bob's back and legs. Dark stuff. Same dark as the sacks. Like they were leaking . . .

And then Bob turned round.

Mayor snatched his head back.

"Mayor? . . ."

"Ssh!"

Mayor, Josh, and Doc waited for a small eternity to yawn and close its mouth. No need to ask Mayor if they were in danger. No need to ask if he thought he had been spotted. All they could do was wait for approaching footsteps.

Josh closed his eyes. He didn't want to see Death coming. He wanted to greet the Reaper with his eyes tight shut and his back turned. He just wanted to hear the brief swish of Death's scythe, and then it would all be over.

12

Now, that was funny. Bob could have sworn he felt someone watching him. That uncanny, prickling certainty, as if a gaze were a needle that printed a tattoo on the back of your brain; the harder the gaze, the deeper the prick of the needle's point.

He dumped the two sacks down onto the sidewalk and looked back along the street. Sleeping houses joined by crisscrossing telephone wires. Shrinking shadows beneath their eaves. The loop and dart of early birds catching early insects.

Probably someone had just opened their curtains, caught sight of Bob Tremaine carrying a couple of sacks, perhaps assumed that Bob was off to Ike's place to make sure Ike's cattle were okay, maybe fetch Ike's mail, because they'd heard Ike was ill. A good friend to his good friend, that Bob Tremaine. Yeah. The kind of guy that made you proud to be an American.

Then Bob remembered that there weren't many Americans left except him.

He groped for his gun. When his hand couldn't find it right away, he glanced down and noticed that one of the sacks had fallen open, to reveal a twist of blond hair matted with dried blood. Bob investigated the sack further, and then he began to chuckle. Heh. Of course he had thought he was being watched, that eyes were following him along the street. The Alice-impostor's eyes were. Her eyes were boring through the burlap into the back of his head.

Heh.

Bob shouldered his burden again and set off.

13

Mayor hardly dared look.

He was thinking, *It's Bob Tremaine, Doc. You know— good ole Bob, big as a house, tall as a wall, wide as a river, who slaughtered your beloved and pounded Ike Swivven's brains to mush and knocked you upside the head for good measure, and he's coming this way. What are you going to do about it? What are you going to do if he comes 'round the corner? Are you going to shake his hand and say, "Well, hi, there, Bobby boy, and how are you this fine morning?" Or are you going to throw your Hippocratic oath to the winds and leap on him and try to rip his gizzard out? I think I know which it's going to be, Doc, so please God, please God, let Bob go the other way, let him have not seen me, let us get out of town alive, please God, please. . . .*

Mayor looked.

South Street was empty. Of Bob Tremaine there was no sign. Mayor wanted to sigh and cry, leap and dance, holler and hum.

Josh and Doc, seeing that the danger was past, rolled their eyes at each other. Doc was about to pat the lad on the head, then thought better of it. He biffed him on the biceps instead.

"Reckon *someone's* on our side today," he said with an upward nod.

Josh wished he could share Doc's confidence. But it wasn't confidence, really. Doc's mood was swinging between desperate bravado and brave despair with a frequency that indicated a mind no longer completely on an even keel. Josh had an idea that he would have been acting pretty much the same way if he had known for certain that Grampa was dead. As it was, he had a hope to cling to, however slim, however frail. That was all that lay between Josh and madness. The thought of Grampa alive. Grampa in the clutches of the Company, but alive, alive, alive.

Mayor gave a wagons-ho wave, and the three of them crept out onto South Street.

14

The train squatted in the siding. The locomotive radiated malevolence in black waves shot through with lightning streaks of silver, a storm cloud in iron and steel. As Bob approached, he became aware of soft rumbles and groans coming from the boiler, and from the carriages scurries and liquid whispers. And another noise:

Chitter-clack.

When the three women emerged from behind the locomotive, Bob couldn't hold back a gasp. The loveliness of them! No one had told him Russian women could be like this. He had imagined them all alike: walking potatoes in headscarves, with piggy little eyes, hairy upper lips, wart-festooned noses, slablike cheeks and vast brick red forearms. These here were beauty incarnate, slender as saplings, but curvaceous in all the right places.

"My God . . ." Bob had to pinch himself. Surely this was some kind of thought control, an attempt to cloud his mind, leave him vulnerable. Maybe the women were wearing some kind of hallucinogenic perfume. Anything was possible.

The women clutched at one another and gesticulated at the sacks and at Bob, and their chitter-clacking reached fever pitch, sounding like a hundred castanets clattering at once.

"Oh, you know what's in here, do you?" said Bob, drawing and cocking the revolver. "More Sisters of the Revolution, right? Well, if you want them so bad, you can come and get them."

The women wanted them bad, all right. They wanted to taste that sweet flesh, drink that delicious blood, slurp the marrow from the bones like tomato juice through a straw. They wanted Bob bad, too. They wanted him to watch while they peeled his dick like a ripe banana and sucked the sap from his *cojones*. Then they wanted to tear him to pieces, and tear those pieces to pieces, and tear the pieces of the pieces into yet tinier pieces. But he had a gun, and they knew that guns spat white-hot death.

Cowering, but not cowed, the three women watched Bob, looking for an opening, that split second when he dropped his guard, when they could fall upon him, and they would make sure that he took an hour to die (and unlike Clem Stimpson, not one minute of that hour would he spend in ecstasy).

"Now, listen here," said Bob. "I want to see Jeremiah Rackstraw and I want to see him now. Any tricks, any sneaky moves, and I shoot first and ask questions later."

"That won't be necessary, Mr. Tremaine."

No prizes for guessing who had just stepped down from one of the carriages. The eloquent, elegant, black-clad leader of the Company smiled cordially at haggard, hollow-eyed, gun-toting Bob Tremaine. Bob looked over at him, but kept the gun trained on the three women. "You're Rackstraw," he said with certainty.

"That I am."

"I've heard a lot about you."

"All of it good, I trust."

"Rackstraw . . . That's your real name?"

"How interesting that you should ask. As a matter of fact, it isn't. It's a traveling name, a nom de plume, one of many. Every time I go somewhere, I pack a new name in my bag, one to suit the climate and the temperament of the locals. My true name you would find almost impossible to pronounce."

"Vladimir Something-ovitch Something-ski, eh?"

"No, Bob. To pronounce my true name requires the ability to talk in seventeen tongues simultaneously. I must say, I have trouble with it myself on occasions."

"Well, forgive me if I don't try." Bob nodded at the women. "Now, call them off."

"I'm afraid that's impossible," Rackstraw replied. "They're guard dogs, not lapdogs. I can't simply forbid them to do something, especially now that they've got the scent of blood."

"Call them off," Bob reiterated. The gun remained leveled steady at the navel of the middle of the three chitter-clacking women, the brunette.

Rackstraw spread his arms in a gesture of helplessness. "I wish I could, Bob."

"Mr. Tremaine, if you don't mind."

"Mr. Tremaine," said Rackstraw patiently, "I wish I could, but women are a law unto themselves, as well you know." He gestured at the sacks. "Speaking of which—that's your wife and daughter in there, isn't it?"

"Yes," said Bob. Then, "No. No, it ain't. It's two of yours."

"Two of ours? I don't think it can be. We're all accounted for, all present and correct."

"That a fact?"

"It's a fact."

"Don't play games with me, Rackstraw."

"The only one playing games here is you, Mr. Tremaine. Russian roulette, by the look of it."

"Joke all you want, *comrade*. What I did to these two, I can do to you."

Rackstraw gave a carefully considered rendition of nervous fear. He raised his hands as far as his shoulders. "You must have been a very big, brave man to have done that to two defenseless females," he said.

"Two spies."

"As you wish. Two defenseless spies."

"They could have defended themselves. I just didn't give them the opportunity."

"May I ask, Mr. Tremaine, what brought this on?"

"Brought what on?"

"This psychopathic paroxysm."

"Use words I can understand."

"This murderous fit."

"I ain't murdered anyone. I have legitimately killed in war two enemy subversives."

"A deep-rooted mental imbalance," Rackstraw diagnosed. "But what was it that tipped the scales in lunacy's favor?"

"Speak plain English, goddamn you!"

"What happened to you, Bob?" said Rackstraw. "What turned you from ordinary family man to self-styled soldier?"

"You want me to say it, I'll say it. I've seen what goes on. I've been out into the desert. I know the score. I know about the atomic war."

Rackstraw's face clouded, then cleared, light dawning miraculously. He began to laugh. Mindful of the Colt, he kept it a cautious, controlled laugh, but it was nevertheless mocking and contemptuous.

"Shut up," Bob told him.

"Oh, poor old Bob!" said Rackstraw. "Poor old misguided Bob Tremaine! Incredible, isn't it, how you fit the facts to suit your beliefs, and not the other way 'round. You bear witness to what you *think* you see rather than what is actually there."

"Shut the hell up, Rackstraw, or so help me I'll blow that grin clean off your face!"

"You think the Russians have nuked America, don't you, Bob? That's it, isn't it? Your private nightmare has come true."

"*Mr. Tremaine.* How many times do I have to keep telling you?"

"Forgive me."

"That is what's happened," said Bob. "Ain't it?" He frowned, and the barrel of the Colt drooped, nosing down to point at the ground. The redhead feinted forward and Bob brought the gun up again. The woman drew back with an angry snapping of her nether teeth.

"No, that's not what's happened at all, Mr. Tremaine. What you have seen is just a simple, practical expedient, something to make our task a little easier. What word can I use that you'll understand? Aha! A corral. That's the word. We've established a corral around Escardy Gap to keep you all in your rightful place."

"Damn, you talk craziness," said Bob.

"Oh, I admit that," replied Rackstraw, "but isn't it *nicely phrased* craziness?"

15

They reached the hospital without further incident. That is not to say that they didn't jump at every sudden sound and didn't halt whenever they came across a shadow that hid just a little too much in its black wings. The main thing is that they made it to the outskirts of the still-sleeping town alive.

By the side of the peppermint green, snow white building they stopped. Over on the other side of Delacy Street the Evett brothers' grain silo stood tall and gleaming, its silvery skin reflecting nothing but perfect blue so that it looked as if it were a cylinder of solidified sky.

"Oh, my good God," said Doc suddenly, slapping his forehead. "How could I be so danged stupid?"

"What is it, Doc?"

"Mayor," said Doc, gesturing angrily at the house, "I've left a patient in there."

"I thought you said Ike—"

"Not Ike. *Sara.*"

"Sara Sienkiewicz is ill? You didn't say anything about that."

"I had other things on my mind," said Doc sullenly.

"What's wrong with her?"

"Some kind of collapse. And I left her there all night! What kind of a physician am I?"

Mayor's conscience wrestled with his instinct for survival. Time was getting short. The sun was fully up and the Company would soon be abroad, if they weren't already. However, Sara was lying inside the house, perhaps in need of medical attention.

"Damn it, Doc!" Mayor exploded in pure frustration. "Couldn't you have thought of this earlier?"

"It's not his fault," Josh pointed out.

"Yeah, I know," said Mayor. "Sorry, Victor."

"I ain't going inside," said Doc in answer to an unspoken question. "Not inside that place."

"But someone's got to see how Sara is," said Mayor, "haven't they?"

"Not me."

"I'll go," said Josh.

"I don't think that's such a good idea, son," said Doc.

"Why not?"

"What's in there . . . ain't a pretty sight."

"What we found at Miss Ohllson's wasn't any too pretty," Josh replied matter-of-factly.

"Yeah, but—"

"I'll go too," said Mayor.

"But it could be dangerous," said Doc. "Tremaine might have gone back in there."

Mayor hesitated, nearly said something he might have regretted, then said, "We'll take that risk. Tell us which room she's in."

Doc gave them directions to the room where Sara was. There was no other way to reach it than by the main stairs. He told them what they could expect to find at the top of those stairs, although he couldn't bring himself to refer to it using Nurse Sprocket's name. He couldn't associate Nurse Sprocket with the mangled thing that lay sprawled across the upper corridor.

"We won't be more than ten minutes," said Mayor. "We'll just see if she's okay, then come back out."

"Look for irregularities in her breathing. It was steady when I last checked. See if her pupils are still dilated. Take her pulse. You know where the pulse is found, don't you? It should be around forty beats per minute."

"What if it's not, Doc?" Josh asked. "What if it's faster? What if it's much slower? Will you come in then?"

Doc thought for a moment. "I don't know, Josh. We'll have to see."

16

Does the phrase Mexican standoff mean anything to you?" Jeremiah Rackstraw asked Bob Tremaine.

"It kind of describes the situation we're in now," said Bob. "Except I've got a gun and you haven't."

"But I have Alecto, Atropos, and Aegle. If you shoot me, they'll have ripped your heart out before my body has even hit the ground. Equally, if you shoot one of them, you won't be given the chance to get another bullet off."

It wasn't hot yet, the sun was still low, but sweat was brimming in Bob's eyebrows and threatening to spill down into his eyes. "So what do we do?" he said, blinking hard.

"You're the one who came here. *You* wanted to see *me*. You come up with a suggestion."

"Once, just once, I'd like a straight answer from you, Rackstraw."

"What, and have me break the habit of a lifetime?"

"God*damn!* All I want is my wife and daughter back. That's what I came here for. A swap. Your people for mine."

Light was blazing in Rackstraw's eyes and his grin couldn't have gone any wider without splitting his head in two. He seemed to find the whole situation an amazingly funny joke, a rib tickler of epic proportions, a monumental cosmic belly laugh.

"You're keeping them in that train, aren't you?" Bob went on. "Bring 'em out. Bring 'em out where I can see them, and you'll get what's left of your comrades back."

"What a bargain," said Rackstraw. "And if I refuse?"

"You die."

"And then *you* die."

Bob shrugged. "That's the stakes we're playing for."

"It is Russian roulette after all," said Rackstraw. "Very well. It just so happens that your family *are* inside the train. Would you like me to go and fetch them?"

"Damn straight I would. But I'll be keeping an eye on you all the way. First sign of any funny stuff—*bang!*"

"Funny stuff!" said Rackstraw, turning toward the train. "It's *all* funny to me."

17

Just one day earlier, Bob Tremaine had been here. He had crept stealthily, treading the same carpet and stairs; had breathed quietly, swallowing the same air; had touched the same doors, brushing alongside the same walls. Like a germ in a system, he had infected the cleanliness of the hospital with his presence, brought brutality into this place of nurture and healing.

Mayor and Josh found the body of Nurse Sprocket where Doc had said they would. From the neck up she resembled a broken meat pie. Her blood had dried black on the floorboards. As with Walt and Miss Ohllson, there were flies. Here, in this cool sanctuary of cleanliness and sterility, there were gorged black flies.

Both Mayor and Josh managed to avert their eyes. The wet-earth stench coming from Nurse Sprocket, however, was harder to ignore. If it hadn't become so familiar recently—since yesterday morning, in fact, when the mist unveiled Century Cedar and all that it carried—that smell would have had them gagging and retching. Covering their faces, they made it past.

The room where Sara lay was white. The walls and ceiling were whitewashed. Embroidered white curtains floated in front of the windows. Simple white furniture was placed spartanly around the room. Ice white sheets and vanilla white blankets covered the bed. Her very skin was white as a glacier. The only spots of color in the room were her eyes, her red lips, and her hair, which had been unfastened to flow in all directions over the pillow in dark brown tendrils.

She was awake, and yet not awake. There were no thoughts or dreams going on behind those big dark empty eyes, no shadow plays, no mind movies. The fictional lands where her characters dwelled did not, at present, exist. Nothing lived in there. Nothing *could* live in there. Her brain was as barren as an arctic waste, as a desert, as space. The mind that turned words into worlds had been sucked dry.

"Guess we'd better do as Doc said. You any good at this sort of thing, Josh?"

"No, sir."

"Me, neither."

Her breathing was long and shallow and so quiet that Mayor had to put his ear right by her lips to hear anything. The rise and fall of her chest seemed even and regular to Josh's untrained eye. It reminded him of the way Grampa slept in his rocking chair, chin on collarbone.

"Now, which is dilation?" said Mayor, examining Sara's eyes. "Is that when they get bigger or smaller?"

"Bigger," said Josh. "I think."

"They can't get much bigger than that," said Mayor, peering into pupils so enlarged that hardly any iris showed, just a flare of violet around the rims like a pair of suns in eclipse.

Josh took one of Sara's wrists and felt for the flutter of life. His thumbs seemed far too big and clumsy to find anything in that piece of delicate bone china, but finally he felt it, a moth's wing of a heartbeat, like her breathing shallow but regular. He timed it by his watch, counting ten beats in fifteen seconds, forty per minute.

Both of them then stood back from the sleeping beauty, feeling as if just by touching her they had committed some indignity.

"A fairy princess," said Josh, and almost immediately regretted the way it sounded: kind of wishy-washy, the sort of thing that would have made the other kids turn on him and call him a sissy. And yet it was true.

"Ain't she just?" said Mayor. "Almost makes you want to lean over and kiss her, see if she wakes up."

"Yeah."

"Go on, then."

Josh looked at him. "What?"

"Go on and kiss her."

"You're joking, right?"

"Only half."

Josh hesitated. "I couldn't. You."

"She wouldn't want a leathery-skinned old coot like me kissing her. A fine-looking young fella like you, on the other hand . . ."

"No, it wouldn't be right," Josh said. But he almost wanted to. Even comatose, Sara Sienkiewicz was breathtakingly beautiful, and her lips were like small rounded rose petals that just begged for another pair of lips to alight like a butterfly on them. To the best of his knowledge, none had. Those lips of Sara's were terra incognita, an unknown continent waiting for the Columbus bold enough, brave enough, to come and explore them and discover their delights.

Josh didn't think he was that man. He didn't think Mayor was that man, either.

But he was sorely tempted. What were a woman's lips like? How did they feel? What did they taste of? Kissing was rumored to be one of life's greatest pleasures. What magic took place when mouths met? What messages were passed? What secrets were shared? What was it all about?

"Come on, lad," said Mayor. "Nothing more we can do here."

But Josh was convinced that there was something they could do, that maybe kissing Sara wasn't such a dumb idea, maybe it would bring her 'round like Snow White, like Sleeping Beauty, like a character out of one of her own stories. . . .

Mayor was at the door. He cupped a hand over his nose and mouth and slipped out into the corridor.

Josh turned back to the sleeping Sara. He gazed at her. And then, obeying some secret impulse he would never understand, he bent down and pecked her lips with his.

They were cold, ice-cold, and Josh snapped his head back in a shock of disgust. He swiped at his mouth with his shirt cuff.

Mayor's hand-masked face appeared in the doorway. "What are you doing, son?"

"Nothing, sir," said Josh, hurriedly adjusting the corner of the pillow. "Just making sure she's comfortable."

"Come on," Mayor said, beckoning for Josh to follow.

18

"Alice!" cried Bob.

Alice, the love of his life. Alice, his true wife. Alice, no great beauty, but a fine woman, a woman you could depend on with your life. Alice, who took his secrets in the night, listened as he poured out his fears, wiped his tears, then told him everything was going to be all right (even if it wasn't).

Alice Tremaine smiled at her husband as Jeremiah Rackstraw raised an arm to help her down from the carriage. She scooped up her skirts and negotiated the steps carefully, aided by the ever-unctuous leader of the Company. When she reached the ground, she skipped over to Bob and hugged him.

"Alice, honey," said Bob, burying one cheek in her hair (but keeping his eyes and gun trained on the three women). "Are you all right? Have they been treating you right?"

He felt her nod. He was flooded with love and gratitude and a whole passle of other emotions, foremost among them relief, relief that he had been right all along, despite the gnawing doubts, the nagging fears that he might, just might, have been making a terrible mistake.

He addressed Rackstraw. "And Sandy. Where's my kid?"

"Sandy's in there, too," said Rackstraw. "But don't you think you should have a proper reunion with your wife first?"

"A proper? . . ."

"A kiss, Bob, a kiss. I think the very least Alice deserves after her ordeal is a whopping great smackeroo on the lips."

"Mr. Rackstraw, I don't care much for your tone. Whether I kiss my wife or not is my business. Now go fetch Sandy." Bob brandished the Colt briefly in Rackstraw's direction, training it back on the women before any of them could make a move.

Rackstraw was unimpressed. "At least a peck on the cheek, Bobby boy. I'd hate Alice to think you weren't glad to see her."

"Mr. Rackstraw . . ."

"No kiss, no daughter."

Bob weighed this. Even though he had the gun, Rackstraw still had the upper hand. The man was cunning as a fox, no doubt about it. Crazy as a loon, too.

"Okay, honey," Bob said to Alice, "let's just do as he says. If it makes him happy. If it means he'll go get Sandy."

He felt Alice nod again, and he bent his face down and kissed the crown of her head. "Satisfied?" he asked Rackstraw.

"Not really, but it'll have to do. Come on in, then."

"What?"

"Sandy's inside. Come in and fetch her."

"You bring her out."

"She's sleeping. I think *you* should be the one to wake her."

"Jesus H. Christ!" Bob exclaimed. "All right, all right. Stay here, Alice, and don't worry. They're not going to hurt you. I've got a gun."

So saying, Bob approached the carriage. The darkness he could see through the open door was about as complete as darkness gets. Even so, he could sense movement within, vague flittings to and fro, darker patches of darkness within the darkness, and he caught the sound of hisses and titters and shuffles. He grasped the inside of the doorway and hauled himself up onto the lowest step.

"Sandy?"

He climbed the next two steps.

"Sandy? It's Daddy, Sandy. It's time to get up, honey. Time to go home."

He leaned back, turning his head.

"If this is a trick, Mr. Rackstraw, so help me I'll . . ."

"You'll do *what*, Mr. Tremaine? Fall for it?"

Bob turned to face the pitch-blackness again, and his heart was beating nine to the dozen, and he told himself, *They're just a bunch of Russkies, they're just a bunch of lousy Russkies, you've got a gun, they ain't gonna hurt you, you've got one of Mr. Samuel Colt's finest.*

"Sandy, I'm coming in."

And with that, Bob lunged forward and left the daylight behind.

Ever swum in a lake at night? Ever plunged deep down into

the icy water and opened your eyes and for one awful, delicious moment found you don't know which is up, which is down, where north or south are, what's right, what's left? The surface and the real world could be miles away rather than inches. You might never draw another breath, and yet you are content just to float and listen to the bubbles burst around you and hear your thoughts echo cavernously in your head. And everything happens slowly, so-o-o slo-o-owly. . . .

So it was for Bob. It seemed to take forever for his eyes to adapt to the darkness, and while he waited he felt dizzy and detached, having no proof from any of his senses that his body still existed, that he hadn't become pure thought floating in a void. Finally the nascent sunlight from outside began to limn the outlines of people, all of whom appeared to be watching Bob intently. When Bob waved the gun at them, they neither flinched nor recoiled. They merely watched.

"Where is she? Where's Sandy?"

Someone pointed to a heap on the floor a few yards away. It was a body, a small body, covered by some kind of canvas tarpaulin. Bob waved his gun along the line of figures, making sure each and every one of them got the message, then went over and picked up one corner of the tarpaulin.

A small hand came up on the end of a short arm. The hand was holding a tobacco pouch. A tiny, whiny voice said, "Smoke, Mr. Tremaine?"

"Rackstraw!!! You lying son of a bitch!!!" Bob yelled, whirling around. He raised the Colt, took aim at Mr. Olesqui, and cocked the hammer.

Mr. Olesqui chuckled.

"Yeah, mighty funny, short stuff!" said Bob. "How's about I give you another mouth to laugh out of?"

Jeremiah Rackstraw appeared to Bob's left. With him was Alice. Alice's face looked all kind of wrong, kind of puffy, as though she'd been stung by a couple of dozen hornets.

Bob pointed the gun at Rackstraw, and was alarmed to see how much the barrel was trembling. There were six bullets in the gun, another eighteen in his pocket. Assuming he got the opportunity to reload three times, twenty-four bullets. Assuming each one found its mark, he might be able to do it: he might be able to kill them all.

"That's enough, Bob," said Rackstraw. "I'm bored with all this." He gestured casually, and the carriage door began to close. The bright rectangle of early-morning Escardy Gap narrowed as the darkness consumed it. There went the Evett brothers' grain silo. There went the top of the sign on Billy's Bar & Grill. There went the station roof. Then there was only a sliver of daylight, as cherishable to Bob as if it had been a gold ingot.

Then, with a loud thump, there was nothing but darkness.

Bob loosed off a round. The flash was blinding, the detonation deafening.

Then someone started screaming.

It was not any member of the Company.

19

Less than half a mile away from the rail yard, the fugitives were too absorbed in their own problems to notice the faintest of faint sounds that floated through the early morning air: a man's terrified scream, muffled but nonetheless unmistakable.

Mayor and Josh finished their report on the state of Sara Sienkiewicz. Doc received the news solemnly, and said, "No change, then. But I still feel bad about leaving her. I feel like I'm not doing my duty."

"It's only for a few hours, Doc," said Mayor. "We'll be at Grant's Crossing by midday, probably back here by late afternoon." He hoped he sounded encouraging.

"I know, I know."

"Of course, if you *must* stay . . ."

"No. No, we've got to keep going. So long as she's stable."

"On we go, then," said Mayor.

The three ill-assorted would-be saviors of Escardy Gap turned and faced south. The badlands awaited. Hot dust, scrub, sagebrush, insects, broken stones, dead grass, and hardbaked mud. Twenty rough-and-ready miles of earth that God seemed to have forgotten about halfway through the making. In a few hours' time they would be walking through the hottest part of the day, and the sun would be burning down on them in the cauldron of the sky, blistering the air, searing their eyes. They were poorly clothed, shod, and equipped for the ordeal. All they could do was trust in themselves and the great guiding hand of the Creator to get them where they wanted to go.

It was time to depart. There was the signpost marking the boundary.

YOU ARE NOW LEAVING
ESCARDY GAP
PLEASE CALL AGAIN SOON!

Mayor took one last look at his town, not a long lingering gaze but a quick over-the-shoulder glance (for a long lingering gaze would have caused too much pain). "See you soon," he said softly.

Neither he nor Josh nor Doc would ever know that Bob Tremaine had, albeit unwittingly, done some good before he died. He had delayed the Company by a few minutes, and that delay almost certainly saved the three refugees from being detected. Thanks to Bob, they were able to slip out of Escardy Gap unseen and unscathed. In the cosmic scheme of things, it might even be said that Bob had redeemed himself, or at any rate somewhat righted the balance of his wrongs.

Seventeen

1

Up in the glacial cool of the white room, the woman on the bed . . .
. . . stirred.

2

The occupants of both carriages assembled in the rail yard, blinking up at the brightening sky.

Jeremiah Rackstraw climbed up onto a small grassy knoll and surveyed the Company, his gaze passing from head to misshapen head. Not a word was spoken, not a sound was heard save for the occasional crackle from Buzz Beaumont's solenoid suit, all charged up and raring to go.

It was a moment for reflection, a time of endings and beginnings. The first act was behind them. The interval was over. Now came the second and final act. The lights were up, the exits closed. The costumes were on, and the audience was waiting and listening and wanting to know (and the wiser ones among them dreading) what was going to happen next.

"Anyone else," said Rackstraw, "would take this opportunity to congratulate you all on a job well done and wish you success in the various tasks that lie ahead. I am not anyone else, and we have rehearsed too long and too hard for success to be anything other than a foregone conclusion. Ladies, gentlemen, Escardy Gap awaits. You know what you have to do. Do it."

He raised an arm and arrowed it in the direction of town, and in a leaping, loping, lolloping crowd the Company began to move off.

"Buzz!" Rackstraw called out, and gestured to the electrical wizard to come over and join him. "Buzz," he said, "wait for me in the town square, would you?"

"Sure, Mr. Rackstraw. Why?"

"I have a feeling I might have a job for you."

"Right!" Buzz Beaumont gave Rackstraw the thumbs-up, flashing his trademark bright blue grin, then set off eagerly after his companions.

3

A tiny breath drifted from the lips of the woman on the bed, hardly more than a zephyr in the arctic wastes of the white room.

4

C arroll Evett knew that his twin brother was dead. He had felt it happen.

Yesterday afternoon, as he was tinkering with the engine of the Kaiser sedan—he and Earl kept promising themselves they would get it on the road one day, one fine day in the middle of the month of Never—and trying hard not to think about what had been done to Tom Finkelbaum (that kid had been tinkered with, all right), he had felt a sudden impact slap bang in the middle of his forehead. The shock had made him jerk his head up, knocking it hard against the underside of the Kaiser's hood, and giving himself one heck of a bruise at the base of his skull. Stunned, he had reeled away from the car.

Earl's dead.

A sudden breeze had swept southward along Delacy Street, heading out of town, drawing signs, sigils, and swirls in the road dust. Then stillness.

Earl's dead.

When they were kids, Carroll had gashed himself badly out playing in the woods. He had got his foot caught in a rabbit hole, tripped, and torn the side of his calf on the jagged edge of a splintered tree trunk. He had howled, bawled, hollered for what had seemed like hours, clutching his bleeding leg. He had tried to stand and walk but the pain was as big as a house. He had felt sick. He had truly believed he was going to die.

And then Earl had arrived with their father. And the first thing Earl said to his brother was, "I knew you were going to be here."

They were twins. They were joined by something stronger than mere brotherly love. There was a secret bond that stretched like a silver thread between them. This was why they had neither of them ever married. A woman would have come between them and, through no fault of her own, tried to snap that silver thread.

And it was through the subtle tingling of this thread that Carroll knew that Earl was dead. Not only that, he knew how Earl had died and he knew where Earl had died.

And Carroll had gone indoors, and had sat down, and had wept, and had sat and wept all afternoon.

Several things had happened outside while Carroll had sat there and wept. Josh Knight had come and gone and come back again, much more quickly than he had gone. Jeremiah Rackstraw had appeared and talked to a squirrel that was not a squirrel, a squirrel that became a monster and then a perfect copy of Rackstraw, and then, when Rackstraw was gone, a squirrel again. Bob Tremaine had entered the hospital across the way, wrought havoc, and left by the somewhat unconventional method of an unopened upstairs window and the branches of a tree, leaving Doc to lament the death of love.

All this had happened, and Carroll had not even noticed.

Evening had fallen, and Carroll had fallen asleep where he sat. And he had dreamed of Earl, vividly. Earl had appeared in the room, right in front of him, so real looking Carroll could have reached out and touched him.

In the dream Earl had had a third eye, or at any rate a hollow, red-rimmed socket where a third eye could have slotted in. And in the dream Earl had told his twin that death was nothing to be scared of. What lay beyond death was very much like life, but lonelier. To both Earl and Carroll, solitude was almost inconceivable. They had never been able to imagine a time when they wouldn't have each other to live with, when they wouldn't be fixing the Kaiser and downing the beers at Billy's and running the grain and feed store, together.

"It's kinda dull here, little bro," Earl had said in the dream to Carroll, his younger brother by four minutes. "It's kinda like watching a very boring movie, one where you know exactly what's going to happen before it happens."

And Carroll had asked, "You want I should come and join you?"

And Earl had thought about this and said, "Nah. Not right now. You wait. It won't be long. . . ."

The drapes were not closed, and Carroll had awoken with the arrival of dawn, secure and content in the knowledge that today was the day he was going to die. He had eaten a cold, solitary breakfast, drunk a single mug of coffee, then had gone out to work some more on the Kaiser. And he was working on it when one of the Company arrived and tapped him on the arm.

Carroll pulled himself out from under the hood, a monkey wrench in his right hand. He found himself gazing into the blank, black, lidless eyes of the Boy.

"Morning," Carroll said, warily.

"Car," said the Boy.

"Yeah, a car."

"Good car?"

"The best. At least, it will be. One of these days."

"Man like car?"

"Me? Love it. Love it more than life itself."

"Man like to be with car?"

"How d'you mean?"

Slowly and deliberately, the Boy began to remove his gloves.

5

The woman in the white room twitched a finger—the index finger of her right hand, the hand that held her pencils, the finger that guided the pencils across the page, navigating the shoals, rocks, and reefs of storytelling.

6

Billy Connors stopped sweeping the stoop of the Bar & Grill and bid the big, big-headed man with the bottles on his coat a very good day.

"Gonna be a warm one," he said, adding calmly, "You here to kill me?"

"Whatever made you think that?" said Felcher.

"Just a hunch."

"No, I ain't here to kill you. The opposite, in fact. I'm here to discuss your *life.*"

"Oh, yeah?"

"Oh, yeah. There's a lot to talk about, ain't there? A lot of things you ain't been able to talk about before, not even with your pals." Felcher rolled back his big head so that his vast and ugly face looked straight up to the sky. "Boy, this heat. Reminds me of when I was in Hungnam . . ."

"You were in Hungnam?" said Billy, trying to hide his surprise but not succeeding.

"Weren't you?"

"Hungnam, Seoul, Imjin River, the Thirty-eighth Parallel . . . Shoot! Which division were you in?"

"Why don't *you* tell *me?*" said Felcher. "Over a coffee, maybe? Or a beer."

"Sure," said Billy, pushing open the glass swing door and ushering Felcher inside. "And while we're at it, you can tell me all about those bottles."

"Mmm, I might just do that," said Felcher. "I might just do that."

7

Her nose twitched, and the hand went up and scratched at it with the small, delicate, unvarnished nail of its littlest finger. The tube inserted into her forearm flexed and wriggled.

8

Dad?"

Moose Rollins, Jr. shook the snoring, snorting leviathan beneath the counterpane that was his father, Moose Rollins, Sr.

"Dad? Wake up."

"Ggggghhhhmmmmfffff . . ."

"Wake *up,*" insisted Moose, Jr., who was the spitting image of his father, only smaller. Moose Rollins senior and junior were like a pair of balloons, one slightly less inflated than the other.

" 'M awake. Whassup, son?"

"There's a man at the front door. He's got a bag. He says he's a doctor. Dr. Candle, I think his name is. Says he's making a house call."

"I don't know nobody called Dr. Candle. Tell him to go away."

Moose, Jr. hurried out of the bedroom and along the corridor to a window, which he flung up with all the considerable might in his great fat arms.

He called down, "My dad says go away."

"Doesn't he want to be cured?" asked the man at the front door with the heavy carpetbag sloshing at his side.

"Cured? What of?"

"Why, the greatest disease of all," said Dr. Canker.

"Which is?"

"Life, boy! Life!"

Moose, Jr. had never considered life a disease before. How could it be? After all, a disease was something that happened to only a few people, whereas life happened to everyone.

"You look like a fine, well-fed lad," Dr. Canker went on. "I think you might have the disease, too."

"Me? I don't think so. I don't *feel* sick."

"Why don't you come down and I'll show you what I mean."

"Well . . . Okay."

Moose, Jr. ran downstairs as nimbly as a hippopotamus and unlatched the front door. So that he couldn't be shut out again, Dr. Canker stepped smartly over the threshold, patting Moose, Jr. on the head. He set his carpetbag down and undid the clasp.

"Which part of you are you most proud of, son?" he asked.

"Which part? You mean, like, of my body?"

"Of your body," Dr. Canker repeated gravely.

"Oh, my stomach. No doubt about it. All the other kids say it's my outstanding feature."

"I'm sure they do." Dr. Canker drew apart the mouth of the bag, and a hot stench crept out through the opening. Moose, Jr. wrinkled his nose.

"Pee-yoo! What you got in there, mister—a dead cat?"

Dr. Canker delved in and pulled out what looked to Moose, Jr. like a fat, sticky black mushroom. "Colon," he said.

"Sorry?" said Moose, Jr.

The mushroom leapt from Dr. Canker's palm as though it had been resting on a coiled spring. It flew unerringly into Moose, Jr.'s gawking mouth and had slithered down his gullet before he could so much as gasp.

"You'll find that you and that tumor have a lot in common," said Dr. Canker as the boy began to groan and clutch his enormous gut. "You both grow too well."

9

The woman in the white room yawned softly, and her eyes fluttered behind their pale blue-veined lids like two trapped butterflies. A ripple of life passed down her smooth white throat, and she uttered her first sound in two days: a wispy, inarticulate hiss of air.

10

Good morning, good morning!" Jeremiah Rackstraw cried into the echoing vastness of the town hall's vestibule.

Good morning! the rafters sighed in reply.

Good morning! the highest corners sang.

Good morning! the dusty eaves crooned softly.

"The time has come, my laudable friend, to pay the piper," said Rackstraw, striding across the chessboard floor, his heel taps tocking imperiously on the marble tiles. "Mr. Mayor? Can you hear me? Are you listening?"

At the foot of the stairs he halted, knuckles on hips.

"Oh, come now, Mr. Mayor. I thought after our little chat that you might at least have prepared a welcome for me—a crucifix, a string of garlic, something of that ilk. I really am most terribly disappointed. Oh, Misterrr Mayo-o-o-o-r!"

Errrmayo-o-o-o-r! Errrmayo-o-o-o-r! Errrmayo-o-o-o-r! sang the echoes.

"Now where can that wascally wapscallion have got to?"

Rackstraw mounted the stairs two at a time with the effete inelegance of one not accustomed to physical exertion.

"Not a single silver bullet," he muttered, "not so much as a splash of holy water! I deserve better than this."

At the top of the staircase Rackstraw cast left and right, then darted along the corridor to Mayor's office. He flung the door back.

"Go-o-ood . . . *morning!*" he said with a flourish of his hand.

His face fell.

The office was empty.

"Oh, really, Mr. Mayor, I'm beginning to lose patience with you. You don't honestly think you can *hide* from me, do you? I'll give you just this one chance. Come out, come out, wherever you are!"

From the adjoining bathroom, from behind the desk, from beneath the couch, from the tall cabinets, no one emerged.

"Hide and seek, is it?" said Rackstraw. "Very well. I'll play it your way. I'll seek. But be warned," he added with a sly sneer, "if I feel I'm in any danger of losing, I'll cheat."

11

The first intelligible word Sara Sienkiewicz said as she swam her way up from a deep dark lake of sleep was, "Pause?"

12

No sooner had Rackstraw said the word "chapel" than he was there, halfway down the aisle, facing the altar and the dangling, decomposing body of the Reverend King. He glanced around the rows of pews that thousands of God-fearing backsides had polished to perfection, then licked a finger and held it up. There was no life in the air currents that swirled through the chapel apart from the flies that hummed and fussed about the business of decay.

"We're alone," he said to the reverend. "I suppose it's unlikely, but I thought Mayor might have barricaded himself in and staged a last-ditch defense here. You haven't seen him, have you?"

He pushed up the closed lid of the reverend's one good eye, but even if it had been open it couldn't have seen anything through the opaque layer that had formed over its cornea, and even if the reverend's dead ears had heard anything, his unworkable tongue would have been incapable of telling.

"But the dead can give up their secrets," said Rackstraw to the corpse. He raised his hand to the reverend's purplish fly-specked face, the tips of his index and little fingers touching each of the eyes, his other two fingers covering the nostrils and his thumb thrust into the mouth. "I want you back, John King. I call you back. I summon you back. I *demand* you back."

For a moment nothing happened. Then there was a series of clicks from the reverend's throat as his neck bones began to knot together and gurgles as his disused digestive system geared itself up and great rattling heaves as his lungs groped for breath through his crushed windpipe and loud lub-dubs as his heart attempted to clear the clotted blood from its chambers. Tiny little snaps announced the bursting of blocked veins. His drained liver and bladder squeaked.

Abruptly the reverend's head started to twist and turn on his neck, writhing like the head of a flower whose growth pangs are captured and sped up by time-lapse photography as it gropes blindly for light. He opened his mouth and tried to scream, but the bell rope prevented him, holding back the release of agony. The lips opened and closed, sending out soundless air yells and affording Rackstraw glimpses of a fat black tongue spotted with fly eggs. The reverend's toe caps slithered and scraped across the floor, where the mottled stains of his semen were old news but still fascinating to the flies.

"Welcome back, Reverend," said Rackstraw. "Hurts, doesn't it? Hurts like a bitch, and there's nothing you can do about it. Can you hear me, John? Can you understand what I'm saying? Nod if you can."

The reverend's head lolled forward onto his breastbone and then creakily cranked itself upright again.

"I'll take that as a yes. Now, John, just a few questions, and then I'll let you go. Not much fun over on the other side, is it? Not the harps and flowers you expected."

The reverend's head flopped onto his left shoulder, then onto his right: *No*.

"Still, you can't have everything. The man I'm looking for, John, the cracked actor—have you seen him? Has he been in to pay his respects? Pray for help?"

The reverend did his best impression of head shaking.

"You're sure about that?"

A clumsy nod.

"And you wouldn't be lying to me?"

A slow, painful shake.

"Trying to protect him?"

Shake.

"Because if you're lying, I could leave you here for a very long time."

Shake, shake, shake.

"I might do that anyway, since I'm feeling particularly unkind this morning," Rackstraw mused. Then: "John, as a dead person you're privileged to learn a few things, pick up a few scraps of understanding in the last few seconds of your existence so that your life doesn't seem entirely worthless and pointless. Tell me, where is our friend hiding? Do you know that?"

The shake of the reverend's head was a long time coming.

"Had to think about that one, didn't you?"

Nod.

"Could that be because you were debating whether to tell the truth or not?"

Oh, no, no, no. A series of emphatic shakes.

"Once more: do you know where he is?"

Shake.

"You're lying."

Shake, shake, shake.

"Well, *I* think you are lying, John. There's no point trying to protect him, you know. I could find him on my own, if I wanted. I'm just playing his game. And enjoying it immensely, I might add. So, one last time: do you know where Mayor Douglas B. Raymond is?"

No.

"Oh, dear, John. To lie to me. To *me*, the master of mendacity, the emperor of untruths, the supreme ruler of falsehood! You really must like hanging here in this rotting body. I think I *will* leave you. . . ."

The reverend's head was flopping from side to side like that of a marionette in the power of an inebriated puppeteer.

"Yes. It's only fair. But don't worry. The maggots will chomp on you and bits will drop off you in the natural course of events, and in a few months' time you'll be bones, John. Clean bones. Dry bones. 'Dem bones, dem bones, dem *dry-y-y-y* bones.' And bones can't cage a soul. So the torment won't last forever, John. Just long enough to make you regret trying to bamboozle the nabob of meretriciousness."

The head shaking became weaker, wearier.

"Anyway, John, I can't hang around all day. Unlike you." Rackstraw folded his arms and wondered where to go next. "Town square," he said, and was gone.

The flies descended on the reverend again, repeating Rackstraw's last word over and over in their contented drone.

If his tear ducts hadn't withered and dried up several hours ago, the reverend would have been weeping.

13

She clambered slowly from beneath the covers and sat on the edge of the bed. She was momentarily overcome with dizziness. It seemed a long way down to the floor. There was something stuck into her forearm. She looked at the harmless rubber tube with as much disgust as if it were a worm. Gingerly she peeled off the tape that kept the intravenous needle in place. Then she tore off a strip of the bedsheet, which she held in her teeth. Wincing in anticipation, she tugged the needle out of her vein. There was a spurt of blood, but she stemmed the flow with her thumb and, wrapping the strip of bedsheet around her arm, made an effective bandage.

Now she felt at liberty to take stock of her surroundings. This was Doc Wheeler's place, commonly (though inaccurately) referred to as the hospital, and she was clad in one of the flimsy cotton nightgowns that were bestowed upon patients as a prime example of medical humor: *see if you can walk around in this and keep a straight face!* A quick scan of the room revealed none of her own clothes, which she supposed had been cut from her and possibly burned to lessen the risk of infection.

She called Doc's name querulously, and there was no reply. Nor did Nurse Sprocket's name bring any response.

I don't feel completely awake, Sara thought to herself. *Neither am I asleep. In fact, I am somewhere in between. This is the same spell I sometimes fall into while I am writing, when, even though nothing I write is real, it is the real world that appears to be the dream.*

She rose up from the bed and a wave of lightheadedness washed over her. When it had passed, she moved to the door and listened. There wasn't a sound in the house except the distant humming of . . . a refrigerator? Or was it a chain saw somewhere outdoors?

She drew open the door with a soft click and the hum grew louder. She found its source soon enough: Nurse Sprocket's battered body lying in the middle of the corridor, although beneath a crawling carpet of shiny black flies it was not easily identifiable as such. It was barely recognizable as human.

Sara covered her mouth delicately with her hand and side-stepped around this horror that had entered, unbidden, into her dream world. She drifted, white clad, white limbed, down the stairs, her fingers brushing the walls not for their support but for the elusive reassurance of their solidity. When she reached the front door she hesitated briefly, worried by her near nakedness. Her arms were showing, all of her legs were showing, and the loose ties at the side of the nightgown revealed far too much of her hips, ribs and . . . other parts. Silly! This was a dream. No one would notice. People often went naked in their dreams.

Gently the beautiful Sara pushed the door open and stepped out into an equally beautiful day.

There was another horror awaiting her on the other side of the street. A car and a man. A man and a car. Where car ended and man began was almost impossible to distinguish. Was that a hood ornament or a skull? Was that leather upholstery or skin? Were those tires rubber or intestine? Was that gasoline leaking from the gas cap or blood? Had the windshield wipers really been replaced by two forearms? Had someone really had the effrontery to attach eyeballs to each headlight? Was that a mouth on the radiator grille? Was that a pair of *buttocks* lodged onto the exhaust?

Sara smiled at the grim twists and turns of her imagination, and hoped she would remember this image when she woke up: she might be able to use it in a story one day.

For no particular reason at all Sara turned right instead of left, east instead of west, to face out of instead of into town. Because she was facing in that direction, that was the direction in which she began to walk. It didn't make much difference which way she went. Wherever you walked in dreams, you always woke up exactly where you had fallen asleep.

Barefoot, begowned, Sara Sienkiewicz headed away from Escardy Gap, out into the desolation surrounding that doomed town.

Eighteen

1

At first it sounded like a large bee. Then a small plane. Then a combine harvester. Only when Mayor, Doc, and Josh saw what it was did it actually begin to sound like a car.

A car? Should such a magnificent specimen of automobilia be tarnished with so gross and inelegant a description? As the Viking longships of old to the stunning opulence of the *Queen Mary* herself was the common four-wheeled vehicular transport when compared with Wilbur Cohen's Hudson Hornet Hollywood hardtop.

It gleamed. It hummed. It spoke in ringing tones of craftsmanship, commerce, and confidence, from the tread on its tires to the lime green sparkle of its bodywork. Its headlights were twin moons and its twin-pronged radiator grille had the grin of a giant, greedy catfish. It was a legend brought to life, a fantasy made real on the production lines of America's automobile industry. It was made for the road and the road was made for it.

The three fugitives stood their ground and watched the Hudson Hornet grow larger and nearer, trailing its peacock's fan of billowing dust. They didn't even think about getting out of the way. They simply watched that miracle of mechanical engineering roll toward them, and finally begin to decelerate, to slow, to stop.

The dust drifted on past them, sweeping into their eyes. They blinked, and the spell was broken. The Hudson Hornet was just a car again, thrumming quietly to itself in the roadway.

The occupants of the car—Wilbur Cohen, Rebecca Cohen and young Josie Cohen—stared through the windshield at Mayor, Josh, and Doc. Wilbur was chewing mechanically on the end of the thickset Havana that smoldered between his lips, rolling it from one corner of his mouth to the other and back again. Kneeling up between him and her mother on the front seat, Josie clutched a large raspberry lollipop, and with her big bright eyes and her red-smeared mouth she looked clownish, comical, and absurdly serious.

The car's engine idled, its pistons and valves chugging smoothly but impatiently—*come on, come on, come on....*

Finally Wilbur rolled down his side window and leaned out. "You gonna move or what?" he shouted.

"Beg pardon?" said Mayor.

"I *said—*"

"I heard what you said."

"So?"

"So what?"

"*Are* you *gonna move?*" Wilbur reiterated, his voice traveling up and down the register as though he were talking to a backward child. He muttered something to his wife, who flapped a hand at him and frowned hard.

"And a very good morning to you, too, Wilbur Cohen," said Mayor, approaching the car.

"Yeah, well," said Wilbur. "I wish I had time for the niceties."

"Rebecca," said Mayor, bending down beside the car. "Miss Josie."

"Good morning, Mayor," said Rebecca. "Please forgive my husband. The urgency of the situation has deprived him of his usual manners."

Wilbur rolled his cigar from cheek to cheek and gazed blithely into the middle distance.

"I never knew he had any manners," Doc muttered to Josh

out of the side of his mouth. Josh knew he shouldn't laugh, so he didn't. But he wanted to.

"It's not a problem, Rebecca," said Mayor. "We're all a little highly strung at the moment. So, which way are you headed, Wilbur?"

"Which way does it *look* like we're headed?"

"Grant's Crossing."

"Then that's the way we're headed, Mayor. Grant's Crossing, pick up the interstate there, and drive on down to Wayneville. I have a brother in Wayneville. He'll put us up for a few days. Owes me a favor. Several, in fact."

"You've got kind of a full house there, haven't you?" said Mayor, nodding at the back seat, which was loaded with packing crates and suitcases and cardboard cartons of tinned food. "You planning on a *long* holiday?"

"You could say that."

"Where are you three going, Mayor?" asked Rebecca, leaning across her husband.

"Just as far as Grant's Crossing."

"You planning on a *long* holiday, too?" asked Wilbur with a hint of a sneer.

"Planning on getting help," Mayor replied.

"And you mean to walk all that way?" said Rebecca incredulously.

"We figure we have to," said Mayor. "It's better if Jeremiah Rackstraw and Company don't get wind of what we're doing."

"But to walk across the desert—that's crazy! You'd be better off coming with us. Isn't that right, Wilbur?"

Wilbur looked at his wife as if she had just asked him to strip buck naked and dance a jig in the middle of the road. "Becca, are you crazy? There's not enough room for all of them!"

"There would be, if we unloaded everything."

"Which we're not going to do."

"Wilbur, dear, it's crazy that we're all going the same way and they should have to walk. We don't need all of that stuff in the back. We don't need half of it. I can't think why you insisted on bringing so much. They're just possessions. If nec-

essary, we can leave them by the side of the road and pick
them up later."

"Pick them up later! Even if we *are* coming back,
Becca"—and Wilbur had no intention of returning to Escardy
Gap until the situation there had improved considerably, and
maybe not ever—"either we'll find them all ruined by dust
and ripped up by coyotes, or else we'll find nothing there at
all. There are such things as thieves, you know."

"These are our friends, Wilbur."

"And this is my car, and I say we're not unloading it and
we're not taking them with us."

"Wilbur Cohen, don't you have a charitable bone in your
body?"

"I have bones full of common sense, Becca. Those are the
only kind of bones I need."

"Ahem."

"I'm sorry, Mayor," said Rebecca. "My husband can sometimes be very set in his ways."

Wilbur said nothing but gunned the motor, raising a small
storm cloud of fumes.

"I guess that means you're not going to take us."

"That just about the long and the short of it, Mayor," said
Wilbur.

"Okay, that's fine," said Mayor. "But would you at least do
me this favor? When you go through Grant's Crossing, would
you let the authorities there know we're coming and give
them some idea of what's going on in Escardy Gap. Prepare
them."

"That we certainly will do, Mayor," said Rebecca. "I
promise." She rapped her husband on the arm. "Wilbur, there
are two canteens of water in the back, and we don't really
even need one. Perhaps our friends? . . ."

Wilbur chewed on his cigar some more, then slowly, reluctantly, inclined his head forward a fraction of an inch,
which no one except Rebecca would have recognized as a
gesture of consent. Rebecca turned to Josie and told her to
pass one of the canteens, which she then handed across her
husband to Mayor.

"Water," she said.

"Much obliged, Rebecca," said Mayor, taking the canteen

and straightening up with a grunt. All that bending down had set his back aching.

"You're doing a brave thing there."

"Just my job, ma'am. It's Doc and Josh are the brave ones. *They* had a choice."

"I just wish there was some other way we could help."

"Becca, we're wasting time." Wilbur began rolling up his window.

"Good luck, Mayor," said Rebecca Cohen. "God go with all of you."

Wilbur wrenched down the hand brake and stamped on the gas pedal. Mayor had to pull sharply back to avoid losing a toe.

The Hudson Hornet purred with joy to be on the move again. The sunlight winked off its fins and chrome trim.

Josie squirmed around to wave at the three fugitives. She waved as if she was embarking on a great adventure.

And perhaps she is, thought Josh, and waved back.

All three of them watched the car glide away like a lime green ghost.

All three heard Rebecca Cohen say, "Wilb—"

All three saw the car vanish into thin air.

2

To her side, bushes rustled conspiratorial encouragement. Beneath her feet, the ground rippled, wave after wave (she felt it through her soles, a vast soil-capped sea). Overhead, the trees beckoned her on like big-city traffic cops, swaying their huge heads to check the roadway ahead and behind. She felt the earth accept her tread, felt coming up from deep down and distant the scurryings and scufflings of all the tiny creatures and insects who traveled through the labyrinthine dark.

A pair of magpies swooped past, chattering, coaxing, their wingtips riffling the air. They were headed east. The wind was headed east. Everything was headed east. Including Sara Sienkiewicz.

She knew what this was called. Even in her half daze/half

doze, she knew the word that described this phenomenon: *serendipity*. That sweet double blooming when nature suddenly opens up around you and inside you at the same time. That sense of being a part of the world and yet apart, detached, able to observe and record the beauty of it all. The gut-driven surge that signals true creativity. On certain rare occasions Sara had slipped into this golden mood while at her desk, pen in hand, and the pages that had followed, *flowed,* were among the best she had ever written. Not so much as a comma needed correcting. The prose seemed to have issued forth from some deep wellspring whose water was always clean, always sharp, always crystal clear, and the story had taken on a life of its own and skipped across the paper from start to finish without her even once having to wonder where it might all be leading. Nothing had needed to be forced. The mood, in fact, in which she had written her last story, the one about the man in the futuristic city with the roomful of clocks.

That is what she felt now: a certainty, an abiding conviction in the purpose of life, in the directedness of things. She was aware that all around her were signs and symbols, covenants and compacts between the eternal and the mundane. Everything was waving her, swaying her, coaxing her eastward, so eastward she must go, and eastward she went.

In some dim recess of her mind she wondered why she should want to leave town at all. She loved Escardy Gap. This was and always had been her home, and would be where they buried her. What *was* she thinking?

But it was the nearest flicker of doubt, and soon passed.

She walked on, and shortly she came to a fork in the road, where she halted. The wind swirled playfully around her ankles, whispering *This way*. But which way? Planted at the fork was a mailbox with the name Swivven painted on it. The track to the right led up to Ike's place; the road to the left went on out into the desert. But which *way?*

The wind snaked forward and the mailbox post shivered. There was a flurry, a knotting of air . . . and all of a sudden the mailbox swiveled around in its hole, lining itself up parallel with the narrow track. The tiny flag clicked up and the lid popped open like a laughing mouth.

That way! Up the path to the Swivven house!

But why? Surely she should stick to the main road.

No whys. No wherefores. Serendipity had no time for questions. Questions only broke the spell. The Swivven mailbox had swiveled, had pointed, therefore that was the way she should go.

Sara pulled her white surgical gown more tightly around herself. She prickled all over with gooseflesh—but it was delicious gooseflesh, the sensation that comes of being in the presence of something great and good and majestic and divine.

She set off up the path.

3

Young Joshua Knight, the much respected Dr. Victor William Wheeler and His Actorliness Douglas B. Raymond, Mayor of Escardy Gap, stood rooted to the spot as securely as three coconuts in a shyster's carnival booth.

It was the damnedest thing. If they had not seen it, if they had not witnessed it with their own bulging eyes, they surely would have believed it impossible.

One moment, a fully-functional Hudson Hornet rolling smoothly along the road. The next, nothing. One moment, the steady purr of a well-tuned carburetor. The next, engulfing silence. One moment three human lives. The next, three souls in oblivion.

There had been no crash, no wail of twisting metal, no caterwaul of bending chrome. There hadn't even been time for a scream, unless you counted Rebecca Cohen's choked syllable. It had been as abrupt as it was inexplicable.

Josh moved first. His limbs were younger, his reactions quicker. He sprinted along the road between the tire tracks, skidding to a halt a good yard or two before the spot where they vanished. Caution was Josh's middle name. He advanced the last few steps exaggeratedly on tiptoe like a cartoon spy, alert to every possible danger. Doc and Mayor were lumbering up behind him and he spread out his arms to ward them off.

"What the hell do you think—?" puffed Doc.

"Ssh!" Josh slipped the toe of one sneaker forward. There were now only a couple of inches between its ribbed rubber rim and the razor-straight end of the tire tracks.

The two elder men watched Josh look up, heard him gasp, and were just able to catch him as he backpedaled desperately into their arms.

"Holy moley!"

"What is it, son?" Mayor asked, feeling the boy's body shudder mightily within his embrace.

Josh gulped a couple more lungfuls of air, then said, "Nothing."

"What? Nothing couldn't have given you a fright like that. What do you mean?"

"I mean, nothing! There's nothing there."

"Don't be ridiculous," Doc snorted.

"Calm down, son," said Mayor. "Explain."

"I don't . . . I don't know if I can, sir. I think you're gonna have to see it for yourselves."

Doc stepped forward to do just that.

"Be careful," Josh warned him.

A second later it was Doc who was teetering backward and gasping in disbelief.

"Shit on a stick!"

"Watch that mouth, Doc," snapped Mayor. "Young folk present."

"This is mad! This is insane! This ain't happening!"

"Slow down, Doc. Tell me. Tell me what's there."

"The kid's right. You've just got to see it to understand."

Given the reactions of his two companions, it was with some trepidation that Mayor moved forward to take a look.

And saw whiteness. Blankness. Emptiness stretching to the periphery of vision, and huge, reaching up skyward beyond reckoning. No trees, no cactuses, no thornbushes, no tumbleweed. Not a rock, not a grain of sand, not a lizard, not a bird. Not an inkling of life.

And staggered back pale cheeked and reeling.

"Jesus H. Christ!" Mayor pinched himself a couple of times. No luck. He was awake. "What in hell is this? What in damnation is going on here?"

4

Neville N. Nolan, who in fly form had trailed unseen in the wake of the Hudson Hornet, could have told them. He could have explained to these puzzled people, in aptly alliterative and tautologous terminology, the nature and purpose of the barrier. But to manifest as a man now would have been undoubtedly unwise, exposing himself to excessive risk. He chose instead to observe the unfolding of events, squatting circumspectly on the crown of a cactus. Jeremiah Rackstraw would indeed have to be told what was happening here. When the time came, Neville would whiz off to warn his sesquipedalian superior. But no need to yet. Not yet.

He watched the hapless humans stutter and stagger and struggle with their stupefaction. For several gloating moments he watched these guileless, guiltless gentlefolk grapple with the cunning, comprehensive cruelty of the Company's plan.

It was wonderful.

5

Ideas, anyone?"
Josh, who had settled himself down cross-legged in the dust, squinted up at Mayor. "I think I have one. But it's a little bit crazy."

"Let's hear it anyway," said Mayor. "Right now, I'd believe in fairies if you told me you'd seen one."

"Well, I don't know if this makes any sense, and I don't know if this is just because I've read too many comic books or seen one movie too many . . ."

"You can never see too many movies," Mayor assured him.

". . . but I reckon it could be a force field."

"A force field," Doc repeated. "Yup. Sure. Riiiight."

"Carry on, son," said Mayor.

"Well . . . They put them around the town when they want to keep everybody in."

"They? Who's *they?*"

"People from space, I guess. Aliens. Bad guys."

"The Company."

"Yeah."

"They're from another world?"

"I don't know. I mean, it's not like they have bug eyes and tentacles or anything, but they're sure *different.*"

"But what I don't understand is that from here it looks just like desert, like the desert's always looked," said Mayor. "That butte on the horizon. I move my head, and it moves too. If it's an illusion, how come the perspective's all there, how come there's depth of field and everything? How did they manage to fake that?"

"Maybe they've got some kind of projector and they can make three-D movies like we can, only better, completely realistic, 'cause their science is much more advanced than ours."

At the words "projector" and "movie" Mayor felt a frisson of recognition trickle down his spine. He couldn't get out of his head the notion that a few moments ago he had walked right up to a screen and had been standing too close and the picture was too large for the image to be comprehensible. In that respect, Josh's explanation made a chilling kind of sense. But it seemed wholly nonsensical that people who were capable of such a feat of technology should have chosen to travel in a huffing, lumbering old locomotive, and Mayor voiced this objection, adding, "And why go to all the bother of pretending to be our friends and coming into our homes when they could've just waltzed down Main Street zapping us with their ray guns? They've got to be the dumbest aliens in history."

"It's only a theory," said Josh, accepting the logic of Mayor's argument.

"And a pretty damn-fool one at that," Doc grumbled.

"And you've got a better suggestion, I suppose?" said Mayor.

Doc shook his head. "No, I don't. I don't profess to have a clue as to what's going on here. This is completely beyond my experience. They don't teach you anything about aliens and force fields and three-D illusions at medical college. Though, now that I think about it, it does make sense of something Bob Tremaine said just before he whacked me up-side of the head and . . ." The thought of Nurse Sprocket had to be dismissed swiftly. "Well, anyway, he was yelling stuff about Russkies and the A-bomb and the end of the world. It must have been this he was talking about. He had some pretty darn wild ideas, did Bob. I guess finding this whatever-it-is is what tipped him over the edge."

"Stands to reason," agreed Mayor.

"Just tell me this, Josh," said Doc. "If it *is* some kind of a force field and it's supposed to be keeping us in, why isn't it doing its job? I mean, Wilbur just drove right on through it and is probably tootling along on the other side right now, not even realizing he just played his Get out of Jail Free card. Some barrier."

"But we don't know that he got through," said Josh. "And we don't know what's on the other side. What if there isn't anything? What if it all just stops there? They could've transported the whole town, lock, stock, and barrel to . . . somewhere else, I don't know, the fifth dimension."

"I was just thinking that," said Mayor. After all, what was there behind a movie screen? Nothing worth mentioning. Cobwebs and dustballs and fly husks and darkness. The world began and ended on those few square feet of white canvas. "I'm glad you said it, though, not me."

"How do we test?"

By way of a reply, Mayor bent down as elegantly as his creaky joints would allow (and that was not elegantly at all) to pick up a small rock roughly the size of a baseball. He tossed it up and caught it a couple of times to get the feel of its size and weight, and then he drew his arm back and threw what Josh considered to be a pretty darn good pitch for an old man. The rock spun straight through the air and then was plucked out of existence directly above the point where the tire tracks ended.

They waited, listening.

No thud of the rock hitting the ground. No click of stone on stone. No rustle of leaves and branches. No scurry of disturbed animals. Not even the *clank-clunk* of a dent appearing in the polished metalwork of a cherished Hudson Hornet.

Mayor threw some more rocks at a variety of angles and

trajectories, high, low, steep, shallow, and all of them disappeared soundlessly into the barrier.

"Doesn't prove a thing, not a damn thing," said Doc finally. "There's only one way to be absolutely, a hundred percent sure."

"And that is?"

"One of us goes where those rocks have just gone."

6

Rackstraw appeared out of nowhere on the steps of the town hall.

"Buzz?"

"Mr. Rackstraw," said Buzz. "I take it you've dealt with the mayor."

"No," said Rackstraw, his lips thinning. "The little fool wants to play games. So I'm humoring him. For now."

"Forgive my asking, but if you want him so bad, why don't you just say his name in that, you know, that special voice of yours you use when you want to transport yourself somewhere?"

"Ah, Buzz, if only, if only. Unfortunately, the Traveling Tongue is confined to moving between places, not people. People are rootless and inconsistent. Places are not."

"Oh, yeah," said Buzz, although he had known this already. He was just trying to be helpful.

"About that job I had for you, Buzz. Are you still interested?"

Buzz perked up. "Mr. Rackstraw, you may not realize this, but wearing this suit when it's pumped up with juice is kind of like having a full bladder and not being able to piss. It'll be a relief to let some of it out."

"An intriguing simile, but the point is well taken."

"Where do I start."

"Right here. What's the best way to catch fish that don't want to be caught?"

Buzz frowned.

"Dynamite," said Jeremiah Rackstraw. "Make a big enough bang, and they'll just float up to the surface."

7

A nd just who should that one of us be?" Mayor asked Doc.
"I'd have thought that was obvious," replied the portly
practitioner.

Mayor looked at Josh. Josh looked at Doc. Doc looked at
them both.

"Why, me, of course!"

"You? But Doc—"

" 'But Doc' *what,* Mayor? 'But Doc, you're too old and fat
to make it a couple of yards through an invisible barrier?' "

"But Doc, we need you. We need you here."

"And what if I'm needed more on the other side? What if,
for instance, Wilbur Cohen's lost his way in all that whiteness
and crashed the car? Have you thought about that? I'm the
only one here with medical expertise."

"I played a doctor once," Mayor pointed out. "Well, he
was more of a scientist than a doctor, but—"

"It ain't just that, Mayor." Doc drew Mayor to one side, out
of earshot of Josh. "You know, ever since what was done to
Nurse Sprocket . . . She was all that mattered to me, *really*
mattered. I've been thinking about this while we've been
walking. Now she's gone, I don't care anymore, I don't care
about anything. I'm a shell. I'm just going through the motions of living. So, if there is any risk involved, which I'm
pretty sure there isn't, but if there is, then the most expendable person here is me. I've got the least to lose."

"What about me?" said Mayor. "If you want expendable,
look no further. What use is an old washed-up character actor
to anyone?"

"A whole lot of use, if he's the mayor of Escardy Gap.
Let's face it, Mayor, you're the heart and soul of this town.
Without you, we'd be just another pissant little burg in the
middle of nowhere. Well, maybe we are anyway, but you give
us our pride, Mayor, you give us a reason to respect ourselves."

"Hogwash."

"So you say, but I know better. Folk look up to you. They

like you. They like you because you remind them that it's not so bad being human, that there's nothing particularly awful about failing, and there's nothing so damn special about being a success."

"That's a compliment?"

"Heck, yes. And there's another reason you should stay." Doc lowered his voice yet further. Boys had preternaturally sharp ears. "The kid needs you. Until you find Grampa Knight, assuming you do find Grampa at all, Josh is your responsibility. Whether you want to or not, you're going to have to look after him."

Mayor took this information on board solemnly, scratching at the whiskery stubble on his chin.

"That's a mighty big responsibility," he said. "I don't know if I'm up to it."

"Let me tell you something I've noticed, Mayor. I don't think you've even realized this yourself, but since yesterday night, you haven't slipped into character once. You've been *you* constantly."

Mayor was ready to object, but Doc raised a hand.

"No use denying it, Mayor. And I think I know why you've stopped playacting. Because you don't have to. Because you have a reason to be yourself."

"I don't understand. What reason?"

"You'll see what I mean soon enough." Doc raised his voice again, giving Mayor a hearty slap on the back. "Just a quick look-see, Mayor! I'll be gone a couple of minutes. You won't even have time to miss me."

"But are you sure?"

"Sure? I've never been surer!"

"You don't have to do this, Doc. We could go along, follow the edge of this barrier thing. Maybe there's a gap somewhere, a gateway. The Company must have got in somehow."

"And maybe there isn't," said Doc. "Maybe we'll just go walking in a big circle like mountaineers in a snowstorm and find ourselves back where we started. At least this way we can say we've tried. Besides, my mind's made up, and you know what an ornery cuss I can be when I don't get my way.

Would you be so kind as to give us a shot from your hip flask, Mayor? My mouth's gone strangely dry."

Mayor obliged, and Doc took a long, relishing swig, smacked his lips, and let out an "Ahhhh!" of profound satisfaction. Nobody was fooled.

Josh held out a hand. "Best of luck, sir."

Doc, touched by the display of adulthood, shook the hand warmly. "Save it, Josh. I'll be fine. I was born lucky." He turned and squared up to Mayor. "And you, you old shamster . . ." The two men embraced, and when they drew back Doc's glasses had misted up, while the moistness at the corners of Mayor's eyes was definitely not glycerin. "You make sure there's some of that whisky left for me when I come back. I know you."

Doc wiped his spectacles on the front of his shirt, then positioned himself between the twin treadmarks of the lost Hudson Hornet, stuck out his chin, hoisted up his belt, settled his shoulders, and took his first tentative step toward the unknown.

A second step.

A third.

Mayor and Josh saw him crane his neck, look left, look right, and heard his soft hiss of amazement. "Good Lord," they heard him say, "it just goes on and on forever." And they saw him reach out a tremulous, questing hand. Saw the fingertips disappear. Saw thin air engulf the knuckles one by one. Saw his arm sink in up to the wrist. To Doc, it looked as if he was burying his hand in smoke or thick fog. To Mayor and Josh, a few yards behind him, the hand seemed to have been dipped into a vertical pond in whose surface all of Creation was reflected. Doc's shirt cuff faded from existence, then the sleeve of his jacket up to the patch on the elbow. And Doc said, with mild surprise, "Say, it tickles!" He glanced around at his friends. "This is great," he chuckled. "It's just like sticking your hand in ether. Look."

And he drew his arm back to show them that no harm had been done. He waved it toward them, and blood sprayed across their faces. He blinked at their shocked expressions and their blood-spattered skin. Where had all that blood come from? He peered down at his arm in puzzlement and confu-

sion. But of course, he had no arm anymore. From below the
elbow there was just a lithe, twisting red rope, spattering its
bounty into the dust.

The amputation was precise, near perfect. Doc would never
have managed one so clean even with his stainless-steel surgical saw. He saw purple muscle neatly bisected, tidy ovals of
tendon and gristle, the bone cross-sectioned, marrow oozing
out. The blood arched through the air in heart-driven spurts
and bursts.

Doc's eyes rolled white. He crumpled to the ground.

8

Rackstraw moved a goodly distance away from Buzz as
the man with the solenoid suit began marshaling his
power. Arms spread, Buzz positioned himself at the bottom of
the town hall's stone steps, gazing up at the facade, scanning
for defects, structural weaknesses, hairline cracks in the masonry, chinks in that whitewashed armor. Extraordinary siz-
zles and pops issued from the suit. Electricity played over
the copper pinstripe in moving marble patterns of living blue.
Coils of it flickered out along his arms, ending at his fingertips in Kirlian flares.

Suddenly Buzz's feet lifted off the ground and he rose into
the air and floated there in a coruscating nimbus of blue. His
hair stood erect in a frizzy fright wig. Although nothing was
on fire yet, the smell of burning reached Rackstraw's nostrils.

Buzz brought his arms forward and aimed at the town hall,
and a sizzling bolt sprang from his hands, arcing through
space and striking the foot of one of the pillars. Plaster flew
in lumps. Stone shattered. With an almighty creak the pillar
sagged on its broken base and fell, taking a section of the roof
with it. Stonework, glass, and masonry came crashing
down together in a thud of flame and white dust. Buzz aimed
again, and another bolt took care of the next pillar along, reducing it to rubble. Then he directed his attention to the double doors. The bolt of electricity struck dead center and blew
both slabs of oak inward, melting their brass ornamentation
to slag. The jagged-edged hole in the front of the building re-

sembled a screaming mouth. Buzz fired a bolt through the gap, and for an instant the interior of the vestibule was lit up in wild blue, then burst into flames. Smoke poured from the entrance.

Jeremiah Rackstraw rubbed his hands.

A few more carefully placed bolts took care of the rest of the town hall's exterior. The last pillar came thundering down, and with it most of the roof. Slates darted across the square like arrows, and several of the windows of the library were shattered, as was the main window of Old Joe Dolan's Merrie Malted, sending broken glass into the sloppy ice-cream stains and the puddles of stale dried vomit on the floor. Old Joe himself, still sitting on a stool at the counter, was hit by a shower of pin-sharp shards that spiked his back like porcupine quills. Though not dead yet, Old Joe was way past caring.

Again, again, again, the man with the solenoid suit unleashed high-voltage bolts at the town hall, blasting the architecture away piece by piece into a confusion of bricks and mortar, dismantling thousands of man-hours of work, annihilating decades of municipal government. Walls came tumbling down. Floor collapsed onto floor. Partitions with nothing to divide came together. A jet of water gouted into the air as a pipe burst. A drinking fountain hurtled toward Century Cedar and was caught and held in that giant catcher's mitt of a tree. A whole section of the vestibule's chessboard floor found itself resting on the roof of Wilbur Cohen's store (but then, people always did say Wilbur had a tendency to see the world in black and white).

9

Ripping off his string tie, Mayor hurriedly applied a tourniquet around Doc's upper arm. This was something Mayor had had to do to a fellow actor when he had played a doctor in *A Bouquet for Sister Rose,* and over the course of eleven takes he had become quite proficient at it. Of course, in the movie there had been very little fake blood, and not a drop of real. Now Mayor was kneeling in a growing puddle of the genuine article, could feel it oozing through the fabric of his pants to his knees and shins, and it was warm, God help us, fresh and full of life, and it was the blood of his friend, his best friend, spilling wantonly into the dust. . . .

But he mustn't think about that. He must think only about knotting the tourniquet as tight as he could, about saving Doc's life.

Josh also knew what to do, even without the benefit of a celluloid medical training. He squatted down and lifted Doc's head into his lap. He removed Doc's spectacles (one of the circular lenses was cracked, scars across a moon) and sprinkled water into his face from the canteen Rebecca Cohen had given them. Neither Josh nor Mayor seemed aware of the drying droplets of Doc's blood on their own faces. Nor did they hear the muffled whump of a distant explosion or the firecracker chain of secondary detonations that followed.

When Doc finally began to stir, Josh asked Mayor for his hip flask. As the injured man's eyes fluttered open, Josh unscrewed the cap and placed the neck between his lips, which were blue with blood loss. Obeying some primal instinct, Doc suckled on the whisky. A trickle of its medicinal fire rolled down his throat. He coughed. Seconds later, vomit bubbled up and spilled out of his mouth, geyserlike.

Ignoring the hot liquid on his leg, Josh wiped Doc's chin with his shirttail.

"Oh, God . . ." Doc groaned weakly. "Oh, God, it hurts."

"Hey, now, no talking," said Mayor.

"And why in hell not?" said Doc, regaining a trace of his usual irascibility. "It sure beats listening to *you* jabber. Touch more of that whisky, son?"

Josh obliged, pouring the precious liquid sparingly, but Doc managed to keep this mouthful down.

"That's more like it." Doc sighed, and then a spasm of pain shuddered through him. He creased up his eyes and emitted a weird, high-pitched whine.

"How does it look?" he asked when the worst of the pain spasm had passed.

"Put it this way, Doc," said Mayor. "You won't be playing the piano again."

"I never did play the piano."

"Then you won't be starting."

"Have you tied a tourniquet?"

"I certainly have."

"Good for you." Doc felt the knots with his remaining hand. "Feels like a halfway decent job, too. I'd look, but I don't seem to be able to move my head."

"Don't try," said Mayor. "Old fella, we've got to get you back into town. Do you think you're going to be able to walk?" Doc looked at Mayor as if he were mad. "Okay, okay. Dumb question. Do you think you can survive us carrying you?"

Doc snorted out a laugh through his nostrils, along with a stream of mucus. "You ain't taking me back," he said, "and you ain't staying here with me, either. You're carrying on. You're going to find the way outta here."

"But there is no way out. We're trapped. That stuff, that screen, that force field, that whatever-it-is, there's no way through."

"Guess I proved that, didn't I?" said Doc with a wince that could have contained a smile. "But there ain't no way you're going to get me back to town. Way too far."

"What do you suggest, then?"

"I suggest you just move me up against that twisted old Joshua tree there, and make sure I'm facing toward Escardy Gap and not toward that desert fakery, and then you leave me, and I'll sit awhile in the shade and just watch the world, and by and by my eyes'll close and that'll be it."

"No, Doc."

"That's not a request, Mayor. I'm telling you what you're going to do, and you better do it or else, I swear, I'm going to come back and haunt you for the rest of your days."

"Maybe we should do as he says," said Josh. "It'll help if he's out of the sun."

"Listen to the kid, Mayor. He's got a wise head on those young shoulders."

Mayor was all out of options, and as he and Josh began hauling Doc between them over the jagged ground to the tree (and they tried to be gentle but all the same they couldn't prevent jolts and jounces sending flashes of pain through his nervous system and causing him to yelp), he wondered how many times he had acted in *this* scene before: the mortally

wounded man urges his fellows to go on without him. Oddly
enough, although Mayor had "died" on numerous occasions,
none of his "deaths" had been of the heroic variety. They had
been coward's deaths or innocent's deaths or victim's deaths,
and all of them had been tastefully handled and just about
blood free. This—all this mess, all this waste, all this
courage—was a real death. This was death's true face, and its
grin was both brave and mockingly futile.

And how was Josh to know, how could Mayor have possibly suspected, that this roadside Joshua tree was the selfsame
tree into which Josh's parents' car had driven some eleven
and a half years ago? Perhaps the trunk could have told them,
although the fender-torn scars had long healed. Perhaps the
stumps where there had once been branches could have given
the game away. But even then, would anyone have believed
them? Would anyone have believed that Fate could be so malicious, so darkly ironic, so openly cruel?

10

Buzz, his duty done, drifted down to his knees. The solenoid suit gave off a few last spits and hisses, but for all
that it sounded like a furious wildcat, the fight had gone out
of it. Wan and disheveled, Buzz looked around at Rackstraw,
seeking approval, which Rackstraw gave with a slow sincere
handclap. Buzz offered a smile.

"Excellent, my friend," said Rackstraw, surveying the
burning rubble, the roiling belches of black smoke, the splintered spars jutting up from the wreckage, the pieces of
incongruous debris littering the steps: a blank blotter, an
official rubber stamp, a smoldering loose-leaf file, the plug
and chain and a single faucet from a sink, a broken bottle
that had once contained Wild Turkey. "Excellent, excellent,
excellent. Take a rest. You've earned it."

Buzz staggered gamely to his feet and made his way to a
bench beside a lamppost. His suit sproinged and boinged as
he sat down.

"What now, Jeremiah?"

"Now, Buzz, we wait for the mad mayor to come running."

"What makes you so certain he will?"

"These people are nothing if not predictable, Buzz. They run according to an inner clockwork of wholesomeness and gullibility, which means they can never do anything that isn't preordained by the despicable decency of things. Mayor will hear his beloved town hall being demolished. He will see the smoke. He will come. He will come even though he realizes there is nothing he can do to save the building. Short of a miracle, there is nothing anyone can do to resurrect this architectural Lazarus. He will come because something near and dear to him has been destroyed, and he will weep over the ruins. And he will be vulnerable then. I will merely have to say the word, and he will be dead. In a way, he's done me a favor by hiding. He's made the prospect of killing him that much more satisfying. There's an element of challenge to it now that was lacking before. I have had to use my wits, and for that I am grateful."

"So we just sit tight?"

"It won't be long, Buzz. He'll be here as fast as his spindly little legs can carry him."

"Well, in that case . . ." Taking a screwdriver out of his pocket, Buzz undid a plate near the bottom of the lamppost to reveal its insulated-wire intestines. He selected a red wire, extracted it, and snipped it neatly in two with a pair of pliers. Then he attached the exposed end to one of the copper buttons on his jacket, and sat back and sighed as his solenoid suit slowly recharged itself.

11

How are you feeling now, Doc?" Josh asked, when Doc had been propped up against the Joshua tree's trunk.

"I'll tell you how I'm feeling, son. I'm feeling damn stupid. I should've listened to you. You were right and I was wrong, and I guess I had to find that out the hard way."

"No, I meant the pain."

"I know what you meant," said Doc impatiently. "And to answer your question: I'd feel way better if you gave me some more of that corn-mash anesthetic. Hell, just pour the whole thing down my throat and let me die in peace."

"No one's going to die," said Mayor with conviction, as if saying it with conviction would make it true.

"You ain't in this goddamn body, Mayor. You ain't hearing the things it's telling me. 'Nearly time to give up, Victor,' it's saying. 'Nearly time to go.' " Doc lolled against the tree, his truncated arm dangling pathetically by his side. The tourniquet had slowed but not stemmed the flow of blood, and the precious fluid still seeped out in dribbles onto the ground. "Anyone seen my glasses?" he said. His voice had paled to a rasp.

Josh unfolded the cracked glasses and settled them on Doc's face. Doc peered through one eye, then the other. "These cost me a buck and a half," he said. "I was told they were unbreakable. I'm going to ask for my money back, and if they refuse, hell, I'll just have to set Nurse Sprocket on them."

Mayor hunkered down beside his old friend and placed the hip flask in Doc's remaining hand. The flask slipped out, but Mayor put it back again and clawed the nerveless fingers around it and held them there until it stayed.

Doc turned his head abruptly, as if coming around from a dream. "Is that a tear I see in your beady eye, Mayor?" he said.

"Of course it is, you old goat."

"Well, what the hell's it doing there?"

"It's there 'cause I know I ain't ever going to see you again."

"I never heard such nonsense. Of course you're going to see me again. We're *all* going to see each other again. What's the point if we don't? Why bother having friends if all they're going to do is turn to dust? What good is love if it dies along with the body? I've seen my fair share of corpses, Mayor, starting way back with Abby Hogan and continuing through more postmortems than I care to count, and take it from me, there's more that separates a living body from a dead one than a beating heart and a working brain. Life is the smile behind the eyes, the glitter in a laugh, the glow that fills a face. *That's* what life is, not just a bunch of cells bagged up in skin.

Life is a light. And that light leaves the body when the body dies, but it doesn't vanish. It's still there, somewhere. It's still in the air . . ." He broke off. "Say, can you see that?"

Far off over town, a column of greasy black smoke was churning up into the sky, fanning out, and thinning in the prevailing easterly wind.

12

At the sound of all that thunder and fury of destruction, a handful of curious townsfolk had begun poking their noses into the town square. Catching sight of the ruined town hall, they cried out in amazement and dismay. But none of them seemed able to screw up enough courage to approach. They regarded the ruins with an almost reverential awe and kept their distance.

It was left to an indignant Jed the barber, armed with his best straightedge razor, to go over and remonstrate with Rackstraw.

"Say, you!" he yelled as he strode across the square.

Rackstraw and Buzz Beaumont shared a quick smirk, but the face Rackstraw then presented to the oncoming barber was stony, devoid of mirth.

"You did this?" said Jed. "Did you? Did you? Oh, you've gone too far now, sir. Way too far. We don't stand for that kind of behavior in this town." Halting an arm's length away from the leader of the Company, he unclasped the razor. "Well? Are you going to tell me you're not responsible?"

"But I'm not," said Rackstraw, sliding his eyes sideways. *"He* is."

Jed followed the line of Rackstraw's gaze to find Buzz, who had unplugged himself from the lamppost and, fingers steepled a few inches apart, was observing minutely the flickering cat's cradle of voltage that jumped back and forth between the tips. Satisfied that full power had been restored, he turned his attention to Jed and smiled his trademark bright blue grin.

"I doubt he managed it all by himself," Jed said, the remark addressed to Rackstraw.

"Oh, Mr. Beaumont doesn't need *my* help, or anyone else's for that matter. He quite excels at death and destruction. Are you intending to threaten me with that razor, Jed, or shave me?"

Jed glanced down at the trusty straightedge razor as if he had forgotten it even existed. The blade, daily stropped and sharpened, caught the sunlight and became a solid lozenge of light.

"Depends," he shrugged. "I'm not a violent man by nature."

"Well, if violence is out of the question, what does that leave?"

Jed seemed to consider this thoroughly. "I never said it was out of the question. However, I think it'd be easier if I just report you to the appropriate authorities."

"A sensible decision. Deadly dull, but sensible." Rackstraw reached out, lazily, without menace, and plucked the razor from Jed's fingers, Jed looking calmly on as if hypnotized. Only when Rackstraw had laid the blade in his lap and was reaching out again did Escardy Gap's barber raise so much as a murmur of protest.

"What are you doing?"

"Me?" said Rackstraw. "Nothing. It's what *you're* going to do that counts." And with his slender forefinger he wrote the word "CUT" on Jed's forehead. "You're going to help me pass the time. You're going to slice a little deeper than you're accustomed to, hair man. You're going to do a little skinning. First, you're going to peel back that worthy foreskin of yours, squeeze out your pecker head, and carve your name in letters a quarter-inch deep. Then you're going to slice and dice those two sweet little nuts nestling at your crotch like a squirrel's hoard, to make fine candies we can feed to my friends. Then you're going to run your blade through the soft virgin skin between your fingers and toes, you're going to slice through your nose until you can lift it up on a hinge of cartilage and touch your forehead with the tip, you're going to spill your eye milk like egg yolk, and then, the grand finale, you're going to slice open your proud belly and hoist your guts out into the sunshine to dry." He offered the razor to Jed. "And you're going to start right away."

Shaking his head and whistling with disbelief—*Lord, did this fool really expect him to do all that to himself? Crazy!*—Jed accepted the blade and set to work.

It passed another ten minutes or so, although for Jed it seemed more like ten years.

When the one-man sideshow was over, Rackstraw got up and went over to stand at the edge of the pool of oily gore that had spread like angel's wings around the supine, mutilated form of Jed the barber. Jed's right arm was still twitching, the fingers of the hand that had held the razor quivering in supplication to the sky like the legs of an upturned beetle. Rackstraw stamped on the hand and stamped on it and stamped on it until it no longer moved.

Faint cries and screams could be heard coming from all directions now, borne on the wind like fragrant, fragile seedlings drifting in search of rest. The sky was dark, and the sun could be glimpsed only palely through the thickening smoke.

13

Somewhere's burning," said Mayor, but the town was too far away, huddled too low on the horizon, for them to tell precisely which building was ablaze.

At the word "burning" Doc mumbled something. Mayor asked him to speak up.

"Cauterize the wound, Nurse," Doc repeated slurrily.

"I don't see as we can, Doc," Mayor told the dying man. "Josh, do you have any matches on you?" Josh shook his head. "Me, neither."

"Whassat?" said Doc. Bleary eyes lolled in their sockets. Their gaze falling on Mayor, they gave the merest flicker of recognition. "Are you two still here? What're you hanging around for? Get going!"

"He has a point," said Josh, eyeing the black feather of smoke uneasily. "They're on the move. I think they may be onto us." His eyesight, sharper than Mayor's, had detected an absence among the roofs that rose among the distant treetops. He had a pretty good idea where the smoke was coming from.

"Damn it all to hell, son, this is one of my oldest friends you're asking me to leave here!"

"It's not just me who's asking you," Josh pointed out matter-of-factly. "Doc says you should go, too."

"I know!" snapped Mayor. Then, more of a sigh, "I know."

"You listen here, Mayor . . ." Doc was finding the words difficult to frame. His lips grudged him the work, and his tongue was big and sandpapery and hard to manage, but he made the effort because what he had to say was important; it was perhaps the most important diagnosis he had ever had to deliver. "The kid has more sense in his pinky than you'll ever have in that big empty head of yours. But you, you've got age and a whole wealth of experience on your side. And fine as each one of you is, together you have the makings of a real winning team. Together, there's a chance you can beat these strangers, run 'em out of town. You'll find a way how, you'll fetch the cavalry. I just know you will."

"Doc . . ."

"Now be off with you, 'fore I get sick of the sight of your skinny face."

"Doc . . ."

But Doc's eyes had glazed over again and he was moving his lips soundlessly, holding an inaudible conversation with himself.

Mayor's shrug of resignation was huge and brought his shoulders somewhere up around his ears. It was a despairing Mayor, a Mayor reaching the end of his spiritual tether, who clambered to his feet, brisked the dust from his palms, settled his hat back on his head. A Mayor on the verge of abandoning all hope.

"Come on," said Josh gently, locking a hand around Mayor's elbow. He looked right, looked left. He saw Boundary Hill. Maybe, if there wasn't a way through the barrier, there was a way over. A hill seemed as good a place as any to try.

"Bye, Doc," he whispered, but the old medicine man was way past hearing or caring.

14

Up on Boundary Hill, Sara Sienkiewicz settled herself into the rocker out on Ike Swivven's porch and laid her bleeding feet gingerly on a small wooden three-legged stool that seemed to have been left there for that very purpose. She winced with the pain and with surprise that one could feel pain in dreams. Perhaps it was simply the illusion of pain she was experiencing. Pain, after all, was only in the head. Like so many other things.

When she bent to examine her wounds, she found that the bleeding was not so bad as she had feared. There were only a few cuts, none of them deep, and already the flow of blood had slowed to a gentle weep. She would live.

She was here, now, at any rate. She was where she was intended to be. Here she must wait, wait for something to happen, for someone to come. Here she must live and dream until the time came to wake up. Not long. Not long now.

Sara gazed down on Escardy Gap, a municipal oasis in the midst of the harsh desert, nestling in its bed of greenery—the heads of cedar, cottonwood, and blue spruce—and her heart went out to the little town.

15

He hasn't come," said Buzz Beaumont.

He had considered crowing the statement mockingly but had decided that this would not be such a good idea. During the past quarter of an hour Jeremiah Rackstraw's face had been hardening like quick-drying cement as Mayor didn't appear, didn't appear, still didn't appear. So Buzz settled for the straightforward, straight-faced iteration of a fact: "He hasn't come." It was safest that way.

"I'm perfectly aware of that fact," replied Rackstraw. He was sitting on a jagged lump of masonry, staring off along Main Street and reading the rippled light with eyes that blinked less than an alligator's. He lifted his head and allowed a passing breeze to ruffle his long, sleek hair and lift it in wisps, like the languid fronds of a sea anemone lulling prey in gentle currents. "No, and tiresome though it might be, I think I'm going to have to go looking for him."

16

"Nurse Sprocket, hand me that towel."

"You fetch it yourself, Doctor."

"I'm not asking for your permission, Nurse. I'm giving you an order, surgeon to assistant. We have a crisis on our hands here. We are in danger of losing the patient."

"Sometimes they're better off lost, Doctor. Sometimes life becomes just not worth living anymore."

"I'm going to save him!"

"No, you're not, Doctor. There's no use trying. He's a terminal case. Let him be. Let his last few moments be peaceful ones."

"Goddamn it, I have a duty! . . ."

"Yes, you do, and for nigh on forty years you've been doing that duty and doing it well, but now it's time to let go. You can't save everyone. That's not your duty. That duty belongs to someone else, a greater healer than you or I will ever be."

"But . . . But ever since Abby Hogan, I vowed that no one would die while it was in my power to help them."

"And that made you a fine doctor, and a good man, the good man I love. But it also made you an angry man and a sad man, because you couldn't hope to live up to that vow. You set yourself an impossible goal, and then grew bitter when you found you couldn't achieve it."

"But what's wrong with wanting to try?"

"Nothing, Doctor, as long as you're prepared for failure. Which you weren't. You could never accept that you would never be perfect. But it was for your imperfections that I loved you."

"The patient—"

"Is slipping away, Doctor, inch by inch, breath by breath. But he should be glad. He's had a life anyone could be proud of."

"But he was irritable, he was selfish, he drank too much, he drove people close to him nuts. . . ."

"Vital signs are weak."

"Nurse?"

"Pulse is very slow."

"Nurse? Why do I feel like this?"

"Let him go. Let him go, Doctor."

"Nurse . . ."

"It's easy."

"Drifting . . ."

"He's gone."

"Oh, Lord. Oh, sweet Lord."

"Come on, now, Doctor. This way. Follow me."

"Where are we going?"

"There are other sickbeds, and other patients. They all want to meet the great Doc Wheeler."

"Let's hope they're not disappointed."

"Oh, they won't be, Doctor. They won't be."

And in the shade of the gnarled Joshua tree, with the sun at his back and Escardy Gap before him, Doc Wheeler's chin sank into folds of fat and his cloudy eyes drifted shut and his chest ceased its labored rise and fall.

Nineteen

1

The Knight house was as silent as the grave, and smelled faintly like one, too.

Jeremiah Rackstraw shook his head and, eyes half-closed, breathed the aroma deep into his lungs.

"Hello-o-oh?" he called tunefully. "Anybody home?"

The house remained silent, waiting.

As did Grampa's body, still in the broom closet.

"Ah," said Rackstraw upon discovering the door still closed. "I see we haven't played our little joke yet." If he was annoyed, no trace of it showed in his face or voice.

Somewhere, in the stillness of the house, a clock was ticking. Rackstraw cocked his head and listened to the clock for several moments, several long ticks and tocks, before remembering why the sound held such significance for him.

He climbed the stairs three at a time. Bursting into the boy's bedroom, he surveyed the carnage, the ripped comics, the smashed models, the overturned chair. . . .

The gutted clock, its insides spilled out, rancid, sticky, pustulent.

"You little *bastard,*" hissed Rackstraw. "That was a gift!"

He went back downstairs, unpegged the broom closet door

and opened it carefully, catching Grampa's corpse as it lurched drunkenly out. He lowered the body down to the floor and knelt beside it. With surprising gentleness, he brushed the hair away from the old man's face and stroked the cold leathery cheek.

"Of course," he said, "*you* might know where they are."

He went to the kitchen and found what he was looking for in the second drawer he tried. Smacking the rolling pin into his palm, he returned to Grampa.

"Up you get, you old fucker. No sleeping around on the job."

Amid creaks and snaps and sloppy flatulent noises, Grampa's body raised itself until it was standing erect and stiff as an ironing board against the door to the broom closet that had for a while been its inelegant coffin.

"Just a little tenderizing first," said Rackstraw, and began to wield the pin.

The sound of Grampa Knight's mortal remains being relentlessly pummeled drifted through the hollow spaces of the house, interspersed with Rackstraw demanding, "Where did they go? Where did they go?" Eventually the sound ended with the clatter of the rolling pin hitting the floor. Then, softly, with a sigh like exhaustion, came the words "the hospital" in a cracked and arid parody of Grampa's voice.

Almost immediately after that, there was a pop as Rackstraw disappeared.

And then there was silence again. A sadder, more solemn silence.

The dead can give up their secrets. But the dead, if they are brave enough, if they have enough love left for the living, can also lie.

That might explain why the expression on Grampa's dead face seemed so strangely happy.

2

Neville N. Nolan had seen enough to convince him that a serious escape effort had been embarked on. He lingered, however, delaying his departure, because the sight and scent of Doc's blood was so maddeningly mesmerizing. The second Doc succumbed to death, Neville was there, crawling over the cadaver's amputated arm, wallowing wildly in the sticky cess in and around the stump, frenzying in the thickening fluid, coating himself in congealing clumps of corpuscle, munching down mouthfuls of that nutritious nectar.

Finally, sated, Neville scrupulously washed and wiped the blood from his bejeweled body. Then he tensed, sprang like a sprung spring, and soared up, up, up into the sky until he was a tiny black dot in that tremendous blue dome, then meandered momentarily, deliberating on his direction, and then wheeled westward and raced toward Rackstraw.

He was drawn to the town square by the sight of the burning rubble of the town hall, reasoning that wherever there was ruin, there was bound to be Rackstraw. He floated down in front of Buzz Beaumont and metamorphosed into human form.

"Rackstraw! Right away!"

"Ain't here, my friend," Buzz said.

"Why? Where?"

"Other business."

"It's unusually urgent."

"Well, he headed off for the Knight place, and that's the last I saw of him."

With a whoosh, Neville changed back into fly form and was gone. He rode up into the smoky air, then hovered hesitantly in a complex configuration of twists and turns, as energetic as an electron in an atom, before hurtling eastward and downward, descending straight to the Knight house.

3

Mayor and Josh trudged through the scrub toward Boundary Hill. Barely a word was spoken.

Keeping the barrier to their left—close enough to remain within sight but not so close that a slip, a stumble, an accidental sidestep might pitch either of them headfirst into that lethal whiteness—they went, moving along that narrow band where the illusion of reality failed and the reality of the illusion became clear.

Josh walked a few yards ahead of Mayor. It had fallen to him to act as guide, for two reasons: one, his senses were sharper; and two, Mayor was too lost in grief to be of much use. His head was bowed and he had eyes only for the ground. He followed in Josh's footsteps, and matched his right to Josh's right, his left to Josh's left, hypnotically, mechanically, but his thoughts were elsewhere, and his heart was back near the Joshua tree where they had left Doc.

It was slow going and it wracked the nerves, keeping to the edge of that barrier—as lethal now as a canyon precipice or the rim of an active volcano—and the sweat was soon pouring into Josh's eyes, even as his mouth grew dry and salty. Halting, he tore a strip from the tail of his blue shirt and wrapped it around his head in a bandanna. Then he uncorked the Cohens' canteen and swilled lukewarm water around his tongue. He offered the canteen to Mayor, saying, "Let's go easy on it, huh?" Mayor nodded agreement, then gulped down a huge mouthful.

And on they went.

All around the desert shimmered as the heat swam up from the ground in gasoline-fume ripples. The sun hammered down like a timpanist on their brain pans. The song of the cicadas rose with the temperature, building up into an insistent band-saw whine. The air was fire. And no sign of a gap in the barrier. It stretched ahead as far as the eye could see, a curving, unbroken wall of milky whiteness.

What was on the other side?

The question buzzed around the inside of Josh's head, evolving, growing more complex.

Assuming they managed to get through the barrier, what would be waiting for them on the other side? Naturally, he hoped it would be the world, the world just as he knew it, with Grant's Crossing a long but not impossible walk away. And he even dared entertain the hope that reinforcements would be waiting on the other side, too; that the police and the army and the air force and the National Guard and the FBI and Project Bluebook would all be there, puzzling over this extraordinary phenomenon, this town that had been fenced in by technology way beyond primitive Terran science, for motives way beyond human comprehension, and when he and Mayor emerged they would be hustled straight to the nearest general to tell him how they had managed to escape, and then the general would send in the marines, and Rackstraw and Company would last a little less than five minutes against trained American combat troops, hooray!

But that was childish.

Okay, then. The whole town had been transported to another planet. An alien sun would greet him and Mayor as they stepped out. Alien soil would grate beneath their feet. Alien air would choke them to death.

Yeah.

Josh didn't know which sounded dumber: the amazing victory or the ignominious death.

He was finding it hard to suppress a clawing sense of claustrophobia. He knew now how the convict felt on his first day in jail, discovering the limits of his confinement; how a goldfish constantly felt, bumping brainlessly up against the glass of its bowl.

The other side: for all that it was just a few feet away, it might as well have been a million miles.

The same could be said for Mayor.

In fact, Mayor was lost in time rather than space. He had traveled back across a couple of decades to the days when he and Victor William Wheeler, though no spring chickens, were, by Escardy Gap's standards, Men about Town. And while Doc was spoken for, and perhaps on account of this fact, there was no lack of ladies who set their sights on a ruffled but still handsome ex-character actor as a worthy husband. Oh, yes, no lack of ladies! (But never one of them quite right. Never one.)

It was Doc who had suggested Douglas B. Raymond audition for the part of Mayor, and it was Doc who had supported him vociferously throughout his campaign, and it was Doc who had cheered loudest when the votes were in because, even though the election was uncontested, virtually everyone who was registered to vote turned out, sweeping into office the closest thing Escardy Gap had to a star—a man who had braved Hollywood and had failed and had returned home in shame but had brought back with him just the merest glimmer of Tinseltown.

And further back through time Mayor traveled, to the end of an era, when Douglas B. Raymond's acting career stalled, the stream of roles dried up like a creek in a drought, and his agent—that rarity, one who spoke plainly to his clients—suggested to him that he perhaps ought to think about pursuing another career, and Douglas B. Raymond thought about it, and went back home, back to the little town he had left in his midtwenties when the dream of Hollywoodland was just a glimmer far off over the hills.

So lost was Mayor in the past that he didn't realize that the ground beneath his feet had begun to slope upward. Back through his life he tumbled. Back like a sky diver in free fall. Back through the well-thumbed pages of the script. Back, with numbered leaves flocking onto the calendar on the wall. Back, back, back down that much-traveled route, along old familiar pathways, past the divergences, each decision made determining the future course, so many choices . . . There had to be a pattern to it all, if only he could divine it. There had to be a story behind the story, a story with a beginning, a middle, and an end. Otherwise, otherwise . . .

Otherwise, when he ended up like Doc, he would look back on his life and see it as a brief, merciless forced march from birth to death, a short hop between two oblivions, a flash of awakening in the middle of a long, long night.

Colliding with Josh brought Mayor abruptly and efficiently back to the present. He blinked around him, while Josh picked himself up off his knees.

"What is it, son? Why'd you stop?" he said, his voice croaky from the dust and despair.

4

Rackstraw pinwheeled out of thin air into a small oak table, smashing it against the wall, which in turn caused Nurse Sprocket's Stormoguide barometer (reading: change) to slip from its hook and stab itself into the floor.

He steadied himself. Control, control. At all times, under all circumstances, control.

But he was panting hard and couldn't stop it. Because the hospital was filled with the reek of hope, of people believing there were possibilities, actually thinking there was a chance of success. Such audacity! Such temerity! Such a stench!

But death was here too to balance the scales; death aplenty, and death's little helpers, hard at work in service of their master, busily processing the rancid flesh of the corpses of Nurse Sprocket and Ike Swivven, as Rackstraw discovered to his delight when he had investigated the rooms and corridors of the house of healing. Ants were trooping back and forth in a long column from a crack in the floorboards to the remains of the nurse's head, lugging away that no-nonsense brain in crumb-sized portions. Flies swarmed around the head of the old-timer, the Company's first victim in Escardy Gap. Maggots squirmed inside him, born into a rich, rancid loam and reveling in it.

But there was no Doc, no Mayor, no one alive here at all. Not even the writer woman, whom Rackstraw had been saving for the sweet joy of bursting that unbroken hymen, popping her cherished cherry and stealing her magic. Neville had failed to snare her properly; either that, or her will was too strong to be subdued for long.

Rackstraw was philosophical about this. He made a mental note to talk to the fly-man about the need to do a job well, but it wasn't as if he wouldn't get Sara Sienkiewicz in the end.

That was for later. For now, there was a mayor and a boy to track down and eliminate.

"After all," Rackstraw said to himself, "how often is it that the victim twists out of the predator's clutches, once the predator has a good grip? Once in a blue moon? Never? Any other way isn't natural. Why else is there a food chain? What else is a pecking order for?"

Out in the corridor, oblivious, the ants continued their two-way trek between their nest and the cornucopia of Nurse Sprocket's shattered cranium.

5

Mayor resisted the urge to slap his forehead (which any self-respecting director would have told him was the appropriate action at this juncture in the script).

"They came *in* through it, didn't they?" said Josh. "Stands to reason we can get *out* the same way."

"Well, now," said Mayor, "that's not necessarily true."

"The barrier goes *over* the ground, but it doesn't go *under*."

"We can't be sure of that."

"But it's *got* to."

A pause.

"Son, I sure as hell hope so."

The topic of discussion was the Snake, that venerable, sinuous railroad tunnel that fed through the northern tip of Boundary Hill. Following the barrier had led Mayor and Josh to the point where the tracks emerged from that black maw to pass along the foot of the hill and on into town. Looking back from where they stood they could see the beginning of the escarpment that ran beneath Ike Swivven's farm (but not the farm itself, which was hidden on the far side).

When he had first caught sight of the mouth of the Snake, it had taken Josh a moment or two to realize what was so wrong about it.

The Snake's arch was standing proud from the whiteness, like a stone rainbow. It was as though the tunnel had actually been built into the barrier. It did not vanish when Josh went up close. The tracks ran into its mouth, and continued. They continued until they disappeared into the darkness. Deep.

There was a further test.

Josh hefted a rock and pitched it into the Snake's black mouth.

The rock flew, descended. . . .

And there was a click, a skitter, and then a most definite iron clunk!

"This is it, son. This is it." Mayor clapped Josh on the back with as much enthusiasm as he could muster. "You surely are one smart son of a"—a quick amendment—"gun."

"Dumb luck." Josh shrugged.

"So we go in."

"We go in," Josh agreed glumly.

"What's the matter?"

"I don't know." Josh gave Mayor a frank look. "No, I do know. I'm scared."

"It's okay to be scared, kid."

"But that's not all. I'm kinda unhappy about leaving Escardy Gap."

"So am I," Mayor confessed.

"Are we doing the right thing, Mayor?"

"We're doing what we think's right."

"That's not the same."

"Way I see it, we don't have a choice in the matter. Not any more. It's too dangerous to go back. Otherwise, I'd suggest we do precisely that. Go back and face whatever's coming to us. Which isn't really a consideration at all. So the choice has been made for us, and I'm relieved, I'm glad. I've had too many choices to make in my life, and each time I've made one, I've spent weeks, months, *years* afterward agonizing about whether it was the right one to make, whether I was better or worse off for having made it. Fact is, you never know until you've chosen, and even then, you're never sure. And now, for once, I don't have to flip a coin or draw a straw. Believe me, Josh, that's a blessing."

Josh understood. The only way out, the only way to go, the only way to save Escardy Gap, was through the Snake. This was the corner into which events had painted him and Mayor. This was the cul-de-sac down which fate had shepherded them.

"And by the way," Mayor added, "I'm as scared as hell about going in there, too. I'm scared stiff. I'm so scared I think I'm gonna wet my pants. Who in his right mind *wouldn't* be scared? But I'm scareder still of staying put."

A cool waft of musty air breathed out of the Snake, and from somewhere deep within its gullet came the sound of dripping water and the wind gently fluting. Sunlight made inroads for a few yards, glinting on the surface of the tracks so that they resembled a pair of fangs, casually retracted. Beyond, there was only darkness and the unknown.

"Don't suppose you've got a flashlight on you?" Mayor asked, and when Josh said he hadn't, Mayor nodded and admitted that it had been just a little too much to hope for.

"After you, Tonto."

"Age before beauty, *kemosabe.*"

They hesitated, their laughter floating ahead of them into the tunnel on weak wings.

"Together, then," said Mayor. He held his hand out to Josh.

"Running," said Josh, taking Mayor's hand.

The old man with the excitable, thrillable heart of a boy inside his hoarfrost shell and the boy with the pondering, steady heart of an old man beneath his summer skin stood side by side on the track at the mouth of the Snake and listened to the titters of distant echoes. And then . . .

A mutual squeeze of their fingers.

A simultaneous cry of "Now!"

And they ran.

Sprinted forward like athletes from the gun.

It wasn't just a leap in the dark; it was a leap of faith. They had no idea what might be waiting for them, either in the Snake itself or at the other end. Nevertheless, as they raced across the threshold, Josh turned to Mayor and Mayor turned to Josh, and between them they smiled the biggest, most forthright, warmest, most generous smile in the history of smiles, the great-great-great-grandmother of all smiles, and that smile said, *I don't know if I am going to live or if I am going to die, but for once, in this moment, in this split instant of terrifying uncertainty, for once in my life I actually, honestly don't care!*

Then everything cooled and darkened around them.

The darkness deepened, and the cool got colder.

6

The trail left by the Traveling Tongue—an echo in the air, inaudible to all but the initiated—led Neville to the hospital. There, a windowpane was penetrated, and even as the glass shards fell to the floor in a glittering shower Neville was racing along the upper corridor, compound eyes scanning and searching. The sweet temptation of the nurse's rotting remains was nearly impossible to resist. A perfunctory flirtation with that putrefying flesh would have been lovely. Later. First, find Rackstraw.

There.

Neville whirred into the empty room where the writer woman had lain, and manifested himself as a man.

"Neville," said Rackstraw, raising his eyebrows, "you have something to tell me?" He was expecting an apology for the missing Sara.

The werefly collected his thoughts, then began. "Just after dawn, Jeremiah, I happened upon a Hudson Hornet Hollywood—and I think it was a hardtop, too—I've decided that's the kind of car I'm definitely going to get—"

"Come to the point," Rackstraw growled.

"An escape attempt, an effort at absconding."

Rackstraw's voice fell, along with his eyebrows. "Who?"

"The mad mayor, the bereaved boy."

"What?" Barely a whisper, a sigh like cyanide gas.

"The demented doctor, too, but he's dead."

"Where?"

"Beside the barrier. The other two are traveling toward the tracks."

"How long ago?"

"I hurried here as swiftly as my shimmering wings would allow," Neville said.

He should have known better than to lie to the master of mendacity.

Rackstraw's hands clenched into fists as hard as marble. Two blotches of red stood out fierily on his livid cheeks. His pupils were darker than the depths of an ocean trench.

Control, control, control.

"Neville . . ."

Control. Calm. Command.

"Neville, this won't be forgotten."

Then he said, "The mouth of the Snake."

7

The instant that Rackstraw materialized at the mouth of the Snake was to all intents and purposes the same instant that Mayor and Josh disappeared into the tunnel. The overlap between these instants was gossamer, the cell wall dividing them wafer thin. They couldn't have been closer if they had been Siamese twins. The molecules of air expelled by the fugitives' lungs as they launched themselves into the unknown were the very same ones that their pursuer's lungs inhaled with his first breath upon manifestation out of nowhere. The air whisked by the motion of two bodies through space eddied around the clothing of the single figure who arrived in their wake.

Fingernails. Hair's breadths. Whiskers. Skins of teeth.

Mayor and Josh would never know how close they had come, how the tiniest trick of chance, the merest fancy of fate, had saved their lives.

Rackstraw, on the other hand, was only too aware.

As two pairs of heels flickered from view, he raised his fists to heaven and shook them impotently at God. He ground his teeth together until the enamel splintered. His boots dug grooves in the rock-hard earth.

They had gone. They had found the only possible means of escape. They were beyond his reach. He couldn't pursue them into the Snake because that would mean moving outside the limits of his power, the sphere of his influence which was demarcated by the white barrier. Somehow, they were *safe*.

Damn them!

Damn them!!!

DAMN THEM TO HELL!!!!!

If there had ever been a trace of humor in Jeremiah Rackstraw's face, it was gone now. If those charnel-pit eyes had ever held the smallest twinkle of mirth, darkness had thoroughly blotted it out. If that slitted mouth had ever turned up its corners in anything approximating a smile, it would remain perfectly straight from henceforth. Before, it was almost possible to believe that Rackstraw was someone who might be reasoned with, someone who might listen to an opposing argument with an attentive ear even if he had no intention of deviating one degree from his own opinions, someone who had a concept of what humanity was even though he had never practiced and would not ever practice it. Not anymore.

Now he was a thundercloud boiled down to the shape of a man. He was distilled anger, one hundred-proof fury. An apocalypse in human guise. Plague, Pestilence, War, and, yes, Death, rolled into one.

As far as he was concerned, the show was over. The script had been thrown out of the window in a thousand confetti tatters. The masks were off.

This wasn't a performance anymore. This was the real thing.

Facing west, Jeremiah Rackstraw threw back his head, bent his spine like a longbow and stretched his mouth open wide, wide, wider than any mouth had a right to go, and then, in a voice loud, loud, louder than any voice had a right to be, said, *"ESCARDY GAP!!!"*

The shock waves from this monumental shout rippled out in wave upon momentous wave, scouring through the dust, tearing out the scrub by its roots, shattering stones into pebbles and grinding pebbles into gravel and pulverizing gravel into sand, sending tumbleweed hurtling a mile in all directions, splintering the old sleepers and warping the lengths of rail, tearing them free from the ground and curling them up into clutching claws. Chunks of rock were vibrated loose from the side of the cut, to slither down on a mat of rattling scree, bouncing and bounding and rolling to rest beside the track. Insects were thrown over onto their backs and writhed and clawed at the killing air. Beneath the ground, a cool fresh aquifer turned to boiling poison and a colony of prairie dogs died in shuddering agony. Birds, stone dead, rained down from the sky, striking the earth in a series of feathery impacts, some heavy, some soft.

Then silence.

Ending

Ho fucking ho," said Chip, striding across the threshold without troubling to close the door behind him.

I leapt out of my seat to rectify his error. Hudson, a feline Houdini, was always on the lookout for an escape route, which I preferred to put down to natural curiosity rather than an abhorrence of living with me. Squatting on the windowsill, she blinked in annoyance as the door flew shut, then calmly resumed her survey of the writhing winter-bare branches and the scavenging wind-torn pigeons and the clouds of ink and water flowing across the city skyline.

Chip, cheeks aglow, tore off his hat, coat, and gloves to reveal the bright scarlet-and-white Santa costume beneath, with its broad black belt encircling his girthsome waist. He stood for a moment slapping the cold out of his hands. Then he drew a pint of whisky out of his jacket pocket, uncapped it, and filled two glasses. The bottle was half-empty. It was the only way Chip knew to get through an afternoon at the department store grotto settling kid after bawling kid on his lap and inquiring gruffly what they wanted for Christmas. How many parents, I wondered, would be shattered to learn that Santa was a lush? Not many. They probably knew already.

"Does it ever worry you that we drink too much?" Chip said as he handed one of the glasses to me. Had he read my thoughts?

"Sometimes," I admitted.

"Never worries me. Nope. Way I see it, at our age, what have we got left to destroy? Our brains are half-dead and our blood has slowed down to a crawl. Being good, temperate citizens will only prolong the agony."

"I'll drink to that," I said, raising my glass.

"I'll drink to anything," said Santa Chip. "Mud in your eye."

We sipped in silence.

"So, no verdict," he said.

"The jury is still out."

"There's a lot to deliberate. I nearly strained a testicle carrying that pile of paper up to her."

"There is too much," I agreed.

"A story will always find its own natural length."

"Bullshit. Are you saying that *Moby Dick* isn't a miracle of discursion and padding?"

"Are *you* saying that *Moby Dick* could have been told in twenty pages?"

"It can be told in one sentence. 'Once upon a time a big bad fisherman goes after a big bad fish, but he doesn't catch it and gets fucked trying.' *The Old Man and the Sea* tells pretty much the same story, and in a fifth of the space."

"That's not the point. You yourself said that there are only, what is it, seven stories in the entire world? You said a plot is just a clumsy wooden instrument, an armature over which you can stretch your sentences."

"I don't remember saying that, but it's nice to know I'm quotable."

"Don't get swellheaded. Could have been someone else. Now that I think about it, I read it in *Kirkus* last month."

"Thanks."

"Prima says we should always keep your ego in check."

"*Thanks.*"

"It's for your own good." Chip managed to sound both aggrieved and patronizing at the same time.

"That's just what my mom used to say as she waved a spoonful of cod-liver oil in front of my nose."

"Your mom was clearly a very wise woman. God knows how she could have had a son like you."

Silence fell, broken only by the tick and thrum of the central heating struggling to keep up with demand and the muffled barks of a marital row next door (the season of goodwill always brings extra pressures). I watched Chip watching Hudson. His Florida tan had long faded: his skin was as blindworm white as mine. His belly had bloomed again, and his beard had flourished, but his eyes were wet and rheumy and yellow. He seemed older than ever. What was he now? Fifty-eight? Fifty-nine? Had he crept past the sixty barrier without either of us noticing?

His third rejection by the Hemingway judges had affected Chip more deeply than even he realized. A few months on, and he was still brooding on it, as if it had been a deliberate insult, as if by denying his marked resemblance to the great man the judges had been mocking not just Chip but his entire genealogy, and had in the process dashed all his worldly ambitions and damned every dream he had ever dreamed. They should have just taken him outside and shot him with a real Mannlicher then and there.

Worst of all, I knew how he was feeling. For some reason I had no desire to finish the novel, and this itched, scratched, clawed, and gnawed at me: a failure to come up with the goods when it counted, like a stud in a sex show afflicted with terminal droop.

We were a pair, Chip and I. A sorry pair of impotent old fucks, lurking in the gloom of our apartment building like moles, nursing our own private despairs, strangers to sunlight and enemies to happiness (except the grim and thankless pleasure of drunken badinage).

"So it's nearly finished?"

I started out of my reverie. "Nearly finished? What's nearly finished?" For one perplexed moment I thought Chip was talking about my life.

"What do you *think,* shit-for-brains? The book! The goddamned book you've been worrying over and killing yourself over and pissing us off over for the past century!"

"Oh," I said, with expert nonchalance. "That."

"The book we were talking about a little less than five minutes ago. It's true what the doctors say. Memory *is* the first thing to go."

"Yes, and memory's the first thing to go."

"Ho ho ho."

"To answer your question . . . What was the question again?"

"Christ, stop him before I split my sides."

"To answer your question, Chip, I don't know."

"You gotta know," said Chip, curiously irritable. "If you don't who does? I mean, surely when you started, you had a pretty good idea of where it was all going to end up."

"Not necessarily. Sometimes it's like a love affair. You embark on it not having a clue whether it will all turn out right or collapse in tears and recriminations."

"I'd believe you if I thought you had any idea what a love affair was."

"Okay, then, it's like church. You go in with your eyes closed, on your knees, praying."

"So they escape from the town," said Chip, leaning forward in his seat with a sudden air of intensity. "They go through the tunnel, and what do they find on the other side? That's a mighty cliffhanger you've left us on, buddy, and I for one can't wait till next Saturday morning to find out. I want to know *now.* Is it the army? Or is it the planet Jeezamaroonie?"

"I put them in there hoping they'd find out for me."

"What, the old man and the kid are gonna walk through and tell you?"

"That's how it works. Characters determine where a story goes."

"Well, look."

I could see that Chip was warming to the role of aide-de-author. Charitably: he was keen to see the book completed and me happy. Cynically: he was looking forward to holding a copy in his hands and being able to say, "I helped him with that. I was the midwife who held the forceps and brought this difficult baby out sideways into the world."

"Well, look," he said again, scratching his beard. "Obviously they're not going to be able to beat the bad guys without some kind of a weapon."

"Who says they have to beat the bad guys?"

"Who says?" Chip exploded. "Why, history says! Experience says! A million fictional precedents say! The good guys *always* beat the bad guys. The bad guys win for the first two reels, kick the living shit out of everybody, rob the women, rape the bank, and then in the third reel, the good guys rally 'round and bang, bang, bang! Bye-bye, bad guys. *Adios, muchachos.* Better luck next time. Now, the old man and the kid aren't going to be able to do that if they don't have some kind of secret weapon."

"A magic cloak. A talisman. A lucky charm. An enhanced Mexican jumping bean."

"Preee-cisely! Or they discover that the bad guys have an aversion to, I don't know, sea water."

"So they fetch a dozen buckets of sea water and throw

them over the Company and they all sizzle down to nothing, wailing like the Wicked Witch of the West."

"Yeah! Or the bad guys all die from pollution."

"There's no pollution in Escardy Gap."

"A common cold, then. They've got no resistance because they don't have the cold virus on their planet."

"Come back, H. G. Wells, all is forgiven."

Chip looked at me askance. "Somehow I get the feeling you're not taking my ideas completely seriously."

"Oh, no," I said, suppressing a giggle, "they're very good ideas, Chip. Very interesting. Eminently plausible."

Chip grinned like a happy puppy.

"And," I added, "a vast reeking pile of pure unadulterated horsecrap."

Chip scowled like an angry gorilla.

"I'll pretend you never said that."

"Why bother? I said it and I meant it."

"Then I'll pretend you're suffering from terminal cancer. That way I can pity you and be glad at the same time."

"You're an evil motherfucker, Chip."

"Get used to it. You and me are going to have adjoining rooms in hell."

"The trouble is, by some quantum leap of thought, like the ape with the bone in *2001,* you've hit on the exact problem. Do you know what I really hate about most books?"

"The fact that they sell more copies than yours?"

"Happy endings. Sudden, impossible reversals of fortune. Penniless, handsome hero ending up wealthy and married to the beautiful heiress. Lone cop beating the system, bringing the serial killer to justice and getting back his badge. The monster defeated and life returning to normal in the sleepy New England town. It's bullshit! All of it! Life's not like that. The truth isn't like that. The truth is, the beautiful heiress marries some fat ugly hotshot lawyer and becomes an alcoholic. The truth is, the lone cop accepts a bribe and rises up to become commissioner. The truth is, the monster eats everybody in the town and then moves on to another like the next dish in a smorgasbord."

Chip gave a sigh of such profound weariness I thought he

had just exhaled his final breath, and I looked anxiously over at him; unfortunately, he was still alive.

"Listen," he said, "I don't know if you've spent most of your life in a monastery or what, but I think you've missed out on a vital piece of information. We read novels precisely because they *don't* tell the truth; they tell long, elaborate, elegant lies. Why do we fall for the lies? Why are we so willing to believe them? Because we *like* having the wool pulled over our eyes. Why? Because most of the time we look at the world clearly and we see it's full of shit and suffering and death and more shit, but you writers, you draw a veil over that and you say, 'Here, forget that for a while, look at this. It's still the same shit you know, but I've polished it up and molded it with my bare hands and, hey, doesn't it look great? Doesn't it look good enough to *eat?* Couldn't you just gobble down this glorious, delicious shit forever and ever?' That's what stories are. That's what myths are. That's why we create these symbols and signs and use them to illustrate life. And I think you've lost sight of that fact, pal. I think you've forgotten why you started writing fiction in the first place. I think you've fallen out of love with the lying."

I raised my hands like a boxer, ready to defend my corner, but sizing up Chip's heavyweight argument, I could only lower them again and place them in my lap, where they lay like a pair of exhausted kittens. "I want to tell the truth, is all," I said lamely.

"And no harm in that," Chip replied. "But the truths you tell have to be wrapped up in lies. Somehow, the lies make them palatable. Everyone knows that in real life the bad guys hold all the aces. The bad guys murder you on the streets, the bad guys take the steroids and win the hundred meters, the bad guys run for president and get elected. Nice guys finish last. Fact. But everyone knows also that the good guys win through in the end. They have to! Otherwise, what's the point? What's the point in carrying on living if you don't hope, hope in your heart of hearts, that sooner or later, eventually, inevitably, the good guys are going to come out on top?"

Enter Prima, bearing manuscript, dressed (suitably, as it turned out) in black.

"Say!" Chip jumped to his feet and took the solid ream

and a half of typescript off her. Gratefully, she shook out her aching arms.

"It looks lovely," she said, casting an eye over my desultory Christmas decorations: a few yards of wrinkled paper chain left over from last year, a homemade tinfoil star dangling from the ceiling, and a snowman candle I had never got around to lighting. There were a few gifts so hamhandedly wrapped they seemed to be hiding in shame beneath the dwarfish, unadorned plastic tree. My motto, when it came to giving and receiving at Christmas, was that the best-wrapped parcels always contained the least-wanted gifts.

I offered Prima my armchair and she drifted into it, composing herself with a grace most women her age would have given a tit to possess. Gesturing at our empty glasses, she said, "I don't suppose you'd let me join you? Reading *is* awfully thirsty work."

Chip hastened to pour her out a glass.

"Well?" I said.

"Patience, honey." She raised the glass, inclined it to her pursed lips and took a delicate sip of the whisky. Her features rippled in a pleasurable wince.

I could barely contain my frustration. It was all I could do to keep myself from grabbing Prima by the neck and wringing her opinion out of her. Instead, I paced across to the window and subjected Hudson to a furious stroking.

"Calm down," she told me. "Shall we have a snack?"

Chip thought this was a good idea.

"Well, if it's such a good idea, Chip," she said, "you can make them."

"Awwww . . ." said Chip like a little kid being told he can't stay up late to watch the creature feature. But he clumped into the kitchen anyway, and set about diligently slicing and buttering.

"Now," said Prima, turning her gaze squarely on me so that there was nowhere else I could look but into the aquamarine glitter of her eyes. "Tell me straight. Are you sure that that's it?"

"You mean, is that all there is?"

"That's what I mean."

I hesitated long and hard before committing myself to an ambiguity. "I think so."

"Don't get me wrong, honey, I'm not saying it *shouldn't* end there. What do I know? I'm not a writer. But I've never thought of you as the experimental type, you know, the kind who've forgotten that writing is supposed to be about entertaining, who've never learned how to tell a story—avant-garde amateurs, whizz kids tinkering around with the machinery, too busy making it run in strange ways to appreciate the gift of strong, solid, simple narration."

I listened to this sideways compliment with a leadening stomach, a sickening sense of the guillotine blade about to fall.

"And," Prima went on, "I don't believe *you* believe it's finished, either. There's a fiery finale due. That's what everyone will be expecting. That's what everyone will want to read. A climax. A resolution."

"That's what I was telling him," came Chip's voice from the kitchen, "but he wouldn't listen to me."

"Chip, is there any mayonnaise in the refrigerator?"

Chip checked. I could have told him there wasn't, but I didn't. Prima, somehow, knew.

"Oh, and I do so feel like having some mayo in my sandwich," she said. "Would you be a sweetheart and pop down to Gristede's and get some?"

Chip took long enough about putting on his hat and coat to have a thorough grumble.

When he was gone, Prima reached out and clasped my hand. The coolness and firmness of her grip were unaccountably reassuring. She smiled, showing a set of perfect teeth, all her own.

"Honey, you can be honest with me now. You've given up, haven't you?"

God, how close to the surface those tears must have been, to pour out so readily, to flood with such unmanly ease from my eyes.

"It's okay," Prima cooed, moving her hand to my arm and squeezing gently. "It's okay. It's okay. Everything's fine."

"I feel such a *sham,* " I blubbered, peering at her through misted glasses.

"No one thinks that," she said. "*I* don't think that."

"Pretending it was all going well when it wasn't."

"Not for the first time."

"Smiling, lying."

"White smiles, white lies."

"I don't know what's going to happen!" I boomed. "I don't know where they've gone. They were inside my head for a while, and now they're not. They've been stolen away. I can't hear their voices, I can't see their faces!"

"They'll be back. They always come back."

"I don't think so. Not this time."

"It seems a pity," said Prima, choosing her words carefully, "to have gone so far and not to be able to go that final mile."

"Pity?" I sniffed. "It's an absolute fucking disaster!"

Prima delved into the pocket of her black skirt and brought out a white, lace-trimmed handkerchief the size of a postage stamp, with which I attempted to dry my face. Within seconds, it was wringing wet.

"I think I need some air," I said, resorting to my sleeve.

"That's a good idea."

"Would you and Chip mind?"

"We'll wait."

"Just a quick stroll around the reservoir," I said, shouldering on my overcoat and slinging a scarf around my neck in preparation to meet the merciless subzero city.

"Don't forget to take some money with you," Prima warned. "Nothing annoys a mugger more than wasted effort."

Wasted effort.

I laughed hollowly and said so long, took the elevator, and hurried out the back entrance to avoid meeting Chip coming the other way.

It was late afternoon, almost evening, and snow had been forecast, and the clouds over the city were dark bellied and flowed with a sinister greasiness. A fierce hawk howled straight off the river and onto the streets, bounding off the sides of the buildings and rattling the lampposts with a vengeance. Its talons cut icy tracks through my face. The waft of its wings hauled my scarf and coattails horizontally out behind me. Bending low into the wind, I staggered like a snow-blind explorer, all sense of direction ripped away. My quiet stroll had suddenly turned into an adventure.

I fought my way along to Central Park West and crossed over, dodging around the fenders of a couple of trawling cabs. I entered the park.

Central Park *is* the Big Apple. It's green, it looks appealing, but it's poisonous. Even in winter, when the paved paths seem darker and the skeletal trees and shrubbery no longer mask the tumors of primal bedrock that thrust up from deep within the body of the island, the park offers an alluring, irresistible combination of beauty and danger, as though there is some lethal spirit that dwells beside the pathways and in the stony ornate castellations of Belvedere, constantly summoning, enticing.

I wasn't alone. Despite the threatening weather, there were others like me responding to that summons, only a few of them with their dogs (it amused me to see them bend down every so often and distastefully fulfill their obligation to pick up their pets' warm fresh shit with pooper-scoopers). There were a couple of bums huddled on a bench, drinking from brown paper bags and spitting invective at a hapless bag lady who had had the nerve to turn down their generous offer of a threesome. There were joggers in Lycra and crazies in next to nothing. A cop on the back of a beautifully groomed horse trotted by, and paused a little farther on to commiserate with the driver of a buggy that stood empty with a pair of blinkered nags nodding in the traces.

I staggered on along the dark pathways of the park.

New York's Receiving Reservoir—their capitals, not mine—was built (or, more accurately, dug) in 1862. It covers virtually the entire width of that park, running way up to Ninety-sixth Street. *Mucho* water. But if it was ever intended to be a beauty spot as well as a functional piece of civic apparatus, time and the habits of New Yorkers have put a stop to that. The perimeter has been claimed as a running track by the health freaks, which, for the sedate devotee of the aesthetic, ruins much of the reservoir's charm, but which, to a contrariwise creature like me, makes the reservoir a fine place to be.

I settled into the flow of joggers, relishing the fact that they had to sidestep me and laughing inwardly at their panted, steaming curses. In order to be the greatest possible inconvenience to everyone, I kept to the middle of the potholed path, pausing now and then to gaze out over the brown water and cackle as ducks mistook Styrofoam lumps for bread and seagulls squabbled over a soggy chunk of Big Mac bun (making virtually the same mistake as the ducks).

I began to feel better. And I began to feel ashamed to have cried like that in front of Prima, letting her see a side of myself I preferred hidden. Until now, I had never as an adult blubbered except in privacy, over the ending of a book, or occasionally in the darkened anonymity of a movie theater (I cried during *E.T.*—honest!). What must she think of me? I imagined her grinning with contempt. It was an awful picture. Worse: she would always have this little secret nugget of knowledge to use against me in the future. She could allude to it whenever she wished, however subtly or unsubtly she liked.

Then my heart went as cold as the wind.

What if she should tell Chip?

This is Prima, I told myself. *If you can't trust Prima to keep a secret, why not just hurl yourself into the water right now?*

I stopped and pressed my nose up against the fence, clawing my fingers through the chain-link diamonds. The water was brown, overlaid with wrinkles from the scouring, hunting wind. It looked horribly tempting.

Headline: "Author, Drab, Little Known, Critically and Commercially Ignored, Found Face Down in Reservoir."

But at least if I was dead (*were* dead), my sales might perk up. There might be a wave of curiosity about this tragic, suicidal writer. Dark, fatalistic undercurrents would be discerned in my books that had been hitherto invisible, and the postmortem on my body of work would begin. Consequently, my publishers would reissue everything I had ever written in an immaculately designed matching set. In fact, all in all, I'd be doing everyone a favor. . . .

And I'd never have to finish *Escardy Gap*!

Wouldn't that be glorious? To be freed from that awful responsibility, that millstone? It could be my very own *Edwin Drood,* tantalizing in its inconclusiveness. My very own Venus de Milo, truncated but somehow still exquisite.

I began weighing up the possibilities. Would I, at my stage of life and at a level of fitness only somewhat superior to a slug, be physically capable of scaling the fence—a fence that was put here, moreover, precisely to prevent people scaling it? And would I be able to get to the top without being dragged back down by the cop on horseback (because it was his job) or a couple of the joggers (because misery loves company)? And after I had jumped, how would I go about drowning?

How *do* you go about drowning?

The water was surely icy cold. Shock would therefore do most of the hard work, and my overcoat, sponging up several gallons, would finish off what shock had started.

Floating down while the pale disc of the sun rippled far, farther, irrevocably far above.

My last link to life a solitary chain of silver bubbles.

The brown deepening around me to black.

Cold, cold, cold.

". . . Hey! . . ."

When I first heard the voice, I thought it was coming from inside my head; I thought it was my conscience piping up with its objections. My conscience was a pallid, whimpering thing that had faded through disuse, and this voice was suitably thin and faint. Its lack of cogent argument was similarly suitable. ". . . Hey, somebody! Please! Somebody help! . . ." it shrilled.

Still clutching the fence, I looked around.

". . . Hey! . . ."

A rape. A mugging. A jogger who had stumbled and grazed his knee. Whatever it was, my good-citizen instincts told me not to get involved.

". . . Help! . . ."

Cautiously I moved to the outer edge of the path and scanned the park.

". . . Somebody! . . ."

"Who's there?"

A brief, incredulous silence, and then, louder and more urgent than before: "Down here! Down here!"

"Where?" I said, leaning on the rail and bending down.

Beneath my feet a twenty-foot embankment fell away. This embankment encircles the reservoir. Into the rock are set locked barred gates that cover the mouths of tunnels whose purpose has long been a mystery to me. The voice was coming from one of these. The one directly below me.

My tired, word-worn eyes peered and made out a pair of hands grappling with the bars and a pair of badly laced sneakers down on the ground among the Snickers wrappers, twisted Coke cans, and discarded prophylactics.

"Who's that?" I said. "What are you doing there?"

"We're kinda stuck," came the reply. "Can you give us a hand?"

"I'm not so sure. . . ."

A jogger thundered past, giving me a queer look. I could see what he meant: *This old loon is talking to his brogues.* I shrugged to him matter-of-factly.

"We've got to get out," said the voice. "We've got an important message to deliver."

Then there was another voice, this one lower, hoarser, and better articulated. "What's happened to the goddamned weather? Why's it gone so goddamned cold all of a sudden?"

"Please, mister, whoever you are," the first voice called up imploringly, "you got to get us out of here."

"Well, now, look, listen," I said. "How come you're stuck down there at all? How on earth did you get in?"

"From the other end, you damn fool!" snapped the elder voice. "How do you think we got in?"

"Well, can't you get back out that way?"

"We're in danger," said the younger. "Everyone's in danger."

They were not East Coast accents, that much was certain. They came from somewhere out West, where the vast landscape drew out vowels to twice their natural length. It was this, more than anything else, that inclined me to believe them; to *trust* them.

"Hang on a minute," I said. "Just let me find a way down."

* * *

A boy and an old man, an old man and a boy, imprisoned behind the rusty bars of the gate.

The boy was around twelve or thirteen years old, wore a dark blue shirt, and had a strip of that shirt tied around his forehead in a bandanna. The old man was in a suit with a white shirt (no tie) and his hair was fine and silvery. Both had well-tanned faces, but there was a red rawness to the skin, as if they had recently spent a little too long in the sun. Dust caked their clothes and hair.

I stood and stared at them from my side of the gate, in the safety and warmth of my overcoat, while they shivered uncontrollably in the darkness of the tunnel.

But I was shivering, too.

I said, "Oh, my God . . ." but the words were too frail to make any impact on the air.

"What's up?" said the old man. "Why're you gulping air like a stranded catfish, man?"

I began to back away, murmuring, "This is crazy, this is crazy, this is completely fucking crazy. . . ."

"We aren't going to hurt you, sir," said the boy.

"Fella looks like he's seen a ghost," said the old man.

New York whirled around me. The buildings above the scorched black skeletons of the treetops danced a tarantella. The charcoal sky raced in a roaring vortex, pivoting on the pallid sun.

The world had stopped turning, and all those eons of momentum were catching up.

I fell to my knees.

I heaved.

I vomited.

In the crystal-clear, bile-tasting aftershock, I looked up at the tunnel again, fully expecting the apparitions of Josh and Mayor to have disappeared. They had not. They were staring at me with surprise and disgust. It's not every day that strangers throw up at the sight of you.

"Mister," said Josh eventually, "are you all right?"

"Central Park," murmured Mayor, glancing up through the bars at the Manhattan skyline. "I don't even want to know how we got here."

"Mister?"

"And this is the famous New York summer. Brrr."

"Mister?"

"I should have known. Jeremiah Rackstraw wouldn't leave a simple way out. That's not him, that's not him at all. Trick upon trick."

There they were, characters of mine, beings I had created, talking, breathing, living, right before my eyes.

I almost, for a moment, but just for a moment, believed they were real.

"This is a joke, isn't it?" I said. "Chip put you up to this. You're a couple of actors, right?"

"One of us is," said Mayor. "Least, one of us *was.*" And under his breath he added, "Goddamn New Yorkers. Crazy as loons."

"Who's Chip?" said Josh.

"Mr. Charles 'Chip' Haroldson," I said. "The guy who paid you."

"No one's paid us," said Josh.

"Yeah, yeah . . ." I said.

"No, honest Injun! We're from Escardy Gap. We've escaped. Found a way out and walked here. These guys, you see, they call themselves the Company, they've come and they—"

"Look, the joke's over," I said. "You can stop pretending now. And Chip"—I raised my voice, calling toward the nearest clump of trees—"you can come out now. Very funny. I'm amused. Very clever."

I looked back just in time to catch Mayor tapping his forehead to Josh, who nodded sympathetically.

"Please, mister," said Josh. "It doesn't matter who you think we are, what matters is we're stuck. This gate won't budge." He rattled the gate as proof. "And we've got to get out and—"

"You're genuinely stuck?"

"Genuinely." Josh held my gaze with his big, wide, honest eyes.

"Okay," I said finally. "Okay, let's see what I can do."

* * *

In fact, they weren't stuck at all. The heavy padlocked chain that secured the gate to an iron pin set into the wall had become twisted around itself. With some strenuous prizing, the chain came loose and there was enough slack for the gate to open and provide a narrow gap through which a slender pair such as Josh and Mayor could slip without much difficulty. (How fortunate, I thought, with minimal irony, that Doc is no longer with them.)

I helped Mayor through first, and he thanked me stiffly and formally. Then it was Josh's turn.

As the wide-eyed, cowlicked child actor Chip had hired to play Joshua Knight squeezed himself between gate and wall, I caught a scent off him.

I knew that smell. And I knew, in that instant, that these were not actors at all. This was not a practical joke.

This was true.

New York is full of fairy tales. Ask anybody. It's a big city and a hard city, but it has its soft spots, too.

Ask the Wall Street dealers. Two, maybe three busted marriages behind them, and they're still buying cuddly toys at F.A.O. Schwartz down on Fifth and Fifty-eighth, a silent marker to the birthday of a child they once knew a whole lot better.

Ask the youngsters at an Avenue A poetry reading, who, with their ragged clothing and rings in their noses and lower lips, look like a mutant tribe from some post-apocalyptic future, but who, as they sip from cups of espresso or glasses of carrot juice and listen to verses that tell them about themselves and their place in the world, have the dreaming eyes and hurt but hopeful expressions of maturing adolescents the world over.

Ask the old lady with the dark line over her upper lip and the first (ignored) signs of gangrene in her leg. Ask her—when she stops raving about the secret men who live in the mailboxes and the dummies she's seen move in the windows of Macy's—ask her why she sobs on Christmas Eve. She'll tell you that three years ago a man leaned over her while she lay in a doorway off Times Square and handed her a brand-new twenty-dollar bill, for no reason except that it was Christmas.

There are tiny holes in the ferroconcrete and glass, tiny apertures through which the magic sometimes shines.

It shone on me then, as I breathed in the smells of old laundering, fresh boy-sweat, tree sap, and ancient desert dust, and buried beneath all these but not hidden, singly and in combination, the sweetness of lime, of vanilla, of sarsaparilla, of peppermint, of spearmint, of strawberry, of bilberry, of blueberry, of caramel, of coffee, of fudge, of chocolate, of every ice-cream flavor known to man and some that are the closely guarded secrets of the gods, and I knew, I knew with a certainty that flew higher than the reach of creeping doubt, that these smells could only have come from a little town in the heart of me that had never grown up, a miniature globe of childhood that I had been preserving unknowingly, unwittingly, while age withered the flesh around it, a pearl, a perfect pearl, untarnished by time.

"What's the matter, sir?" inquired a solicitous Josh.

"Nothing," I said, starting out of my reverie. "I'm just going mad. Quietly, certifiably mad."

Mayor cracked his first smile. "Heh. What'd I say? New Yorkers."

"Who *are* you?" said Josh.

"Me?" I hesitated. It was a good question. What was I to say? *Me, Josh? I'm the man who invented you. You sprang from my brain like Athena from Zeus's brow. And somehow— I don't know how, I don't want to know how—you've taken flesh and become real. You look exactly how you're supposed to look, you speak exactly how you're supposed to speak, above all you smell exactly how you're supposed to smell. You stepped into the Snake, out of my head and into the real world. That's who you are. Creations. That's who I am. Your creator.* Oh, yeah. They'd really fall for that in a big way.

"Me?" I said. "I'm a friend."

"You have a name, friend?" said Mayor.

"I do, but let's stick with 'friend' for the time being."

"If you insist."

"Anything else would be too complicated."

Mayor introduced himself and Josh, then said, "Friend, if

you *are* a friend, perhaps you'd be so good as to point us in the direction of the nearest police station."

"I could," I replied. "But I don't think it would do much good."

"How so?"

"You say you've come from Escardy Gap, right?"

"You *know* Escardy Gap?" said Josh, clearly astonished that a New Yorker might be aware of the existence of his fly-speck of a hometown.

"Well, not exactly know," I said, extemporizing quickly. "I've heard of it. I know where it is. So I know that you could never have walked from there to here as you claim you did."

"But we did!" said Josh. "We found a hole in the force field and came through."

"It was a heck of a long tunnel," Mayor remarked, nodding slowly. "Seemed like we were in there for at least a day. But you can't walk to New York in a day."

"I thought we were only in there for an hour. Two at the very most."

"No, it was a heck of a lot longer than that, son. Why else would I feel so dog tired?"

"I don't know. In that darkness . . . Maybe we both lost track of time."

"That still doesn't explain how we managed to get all the way to New York."

"We went through a dimensional warp," Josh decided.

"A dimensional warp," Mayor repeated.

"Something like that anyway."

"I'll take your word for it, son. You're the expert in these matters."

I laughed. "There you are! Can you imagine how the police are going to react to all this business about force fields and dimensional warps? Can you imagine how crazy it's going to sound? They have special cells for people who talk like that. Cells with rubber walls."

"*Someone*'ll believe us," said Josh with a furrow-browed conviction I could only admire.

"No, I reckon he's right, son," said Mayor. "To you and me, it seems perfectly natural. Least, no crazier than what we've become used to over the past couple of days. But coming to it cold, well, would *you* believe us?"

All but imperceptibly, Josh shook his head.

"How about you?" Mayor asked me. "Do you believe us?"

"Oh, yes," I said. "Completely. Unquestioningly. One hundred per cent."

"Well, it's a start," said Mayor, "I guess."

A racking shudder traveled through Josh. His sunburned face had gone pinched and gray, and gooseflesh had erupted over his bare arms. Mayor, too, was showing signs of feeling the cold, though doing his best to hide them, surreptitiously stamping his feet and rubbing his hands behind his back.

"Jeez, how'd it get to be so cold all of a sudden?" Josh asked.

"Because it usually does in winter," I replied.

"It's winter?"

"December, to be precise. A week before Christmas. But don't worry. My apartment's not far from here. Why don't you come with me, sit, get warm, have something to eat, and we'll plan what we have to do."

"Now, why should we trust you?" said Mayor. "You've been acting pretty weird all along, telling us you know us when you don't, refusing to give us your name . . . throwing up! How do we know you're not one of Rackstraw's cronies?"

"Yeah," said Josh.

"That, gentlemen," I said, "is something you're going to have to take on blind faith."

And I turned my back on my creations, confident that— knowing them as I did, with inside-out familiarity—they would follow.

Sure enough, a moment passed, and then Mayor called out, "Wait up! Hey! Friend! Wait for us!"

We crossed the park safely, unhindered. It was when we hit the street that we encountered problems.

Josh had made some remark about the traffic—he'd never seen cars like these before, in such a variety of oddball shapes and sizes, with all those smooth edges and curves, and so *many* of them—and Mayor had replied that everything was more sophisticated in New York than in Escardy Gap. (How he knew this, having never visited New York in his life, was a mystery. I had to assume he was trying to impress and perhaps reassure Josh with a show of worldly wisdom.) We were standing on the corner, waiting for the traffic to thin so that we could cross. We must have looked like a bunch of tourists—which, in a sense, two of us were. We surely looked like easy game.

Three punks swaggered up to us in an expertly synchronized display of the hands-in-pockets homeboy slouch. They were wearing parkas with fur-trimmed hoods, slashed jeans, and the very latest in sneaker technology. They had trouble written all over their sneering faces.

"Yo, bro!"

"Ignore them," I whispered to my creations from out of the side of my mouth. "Keep looking straight ahead of you. Don't respond to them. Don't rise to the bait. Don't jump or run or do anything sudden."

"But they're just boys," said Mayor.

"What do they want?" said Josh.

"With any luck, only money," I said.

The punks stopped about six feet away.

"Hey, old guy!" yelled one. From the corner of my eye I saw Mayor twitch. "Yeah, you. You sure dress funny, man. You dress like my grandfather."

"Nah, Arnie, he dresses like your grand*mother*!"

"Zip that lip, Dodo."

Walk winked at us, but we didn't feel like taking the hint.

"Yo, brothers," said the third punk. "Never mind the old guy, scope out the *kid*. Ain't seen a haircut that bad since my momma got drunk and went after my father with the scissors."

"Wearing a *badge,* too." The punk called Arnie reached out and fingered Josh's dark blue shirttail bandanna. "White-boy thinks he's a Blood."

"Nah, man, Bloods wear red. He thinks he's a Crip."

I bustled forward, slipping my wallet out of my back pocket. "Okay, fellas," I said, "how much do you want?"

They turned to me. The one called Dodo feigned astonishment. "Did you hear that, brothers? Trey, Arnie, did you hear that? Lard butt here just tried to bribe us. Man, I am *insulted.* Do I look like some common street punk to you, mister, huh? Zat how I look?"

I resisted the urge to say yes, that was precisely how he looked. Instead, waving a fifty-dollar bill in front of his nose, I said, "Consider this a donation. Give it to your favorite charity. Season of goodwill and all that. You do have a favorite charity, don't you?"

Dodo smiled brightly at his friends. "Sure, I do!" They all laughed. He took the note. "Mister, I accept your generous offer and I vow that I shall find a good home for this."

"Right," I said. "And my friends and I will just cross the road and be on our way."

"Sure, man. Merry Christmas."

"Merry Christmas to you."

The punks turned to go, and then Arnie pretended he had suddenly remembered something.

"Hey, you."

Josh, thinking we were safe now, dared to look 'round.

"Yeah, you. Tough guy. Gang boy. *Hombre.* Answer me one question. Are you wearing that bandanna as a fashion statement . . . or because you're *stupid*?"

From my position of absolute omniscience, I watched events unfold the only way they could. I watched Josh step forward. No one had ever called him stupid before. He was a lot of things, but he was definitely not stupid. Angry blood swelled the veins in his forearms and engorged his hands into fists.

I watched the punk's blade flicker out in a blurred arc of steely silver.

I saw, understood, *felt* Josh's stab of terror as he realized the enormity of the mistake he had made.

And then, as I had known he would, I saw Mayor shoulder Josh aside and confront the punks with his hands pushing the corners of his coat back over his hips, like a gunslinger without guns.

Arnie snarled and waved the knife at Mayor.

Mayor, God preserve him, did not so much as blink.

"You young whippersnappers," said Mayor.

Arnie frowned at Dodo. Dodo frowned at Trey.

"What'd he just call us?" said Arnie.

"Snicker-snatchers?"

"Oh, yes," said Mayor, "you may dress peculiar, you may think you're big men just 'cause one of you's got a knife, but you're still just snotty-nosed little boys to me. You're not too old for me to take you over my knee and give you a good thrashing."

Arnie grinned incredulously and spectacularly. "Is this guy *for real*?"

" 'Over his knee?' " said Dodo.

" 'A good thrashing?' " said Trey.

A taxi hooted as it rolled past: disapproval, or encouragement?

"Well, hot damn!" said Arnie, laughing heartily. "We got ourselves a—what's the old guy's name?—a regular *Harrison Ford* here."

"Well, I don't know who this 'Harry Sunford' is," said Mayor, drawing himself up to his full height, inflated with self-belief, "what you've got yourselves here, boys, is a regular Douglas B. Raymond."

The knife blade wavered in the air.

"I ain't never heard of no Douglas B. Raymond," said Arnie.

"He's been out of the limelight a long time," said Mayor, "but you could say he's making a comeback."

Arnie was confused. His face registered all the bewilderment of a pea-sized brain being sorely taxed.

"This is bullshit, man," said Trey. "Either stick the motherfucker or let's go, Arnie. What's it to be?"

"Yeah," said Dodo. "We got the money. You gonna stick him or what?"

"Mister," said Arnie to Mayor, "I don't know if you brave or just plain crazy, to talk like that to the man with the knife."

"Both," Mayor replied frankly.

"Yeah," said Arnie, "yeah, that could be. Ain't you scared?"

"No," said Mayor.

"You should be."

"I would have been. Once upon a time. In an earlier reel. But not now."

Arnie closed his eyelids once, slowly, contemplatively, and I foresaw with stunning clarity the knife flashing forward and slipping between Mayor's ribs, straight into that admirable old heart; I saw Mayor tumbling back from an arc of blood, heard it spatter on the cold sidewalk; saw my creation, this living flesh of my mind, gasping its last in the grit and grease of a New York street. . . .

Then Arnie gently folded the knife shut, blade sliding home into handle like husband into wife.

And he held out a paw and he said, "Old guy, you is the dumbest motherfucker I ever come across. I like that."

Dodo and Trey breathed disbelieving sighs of "Shit, man" and "What the fuck?"

Mayor, too, was perplexed, but nonetheless he took the proffered hand and shook it.

"Son," he said, "I can't tell whether you just paid me a compliment or an insult, but I *can* tell you this. Christmas isn't just a time for giving presents and being with your families. Christmas is a time for magic. True magic. It's the one time of the year when we all think about each other instead of ourselves. And I think you and your friends and me and all of us . . . have just been touched by the spirit of Christmas."

Arnie stared at Mayor.

"Man," he said finally, with a broad grin, "you is fucked beyond all repair."

The punks strolled away in a cloud of high fives and shoulder slaps. As far as everyone was concerned, the episode had gone well.

Mayor turned to Josh and myself. He wasn't even trembling.

"Thanks," said Josh.

"Don't mention it," Mayor replied, with a noncommittal gesture.

"No, I mean it. That was pretty nifty."

"No one threatens Josh Knight with a knife while I'm around."

The light was flashing Walk, Walk, Walk again.
"Let's go," I said.

It's harder than you think, communicating using only your eyes. Animals, especially cats, can do it. Humans seem to have lost the knack.

Opening the apartment door, I rolled my myopic pair from side to side trying to tell Chip and Prima to play dumb and ask no questions. When this didn't seem to work, I opened them cavernously wide like Jack Nicholson in *The Shining*. This was intended as a warning: *Heeeere's Mayor and Josh!* Then, as my friends were clearly none the wiser, I crossed the pupils like Ben Turpin, to suggest that something weird was happening.

It was obvious from Chip's and Prima's eyes that they thought I had lost my mind, so I resorted to whispering "Don't say anything until we talk, okay?" loud enough so that they could hear but still so softly that Mayor and Josh, trailing me by a few yards, could not. Turning quickly to usher in my creations, I gestured expansively with one arm and said, "Here we are. Humble and modest, but comfortable."

"Hell," said Chip, "I've been called a lot of things in my time, but never that."

"Guests," said Prima, both delighted and puzzled. "I didn't know we were expecting."

Tentatively and with much craning of necks and general three-sixty-degree peering, Mayor and Josh entered the apartment.

Both my friends gave the new arrivals a long and frank head-to-toe appraisal. Chip was first with a comment, directed at me. "Been hanging 'round the soup kitchens again?"

"Chip!" Prima hissed, and rose from her seat and spread out her arms in an all-welcoming embrace. "How do you do? It's a pleasure to meet you."

Mayor, whose eye for the ladies had not dimmed (had in fact grown hungry through disuse), beamed at the vision of sexagenarian beauty in front of him. "Ma'am," he said, "the pleasure is undoubtedly all mine."

Prima was suitably charmed, although she knew bullshit when she heard it, and this was prime stuff. "Prima Ferlenghetti," she said.

Mayor held out his hand. "Douglas B. Raymond, ma'am. And if I hear you using anything other than that first name, I will be more than mightily upset."

Now Prima frowned. "Douglas B. Raymond," she said. "Where have I heard that name before?"

"I'd hesitate to suggest that you might once have seen one of my movies."

"Oh, my God . . ."

In unison, Chip and Prima's expressions altered; he was amused, she wholly bemused.

"And that, I suppose, is Josh Knight," Chip said, pointing to none other than Josh Knight. "And out in the corridor Alan Funt is waiting, holding a big camera. Am I right?"

"No," I said, "you couldn't be more wrong."

"Well, it's gotta be a setup, hasn't it? I mean, if this isn't a setup, just what the hell *is* it?"

"I wish I knew."

"What does he mean?" Josh asked, eyeing the sandwiches that were piled on a plate on the coffee table and licking his dry lips.

"This is Chip," I said. "I mentioned him to you before."

"The practical joker," said Mayor. "Is that why he's dressed as Santa?"

"No, he's dressed as Santa because, impossible though it may seem, somewhere beneath that grouchy exterior there lurks a heart, and a big one at that. Just don't tell him I said so."

"Douglas, Josh, sit yourselves down," said Prima, taking control of the situation as I had suspected and hoped she would. "Can I get you something to drink?"

"Well, now, ma'am, that would be most kind," said Mayor as he and Josh perched themselves uneasily on chairs. Josh threw another longing glance at the sandwiches.

"Josh," I said, "are you hungry?"

"Well . . ."

"Damn me if the boy isn't ravenous!" exclaimed Mayor. "Growing lad like him. When did we last eat?"

Josh shook his head.

"Help yourself," I said, gesturing at the plate.

No further instruction was necessary. Josh wolfed down one, two, three of Chip's raggedly lumpen pastrami-on-whole-wheat-with-lettuce-and-mayonnaise concoctions, washing them down with a can of Coca-Cola. Prima gave Mayor a coffee laced with Jim Beam, and he told her she must have read his mind: it was his favorite tipple.

We watched them eat, we watched them drink, and all along Prima and Chip kept throwing looks at me, looks that promised mute acquiescence for now on the condition that an explanation would be forthcoming, sooner rather than later. Hudson, meanwhile, seemed to sense there was something not quite right about our guests and glared at them with a cat's astonished unwavering fixity.

Finally, Mayor informed us that the spot had been hit, while Josh claimed he couldn't eat another crumb, thank you very much.

"I don't suppose I could freshen up, could I?" said Mayor.

"Bathroom's through that door."

"Mind if I come, too?" Josh asked Mayor, and I understood why. Who would want to be left alone in a room with three gawking, gray-haired unknowns?

"No problem," said Mayor.

Tension snapped the moment the bathroom door clicked shut. Chip and Prima, and even Hudson, rotated their heads to stare at me, like a jury fixing accusingly on the guilty man when they learn about the most damning piece of evidence of all.

"I swear this isn't a gag," was all I could think of to say.

"Oh, it's a gag all right," said Chip mirthlessly.

"What *are* you trying to prove, dear?" said Prima in her frostiest tones.

"Precisely my reaction," I told them. "It must be hard for you to take on board, but think how much harder it was for *me*. That's Mayor in there, that's Josh. You've been reading about them. I've been *writing* about them. And suddenly they've sprung into life. I mean, I have to keep looking at them just to prove to myself that they're flesh and blood. I keep expecting them to fade away like ghosts. I feel that if I stop believing they're real, they'll cease to exist. It's . . . I can't describe how exhilarating it is. Like being drunk on a roller coaster, absolutely out of control. Wonderful!"

Prima took my arm. "Would you like to lie down?"

"Why? The last thing I feel like doing at this moment is lying down." I examined her expression more closely, scrutinizing the hieroglyphs of wrinkles and eyebrows. "Oh. Oh, that's it, is it? You think I've flipped. 'Poor fellow. All that hard work, all that frustration. He's had a nervous breakdown. He's dressed some actors up as characters of his and he wants us to believe, he's desperate to convince us, they're real.' That's what you think."

"I think," said Prima, "you've been putting yourself under a lot of strain recently."

"I don't deny that, Prima, but you have to believe me, I'm perfectly sane. I've never felt saner. I've never felt this sharp, this clearheaded since I was in college. I've got a diamond for a brain."

Chip muttered a correction. "More like an eggplant."

"And I know," I continued, "I *know* that you, both of you, deep down, realize that these are the genuine article. You just can't admit it to yourselves. Not yet. Nor could I, for a while. But Chip, you recognized Josh, even though you'd never seen him before."

"It was obvious," said Chip.

"And Prima, you made Mayor his favorite drink."

"I was humoring you," said Prima.

Neither of them could give their replies the ring of conviction.

"Yes, it's impossible," I babbled on. "Yes, it defies the laws of nature and physics. Yes, it's absurd and ridiculous and irrational. Who cares? That's what magic is all about: defying everything you've been taught is true. A glorious, incredible lie—the bigger the better!"

"That's the first honest thing you've said all day," Chip grumbled.

"You've chosen these people well, whoever they are," said Prima. "And you've coached them well. They're thoroughly convincing, although, you know, Mayor in the book comes over as much less confident and charismatic than this fellow."

"He's rediscovered himself. That's what I was trying to show. Until the Company came, Mayor had only had this vague responsibility for the town as a whole—not much of a responsibility at all, because it was a peaceable place, easygoing, democratic, safe. A challenge brings out the best and the worst in people. In Mayor's case, the best." It felt weird to be discussing Escardy Gap as if it were still confined to the printed page, when its living symbols were only a few yards away behind a thin door. I lowered my voice, like a confessor in church. "That's the most marvelous thing of all. At the exact point where I stopped writing the book, they stepped out of it. They're not just Mayor and Josh, they're Mayor and Josh as they are at the very moment of escaping into the Snake. The words have lifted themselves off the page, swirled around, gathered, and shaped themselves into human beings." I lowered my voice still further. "I've been wondering whether I have the power to do this to anyone else, whether I could maybe bring Jeremiah Rackstraw out into the world."

"That wouldn't be very wise," said Chip with a slight but unmistakable shudder.

"A*ha!*" I cried, startling him, Prima and, most of all, Hudson, who bristled and hissed on the windowsill. "So you accept the possibility that this might be real!"

"I don't accept anything," Chip replied. "That Rackstraw guy gives me the creeps, that's all. Hey, you should be flattered. Tribute to your art and all that shit."

Prima had picked the ruffled Hudson up and was cradling her, nuzzling the fur on her head, calming the cat and herself. "How long do you expect them to stay?" she said.

I had no idea. I hadn't given the situation much thought. Did that mean she—?

"Because," she went on quickly, "if they really are who you say they are, they can't hope to survive here. This isn't their world. They come from somewhere else, I don't know where exactly, but wherever it is, it's not here and here they cannot stay. You have to send them back, tonight if possible, tomorrow at the very latest."

I glanced at the window. The first flurries of the long-promised snow were swirling down against the dark background beyond, and I thought of a million happy children and a million cursing adults. "I couldn't possibly send them out into that."

"You could if you had to."

"Please, Prima," I said, with a whiny begging note that I didn't like to hear in my own voice. "Can't they stay even just the night? There's so many things we have to talk about, so much I have to ask."

"I thought you knew everything there was to know about them," said Chip.

"Maybe I do," I replied, "but it's one thing to have a vague idea of a character in your head, quite another to be able to ask them about it. For instance, has Mayor been in any movies that I haven't mentioned in the book? Does he know their titles? Does he know only as much about himself as I've revealed, or does he have an entire life history beyond the little I've hinted at? This is such an opportunity! I could find out so much about the creative process! God, I could write a whole book about it!"

"And have you given any consideration to what you're going to do with them when they go back?" Prima asked.

"Do?"

"On paper, on paper!" She sighed testily. "Are you going to carry on with the book?"

"Well, I don't know. This is all highly unusual. I tend not to want to think too much about the consequences yet."

"But you must!" Prima wagged an admonitory finger. "You must send them back and then you must carry on with the book and you must finish it, and that's final."

"But why?"

"Why? *Why?* God preserve us, are you really that dim-witted? Haven't you worked it out yet? Don't you see? They've got to go back and save the town! They've got to go back to a happy ending! You still don't get it. I can tell. They haven't sunk in yet, have they? The implications." She handed Hudson to Chip, then seized me by the shoulders and looked straight into my eyes, so that what she said would drill itself directly into my dull brain. And these were her words: "If they are alive, then wherever Escardy Gap is, it exists. What's happening there is *real*. Everything you've written so far is *real*—every deed, every thought, every piece of dialogue, every death. You're the one responsible. And only you have the power to make sure it all turns out all right."

I must have tried to speak. My lips and jaw certainly went through the motions, but nothing emerged. I had been teetering on a pedestal a thousand feet high, and now I was hurtling down like an angel felled, surrounded by the tatters of my wings. I could hear the roar of the wind that accompanied my descent.

Someone once said that if a child had the power it would destroy the world, and whenever I see a little kid throw a tantrum I know exactly what that wise person meant. When I watch the frenzy of small writhing limbs and purple puffing cheeks and liquid eyes, it's almost as if I am watching that destructive will straining to emerge, the recently born struggling to give birth to a terrible creation of its own.

Parents and schooling curb such displays of emotion (the taming of the expression of desire is called growing up), but it is never beaten; it merely retreats, and hunkers down deep within our adult psyches, enthroned, an angry impetuous vengeful infant-god. And with our imaginations we worship it. To appease it, we offer small tidbits of thought-violence. A man throttles his aggressive boss a thousand times over in his head, where no actual harm is done. A woman disposes of an abusive husband in a dozen ingenious ways, a dozen times a day, inwardly where she will never be caught. TV viewers aim finger guns at the images of the two-bit politicians and tinpot dictators they loathe. Such dreams of retribution keep us safe and sane. Imagination fulfills the role of reality (although for a few, a lunatic few, the imagining is not enough: the deed must be done. Usually, these people make the headlines.)

And perhaps those of us who write the books and direct the films and paint the paintings that seem to celebrate destruction and violence do this not only to satisfy the infant-god in us but also in others, allowing him to roam free for a while, indulge his every whim and appetite, until finally, glutted and exhausted, he falls asleep again, and we are all the better for it. Perhaps.

No one, of course, is confronted with the consequences of their imaginary acts of vandalism. No one is put on trial for crimes committed solely in the mind.

No one, at any rate, until now.

There I was, all of a sudden guilty of at least twenty counts of murder, not to mention rape, child abuse, arson, damage to public property, and several other offenses for which there are no laws yet in the statute books, including use of supernatural tobacco to reduce a human being to the consistency of wet cement, fatal electrocution by means of a copper-threaded solenoid suit, and the unlawful appropriation of memories.

I couldn't even shift the blame for these crimes onto the Company. I had created them. I had sent them into Escardy Gap on an express mission to murder, maim, and mutilate. I was the Godfather, they were my Family. The order to kill came from no one else but me . . . and I hadn't even known I was giving it! I was at once as innocent as heaven and as guilty as hell, as pure as the driven snow and as black as the darkest night, and my Christmas miracle had turned out to be nothing but an elegant confection of tinsel, paper, and ribbon inside which lurked the least-wanted gift of all.

Prima was hugging me. "I'm sorry that I had to be the one to break it to you," she said.

I mouthed some platitude about that not being her fault, and rather her than anyone else.

"But you know, it is for the best. Now you have a reason to finish the book. There are souls in peril to be rescued, and it's up to you, all up to you."

"I can't do it," I whispered into her peach-scented hair.

"Yes, you can. As long as you keep believing. Remember that. Come what may, remember to keep believing."

Chip, still carrying Hudson, leered over Prima's shoulder. "Suddenly my ideas aren't looking so much like horse doo-doo any more, are they, huh? So which is it to be, old buddy? Sea water? The cold virus? The magical Mexican jumping bean?"

"Chip . . ." Prima said quietly as she unlocked our embrace

and took a step back. She clasped Chip's hand, and there they stood, side by side, looking at me, his eyes devilishly mocking, hers sad with the secret depths of the knowledge they held.

"Yeah, Prima," said Chip. "I know."

"Know what?" I asked.

"It's over," Prima said, as if a fever had abated or a life succumbed. "It couldn't have lasted forever, of course. Nothing can. And it's a shame, but it's a blessing, too. Now, at least, you can get on with your life."

"What *are* you talking about, Prima?" I asked.

"The barrier between fact and fantasy has been breached. The river of imagination has burst its banks and spilled over into the world, to purge, to cleanse, and to renew. The old artifices are being washed away, and new edifices will have to go up in their place. That's how it works. Good-bye. I've enjoyed being your confidante, your confessor, your conscience, your friend."

"Yeah," said Chip. "So long, buddy. You're on your own now. Hey, be glad! You won't have me dragging you down anymore."

"Where are you going?" I stammered. "Are you going away somewhere?" Suddenly I could see, dimly through Prima's breast, as though through gauze, the Smith Corona sitting on my desk. I could see, through Chip's face, Escher's eternal cycle of hand drawing hand drawing hand.

"We're finished here," Prima said. "Now that you know what you're capable of, now that you understand the power of your imagination, you don't need us any longer."

"But I want you here!" I cried, and Prima's face was sorrowful and faint, and the snow outside seemed to be falling through it from brow to chin like ghostly tears. "You're my friends. I don't have any other friends. You're all I know."

"You've got friends," said a spectral Chip. "You just haven't met them yet." Hudson mewled softly, then licked the back of Chip's hand.

"There are other places," said Prima, "other worlds than this."

They were fading, losing substance before my very eyes. They were tuning out like the image on an old television set, slipping into mute static. Opacity became translucence. Two pale flickering shadows occupied the air in front of my desk, woman shaped and man shaped, the man-shaped one with a cat-shaped shadow in his arms. They were still talking to me, making their good-byes, bidding their adieus, saying their fond farewells in all the myriad ways the language allows us, but their voices were gossamer faint and growing fainter by the word, until they were no more than a tickle in my ears, and then silence. Chip and Prima were merely outlines of human beings, Hudson just a cat in silhouette. As one, Chip and Prima raised their outline arms and waved. Then, milk-ily, they vanished.

I reached out to touch the air where they had stood. It was chilly, and still swirling with the disturbance of their passing. I wanted to find some outlet for the ache of grief I was feel-ing deep in my gut, but there was nothing, not even an inar-ticulate howl, that would have done.

From the bathroom came a cry, followed by the crash of a body falling.

When I burst in, the bathroom was silent but for the plick, plick, plick of a dripping faucet and the ragged breathing of the body that lay curled on the tiles surrounded by a pool of slick redness. Josh stood poised at the sink, his forearms slick with soap, the water scummy with dirt. He was staring down at Mayor, too scared to breathe.

"What's happened?" I said. "Did he slip? What is it?"

Numbly Josh shook his head.

One side of Mayor's face was rippled and greasy, a little like the skin of a waxwork after a fire. The eyeball bulged out, almost touching his cheekbone, the pupil flicking uncontrol-lably from corner to corner, searching for explanations, find-ing none. The mouth drooped in a lopsided sneer. The hair that straggled on the floor was matted into sticky red rattails. His hand, like some knotty-jointed albino spider, twitched as if luring prey.

Then I noticed the blood spreading across the tiles in a dark, precisely edged pool, oozing toward my toes, reaching my toes, spilling idly beneath my toes. Mayor's blood.

I said his name twice. The first time, there was no response. The second time, Mayor tried to look up. The bony neck clenched and rippled with the effort, but in vain. No engine could lose that much lubricant and still function.

"Mayor, please, say you're all right."

"He was just standing there, talking with me," Josh said, his voice deathly hollow, "and then he just sort of gurgled and fell over."

Mayor shuddered convulsively, squeezing himself more tightly into the fetal position, and coughed and then unleashed a gush of scarlet vomit that washed over my feet and ankles and splashed the cuffs of my pants legs. There were things in that vomit that had no right to be there, blubbery lumps and fleshy morsels that didn't bear close scrutiny.

"He's dying, isn't he?" Josh whispered.

"Is he?" I said. "I've no idea. I'm none too sure what death is anymore. If he was never even alive, how can he die?"

Mayor convulsed, heaved, and retched again, although this time nothing emerged from his mouth except a stream of frothy pink bile. Covering my nose, I crouched down and raised his arm in order to feel for a pulse. The arm weighed no more than a sheet of paper. The pulse was mothlike.

A wisp of wind crawled up from Mayor's throat and, shaped by his tongue and lips, made words. "So this is my death scene, huh?" he said. "Is someone going to shout 'Cut'?"

"Only God can do that," I replied, with a conviction I did not possess but that I hoped would comfort Mayor.

"God?" Mayor sighed. "What's He ever done for me? He's never been any help to me. Not as an actor, not as a mayor. I did it all myself. Ain't gonna let *Him* take the credit for my work. Who does He think He is? A director?" Mayor tried to laugh, and all I could think of was a death's head grinning dumbly.

Then, abruptly, Josh staggered back on his heels, clutching the sides of the sink for support. "I don't feel too good," he groaned. He bent low over the water as if to vomit, but when the spasm came, it was accompanied by the sound of fishermen emptying their nets onto the deck of a trawler. At the same time, blood and bloody matter shot out of the legs of his jeans and sloshed over his sneakers and spread lumpenly across the floor.

Josh peered down uncomprehendingly at what he had done, and then turned to me, cheeks gray with dread. He reached out a beseeching hand.

"What is this?" he said. "What's happening?"

Then he slithered down against the toilet, his heels leaving trails in the blood-washed floor. His eyeballs rolled up to look at me.

"Please . . ." he said. "Do something. Do something. . . ."

So I did something. I did the first thing that came into my head. I did the only thing I could think of to do. I ran.

I ran but I did not flee. I ran with direction, with a purpose. I ran out of the bathroom and over to my desk. There, I snatched the cover off my Smith Corona, unveiling its idiotic, robotic smile. I plumped my backside down in my chair. Fingers tingling and dripping with sweat, I fumbled with a sheet of paper.

Come on, come on, the typewriter urged. *Time is of the essence. This is a matter of life and death here. Come on! Get it together. Get that useless fat ass of yours in gear.*

Tongue tip prodding the corner of my mouth, I jammed the paper into the typewriter and feverishly turned the knob to roll it around the platen. The paper snagged, crumpling in on itself like a crashing car. As I tugged to extricate it, it tore off in my hand. I screamed.

You goddamn loser! the typewriter yelled. *Can't you do anything right?*

"Fuh-uhhhhhh-uuck . . . you!"

I wrenched the rest of the shredded sheet out of the typewriter's teeth, spraying snow-white tatters all over the dark desktop. Another sheet was snatched from the top of the pile and, this time, successfully inserted. The typewriter sighed with readiness.

Okay, it said. *Off you go, Joe. No more blocks. No more staring out of the window. No more getting incapably drunk. There are lives to be saved here.*

And I reached for the keys, and I typed:

Twenty

1

For all his foresight and forward thinking, even Jeremiah Rackstraw could not have predicted how his utterance of the town's name—a great gut-expelled bellow that carried only the minimum necessary amount of the Traveling Tongue to get him to where he wanted to go—would affect his immediate surroundings. All he could think of was progressing with the annihilation of Escardy Gap as quickly as possible, wreaking a terrible vengeance on that town for having the temerity to attempt to thwart him, and the fact that he howled its name with all the venom of a thousand snakes, that the power of his voice caused localized destruction around him, was neither here nor there. Nor did it occur to him that he had not been any too specific in his choice of destination. A town, even a small one, is a big place in respect to a single individual, and the Traveling Tongue could have taken him to any one of the countless man-sized points in space within Escardy Gap. In the event, it transported him to the dead center of town: the town square.

Neither Josh nor Mayor had any idea what caused the sudden explosion that lifted them off their feet and sent them hurtling forward onto their faces. Neither even had time to think about it. One moment they were sprinting into the Snake, hand in hand; the next they were being carried along on an almighty gust of wind that seemed to roar the very name of the town they were escaping.

The unnatural wind, funneled and focused by the Snake, bore them a good ten feet through the air, as though they were no heavier than scarecrows, and then, like a bored child, dumped them unceremoniously onto the track. Josh landed badly, Mayor worse. The clonk that the old man's head made when it struck the rail was audible even above the roar of Rackstraw's rage.

The wind continued down the Snake, scouring the tunnel's walls like floodwater along a storm drain, only abating as it reached the far end, where it spilled out in a cloud of debris into the world beyond the Company's barrier.

Then there was silence—a mean, expectant silence, during which Josh managed to raise his head and in the dim light that leaked in from the tunnel entrance saw Mayor lying beside him, limbs stretched out like a happy cat's, eyes closed, mouth lolling open. Josh had enough time to deduce from the awkward angle of Mayor's head against the rail and the shallow rise and fall of his chest that the old man had been knocked unconscious. Then his ears detected a low groaning sound that he at first thought came from Mayor but then realized had not been made by any human voice.

A sift of dust descended from the roof of the Snake, pattering softly onto Josh's head and hands, and the groan was repeated, and seemed to reverberate the entire length of the tunnel. It sounded like two huge boulders being clenched together, grating against one another like giant pebbles in a titan's fist, and when a further fall of dust scattered itself around Josh and Mayor, Josh had a terrible feeling that he knew what was about to happen, and he struggled to get to his feet. One arm ached dully, there was a sharp stabbing pain in one knee, but Josh ignored both discomforts as he heaved himself upright and then knelt down next to Mayor.

"Mayor? Mayor? Come on, we've got to get out of here!"

Another ominous groan shuddered through the Snake, and distantly but distinctly Josh heard the clatter of rock tumbling to the ground in front of them.

Mayor did not stir.

"Mayor! Come *on!*" Josh leaned down and tugged at Mayor's arm. Mayor's body was just so much deadweight. "Oh, Jeez, Mayor, I think the tunnel's about to cave in. You've got to wake up!"

Mayor exhibited absolutely no sign of independent loco-motion, and from the dark depths of the Snake the loudest groan yet resounded through the solid stone, which had been damaged by the sheer malignancy of the shock waves from Rackstraw's shout and in whose surface deep cracks were appearing. Chunks of loosened rock were beginning to slip, crumble, and fall from the walls and roof of the tunnel ahead of them, and Josh could hear the process gathering impetus as the cracks made more cracks, as cracks met other cracks, as the convergence and divergence of flaws and fault lines in-creased and multiplied. It was a chilling sound, the more so because Josh was unable to move Mayor and Mayor was out cold, blissfully oblivious to the danger they were in.

In the end, there was nothing for it but to slap Mayor. Hard.

This Josh did with some reluctance—hitting anyone, but above all this kindly old man who reminded him in so many ways of Grampa, was wrong—but he did it all the same, two, three desperate open-palmed blows across the face, knowing that the urgency of the situation gave him no choice.

And slowly, painfully slowly, Mayor stirred. A grunt es-caped him, and his hand flew to his head to clutch his throb-bing skull. He coughed a couple of times, then blearily opened his eyes. They took a moment to focus on Josh, and then Mayor said hoarsely, "Am I supposed to be on already?"

"Mayor," said Josh, "you've got to get to your feet. We're in trouble. Please. Come on."

Mayor sat up, in so doing revealing an ugly welt on his temple where his head had struck the rail.

"Trouble?"

And as if in answer to the query, a chunk of rock the size of a football crashed down onto the tie inches away from Mayor's left leg, splintering the aged wood.

"Holy cow!" Mayor yelped, and, galvanized into action, sprang to his feet. He moved more rapidly than was wise, however, and the blood surged from his brain like water down a drainpipe and he teetered on the spot and would have fallen had Josh not grabbed him and held him upright.

"This way," Josh said, supporting almost all of Mayor's weight on his shoulder. "Quickly. We've got to go back the way we came."

"The way we came?"

"We don't have any choice. The tunnel's about to collapse any moment. We can't go forward. We don't have time. We're going to have to go back."

"We can't go back."

"We'll die if we don't!"

Still dizzy, with sparks still cartwheeling across his vision, Mayor turned and began to totter toward the tunnel entrance taking his cue from Josh, using the boy's steps to guide his own. He had no idea why the Snake was collapsing around them. He only knew that it was, and that Josh was right: they had to get back to the entrance *now* if they weren't to be buried alive. The survival instinct blotted out all other considerations. Leaning on Josh, he walked with the staggering gait of a drunkard, one foot slapping the rocky floor after the other in a grim parody of Wile E. Coyote reeling from yet another failed plan to trap the Road Runner, while all around them the dust billowed and the reassuring glow of light from the tunnel entrance gradually became lost in ribbons of thickening, darkening dirt clouds. As the ability to see faded, Josh was thankful that they couldn't actually make out the rocky walls and the huge gashes that must surely be accompanying the bilious rumbling belches from beneath their feet and above their heads.

Mayor tried to say something, but the word was lost in a throaty, spluttering cough.

"Save your strength, Mayor," Josh said, just managing to keep a sneakily growing sense of panic from working its way up out of his stomach and into his voice. "Concentrate on getting out of here."

"Getting out of here," Mayor agreed hoarsely, as he did a quick clumsy do-si-do to the left and then steadied himself. "Yes. Getting—"

His words were drowned by another terrific crack that started somewhere over ahead of Josh, to the right, and traveled like a jet fighter straight over their heads to finish in a huge booming thud behind Mayor, to the left. Josh ducked in expectation of the inevitable shower of broken rock, but fortunately it didn't come. He peered ahead into the blackness, squinting his eyes and covering them with his free hand. "Just a little way farther."

Just a little way farther! That was rich. Josh was no longer even sure that they were going the right way anymore. He could no longer see the entrance. It had to be up ahead, just a few yards, but what if the tunnel had split open and they'd taken an unknown fork? Maybe they were right now heading off into the bowels of the earth instead of following the train tracks, heading down into a lost world that had been hidden for centuries from human eyes—like the one in that movie he had seen at the Essoldo. What was it called? Just then, Josh couldn't recall its name. But just then, remembering the title of a not particularly memorable B movie was not the foremost priority in his mind.

Josh stopped for a moment and Mayor stopped with him. Josh extended one foot to the side, feeling for the rail. There it was. So, at least they were still going in the right direction. For a second, he had been half expecting one of the creatures from *The Mole People*—*that* was what the movie was called!—to step out right in front of him.

But that was a childish fear, he realized, and in the face of adult concerns, in the face of the terrors and responsibilities of the real world, childish fears had to be stowed away in their toy chest and banished to the back of the mind's closet. He knew where the rails were; all he had to do was follow them, and he and Mayor stood a good chance of getting out of the tunnel alive.

Josh wasn't aware of having changed, but all the same he recognized at that moment that he *had* changed. He was not the same Josh Knight who had stepped out of the Essoldo that Saturday morning with an indefinable feeling of *something* in his bones and a handful of loose change in his pants pocket. No longer did he feel like an adult soul seething frustratedly in the body of a boy. No longer did he feel that who he was and how he perceived himself to be were two separate and irreconcilable states. Here, now, with Mayor's life in his hands and his own life in danger, everything was as clear as bird-song on a spring morning. He was just a human being, no more, no less, a human being doing his best in an unjust, in-imical, and deceitful world. It was a revelation of sorts.

The rumbling roars were growing louder, the dust roiling more thickly, as though a thundercloud were gradually insin-uating itself into the Snake. Josh had no idea how much far-ther they had to go or how long they had before the tunnel collapsed in on itself (as seemed inevitable), but grasping Mayor more tightly around the waist, propping his shoulder more firmly into Mayor's armpit, he continued to heave, haul, drag, and manhandle Escardy Gap's thespian town official forward with all the strength in his twelve-year-old body, and Mayor responded as best he could, though his legs were watery weak and unwilling to perform even their most basic function.

And then suddenly they were staggering out of the mouth of the Snake, blinking into the daylight, and behind them, equally suddenly, the fuss and clamor that accompanied the destruction of the tunnel, because it no longer threatened them directly, seemed to subside, as though banished to an-other world. The subterranean groans that made the ground beneath their feet tremble culminated in a last almighty cat-astrophic roar, and this was followed by a sigh of sucked-in air, which in turn was followed by a crash that shook all of Boundary Hill as the roof of the Snake found itself no longer able to support the weight of rock above it and caved in.

A great brown cloud of dust spilled out around the retreat-ing Mayor and Josh like a tidal wave, choking them, darken-ing the air, blotting out the sky.

The subsequent silence was awesome.

Coming to a halt, Josh looked back and saw a fall of bro-ken rock blocking the mouth of the tunnel, like solidified vomit in the throat of a dead man. Tears of frustration threat-ened to come to his eyes. Fighting them back, he snarled, "Some cavalry," then, disengaging himself from Mayor, bent over and scrubbed dust from his hair with quick back-and-forth brushstrokes of his hand.

"What's that you say, son?"

"Remember Doc telling us to bring back the cavalry?" said Josh. "Well, here it is. Here we are. It's us now. Just us."

All Mayor could do was sigh at the abysmal truth of the statement.

As the dust cloud slowly, rollingly settled, thinning, dissipating into nothingness, Josh peered ahead, expecting to see a pair of silvery tracks curving smoothly through the cut that shaved into one side of Boundary Hill. Instead, there was chaos: lengths of rail clawed up like fingers, rocks littering the splintered ties, dead birds lying everywhere in explosions of feather.

Mayor became aware of the carnage at roughly the same time.

"Earthquake?" he wondered aloud.

"Could be," said Josh. "Never heard of an earthquake that killed *birds,* though."

"Rackstraw?" said Mayor, more quietly.

Josh's silence was a reply in itself.

Mayor dropped his voice. "D'you think he's still around?"

The thought had occurred to Josh, but bravely he said, "If he was here, he'd have said something to us by now. Announced himself. Made a speech. A long one."

Mayor laughed, but the laughter, sending a flash of pain through his skull, ended in a hiss of pain. He lowered himself gingerly down onto a large, flat-topped boulder, rubbing the raw-looking bump on his forehead. "Loosened a few more marbles up there, I reckon."

Josh took the opportunity to make a quick inventory of his wounds. His forearm hurt—a dull, iron pain—and his knee also was busy registering a complaint with the management, though the denim of his jeans wasn't torn down there and there was no blood. He flexed the joint a couple of times, and grudgingly it worked. Then, setting his hands on his hips, he examined again the destruction caused by the rockslide. Thin falls of loose scree still slithered down the cut's sloping sides, carrying the occasional clod of grass with them. The rocks themselves were strewn evenly across the track and ranged in size from pebbles to something that would take ten men to lift. Though not impassable, the damage to the cut was going to make the journey back into town even more hazardous. Assuming, that is, that they *were* heading back into town. It seemed to Josh that they didn't have a choice—they couldn't just sit down on their butts there and do nothing, could they?—but he hoped Mayor might be able to offer an alternative course of action.

"Only one thing for it," said Mayor, following Josh's gaze. "We've got to head back into town." He waited for an objection. None came. "We tried to get help. We gave it our best shot. Our escape route's been cut off. We've failed. No shame in that. Now we've got to do what we can on our own. In a way, it seems kind of appropriate."

"But what *can* we do?"

"I don't know, Josh. But if you help me to my feet, we can start walking, and while we walk we can think. I think better on my feet."

Thinking, however, had to wait until they had negotiated their way over the rockslide, which demanded all of their concentration. The rocks were unsettled, treacherous underfoot. A misplaced step could mean a twisted ankle. And then there were the bird corpses to avoid, and the wriggling, upturned, dying insects. And every so often Mayor needed a helping hand, when his legs would not work in quite the way they were supposed to. In all, it took the hobbled pair half an hour to cover a couple of hundred yards, and when they reached the end of the cut, just below the Swivven's place, and were clear of the rubble, both sat and took a rest. Neither had slept the previous night, they had been on foot since dawn, they had witnessed the hideous death of a friend and had narrowly escaped a similar fate themselves: little wonder that the accumulated exhaustion was catching up with them. Nevertheless, the rest stop was brief. Mayor was first to his feet, and Josh found himself marveling at the old man's grit, and his recuperative powers, even as he scrambled after him.

"Where are we going?" he asked as he fell in step beside Mayor.

"Like I said, back into town." Mayor gestured ahead along the sleek straight path of the track to the thin green shadow crouched on the horizon that was Escardy Gap.

"I know that, but *where* in town? And what are we going to do when we get there?"

"Well," said Mayor, almost apologetically, "I was kinda hoping *you* might be able to come up with a suggestion."

The sky above was blue and wide and as empty of clouds as Josh's head was of ideas. It was obvious to him that they could not take on the Company face-to-face. He and Mayor against the whole of Rackstraw's crew? Absurd. One member of the Company alone would make not just mincemeat out of them but a full string of sausages. So, having failed to get hold of any kind of reinforcements, returning to Escardy Gap was little more than a suicide mission. Josh saw knowledge of this fact etched into the creases in Mayor's dust-caked face. But he saw something else there. A steadfast refusal to admit defeat. Sheer, for want of a better word, cussedness. Mayor, like so many of the heroes of the movies in which he had played a small part, had had enough and wasn't going to take any more. And yet Josh knew that this was no act, no role. Not anymore. This was Mayor himself. This was Douglas B. Raymond, pure and simple.

But what to do with this defiant determination of Mayor's? What use was it if there was no target to aim it at? The Company was invincible. Undefeatable. They had to be. Mayor said Rackstraw had told him so. Therefore it had to be true.

Didn't it?

Jeremiah Rackstraw was, after all, an arch-manipulator of words. A twister of truth. Someone for whom the saying was an effective substitute for the doing. What if he had been lying to Mayor? What if his convincing display of serene supremacy had been little more than bravado?

"Mayor," said Josh (they had been walking in silence for several minutes), "what did Rackstraw say yesterday when he told you that the Company was taking a rest for the night?"

"His exact words?"

"His exact words."

There was an almost perceptible ruffling of mental script pages, and then, in a voice all too eerily reminiscent of Rackstraw's gelatinously devious tones, Mayor said, " 'Showdown isn't until tomorrow. The first act is almost finished. The curtain will go down with the sun and rise, after the interval, at dawn tomorrow.' "

"But why?"

"But why what?"

"Why would the Company take a break? I'd have thought, in their situation, they'd want to get things done as quickly and efficiently as possible. What do they need with a rest? What do they get from it?"

"A chance to compare notes, maybe. To gloat over the innocents they've killed." Mayor spat onto the railroad tie that was at that moment passing beneath his heel. "How should I know?"

"Because you used to be a performer, and Rackstraw described this pause as an interval, and you know as well as I do that he's awfully precise in his use of words. An interval, like in a stage play. Now, why should there be an interval in the Company's performance? What purpose does it serve?"

"In the theater it's usually so the set can be changed."

"But the only set here is Escardy Gap."

"So it's an artistic pause, then. I don't quite see what you're getting at, my boy."

Neither did Josh. But he did sense that there was something there, something glimmering at the far end of this line of reasoning. He only had to follow his deductions through logically, intelligently, patiently, and he would get there. Absently he snatched up a pebble as he walked and tossed it ahead of him, so that it landed on the right-hand rail with a *ting* and skittered off into the trackside dirt.

"When you acted in plays," he said, "weren't you glad of an interval?"

"Sure was," said Mayor with a ghost of a grin. "Acting really takes it out of a fella. When I did my Hamlet . . ." And he could almost hear Big Ben Burden cracking his Great-Dane-the-morning gag again, Big Ben on Wilbur Cohen's stoop, Big Ben who was almost certainly dead by now, Wilbur who had driven his car and his family headlong into the force field that had mortally maimed Doc Wheeler, amputating his arm like a butcher's cleaver. . . . And for the first time, a career reminiscence gave him no pleasure. He wondered if anything would ever give him pleasure again. Was this the price you paid for staring evil in the eye and not flinching?

He steadied himself and began again. "When I did my Hamlet, you can bet I was grateful for every moment of rest

I got between acts. Chance for a cigarette, maybe a nip of whisky . . ."

"A chance to recharge your batteries, in other words," said Josh.

"Precisely."

"So what if—and you can shoot this out of the sky if you want to, Mayor—but what if that's what the Company have to do, too? Have to return to the train to recharge their batteries at some prearranged time because all this killing and mayhem really takes it out of them."

"You mean the train is their green room?"

"Yup."

Mayor cocked his head quizzically. "Yeah, I can go with that. I just don't see what use it is *knowing* that. They ain't going to be there now, so it's not as if we can just sneak up on them, stick some dynamite under the carriages, and blow them to kingdom come."

"I wasn't thinking so much about the carriages. I was thinking about the locomotive itself. Mayor, you're probably going to think this crazy—"

"Nothing can be crazier than what's happened to our town these past couple of days."

"Well . . ."

"Go on, shoot."

Josh ran his tongue around the dusty-dry interior of his mouth. "When I said the Company was recharging their batteries, I think I meant it literally. I think what I'm saying is that they need some kind of power source for their talents, abilities, whatever you want to call them, the way the Green Lantern needs that big old lantern to power up his ring."

His ring. Josh thought of Rackstraw's ring, and another bell chimed in his brain. While the ring didn't exactly form what you might call a direct connection, it was yet another symbolic link in the chain of deduction.

"So maybe we've been looking at this the wrong way 'round," he continued. "Maybe the Company isn't simply a troupe of lunatics and murderers who travel around by train. Maybe the train takes them where *it* wants them to go. Maybe the train doesn't belong to *them*. Maybe *they* belong to the *train*."

Mayor nodded noncommittally.

"I'm just thinking out loud here," Josh continued hurriedly. "I could be way off. But the more I run this over in my head, the more it appears to fit. Remember when you first saw the locomotive? Did anything about it strike you as strange?"

"Did anything about it *not* strike me as strange?" Mayor mused. "Let's see. The three women riding on the engine. The way its whistle sounded like a scream. The way all the carriage doors opened at once."

"But the locomotive itself," Josh urged.

"Nope, can't say I . . . Hold on. Hold your horses." Mayor brought a finger up to his lips as he realized what Josh was getting at. "The locomotive. Had no driver. No way in for a driver. No room for a driver."

"No door. Nothing. I took a good look at it later. The cab is completely sealed. So . . ."

"So who drives the damn thing?"

"Exactly. And there's more. And this is where my theory goes further, and at the same time deeper into craziness land." The ideas were coming thick and fast to Josh. He was more or less extemporizing, but everything he was saying felt good, felt *right;* every statement he made locked into the previous one with jigsaw precision. "You remember me telling you about the clock Rackstraw gave me? The clock that tried to kill me?"

"Until you pulled out its innards."

"Right. Now, I'm betting that the clock and the train work along the same principles. That they're two of a kind. The clock *looked* like a mechanical object, it *worked* like one, but inside it was living, organic. And I'm guessing that the locomotive is the same. It looks like a machine but it's more than a machine. It drives itself. And, like the Green Lantern's lantern, it gives the Company their abilities. Rackstraw's ring made me think of this, of the Green Lantern. I mean, I don't base everything I do in life on what I read in comic books, but sometimes . . ." He shrugged, and Mayor shrugged back. "Sometimes you take what you can get. See, my thinking is, the locomotive is probably responsible for the force field too."

"So you're saying . . . you're saying that the *train* is somehow running the show? The Company are puppets and it pulls their strings?" Mayor sounded doubtful. "Judging by what I've seen of those people, that's a mite hard to believe."

"Okay, but let's assume for now that they do owe their abilities to the train. If they have to rely on it for what they can do, then it would make sense that the train expects something from them in return."

"Such as?"

Mayor was so absorbed in Josh's theorizing that he continued on for a good ten paces before noticing that Josh had not replied and was no longer walking beside him. Seized with a sudden panic, fearing that somehow or other the Company had secretly and noiselessly snatched his last ally from his side, he spun around, to find Josh standing a little way back down the track, staring ahead, past Mayor's shoulder, with a look of outright despondency on his face. Wheeling around again, Mayor saw instantly what had caught Josh's attention.

Above Escardy Gap, above the clustered treetops some two miles distant, several bellying black columns of smoke were purling upward, each rising from a separate source, yet, in their spreading upper layers, gathering to form a thin dark mist that hung in the air like a widow's veil. Even as Mayor and Josh watched, a fresh column of smoke erupted from somewhere over on the west side of town, and was soon adding to the looming pall above. It was as though a somber reflection of Escardy Gap was amassing in the sky, a smoke town created by the burning of the original, a soiled soul town escaping from the death of its physical form.

Infinitely saddened, the two would-be saviors resumed their journey with a wearier tread, mutely following the railroad track, retracing on foot the path the train had taken into Escardy Gap. The smoke began to darken the sun and the smell of burning, at first faint, grew strong and tangy in their nostrils. Though it was not yet midday, a sulfurous twilight was descending, and soon the sun was a coppery brown disk through the haze of smoke, and by the time Mayor and Josh reached the splintered remnants of the signpost that marked Escardy Gap's town limits, the air was so dark and tainted it might have been the evening of Judgment Day itself.

The last quarter mile of track lay ahead of them, describing a gentle curve past backyards and scrubland, scything by the lumberyard and over the canal. Mayor and Josh were now only a handful of minutes away from their destination, from a showdown neither believed they had a chance of winning. From far and near they could hear the crackle of burning buildings, like guttural laughter. Every so often there would come to their ears screams or pleading or a shouted prayer, echoing faintly over the rooftops. The town was dying. You could feel it in the air. The town was dying in much the same way that the human body succumbs to a lethal disease: piece by piece, organ by organ, slowly, by degrees, inescapably.

Such was the murkiness of that unnatural twilight that there seemed little need to move stealthily. Though they were careful to keep a wary eye out at all times, Mayor and Josh proceeded along the track confident that the semidarkness gave them a certain amount of cover, a certain shadowy protection. Neither had any idea what they were going to do when they reached the train. Both hoped something would present itself, some obvious means of attack, but neither held out much hope of this. They walked with their shoulders slumped in resignation. Whatever fate offered them, they would accept it. Sometimes compliance was easier than valor.

That did not mean they were not afraid. In Josh's guts, a knot of fear twisted and tightened with every tie he stepped across. It was not something he could talk about, because it was a weakness he did not wish to admit to, but with the station and the train so close, he knew that there was a real possibility that these were the last steps he might ever take on earth, the last breaths of air he might ever inhale. At just twelve years of age, he ought not to be ready for death, but it wasn't death itself that scared him. It was dying. The pain of dying. For he realized that if Rackstraw or one of the Maneaters were to get hold of him, the end would not be swift in coming. And the anticipation of that agony was a tangible ache in his guts, and there were moments when it was all he could do to keep himself from trembling and moaning out loud.

As for Mayor, the same flinty, grim-lipped determination that Josh had seen transfiguring his features earlier had settled there for good, and seemed to be the expression that he would carry with him to his grave. Like Josh, death held no fear for Douglas B. Raymond. Not anymore. He had lived a long and mostly fruitful life, and if it was to be sacrificed in the act of saving his town, that was fine. What Mayor was scared of now was a death that had no purpose, and he was going to do his damnedest to make sure that his end was anything but futile.

So, while both had no wish to die, neither was intimidated enough by the prospect of death to waver from their course. It was almost as if they had met the Reaper already, gazed upon his bony grin, and recognized him for the old fraud he was.

And now the train was in view, lodged in the siding, sitting there snug and complacent in the false dusk. There was the porchlike construction at the rear of its second carriage, there the drawn blinds in the windows of the carriages themselves, there the coal-filled tender, there the silver-and-black locomotive. And there, to the left, was the shrubby bank where Josh had crouched yesterday and from which he had observed the train and the Man-eaters. Of the three women there was no sign, though Josh knew that that didn't mean they weren't hereabouts.

Pausing, Mayor whispered, "I'll go first, you follow. That way I can deal with whatever comes, and you, with your faster legs, can get away."

"No way," Josh replied. "My eyes are sharper. I go in front."

"Son, I ain't going to argue—"

"Then don't." ·

"Then . . ." said Mayor, and spread out his arms.

And so it was decided, without being said, that they would proceed side by side, as they had into the Snake.

Ears alert for the slightest sound, the smallest chitter-clack, they approached the train. To them their footsteps seemed appallingly loud. Past the closed carriages they crept, scarcely daring to breathe. At any moment it seemed that one or all of the doors might come flying open and out would climb, or crawl, or slither, a member of the Company—perhaps one that nobody had seen before, one so hideous it had to be hidden from the daylight, one that no man could look on without going immediately and irrevocably insane.

And as they neared the locomotive they began to sense something that neither could precisely define: a vibration in the air, a tingling that was almost an audible hum, an atmosphere such as you find in old places with dark histories, the accretion of sins committed and evil deeds done. The closer they came, the stronger the feeling grew that here was something that had not just been responsible for wickedness in the past but was constantly on the lookout for more, was insatiably greedy for more. Both had experienced this same sensation before in the presence of the train, but then it had manifested itself as nothing more than a mild disquiet, an unease. Now, barely a yard from the engine itself, they understood that Josh's theory had been correct, that the locomotive was not merely a thing of metal built to travel the iron pathways of America. Just as some insects—scorpions, say, or some of the more formidable beetles—are machine-like in appearance and movement, can even resemble windup toys, so the locomotive belied its own life. Inside that cylindrical body, that closed-in cab, even within those wheels there lurked a living entity that was possessed of a pulse, of energy, of thought, of a great and ancient *hunger.* And now it was possible for them to discern glugs and gurgles coming from within the boiler, secret bubblings, weary sloshings as of a slow but still efficient digestive system. Oh, yes, the locomotive was alive, all right. And it knew they were there. And it knew they were there to destroy it.

Suddenly its hatred for them spilled out from its ironwork in oily waves, which left Josh feeling vertiginous, as though he were teetering on the edge of a vast black abyss, staring down. His stomach lurched biliously. He grabbed hold of Mayor's sleeve for support. Mayor staggered, dizzied, too. Even Rackstraw's volcanic contempt was nothing next to the locomotive's appalling, sucking enmity.

Clutching one another, Mayor and Josh rode out the psychic assault, waiting until the first burst of loathing had died down and all that was left were lesser eddying ripples of resentment.

"Okay," said Mayor, taking deep breaths. "Okay. Okay. Okay."

Josh shook his head, and as the roiling in his stomach gradually dwindled, so a ferocious grin spread over his lips.

Mayor frowned at him. "And what's to smile about, son?"

"Can't you tell, Mayor?" Josh replied through rictus teeth. "It's scared of us. It knows what we're here to do and it's actually *scared* of us."

"Well, I'll be . . ." breathed Mayor. The boy was right. And something flickered faintly in Mayor's heart, a dim flame he had not expected to be rekindled. "Well, then, let's go to work. There's got to be some kind of way to hurt this beast, ain't there? Let's look for it."

"Sure."

They were keeping their voices low, but the locomotive, as if hearing them, offered a response. A short puff of smoke hissed up from its funnel. The slight sound, sudden and sharp in the crepuscular stillness, jolted Mayor and Josh half out of their skins, but when nothing further happened, both came to the conclusion that it posed no threat to them, that it was nothing more than a seethe of frustration and alarm. And glancing up at the rising, thinning skein of smoke, Josh thought he saw (though he would never be sure) faces within it, vaporous faces that swirled and dissipated into nothingness, faces with wide helpless eyes and gaping agonized mouths.

And beneath the rear carriage, in the cool shadows beneath chassis and track, figures began to stir.

Dismissing the faces as a trick of the light, or rather a trick of the lack of light, Josh joined Mayor in examining the locomotive's surface for an opening, a chink, an aperture—for its Achilles' heel. Because, like the clock, it had to have one. If it didn't, why did it need the three women to guard it? If it didn't, why was it scared of them?

Thinking of the Man-eaters, Josh recalled how he had watched them brawl over that critter yesterday before one of them had despatched it up between her legs. He tried not to let himself be distracted by the fact that they must be somewhere in the vicinity. He concentrated instead on running his gaze slowly and methodically over the locomotive's jet black ironwork, paying particular attention to the riveted joins where its component plates overlapped. There, if anywhere, a way might be found through the shell and into the soft vulnerable parts inside.

And all the time, while Mayor and Josh worked with as much calmness as their anxiety would allow them, the locomotive enveloped them in its hatred. But hatred was all it could assail them with. Until its guardians emerged from their resting place, the locomotive was defenseless and, to all intents and purposes, powerless.

Its guardians, however, were already disengaging themselves from their perches, easing themselves out from where they had been sleeping athwart the axles of the rear carriage in a shimmer of gossamer and a slither of pale-skinned limbs.

2

At that moment, Neville N. Nolan was flitting forth and fro in fly form over the tormented town, the embedded rubies of his eyes roving restlessly, facets flashing as they scanned the scenes of street slaughter, the front-porch flashpoints that culminated in Company-committed killing, the backyard butchery. There Dr. Canker dug deep into his carpetbag of bulbous cancers in order to murder a man with melanoma. There Gypsy Zelda predicted the precise details of Davey Higgs's hapless demise, which involved the imminent incision of his epiglottis from ear to ear courtesy of the fiercely curved boning knife concealed in her fine long fingers. There the Boy brutally burst blood vessels within the body of a victim, pinching and plucking them open one by one, before inserting his invisible hands into the victim's intestines and rearranging them like reels of rope. There Big Ben Burden's boy blindly and breathlessly swung a Louisville Slugger at the loose, liverlike limbs of the changeling creature, Clarence, who easily absorbed each assault, until, eventually, annoyed, he extended one awful claw and clasped the broader end of the bat, snatched it sideways, jerking it free from Jim's fist, then brought it back to batter the boy into a bloody, puling pulp. There Buzz Beaumont, the man in the solenoid suit, dispensed luminescent discharges of lightning to the left and to the right, reaping rich rewards of fire and fear as flames hissed forth from houses and human flesh alike. There, in a quiet corner of Poacher's Park, the falsely friendly Felcher fathomed a young woman's thoughts in his thirst for the sour-sweet sensation of loves lost and promises paled and trust twisted out of true, all drained in drooling droplets of gluey liquid from the girl's lips. And there, and there, and there, countless other vignettes of viciousness vied for Neville Nolan's attention and acquired his approval.

And then he spied a strange sight, unexpected and therefore unexplainable: a small eruption of smoke escaping from the ferrous funnel of the living locomotive.

Cruising in for a closer inspection, the werefly witnessed what he would have insisted was wildly improbable, had his own carmine-colored orbits not comprehended it themselves. The mad Mayor and that jumped-up juvenile Josh had not merely journeyed back into town but were busy looking over the locomotive with the mien of those who mean malice.

Madness! What pernicious tinkering with the time-honored plan was this?

Hovering, Neville negotiated with himself. Though his immediate instinct was to swoop down and deal severely with the interlopers, he remembered Rackstraw and the dismal disfavor that had followed his failure to enlighten the master of mendacity early enough of the two townsfolk's escape from Escardy Gap. Neville needed to be readmitted to Rackstraw's righteous reading matter—in other words, to get back in his good books—and here, obviously, was an overt opportunity!

Foregoing further deliberation, he dived straight in the direction of Delacy Street, where he had previously registered Rackstraw's presence, and sure enough, there he was, striding the sidewalk, sidestepping eviscerated corpses and episodes of continuing carnage, looking for all the world like a proud patron presiding over the performance of his pet poet, blood bespattered, beaming, his former fury apparently abated, clearly calmed by the chaos, healed by the horrors all around him.

Neville completed nine narrowing circuits of the Company's silver-tongued spokesman before he was content that he would receive a warm reception. Manifesting in man form, he was glad to be greeted with nothing less than a glutted grin.

"Neville," said Rackstraw, adding with an almost absent-minded sigh, "Isn't it all so *wonderful?*"

The news Neville had for Rackstraw was woefully *not* wonderful. Nonetheless he delivered it in detail. And to his surprise Rackstraw's smile was not reduced; rather, it grew broader and got bigger, while a gleam blossomed in his grimly black eyes. And far from chastising Neville, he congratulated him copiously.

And then, to the werefly's further surprise, Rackstraw summoned the Traveling Tongue, not to say "The railroad siding," but something else, something Neville hadn't expected: "The Knight house." And, as he winked out of existence, Neville also heard him hiss the word, "Excellent!"

3

Mayor and Josh, meanwhile, were no closer to finding the locomotive's weak spot. They had nosed all the way around it, testing the pistons to see if they were loose in their drums, testing the cowcatcher to see if it was anything less than securely bolted to the chassis. Josh had even stepped up to wrench at the handles that sat like the hands of a clock at the center of the domed door that fronted the cylindrical boiler, but the handles would not shift so much as a fraction of an inch. The iron plates that blocked all of the openings that might otherwise allow access to the cab were also fastened tight. Moreover, they didn't look as if they had been added to the locomotive as an afterthought; they looked as if they were part of its original construction—if "construction" is a word that can be applied to the misbegotten birth of this pseudomachine—and so were no more likely to budge than any of its other components.

Refusing to accept defeat so easily, Mayor and Josh began to look again. Josh tapped the side of the boiler to see if any portion of it sounded hollower than the rest. The iron might be thinner there, perhaps penetrable. Disturbingly, his taps did not echo. More disturbingly, the boiler was blood warm to the touch.

And beneath the rear carriage, in the cool darkness down between the bogies, the three Man-eaters were lowering themselves to the track and sliding out into the dimmed daylight, with barely a sound, just the merest click of teeth on teeth.

Lizardlike they began to crawl the length of the train on all fours, the tips of the long strands of their hair brushing the dusty ground.

What about the smokestack? thought Mayor, oblivious to the women's clandestine approach. He made a gesture to Josh, to whom the thought had occurred just a second earlier, and then linked his hands to form a stirrup, which Josh used to boost himself up onto the top of the boiler.

Clambering along on hands and knees, using the silvery steel running rails for support, Josh reached the mushroom-shaped funnel and gingerly peered over its lip and down in. The aperture was five inches in diameter, and he could see nothing but darkness inside. He sensed rather than saw the movement down there, the ponderous slow pulsing as of the beat of a giant heart or the heave of leviathan lungs, but the smokestack was too tall for him to reach his arm down in there and do any damage to the locomotive's innards. A stick of dynamite might have done the trick, but he had no idea where to obtain one or what precisely to do with it if he did get hold of one.

Straightening up into a half crouch, he indicated the confounding of another possibility to Mayor by means of a shrug. . . .

And he saw a sight that sent every organ of his body into palpitations, that made his already erect hair bristle yet further, and that enlarged his already gaping eyes until they were as big as saucers.

The need for surreptitiousness was gone.

A dry throat gulped Mayor's name hoarsely.

A swallow, and Josh tried again.

"M-Mayor?"

Mayor was about to raise a finger to his lips when the full import of the expression on Josh's face struck home.

He turned, knowing, even as he did so, what he was going to find.

The brunette was closest, about twenty feet away. She it was who first rose from her belly-to-the-soil crawl to spring upright into a posture of attack, her fingers clawed, their nails wicked. The blond followed suit. Of the redhead there was no sign.

And Mayor, who had romanced starlets in his time, once again couldn't help but compare the beauty of any woman he had ever known, even Sara Sienkiewicz, unfavorably to the beauty of the pair before him. His heartbeat quickened to triple-time, both in fear and desire, keeping tempo with the volley of chitter-clacks that was issuing forth from beneath the hem of the women's diaphanous gowns, out from between their thighs. And even as they bared their teeth at him, he could only think how desperately kissable those ruby lips of theirs looked. And even as they stalked toward him eager for his death, life twitched and stirred in a region of his anatomy that had long since ceased to take any interest in such matters. Mayor was the helpless thrall of a lust that was as urgent as it was lethal. Right then, he wanted nothing more than to be clawed to pieces by these women, to shudder as their kisses drew blood. It was all he could do not to utter a low moan of longing.

Josh, for his part, found it hard not to succumb to the women's charms, but not impossible. For one thing, they were concentrating their attention—and their power—on Mayor, so Josh was not locked in fiery eye contact with them. For another thing, he knew where that relentless chitter-clacking was coming from and what it implied,

"Mayor!" he yelled, finally finding his full voice. "Move!"

Mayor did not seem to hear, but tossing her head sideways, the blond hissed in Josh's direction: a you-can-keep-till-later hiss.

"*Mayor!* They'll *kill* you!"

The old man's head shook, just once, all but imperceptibly, as though a gnat had whined past his ear.

The brunette glanced up at Josh where he perched atop the

locomotive and snarled a venomous "Sss-*sah!*" Neither she nor her fellow Man-eater swerved one iota from their path as they continued stalking toward the immobile Mayor. The sinister castanet polyrhythm of their chitter-clacking didn't miss a beat.

There was nothing else for it: Josh braced himself to leap down to the ground beneath the women and their intended victim, hoping that he could snap Mayor out of his trance before they reached him.

A hand seized his ankle from behind.

The redhead, clinging with her free hand to the steel rail that ran along the side of the boiler, was sneering up at him, her coppery hair as wild as her green eyes.

Her nails dug deeper into the skin between Josh's anklebone and Achilles tendon, drawing blood. With a cry of anguish and outrage, Josh flailed at her fingers with his fist, but her grip was like the jaws of a mantrap. Hard as he tried, Josh could not dislodge it. Blood streamed down his sock and darkened his sneaker.

Now, twisting his body around, Josh aimed further punches at her head, neck, and shoulders, but she avoided each blow with a contemptuous agility, and all this time the blond and the brunette were closing in on Mayor, fiendishly confident of their prey, mesmerized as he was by their incandescent beauty, like a rabbit in the headlights of an oncoming car.

It was all over, Josh realized, but that did not prevent him from continuing to fight. In fact, despair lent his efforts impetus, if not any greater accuracy. And then, to add insult to injury, the redhead began laughing at the impotence of his resistance; threw back her head and let out a shrill shriek of amusement and scorn.

Enraged, Josh drew back his leg and launched a sweeping, furious kick at her mocking face. Again, she evaded him, but this time the attempt threw him off balance, and next thing he knew, he was tumbling backward over the side of the locomotive.

The redhead's grasp saved him from hitting the ground headfirst. Instead, the back of his cranium struck the edge of the loco's chassis and a white splintering pain filled his brain.

There were moments of blackness, and then, when he finally opened his eyes, it was to find himself dangling upside down, secured by the agony in the ankle and watching drips of his own blood leak from the top of his head and patter down into the dust below. The bandanna slipped from his forehead and fell to the ground with a flop. Too dazed and disoriented even to speak, helpless to interfere, Josh watched—as though from an infinite distance—the two inverted women continued to move in on the inverted Mayor. Suddenly all the pain he was experiencing seemed to belong to someone else, someone who lived on a planet at the other end of the Milky Way.

The blond swiftly covered the last few feet between her and Mayor and clasped a handful of his shirtfront, peering up into his face with feigned adoration. The brunette grabbed herself an arm and teasingly began to run her lips over Mayor's fingertips. A shudder rippled up through his spine. Then, with abrupt savagery, the blond raked her nails down the wattled skin of Mayor's neck. Five parallel trails of blood appeared, and Mayor let out a quivering gasp. The women's nether teeth were now clattering furiously.

Dimly Josh felt something in the region of his trapped foot *give*. Then he was floating to the ground, joining his bandanna and his blood. He landed in a heap, but in his semiconscious state his body was so relaxed, his limbs so loose, that nothing was broken.

At first he thought his leg had torn free of his foot at the ankle, but both sneakers were present and correct when he looked, and then he saw the redhead clambering over the top of the boiler and down the other side, her green eyes shining greedily, her movements so sinuous she appeared to be flowing, while her gown glistened nebulously around her. The sight of Mayor's blood and the sound of his exquisite pain had drawn her, irresistibly, to the orgy, and now she joined her sisters as they slowly disrobed Escardy Gap's thespian town official, stripping him of his jacket and vest, popping the buttons of his white shirt. . . .

And Josh lolled uselessly in the dirt, knowing that he was next.

And then Mayor's head swiveled, and his eyes sought Josh out (the pupils were black with terror and ecstasy), and one eyelid drooped in a slow, sad wink, and then his mouth opened and words oozed out: "It's all right, son. I know what I'm doing. Save yourself while you can."

Josh creased the reluctant skin of his brow into a frown.

"Just go!" Mayor urged while, oblivious, the women set about unbuckling his belt and unbuttoning his pants. "Git!"

The chitter-clacks reached a frenzied peak as the women hooked their nails into the waistband of Mayor's baggy cotton underpants, which bulged dramatically at the front.

And Josh willed himself to move, eager as much as anything to turn away from what was coming. Mayor's death was a sight he did not want to see. But his limbs responded to his brain's command with a torpid, ineffectual writhing, his heels plowing furrows in the dust and propelling him nowhere. His arms flailed, and his left hand struck metal. One of the locomotive's wheels.

It looked cool there, in the dark narrow space between the belly of the locomotive and the track.

It looked safe.

Someone was screaming. A shriek that sounded like a shout of joy.

Josh gripped the rail with both hands and hauled himself forward on his front.

Feminine growls and snarls of approval.

The effort was unbelievable. Just to move a few inches required all the might in his upper body.

The whisper of clothing falling to the ground, three gossamer robes collecting in three separate soft puddles.

Now his head was in shadow, and he was using the underside of the engine, the axles, to maneuver, turn himself over.

A snapping sound, sickening and wet.

It was a tight squeeze, but by angling his shoulder and twisting his torso he managed to flip himself onto his back.

More screaming, and a trio of moist crunching noises.

Raising his less damaged leg, Josh braced his heel against the inner edge of the rail he was lying on and shoved.

Delirious cackles of laughter, and from Mayor a raucous yell of exultation.

Shoved himself deeper into the dark crevice that stank of

engine oil and iron and dirt, until only his wounded ankle and foot were sticking out from under the locomotive.

The screams began again, then subsided into a chain of racking sobs, interspersed with gulps for air such as a drowning man might make.

One last heave, and Josh was fully beneath the locomotive, lying on his back across the ties, panting.

He lay there he didn't know how long.

One thing he did not do as he lay there was listen to the noises coming from just a few feet away.

The munching noises. The sucking noises. The slurping noises. The slobbering noises. The writhing, involuntary, masculine moans.

No, he made a point of ignoring these noises. He had heard enough and did not want to hear any more.

And when the noises ceased—and they seemed to go on for a very long time indeed—he pretended not to realize that they had ceased.

For when the eating sounds and Mayor's sighs and gibbers and groans ended, that meant Josh was alone. Utterly alone.

Alone in the dark, gazing up at the underbelly of the hateful locomotive that had hauled its carriages untold miles across the country to unload its minions in Escardy Gap and spread suffering and death to all four corners of that sweet little town.

Gazing up at a circular panel roughly the size of a car's steering wheel, into which was etched some kind of pattern.

A panel attached not by rivets but by two bolts, which appeared not to have been turned since the day they were first tightened into place.

And the pattern . . . Well, it wasn't easy to decipher at first, since it was caked in the sticky black dirt of years of rail travel, but the outline of an eye was detectable, and then Josh made out the edge of one wavy eyebrow, and then half of a great yawning grin. And then it was only a matter of moments before his mind's eye had filled in the blanks and he recognized once again (how could he ever forget it?) the clown face that had decorated Rackstraw's ring and the lethal clock.

The very same clown face on the clock he had destroyed.

It was hard to believe that he had discovered the locomotive's vulnerable point. It was nigh on impossible. He couldn't allow himself to hope that this was it. No, better to think, after all this suffering, after the many disappointments and disasters he had endured, better to think that this was just another fraud, another trick meant to delude him into thinking there was such a thing as justice in this world. He would be foolish to proceed on the assumption that this was anything other than yet another deception.

Still, he reached up and tried the bolts.

He gripped one between the thumb and forefinger of each hand and twisted.

Nothing happened. Naturally. He hadn't expected it to, had he? The bolts were stuck fast. Over the years they had become fused into place. Even with a monkey wrench he doubted he would have been able to move them.

Nevertheless, he readjusted his grip and tried again.

Of course, he couldn't get any decent leverage, that was the problem. Kinked into a gap of about eighteen inches between locomotive and track, he hadn't enough room to apply his full strength to the bolts. He was never going to get the panel open.

But he kept on trying.

Even when an arm shot from between two wheels and clutched at the leg of his jeans, he kept on trying.

Even when other arms joined it—female arms, their pale skin streaked and smeared with blood—and began clawing at him, he kept on trying.

Even as the chitter-clacks grew louder and angrier, and as a blond head insinuated itself into the space under the locomotive and savage blue eyes flashed at him in the shadows while snapping, bloodstained teeth sought his flesh, he struggled with the bolts, ignoring the danger.

When he died, he wanted to die with the bolts gripped in his fingers so tightly they would have to cut his body loose.

So intent was he on his task that he hardly noticed when the arms and their owners withdrew. Though he dimly registered that the women were no longer trying to get at him, he didn't stop to wonder why they were gone, leaving him with only the half-hidden clown face on the panel for company. He knew they hadn't given up on him; they had left him alone and alive for a reason. He tried not to think what that reason might be.

Just then, one of the bolts budged.

It moved scarcely one tenth of a degree . . . but it *did* move.

And at this point, a very familiar voice spoke to him. A voice he never expected to hear again.

"Hey, young fella. What are you up to down there, for Pete's sake?"

Josh said the name before he could stop himself. He said it in a tremulous, questing tone of voice. In a way that carried much too much hope, a pathetically large amount of it.

"Grampa?"

There was a soft, wheezy chuckle.

"Grampa, is that you?"

"Of course it's me, Josh. Who else would it be?"

Turning his head, Josh saw a pair of legs standing beside the track. The feet were shod in old work shoes whose leather was as wrinkled and cracked as their owner's skin.

"You're alive!" Josh cried. "They didn't get you!" His heart seemed about ready to burst with happiness. Grampa— here! Safe! It was almost too wonderful to be true.

"I'm too old and too ornery to be got by the likes of Jeremiah Rackstraw, lad. You should have known that. Now why don't you come on out so's your old Grampa can give you a hug?"

"I can't, Grampa," Josh replied with genuine regret. Just about then a hug from his old Grampa was all he could ever have wanted. "Why don't you climb in here instead? I need a hand with these bolts here. I'm going to destroy the Company."

"Son, I don't think my rusted-up old joints'll let me get under that locomotive," said Grampa. "Why'nt you climb out so's I can get a good look at you, see you're okay? Destroying the Company can wait. Come on. Boy, have I got some stories to tell you. . . ."

"Grampa, you better be careful. The Man-eaters are 'round about here somewhere."

"You mean those three pretty girls? They've got 'em, Josh. They've got all the Company."

"Who do you mean 'they'? Who's 'they'?"

"The police and the National Guard, Josh!"

Josh let go of the bolts, barely registering the blood blisters that had formed on the tips of his thumbs and on the outside edge of each index finger.

"The National Guard?" he echoed.

"Sure thing! Even as I speak, they're combing the streets, cleaning up the last of the Company. Arresting each and every last one of 'em. It's over, Josh. It's all over. We won. The good guys won! Now come on." Josh saw the legs bend stiffly, with an audible creaking, and heard Grampa grunt as he lowered his knees to the ground. Grampa's arm reached in, but his face—his wise, wizened face—remained out of view. "Give me your hand," Grampa said, "and I'll help you out."

Josh made to take the proffered hand . . . and hesitated.

The hand waved in the air. "Hey, what're you waiting for, son? Grab a hold and I'll haul you out."

Something wouldn't let Josh do it. For all the relief and gratitude surging through him, a limpet of doubt remained, clinging tenaciously to the back of his thoughts.

Why? What was his problem? This was Grampa! It sounded like Grampa, it looked like Grampa. . . . And everything he had said had the ring of truth to it. It was perfectly possible that he had walked all the way to Grant's Crossing and managed to persuade the police and the National Guard to come back with him. But more than that, it was just what Josh wanted to hear. It was everything he could have wished for.

And the clock had taught him to be wary of that. For, in accelerating his life, in trying to make him old before his time, had the clock not simply been granting him his innermost desire? And look what had happened. It had almost killed him, and in destroying it he had unwittingly destroyed the Neverseen Era, the ultimate expression of his longing for a world where the old and the young—represented by dinosaurs and mankind—lived side by side in harmony. No, wishes were not things to be dreamed for. Wishes were things to be scrupulously avoided.

So, having Grampa here, alive and informing him that the town was saved, was all just a little too perfect. A little too Neverseen. A little too implausible.

It all had the air of a cunningly constructed, so-flawless-it-shone *lie*.

And who did Josh know made a habit—no, a *point*—of lying at every opportunity?

"Just let me make sure of things, Grampa," he said, seizing the bolts again. The sting of his blood blisters made him wince. "No point arresting them if they still have their powers. What prison could hold someone like Jeremiah Rackstraw, huh?"

There was a pause, and Josh thought he might have heard teeth clench, and then Grampa said, "I take your point, son. That Rackstraw's a slippery son of a gun, no doubt about it. He could sweet-talk his way outta hell if'n he wanted to. But I reckon Sing-Sing or San Quentin'll hold him long enough to be brought to trial and given the sentence he deserves. Hanging's still legal in this state, you know."

"Imagine that," said Josh, concentrating his efforts on the bolt that had budged. "Jeremiah Rackstraw choked to death. Unable to get a word out edgeways. It'd be sort of fitting, don't you think?"

Again, a pause, as though Grampa—or whoever it was that was imitating Grampa's voice—was taking the measure of Josh's words. Grampa's gnarled, rope-veined hand still hovered close to Josh. The bolt was turning. Slowly.

"Yes, well, hanging's no laughing matter, son."

"I don't know. I think I'd hold a party around Rackstraw's scaffold."

"Josh . . ." There was impatience now in Grampa's voice. "If you want to stay under that locomotive all day, that's your lookout. I, for one, want to see if my one-and-only grandson is safe and sound."

"I've told you I am."

"With my own eyes."

"Lie down and take a look, then."

Shrilling its protest like a mouse under a cat's paws, the bolt was turning. Every fraction of a degree of rotation cost Josh in pain, adding to the ache in his forearms and wrists, to the fingertip fire of his blood blisters (which were close to bursting), but he didn't slacken his efforts one jot. He didn't dare.

"Josh," said Grampa's voice, "you're being kind of impertinent. You know, you're not so old that I can't take you over my knee and give you a good hiding. You've always been a bit too uppity for your own good."

"I was brought up that way." Despite the pain, Josh was close to laughter. Reckless, hysterical guffaws kept trying to force their way out of his mouth. He knew now that this was not Grampa, could never be Grampa. Instead, this conversation was a verbal endgame of insinuations and dramatic ironies that was buying him the time he needed.

"You were brought up to be a good boy who respected his elders," came the reply. "Too bad you didn't stay that way."

"I don't respect my elders, I respect my elders and *betters.*" The bolt was close to the end of its thread. The panel shifted fractionally downward, and all at once a whiff of fleshy stench wafted out.

Grampa's hand balled into a fist and shook just inches from Josh's cheek.

"Joshua Knight, you are sorely trying my patience! I don't know what's happened to you, boy, what those Company folk have done to you, but I don't think I like it. Now come on out here, like I asked. I won't ask you nicely again."

"Come in and get me."

The bolt came free, and Josh tossed it aside. He seized the rim of the circular panel in order to shift it sideways by levering it around on the axis of the remaining bolt. It moved stiffly and reluctantly at first, but he managed, after much straining, to create a narrow, crescent-shaped opening between the panel and the aperture it covered, through which dark vicious fluid oozed out, dribbling down his forearms and into his face. It stank like bloated animal corpses by the roadside. Breathing through his mouth, Josh started twisting the panel this way and that, feeling the weight of the locomotive's innards pressing down on the panel from above.

"Josh . . . !" Real anger now, quivering deep down in Grampa's voice. And his accent was starting to slip, becoming more cultivated. It was amazing that the impersonator still thought he was fooling Josh. Maybe he had just too much self-confidence for his own good. "I've had just about enough of this. I'm a tolerant man, but you can push me only so far.

I'm going to"—he corrected himself—"*gonna* count to three, and after that I want to see you out here on the double, where you'll answer to your grandfather for your disobedience."

Left, right—Josh was steadily working the panel free, helped by the leaking fluid, which acted as a lubricant. The second bolt was swiveling easily, this way, that way, like the needle of a compass. The stench released from within the locomotive was revolting, but Josh, in his triumph, didn't care—perhaps didn't even notice.

"Three," said this bogus Grampa. "Two."

The time had come for the ultimate test of the impersonator's art, the devastating master stroke, the killing blow, the clincher.

Josh said, "I'll be with you soon, June."

And, as he expected, "Grampa" did not come back instantly with a rhyming quip of his own. Instead, he said, "Make it quick."

"No!" said Josh, and the pent-up laughter spilled out. "Unh-unh! Wrong-o! What you meant to say is, 'Make it quick, Rick.' That's the trick, Nick."

"What on earth are you going on about?"

With a last desperate squeal, like a pig meeting its Maker at the abattoir, the panel slewed sideways, clear of the opening it had been covering.

And Josh was gazing up at a bulge of yellow, red, and purple organs, all crowding into the opening like cattle trying to escape the corral. Some of the organs were laced with fine capillaries, others frilled with fat. Even distended by the narrowness of the aperture, they none of them bore a resemblance to any viscera, human or animal, that Josh had seen in his biology textbooks. A string of what looked like gnarled wood softened to a fleshy consistency seemed to be all that was holding them in place.

Gleefully, Josh looped a finger around this string. Warm wetness trickled down his hand.

"It's a game, Rackstraw!" he cried. "A game Grampa and I have played for as long as I can remember. The sort of word game only people who love each other and have known each other for years can play. You almost had me going there for a while with your impersonation—which was very good, I have to admit—but I guess even a smartass like you can't know everything. Tough break, Jake."

Rackstraw struggled to keep up the pretense. "Erm . . . What utter tosh, Josh! What non*sense*, Clemence!" There was something pathetic about his attempts and their lack of spontaneity.

"Too late, Nate!" Josh was all but crowing. "You and the Company are goners!"

The body of Grampa fell to the ground beside the track. Hard. It had been tossed from above. The hand flopped to the track beside Josh's ear.

Grampa's face was puffy and distended with huge blue welts and raw purple bruises, and his eyes stared vacantly from their battered orbits, their pupils clouded a milky white. The skin hung away in slack folds from the ruined bones of his cranium, and his lower jaw lolled from shattered hinges. Teeth were missing. There was a deep dent in his right temple roughly the size of the tip of a baseball bat.

And then Jeremiah Rackstraw leapt down from the lip of the chassis where he had been crouching all this time, manipulating the body of Grampa from above like a puppeteer. Dropping to his belly beside the body, he peered malevolently in at Josh, his eyes two windows into the nether pits of hell.

"I will recall the Man-eaters," he hissed. "What they leave of you will be *mine* to play with."

And he flashed Josh his hyena smile—and then caught sight of the displaced panel and the vulnerable bulge of the train's innards sagging out, with Josh's finger hooked through that supporting string, poised as though curled around the trigger of a gun.

Then the smile vanished.

Then the eyes went dead, like two black holes lost in the depths of the universe.

Then there were no words from Jeremiah Rackstraw, no florid speeches, no eloquently uttered untruths, no toothsome threats.

And all Josh had to do was say, quietly, coldly, jubilantly, "All aboard, Henry T. Ford," and tug on the sticky length of organ like an engine driver on the chain of his whistle, and the membranous string snapped, and out came the locomotive's innards, vomiting out of the aperture in a huge whooping slosh that swamped Josh from head to foot and then flooded out from between the wheels in a tidal wave that struck Rackstraw full in the face, spattered over his shoulders and over the inert form of Grampa, and still kept coming, spilling outward on both sides of the locomotive, organ after organ—green lumpen footballs, scarlet hourglass shapes, straggling twisted cords of a pale ocher substance that looked like ten-foot lengths of knotted mushroom, translucent bags of pus yellow liquid, chains of black fetal objects tied to one another with veiny ropes, nightmarish orchidaceous *things* whose fleshy petals fluttered wanly as they were carried along on the flood—and all of these Josh pushed aside as they poured down onto him, gagging as he did so, his eyes squinched tight shut, and now a vast bulbous lung fell into his hands, dark as soot, and he thrust it out and its outer membrane split open at the side of the track to expose alveoli like florets of rotten broccoli, each coated in bubbling orange mucus, and now a huge object thumped out on top of him, and he struggled to heave it aside but this one was as heavy as a child and its surface had the texture of raw beef, and it was all one muscle, a large hollow muscle from which four thick-skinned tubes protruded . . . the heart!

And instead of tossing this organ aside like all the others, Josh wrapped his slippery arms around it and embraced it. Choking against its putrid reek, he squeezed and squeezed, squeezed hard, squeezed the hardest he had ever squeezed anything in his whole life, and from somewhere far away he heard a shrill whistle, as of pain, and he knew that this was the locomotive's death shriek, and he squeezed harder still. He squeezed, remembering Grampa, and Mayor, and Doc Wheeler, and Tom Finkelbaum, and the Cohens, and Miss Ohllson, and Walt Donaldson. For all these and for the countless others the Company had killed to satisfy the hunger of the damned train, the hundreds, the thousands, the maybe even millions of lives they had snuffed out in the course of their travels, Josh bear-hugged that heart, squashing the blood from its ventricles, closing off its auricles, until its great pulsing weight began to twitch galvanically, spastically, and then, suddenly, it was still.

The last of the locomotive's remaining organs rained down on Josh, pattering onto his grimacing face. Soon there were only dribbles of liquid, and from inside the boiler there came dripping sounds that echoed hollowly in the emptied chamber. Josh was soaked to the skin. He was writhing half-buried in a slather of offal, suffocating on their stink, clutching the locomotive's dead heart in his arms. Every bit of him was in pain. He was blind, his eyelids glued together with gore. But he was alive, and the locomotive was dead. *He was alive, and he had won!*

He shoved the heart down toward his feet, kicked it away, then, struggling to gain a purchase on the slickened ties, he hauled himself through a six-inch-deep soup of nameless inner parts, trying not to think about what he might be squashing beneath his elbows and knees and trying not to listen to the squelches and pops and gristly crunches.

Like an eel he slithered beneath one of the locomotive's pistons and out onto the trackside, where, as muck-encrusted and bloodstained as a newborn infant, he lay helpless in the gore-drenched, viscera-laden dust, face down, exhausted beyond belief.

So tired was Josh that it didn't even occur to him to wonder where Rackstraw might be. He sensed Grampa's body somewhere over to his right, awash with gore like his own body. He knew Mayor lay a little farther off. Rackstraw? The name meant nothing to Josh right about then.

The hand that seized him by the back of the hair and brought his head up out of the dirt was a sharp reminder. Prizing his eyelids apart, Josh saw Rackstraw's face looming inches away from his own. Rackstraw was hunkered down, and his features, beneath their mask of blood and offal, was contorted with rage, and with something else. It took Josh a moment to recognize the emotion, so out of place did it seem on the visage of Jeremiah Rackstraw.

Despair. Abject and utter despair.

"Do you realize what you have done?" Rackstraw snarled, adding spittle to the various fluids and secretions that covered Josh's face.

Josh blinked rapidly, gummily, then nodded.

"Do you understand what you have done to us?"

Again, Josh nodded.

Rackstraw raised his free hand, his left hand, and his clown-face signet ring flashed in the half-light. His hair was sticking out in matted tufts and the fabric of his black suit glistened darkly and wetly. He straightened out a dripping index finger and positioned it in front of Josh's forehead.

"Then," he said, "you will know that you have the privilege of being the very last victim of the Company in this particular world. There are other Companies, and other worlds, but here, Josh Knight, you are going to be our coda. Our last lamb. Our swan song. Our curtain call. Offer up your prayers to whatever deity you believe in, though don't," he added, with a ghost of his former slyness, "hold your breath waiting for a reply. It is time to die, Joshua Knight. Let me tell you that you have been a most *ungrateful* audience. Good-bye, and I hope we never see you again."

Too numb and dazed to resist, Josh felt the tip of Rackstraw's index finger press against his forehead and begin to trace out a word. He didn't know what Rackstraw was doing to him, but he understood it meant his death.

Closing his eyes, he readied himself for the embrace of oblivion.

In a way, it was a relief. And it would be good to see what was on the Other Side.

The finger wrote and, having written, moved on.

The word on Josh's forehead was "DEAD."

Josh, however, was not.

"Too late," Rackstraw moaned, and then uttered a stream of curses.

He let Josh's head fall back to the ground.

"Too late, too late! I'm out of time! The curtain has already dropped!"

With a supreme effort of will, Josh rolled over onto his side and reopened his eyes.

There stood Rackstraw, arms held up to the pallid, veiled sun, looking for all the world like an actor staring into the spotlight and imploring an unseen audience for just one more round of applause, one more encore. Throwing back his head, the Company's spokesman let out a howl that rose into the polluted air and echoed across all of Escardy Gap. Then he fell to his knees and buried his face in his hands.

"Gone," he sobbed. "Our Angel is gone. There is no more. The show is over."

With that, he lowered his hands and stared at his fingers. Josh noticed something different about Rackstraw's skin, but it wasn't until the first flake of skin fell away from his cheek that Josh realized that the Company's spokesman was slowly disintegrating. His epidermis had gone as dry as a riverbed in a drought, and cracks were appearing, running down his neck, over his palms and down his wrists, and down from his hair-line to his chin. His hair started falling out in clumps, and his lips began to resemble old clay.

Faster and faster Rackstraw's skin flaked away, to reveal desiccated flesh beneath, and parched white bone. His cloth-ing grew baggy and began to sag inward, while powdery dust poured from between his shirt buttons and out of the cuffs of his jacket and trousers, collecting around him in small drifts.

But still he was alive, still he writhed as the very essence of him evaporated before Josh's gaze. Still his jaw worked as he mouthed soundlessly, trying to find the right language to describe his own private apocalypse, or perhaps remonstrat-ing with his departed Angel. Even as his eyeballs shattered like porcelain, even as his lungs set puffs of gray dust up out of his windpipe, even as the blood in his veins turned to crim-son sand, Jeremiah Rackstraw fought to find speech and put his plight into words.

Finally, his own skeleton became too brittle to support him, and he collapsed, his dark suit billowing in on itself, crum-pling in a heap with nothing but dust to show for the man who had once worn it.

The dust continued to flow from the gaps in Rackstraw's clothing for some time, mingling with the dust on the ground, the dust that had covered the earth here for thousands of years.

And then, as if from nowhere, a cool breeze started to blow.

4

The wind moved through the streets of Escardy Gap like a pack of dogs, questing into every crack, crevice, and corner, nosing the sidewalks and storm drains, rustling across lawns in waves. It padded through front porches, setting rocking chairs rocking, and sniffed the wheels of parked cars. It leapt up against windows and screens, rattling them in their frames, and disturbed the lids of trash cans, and chased litter over roads and under benches. It pounced through the shattered glass of broken storefront windows and scattered the goods within. It worried at shrubs and saplings, gnawed at loose fence posts, and pawed at unlatched shutters.

And like the master of the hounds, Josh rode with it.

Favoring his damaged ankle, he limped through the streets in a dreamlike daze, searching for life and finding none. On every sidewalk, at every corner, in every house, there were only corpses and more corpses. He knew the names of almost all the dead—those whose bodies he could identify—and he stared into each face, each pair of sightless eyes, unable to imagine how these lifeless mannequins could ever have occupied his hometown, filled it with laughter and passion and dreams and hope and happiness.

The wind fanned the flames of the buildings that burned, encouraging fires to spread like gossip from one house to the next. Gradually, more and more of Escardy Gap caught alight and was reduced to charred beams. The flames burned steadily but not fiercely, and the streets were wide enough so that Josh could walk between two rows of blazing houses and barely feel the heat on the backs of his hands. Everywhere the creak and crack of snapping wood punctuated the slow rattle of the spreading destruction, and firefly swarms of embers gusted from sidewalk to sidewalk, cooling to ash and falling to the road like black snow.

The wind carried the smoke away, too. Now that the force field was no longer in place to contain it, the smoke stretched in a long plume that trailed across the badlands for several miles, and the sun resumed its afternoon duties at something close to full strength, though brown-black swathes occasionally passed in front of it and temporarily dulled its luster.

The gore from the locomotive had dried hard on Josh's skin, but he didn't make a move to scrape it off or even wash himself. He simply continued to walk without direction. Down Delacy Street, up Muldavey Street, along Hampton Boulevard, Belvedere Way, Furnival Street, Carnegie Drive . . . All streets he knew for the people who had lived in them, the kindly adults who had known him and called out his name whenever he passed, the kids who had yelled "Hey, Josh!" and invited him to join in their games. As his green town was slowly consumed by fire and turned black, Josh found himself wandering and wondering as the survivors of the Blitz in London and Coventry must have wandered and wondered, unable to grasp the immensity of their loss.

Every now and then he would come across a pile of clothing that lay amid a small mound of dust. Here was a suit pinstriped with copper wire, and here, atop a mound of women's garb, a pair of smoked-black spectacles. At one point he felt a crunch underfoot and looked down to find a cluster of jewels set in rusted iron in a pattern that vaguely resembled the shape of a large fly. Idly, he mused who might have owned such an ugly and ungainly piece of jewelry. He recognized other sets of clothing from his first-ever sight of the Company when they stepped out of the train. The wind was sifting away the dust that was all that remained of those individuals, mixing it with the commonality of all the dust that had ever crept into Escardy Gap from beyond. Soon the Company would be nothing but clothing, empty costumes littering the stage of their last-ever performance.

On Josh walked, and the sun's glare grew less pitiless as it rolled down from its zenith.

In his hand he held Jeremiah Rackstraw's ring. The yawning clown face looked a little more subdued in Josh's palm than it had on Rackstraw's finger, a little less lunatic. It was as though it recognized its defeat, and while the painted smile remained, the real smile was long gone.

Josh didn't know why he had picked up the ring. He assumed he had wanted it for a souvenir, though why he should want to keep anything that would remind him of the Company he had no idea. It had seemed apt at the time to pick it up and blow the dust off of it, that was all. A trophy, maybe. Perhaps a totem, to ward off such evil if he should ever encounter it again in the future.

Eventually, as evening set in, Josh found himself in the town square. Taking a seat on a bench opposite the rubble that had been the town hall, he lay back and turned his face up to the sky.

The first stars were coming out, twinkling in the dusk's violet dome. Real stars, not the false stars that had formed part of the backdrop that the locomotive had draped about the town. The same stars that people have gazed up at ever since mankind first developed the capacity for wonder.

Josh gazed up from the dead town as more and more stars winked into life. The old familiar constellations. The patterns divined to make sense of the inexplicable, to tame the unknowable, to bring reason to the inordinate chaos of the universe.

For a long time Josh sat watching the stars, and tried to understand.

THE END

Epilogue

It was a hard-fought struggle, but lives were at stake—what else was I supposed to do? Let them lie there disintegrating on the bathroom floor? No, not when I could save them. Not when I could write them back into the book and make them live again.

While I wrote, the Smith Corona was its usual unhelpful self, interjecting comments and queries whenever it could, pretending it was my partner when it was just a pain in the ass, claiming to be the voice of my conscience when all it was the demon Doubt tapping me on the shoulder in time to the tapping of keys on paper. I did my best to ignore it, and most of the time I succeeded, but every now and again its opinions got the better of me and I felt obliged to respond to them—usually speaking out loud.

```
Nor did it occur to him that he had not
been any too specific in his choice of
destination.
```

Who cares? said the typewriter. *As long as he's off the scene, right?*
"Can the smart cracks," I snapped.
Oh, pardonnay moy.

```
His ring. Josh thought of Rackstraw's
ring, and another bell chimed in his
brain. While the ring didn't exactly
form what you might call a direct
connection, it was yet another symbolic
link in the chain of deduction.
```

That's pretty weak, the typewriter whined.
"The drowning man will clutch at anything that floats, be it a lifebelt or a turd," I replied, glancing back over my shoulder at the bathroom door. There was not a sound from within. I could have been failing, but I thought I might be winning. My fingers flew on.

```
"Can't you tell, Mayor?" Josh replied
through rictus teeth. "It's scared of
```

us. It knows what we're here to do and
it's actually *scared* of us."

Sentient machines, snapped the typewriter. *I ask you!*

"Look who's talking," I said, and carried on hammering at
the keys, feeling like Beethoven at his piano, inspiration in
full spate.

The typewriter, as if brooding on the irony, had nothing
else to say until I typed a *2,* beginning the fresh section at the
top of a fresh sheet of paper, as was my custom, and following it with:

At that moment, Neville N. Nolan was
flitting forth and fro in fly form over
the tormented town. . . .

*Haven't we had enough of this alliterative ass wiping al-
ready?* the typewriter sneered then. *And don't you think
you're wasting time? I mean, this hasn't got anything to do
with Mayor or Josh exactly, has it?*

"It's necessary to the plot. Now please, shut the fuck up."

And then Mayor's head swiveled, and his
eyes sought Josh out (the pupils were
black with terror and ecstasy), and one
eyelid drooped in a slow, sad wink, and
then his mouth opened. . . .

You're not going to do this, said the typewriter. *Tell me
you're not going to kill the old bastard.*

If I hadn't known better, I could have sworn it was genuinely concerned.

"I might have to," I said.

But you're supposed to be saving him. Aren't you?

"Sure, saving him *here,* in New York. But in the book . . ."
I shrugged. "I don't know that I have a choice. Josh has to get
beneath that locomotive *somehow.*"

But that's stupid.

"That's fiction," I replied.

The typewriter maintained a surly silence all through Mayor's death scene, piping up again only as I wrote:

```
And then it was only a matter of moments
before his mind's eye had filled in the
blanks and he recognized once again (how
could he ever forget it?) the clown face
that had decorated the lethal clock.
```

Why, it's almost as if you planned this! It snickered.

"Almost," I said.

And at last, some fifty sheets of paper later, I was pounding out the final few sentences, sitting Josh down on the bench and forcing him to turn his head up to the night sky to gaze in uncomprehending wonder at the eternal silence of the stars.

```
. . . and tried to understand.
```

"There!" I cried, and threw myself back in my chair, gazing in uncomprehending wonder at the disheveled pile of paper that had accumulated to the left of the typewriter. My fingertips were sore, there was a burning knot in the vertebrae between my shoulder blades, and my vision was blurred from staring at a fixed point in space for so long, and when I glanced at my watch I could hardly believe that five whole hours had passed since I sat down. Ten pages an hour! When was the last time I had ever written anything that fast, that urgently? Not since I was a lowly undergrad, pumping out short stories late at night after my college roommate had gone to sleep and feverishly hoping each time that *this* would be the one that *Amazing Stories* or *Asimov's* accepted.

I flexed my fingers together, popping the knuckles. I took off my glasses and massaged my eye sockets. I rolled my shoulders to work out the kink in my spine.

Then, and only then, did I get to my feet and move to the bathroom door.

I was almost seasick with terror and hope as I grasped the door handle. Had I done it? Had I really sent them back where they belonged? Or would they still be lying there in a sea of their own lifeblood—my creations, destroyed by my own eagerness to bring them to life?

I held that door handle for the best part of three minutes before finally summoning the courage to turn it and open the door.

The door swung gently inward. At any moment I expected it to encounter an obstacle—a limb, an organ—and judder to a halt. I didn't dare breathe.

The bathroom was empty. The floor was clean. The tiles glinted spotlessly. The faucet dripped into the sink.

Mayor and Josh might as well never have been there.

The days blurred together. Sun and moon spun around the earth, exchanging roles relentlessly. Snow fell, snow lay, snow melted, snow dissolved until only a few hardened piles of grayish ice were left hanging around on street corners, tripping up unwary passersby. December ended. The ball in Times Square descended in a blaze of lights and cheers. Auld acquaintance was not forgot and cups of kindness were taken all across the Northern Hemisphere.

Stubborn in their cheerfulness, as in everything else, the citizens of New York skipped into the New Year, red nosed and laughing in their fake furs and woolen caps and mufflers. Then the holiday season was over, and families divided again. Old folk resumed their solitary independent existences as their children and grandchildren returned to their own homes, their own lives. Shops reopened, decorations were dismantled. The hum of traffic grew louder and busier as the city settled back into its old ways with renewed vigor. The crime rate went up, Wall Street went down, and disgruntled workers went on strike.

Sometimes, on crisp midwinter mornings, the skyscrapers looked strangely flat and unreal against the glacier blue sky, as though they were chipboard pops for some Broadway musical. Other times, on dull overcast days, they huddled together into one looming mass of concrete like a great gray prison wall, glowering down on the convicts below, innocent and guilty alike.

But otherwise, in every other respect, New York life continued much as it had before, as it always did, as it always would. Old year, new year, winter, summer—they were all the same to the bricks and bedrock of the greatest city in the world, bar none. New York shrugged its massive shoulders and watched time go by with its multimillion window-eyes. Time? What's time to a city? Time is a thing that a city measures by its own private clock. Each second begins with a birth and ends with a death—someone's birth, another person's death. On this clockface, a human life is just one second small, just a three-degree increment long. *Tick, tick, tick, tick, tick . . .*

Me? I wrote. Or, I should say, I redrafted. I did little else but edit, eat, and sleep. While I ate, I was reconfiguring the next paragraph in my head. While I slept, my subconscious was working on new wrinkles for the next chapter. Being a writer is a twenty-four-hour-a-day, seven-days-a-week, fifty-two-weeks-a-year job. Even when you're not typing, you're writing. This I understood now. And this also I understood: during the period when I had not been writing, when I had been the Writer without an Idea, my creativity had been forced to find another outlet and had done so, had reached down into itself and had conjured up three companions, three dreams made flesh, three archetypes molded from the clay of the collective consciousness, as real to me as they were invisible, inaudible, and intangible to the rest of the world. An angel, a devil, and something that was a little bit of both. Prima to love and care for me, Chip to bitch and gripe with, and Hudson, both dependent and independent, affectionate and unloving, transparent in her emotions and yet at the same time inscrutable—above all, neutral. A mother, a father, and a child-creature. A family, of sorts. This piece of insanity had kept me sane.

Through the blur of days I typed away, transforming the error-strewn pages of the manuscript into the fairest of fair copies. The Smith Corona and I chattered together. Together, we smoothed out the book, planed away the corners, sanded down the rough edges, until finally, one day in midspring when the pigeons were raising their own particular brand of hell outside my window, I typed once again those two words that usually strike a plangent, bittersweet note in my heart:

THE END

And having typed those two words, I sat back and I stared at the finished manuscript squatting on my desk, and I glanced around the apartment, and I returned my gaze to the manuscript—sloppily stacked, all mismatched corners—and I wondered why I wasn't feeling the surge of pride and triumph that ought to accompany the completion of any Herculean labor, and I looked down inside myself and I found there a beast called Dissatisfaction and it was pacing the floor of its cage and growling and nuzzling the bars, and I looked at the manuscript for a third time and I saw just a bunch of words strung together in random forms (rather like the paper chains that still adorned my walls, this late into April). . . .

Something was missing. Either I had left some vital element out, or else there was a loose end to be tied up somewhere, somehow.

I looked to the typewriter for advice. It offered me its customary smug grin.

"I'm forgetting something," I said.

You sure are.

"But what? I've been through it all. *We've* been through it. I thought we'd got it all straight."

Well, I didn't want to say anything at the time, seeing as you were enjoying yourself so much and all, but . . .

"But what?"

Nah, best leave it as it is. No one'll notice. None of your readers will notice, at any rate. Largely because you haven't got that many.

"*What is it?*" I yelled, and raised a fist at the machine. I swear, even though I knew in my heart of hearts that it wasn't the Smith Corona that was doing the talking, it was my subconscious, still I threatened to hit the typewriter. I guess I should get out more.

Maybe it's better left hanging, said the typewriter. *Maybe you can resolve it in the sequel.*

"That's no good. Even if I have a sequel planned, the novel still has to stand on its own."

Just think about it. Who's left alive in Escardy Gap?

"Just Josh, of course."

Uh-huh? You sure?

"Sure, I'm sure. I planned it that way."

Yeah, you did, only the best-laid plans of mice and men, Mr. Steinbeck, often end up getting fucked with a flagpole.

"Would you *please* put me out of my misery?" I implored the typewriter.

Love to, buddy. The window's over there. All you have to do is step out of it.

I went to the closet where I keep all my useful household items, fetched out a ball peen hammer, came back, and waved it intimidatingly at the Smith Corona.

"One last chance," I said.

You wouldn't dare.

"That's what you think."

Without me, how will you ever be able to write?

"I'll buy one of those word-processor things."

You'll miss me.

"Not if I aim carefully."

I brandished the hammer, and the typewriter was convinced.

Jeez, you're serious! You really would do it!

"Without a moment's regret." And I meant it. "Now, tell me what I've forgotten."

Okay. Okay. Seeing as you asked so nicely. The typewriter ground its teeth, then said, *Sara.*

"What?"

Who else apart from Josh did you leave alive in Escardy Gap? Sitting on the porch at old Ike Swivven's farm?

"Sara Sienkiewicz," I breathed.

I felt sick to my stomach. I prayed it wasn't so.

But it was true. I had left her dangling there, the loosest of loose plot threads. What was she doing at the Swivven farm? Why had she gone there? What purpose was she meant to serve?

I racked my brains, but couldn't think of any way of getting her out of the novel without fatally compromising it. She had to be a part of the story, she had to do everything she did—and yet there was no resolution for her, no closure, no fixed end to her character arc.

All I could do with her was leave her at the Swivven place waiting.

Waiting for what? For the first person to arrive in Escardy Gap from the outside world? Waiting to tell him or her about everything that has happened to the town?

She was waiting for *someone*, that was for sure. The beautiful authoress was there for a reason. She had to be.

That was when the typewriter said something, so muffled that I had to ask it to repeat itself.

I said, shit-for-brains, she's waiting for you.

I had already paid the rent for that month, so I didn't have any qualms about leaving without telling the landlord. The apartment wouldn't stand empty for long. The landlord would have someone new in there the day after my next rent check failed to materialize.

I spent the last of my savings on a new set of clothes, including an off-the-rack suit and a Panama hat from a tailor whose clientele and sense of fashion had changed little in forty years. I also bought a pickax from a hardware store. The proprietor assured me the pickax would get through anything. And it carried a lifetime guarantee.

"I don't need it for a lifetime," I told him.

Back at the apartment, I packed a suitcase.

I wanted to remember the old place in every detail, but as I stood in the doorway with the suitcase in one hand, the Smith Corona in its carrying case under my arm and the pickax slung over my shoulder, as I stood there and cast my gaze around, I realized there wasn't much worth remembering. Gloom, dirt, and shabbiness aren't exactly the stuff of nostalgia, and they certainly had no place where I was going.

"So long anyway," I said.

It would have been just my luck to have been murdered the very last time I ever crossed Central Park, but the god of irony was looking the other way that day. I reached the reservoir unscathed.

It took me a while to find the entrance to the culvert from which Mayor and Josh had emerged. They all looked the same. But there—*there* was the loosely padlocked gate I had helped them through, when the smells of Josh, the smells of my own childhood, had convinced me that he was as real as I.

I pushed the bag and the typewriter through the gap. When it came to pushing myself after it, however, I met with some difficulty. I did not have the strength to force the gate open wide enough to accept a belly and a backside enlarged by years of studious inactivity. I grunted and strained, but it was like threading a rope through a needle. I tried using the pickax handle for a crowbar, but I couldn't prize the gate open and clamber through at the same time. I even tried hitting the chain with the pickax point, for all the good it did me. Redfaced, panting, and close to tears, I cursed myself for not having the foresight to buy a pair of wire cutters at the hardware store as well.

Just when I was thinking of turning round and going home, a rich low voice behind me said, "Having some trouble, sir?"

It was a cop on horseback—perhaps the same cop who had been patrolling the park the last time I was here, although one mounted policeman in a helmet and leather jacket looks pretty much like another.

"Yes, Officer," I said, and quickly spun him a yarn about seeing a kid run into the culvert just a moment ago and I was worried that he might be in trouble and I thought I should go in after him. It was the best I could do at such short notice, and I had to pray that the cop hadn't spotted my suitcase and typewriter and the pickax, all of which were now tucked just inside the tunnel mouth.

"So you thought you'd do your civic duty," the cop said, dismounting.

"That's right, Officer."

"Well, why don't I go in and have a look-see? I think it'll be easier for me to get through than you." He added, belatedly, "If you'll pardon my saying so."

"But . . ."

"But?"

"But I'm pretty certain I know this kid. He lives on my block. That's why I'm so concerned. He's a good kid. Gets into trouble sometimes, but basically good at heart. I know his parents. I often visit the family in their apartment. He won't be scared of me, but he might be scared of you." I added, belatedly, "If you'll pardon my saying so."

The cop pursed his lips and scratched his forehead. His horse blew audibly through its nose. "Well," he said eventually. "Okay. I'll give you a hand. Here."

He grasped a bar, braced a boot against the stone wall and applied all his might to hauling the gate open as far as the chain would allow. Through clenched teeth he said, "Go on. Get through."

I squeezed past him, crouched down beneath the chain, rotated myself sideways, and pushed with all the strength in my legs and pulled with all the strength in my arms. There was a moment when I thought I might be crushed, squashed between gate and wall like a bug between a child's fingernails. My body would have to be transported to the morgue in two bags.

I gave a last titanic effort and, like a sudden squelch of toothpaste out of the tube, I was through.

The cop released the gate, puffed out his cheeks and rubbed rust off his hands. Then he saw me bend down to pick up my bag, typewriter, and the pickax. He yelled, "Hey!" Then, "Hey, what *is* that stuff? What the hell are you *doing?* Come back here!"

But I was running deep into the clammy darkness. I must have been about thirty or forty yards in before I glanced back at the arch of barred light that encapsulated a small section of the park with a few buildings beyond and a gray sky above. The cop was staring after me, one hand on his hip, the other scratching his helmet. Even he, over the course of his career, had probably never seen anything quite so dumb and inexplicable as a man in late middle age running into a dead-end tunnel carrying a suitcase, a typewriter, and a pickax.

I turned and ran on.

* * *

When I looked round again, a measureless distance into the tunnel, I could see nothing behind me. There was nothing ahead either. Pure blackness.

I slowed my pace, expecting at any moment to come face-to-face with a wall of ice-cold bedrock, but expecting also to be able to keep going unhindered for as long as it took to reach the rockfall that blocked the mouth of the Snake.

After a while, I lost track of the time. A day could have passed, a week, a lifetime, an eon, or simply a handful of minutes. A glance at the luminous dial of my wristwatch showed me that it had stopped, and somehow I wasn't surprised.

No longer did it feel like walking. There was something smooth and solid beneath my feet, certainly, but it wasn't stone or rock or metal or wood. I seemed to be traveling through a perfect starless void over a bridge of black glass. My footsteps made no sound, and there was no echo of my breathing. The only things to reassure me that I was still alive were the thump of my heart in my ears and the ache in my arms as my burdens grew heavier.

All the while I waited for the air to change, to grow warmer, sweeter, to fill with the dust that covered all of Escardy Gap, embalming it.

I knew how that dust would smell. It would smell of my childhood.

I knew, too, that if I kept walking, I would sooner or later reach the rockfall.

And I knew that I would be able to hack away at the rockfall with my pickax until I could see a chink of daylight, the bright daylight of another morning in Escardy Gap.

And I knew that beyond that rockfall there would be the cut and the slope up to the Swivven farm, and at the Swivven farm Sara Sienkiewicz would be waiting for me, sitting in old Ike's porch rocker.

And I knew that when I arrived she would greet me like an old friend, ask me how I was doing, offer me coffee, and we would fall to talking, and she would tell me about Escardy Gap, about what happened to her dear sweet hometown, and I would listen sympathetically, painfully, and strive to keep myself from confessing my guilt, and instead tell her how sorry I was that this had happened, and long into the night we would talk—she would tell me she was a writer, I would tell her I was one, too, and this miraculous coincidence would fuel the conversation for another two or three hours, and at some point during this conversation we would both realize that we had come to an understanding, and then a silence would fall between us, and then Sara would say, "Would you like to stay the night?" and I would reply, "That would be mighty kind of you, Miss Sienkiewicz," and she would say, "Please, I insist. Call me Sara," and I would try out her name, "Sara," and try it again, "Sara," this time with a smile, because it's a name you can't say without smiling, and she would smile back and take my hand and lead me indoors. . . .

I had no doubt that any of this would happen.

No doubt at all.